mannequin

m a n n e q u i n

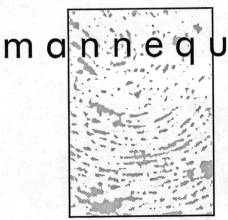

j. robert janes

First published in Great Britain 1994
by Constable & Company Ltd

Copyright © 1994 by J. Robert Janes

Published by
Soho Press, Inc.
853 Broadway
New York NY 10003

Library of Congress Cataloging-in-Publication Data

Janes, J. Robert (Joseph Robert), 1935–
Mannequin / J. Robert Janes.
p. cm.
ISBN 1-56947-129-0 (alk. paper)
1. France—History—German occupation, 1940–1945—Fiction.
2. World War, 1939–1945—France—Fiction.   I. Title.
PR9199.3.J3777M36   1994
813'.54—dc21   98-18970
                                                                          CIP

10 9 8 7 6 5 4 3 2 1

To each the image of perfection idolized until undressed

author's note

Mannequin is a work of fiction in which actual places and times are used but altered as appropriate. Occasionally the name of a real person appears for historical authenticity, though all are deceased and the story makes of them what it demands. I do not condone what happened during these times, I abhor it. But during the Occupation of France the everyday crimes of murder and arson continued to be committed, and I merely ask, by whom and how were they solved?

acknowledgement

All the novels in the St-Cyr-Kohler series incorporate a few words and brief passages of French or German. Dr Dennis Essar of Brock University very kindly assisted with the French, as did the artist Pierrette Laroche, while Ms Bodil Little of the German Department at Brock helped with the German. Should there be any errors, they are my own and for these I apologize but hope there are none.

1 THE GIRL WAS ONLY EIGHTEEN AND SHE HAD been missing for four days. In photo after photo she stared up at them from among the dozens of photographs of herself and others who, like her, had worn the clothes and jewellery of the fashion trade and only by degrees had been cajolled into removing everything.

Now her nakedness, her dawning uncertainty and finally her terror lay underfoot among the scattered twenty by twenty-five centimetre enlargements that littered the parquet floors and staircases of an all-too-empty house.

Every stick of furniture had been removed, every designer blouse and slip or bit of cloth.

'Who blew the whistle, Louis?' breathed Kohler with barely controlled fury. Not a half-hour ago, thinking the girl might still be here, he had broken the lock with their stonemason's hammer, hadn't hesitated.

'So many, Hermann. Ten, twelve—fourteen or fifteen young women,' said St-Cyr, still aghast at what they had stumbled on to.

Breasts, thighs, buttocks, arms, legs and eyes formed a montage that only served to sharpen what must have happened.

'All of about Joanne's age, her hair, her . . .'

'Yes, yes, but *why* was the house emptied, Hermann? Did they fear we would find their fingerprints? Did she cry out to them that Chief Inspector Jean-Louis St-Cyr of the Sûreté Nationale was a friend and neighbour? Did she tell them they had best release her?'

'Don't be a *dummkopf*. If she had yelled that at them, they would have killed her. There's no evidence of that.'

'Ah *merde*, Hermann. To not know what has happened to her is to fear the worst and share the family's agony.'

It was now Monday, 28 December 1942. The girl had last been seen at 11.45 a.m. on Thursday the 24th. Parisian to her very being, she had missed Christmas with her family, had simply not come home.

'Have the others also been declared missing? Have some of their bodies been found? Mutilated? Raped? Sodomized? Tortured?'

'Louis, cut it out! Quit jumping to conclusions. Quit taking it too personally.'

Clearly things had been going on for some time, and just as clearly the house had been emptied in one hell of a hurry.

'*Christ!* What am I to tell her parents?' demanded St-Cyr.

'Nothing. Just progress is being made. You know the drill. You don't need your Gestapo partner to tell you that.'

They began to sort through the photographs. In one photo Joanne Labelle, whose mother took in laundry and who, with her family, lived up the street from Louis on the rue Laurence-Savart in Belleville, lay on a superb Louis-Philippe *chaise-longue* staring up into the camera with so much doubt and fear in her eyes, they both knew she had realized all too clearly she was in too deep.

In another photo, the girl gripped the edge of a very fine Louis XIV commode as she stood starkly facing a wall mirror with her breasts squeezed between stiffened arms. The hair, loose and thick and falling almost to the waist, had been thrown back, the chin uplifted, the lips parted in a gasp, eyes clamped shut.

'The bastards must have told her what was going to happen to her, Louis.'

St-Cyr took the proffered photo. 'She's not bound . . . ? She's not restrained in any visible way . . . ?'

'A gun then,' snapped Kohler. 'That would imply there were at least two of them. One to take the pictures and the other to make certain she didn't escape.'

Joanne stood on tiptoes in the photo and the thick and disconcerting triangle of her pubes was caught in the glass whose richly carved frame spoke of money. Lots of money. Old money probably.

In yet another of the prints, she had turned swiftly to challenge her abductors and must have shouted something, for the photographer had caught her biting back the tears, pinned as she was to the edge of that same commode, again reflected in the glass.

In another, she grovelled on a magnificent Savonnerie carpet. In another, she lay there weeping.

Kohler was grim. 'This wasn't the usual. The clothes are too classy, too damned expensive and hard to come by.'

Ah yes, the shortages, thought St-Cyr. Paris under the Occupation of the Germans in late 1942 was a city destitute and in hunger, yet still it attracted all sorts of 'tourists' from the Glorious Third Reich of the Nazis. Soldier-boys in field grey-green or airforce and navy blue. Rest and recupe' for generals, businessmen from the Reich, spies and fellow-travellers. Fine restaurants, lots to eat, smoke and drink for them, all the clubs doing a roaring business, and any of the forty or so brothels that were reserved for the Wehrmacht, to say nothing of those for the officers, the SS, the bigwigs, their French friends and collaborators *and* the gangsters too.

Joanne had answered an advertisement in *Le Matin*, a newspaper that, like all the others, was now totally controlled and used by the Germans. It was a common enough scheme in pre-war times when a fee would have been charged. Normally the girls didn't disappear but were forced to bear the discomfort of their indiscretion when the photos were sold on the streets and in the bars. But now it was a racket that puzzled if for no other reason than the almost total absence of photographic film unless purchased on the black market at astronomical rates or stolen from the Germans.

St-Cyr took out the torn bit of newsprint and read the advertisement again. *Wanted by a noted fashion house, girls of suitable ability, poise and determination. Ages 18 to 22. Hair long and of chestnut brown, eyes of the same. Please, no others need apply. Height 168 to 177 centimetres, weight 52 to 57 kilos, waist 61 to 71 centimetres, bust 76 to 86 centimetres. No previous training or experience necessary. We will teach you everything you need to know. Apply box 169. Send snapshot if possible and personal details. Responds in two weeks. If chosen for an interview, bring acceptance letter to enclosed address.*

It was the stuff of dreams and aspirations. Though he didn't think it possible, he had to ask. 'Were they being prepared for use elsewhere?'

'In one of the brothels? Raped so as to force them to spread their legs? Hey, come on, Louis. It could only have been for a *clandestin*. An unlicensed house is too risky and definitely not classy enough for a set-up like this.'

Louis's bushy brown eyebrows lifted in acknowledgement. The chubby cheeks that were perpetually touched with shadow, quivered. 'Then did they tell her her lovely hair would be cut off and thrown at her feet to be pissed on? Is this what you're thinking?'

Ah *Gott im Himmel*, the deep brown ox-eyes of the Sûreté's little Frog were misting. Louis had watched the girl grow from a babe in arms. Her younger brother, Dédé, a ten-year-old who adored her, had come down the street to beg help. They had only just got in this afternoon from Lyon, from a case of arson and 183 dead. Shit! Was it all about to start again?

'Look, I have to be honest. She was moved from here. That's all we really know.'

'Are you certain?' asked St-Cyr suspiciously. Hermann seldom told the whole truth all at once.

'Hey, don't be so wounded. I'll take another look. Stay put.'

'How's the stomach?' Hermann hated finding dead bodies, especially those of young women and children.

The Bavarian didn't waver. 'Fine. Don't worry. If it makes you feel any better, I think she's still alive.'

In spite of the war and the conqueror-conquered relationship, they had got on since the fall of 1940. Two detectives of long standing. None of the Gestapo-SS brutality and sadism for them. Just robbery, arson, murder, extortion, other things also, and much trouble with the SS and the Gestapo. These days so many got in the way.

Kohler's storm-trooper's jaw, bulldog jowls and shrapnel scars tightened. The puffy, faded blue eyes that were so often empty but saw everything, passed doubtfully over him. 'Are you really okay yourself?' he asked.

'Yes, I'm okay.'

It would be best to keep Louis busy. 'Then why not collate the photos and spread them out? We've had a break, eh? Someone was thoughtful enough to leave us the evidence.'

'But *why*? That is the question, Hermann, and always with you Germans it's the blitzkrieg for us. *Always!*'

Satisfied that he could safely leave him, Kohler tried to be cheerful. 'Okay, Chief, don't get tough. I'm on my way. I won't be long.'

In rank, St-Cyr was above his partner who was only a Haupsturmführer, a captain and inspector. But Hermann had been a Munich detective long before this war and from there had gone to Berlin, so he knew all about what could happen to young girls who were foolish enough to answer such advertisements.

His pipe alight, St-Cyr picked his way over to tall french windows that were touched with frost. Down across the garden of the Palais Royal, the bare branches of regimented lindens threw their shadows on the sleet-encrusted snow. Not a soul stirred or strolled beneath the arcades to browse in dusty, forgotten shops where old stamps, books, second-hand military medals and lead soldiers were sometimes sold. Staid and eminently respectable, the identical, grey-stone façades and windows of the bourgeoisie frowned on intrusion of any kind. Doctors, lawyers, bankers and men of commerce lived quietly in this quietest of enclaves right in the heart of Paris and not a stone's throw from the rue Saint-Honoré, the Louvre and the Bank of France.

Though he didn't want to admit it, he was forced to tell himself the location was perfect. Who would think it possible such a thing as kidnapping, rape and . . . *yes*, murder, could ever occur in a place like this? Two hundred years ago of course, when the brothels were here, but not today and not for the past hundred years.

He and Hermann had obtained an address from the newspaper but only after threats and much baksheesh. *Le Matin* had run the ad for about a month—a first time for them, so other newspapers must have been used to trap the rest of the victims.

That address had turned out to be nothing more than the box office of the Théâtre du Palais Royal. The custodian there had given Joanne her last letter of instruction, but it was only because the girl had opened it right away that the man had overheard her reading it to herself in the lobby and had been able to give them the final address. A stroke of luck in a world where luck was not common.

No other such letters had been left there, though the theatre often received and held mail for the actors and actresses. Hence nothing untoward had been suspected and the letter had simply been put in with the rest of the mail.

As a result, her family hadn't known exactly where her interview and photo session were to be held and neither had Joanne until the very last moment.

'A house on the rue de Valois whose rear windows face onto the garden, Hermann,' he called out. 'A residence whose owner, I am sure we will find, is still in the south or in the countryside, having felt it prudent to pay off the authorities so as to keep the house, and to stay away from Paris for the Duration.'

'For eternity, you patriot,' came the shout. 'The Thousand-Year Reich is here to stay.'

'Ah *bien sûr*, if you say so, Inspector, but if I might say so without being thrown up against a wall and shot for heresy, perhaps you are wrong.'

The Führer was an idiot and both of them knew it, but baiting

Louis was good for him. 'Quit feeling your oats, eh? Rommel will turn the Allies back in the desert. Stalin's armies will collapse at Stalingrad and my two boys will come home safely. My Gerda *won't* get the divorce so that she can marry her indentured French peasant! It's all a cruel joke.'

Hermann was moving from room to room just begging for an answer! 'A joke God has perpetrated on the two of us because He is punishing *me* for something I did as an altar boy', sang out St-Cyr. 'The stealing of the Blood of Christ and substitution of absinthe. The salting of the wafers with iodine in revenge for punishments received!'

'Admit it, you were unruly,' shouted Kohler, delighted to have stirred Louis out of himself.

It was all a game with them, this banter, to hide the horror of what they might find. Hermann must be on the first landing of the staircase but listening for him now would do no good. He could be far too quiet when he wanted, too noisy also, of course, at other times.

The six-acre quadrangle of the Palais Royal garden was bounded on three sides by identical houses of three storeys whose entrances faced not onto the garden but onto one of the adjacent streets: the rue de Montpensier was directly in front and to the west of him, the rue de Beaujolais off to his right at the far end, and the rue de Valois was behind him, the house being, like most others on that street, directly across from the Bank of France.

Down at the other end of the quadrangle, the original palace had been bequeathed to the Royal Family by Cardinal Richelieu in 1642. As a boy, Louis XIV had sailed toy boats in the fountain and later had played with the daughters of his servants. In 1715, when Philippe d'Orléans became regent, the Palais Royal acquired a rather *risqué* reputation which only increased during the Restoration when whorehouses and gambling dens surrounded the garden and Balzac wrote of them.

But Louis-Philippe put a stop to it all and gradually the garden and the houses, with arcaded shops below and apartments above, had slipped into that genteel quietude of polite insularity that so characterized the place even under the Germans.

Heavy iron gates kept the public out except at certain hours: 7.30 a.m. to 8.30 p.m. in winter, an hour earlier and two hours later in summer.

The custodian of the gates might have seen Joanne, for the girl would have made certain she had plenty of time to spare before her appointment, even after picking up her final letter unless, of course, she had been delayed.

Back came the plaintive voice of her little brother, Dédé. 'The robbery, Inspector. Eighteen million. One for every year of her life!'

The main Paris branch of Crédit Lyonnais nearby had been hit and a teller shot in the face and killed at 12.47 p.m. on that same Thursday. Bundles of 500- and 1000-franc notes had been crammed into two leather suitcases of good quality just waiting to be snatched. Pre-war cases of course. Unheard of now if new, and why would the bank in Lyon not have sent the money in dispatch cases or strong-boxes? Even at the 'official' Vichy rate of 200 francs to the British pound, it was at least £90,000. A fortune.

But had Joanne been a witness to that robbery? Had she been followed by someone connected with it? Had things been interrupted here by them because she could perhaps identify one of the men?

Was that why the house had been emptied in such a hurry?

He's lost to things, thought Kohler. He hasn't even heard me come downstairs. Well, I've news, *mon vieux*. News.

Louis didn't even turn from the windows. 'She would have got here early, Hermann, and come timidly into the garden to have a look at the place. A girl from working-class Belleville would *not* have announced her presence at the front door before having a little look around. She would have been going over how best to behave, and fretting about her atrocious accent, the slang of the *quartier* also, of course.' He tossed the hand with the pipe in salute.

'You heard me come downstairs,' grumbled Kohler.

Again the hand was tossed. 'It's nothing. The eyes in the ass of the trousers, just like the reflections in a shop window, are used to see if the coast is clear or to observe a little something like a bank robbery perhaps.'

The robbery ... 'You're full of surprises,' snorted Kohler. Somewhat diffident, somewhat chubby, a gardener, a muse, a reader of books and a fisherman when he could break the law and get away with it *and* find the time, Louis was fifty-two years of age, himself a little older. The scruffy brown moustache was tweaked, a shred of tobacco plucked from generous lips and examined closely in case it was worth saving. The shortages, the things one did to overcome them.

'Well, tell me what it is you've found, Hermann. Please, suspense I do not need in my life, having had enough of it already with you.'

'She was chloroformed up in the attic.'

The Frenchman spun round. 'She was *what?*'

Kohler grinned hugely and pulled down his lower left eyelid in mock salutation before triumphantly thrusting the crumpled cotton pad at him. 'I found this behind the bathtub. They couldn't have had time to search for it. She may still be alive, Louis. Alive!'

'Chloroformed ...' squawked the Sûreté, alarmed.

'And why not? What better place?'

'Then is it that those who emptied the house in such a hurry were the same as those who abducted the girls?'

Kohler swallowed hard. 'The bastards who pulled off that bank job wouldn't have had chloroform, would they? There's nothing to suggest it was them, Louis.'

'Then why were the photographs scattered if not to tell the police what happened here?'

Why indeed? Surely the kidnappers wouldn't have deliberately left the photos to point the finger at themselves?

Hermann found a broken cigarette and lit up. A giant with frizzy, greying hair that was not black or brown but something in between, the Bavarian had the heart and mind of a small-time hustler and the innate suspicion of the farmboy he had once been. A bad Gestapo—lousy would be a better word—he was a doubter of Germanic invincibility who had suffered for such doubts. The scar down the left cheek from eye to chin and the other one across the chest from shoulder to hip were from another case, a rawhide whip and a lesson he was supposed to learn.

An older brother had inherited the small farm near Wasserburg but, long before the deaths of his parents, Hermann had wanted to become a big-city detective. Now he was no longer sure of this but nothing short of a bullet or the piano-wire garrotte of Gestapo retribution could intervene. He was stuck with it, and with the Occupation, and so made the best of a bad bargain.

He had two women in Paris to warm a bed he seldom used. Giselle, a young and very vibrant hooker from the house of Madame Chabot around the corner on the rue Danton, and Oona, a Dutch alien he sheltered, though everyone in Gestapo circles must know of it.

A man for the times and in his element. A man on holiday. Well, almost.

'Let me keep the pad, Hermann.'

'Certainly. Just tell me where the photographer got the chloroform.'

'And the film.'

Questions, there were always questions.

Patiently they gathered the photographs into a pile for each victim. From time to time they studied them and made terse comments or paused to ease an aching back or knees, but for the most part they were tireless. Two very determined men who knew they had little time in which to find Joanne alive.

All of the girls had good bodies—hell, most of that age were biological honey pots, thought Kohler, and wasn't it a pity so many of the young men were dead or away in the Reich in POW camps or with the forced labour brigades or hiding out in the woods and hills of France with the maquis, the 'terrorists', the fledgeling Resistance? 'But why the stipulation of chestnut hair and eyes, Louis?'

'Such specifics demand a rationale.'

'A sister, a former lover, a mistress or hated mother,' offered the Gestapo.

'Or nanny.'

'Right back to the crib, eh?'

'They've all been photographed in exactly the same poses, Hermann.'

'On or against the same pieces of furniture? Naked and trapped in the same . . .' Quickly Kohler sorted through three of the piles, then sat back on his heels and sighed. 'That corner over there, I think. Behind the armchair and sofa, beside the lamp— squashed in next to the desk and with the vitrine full of porcelain and silver directly behind them so that the light reflected off the curvature of the glass for special effects. Ah *merde*, Louis, with what are we dealing?'

Each of the girls had retreated in shock to cower in that same corner, dismayed and in tears, with a breast clasped hard or the base of the throat and, in two of the photos, the other hand tightly gripping the crotch.

St-Cyr tried to clear his throat, but still a catch remained. 'Surely someone bent on humiliating a succession of young women would have been distracted sufficiently by fear of discovery and would not have chosen the same settings for all fourteen girls?'

Yet when the photos had been spread out in broad arcs across the living-room floor, they realized that, indeed, each girl had been caught in almost exactly the same poses and settings. On the *chaise-longue* and looking up into the camera, most with doubt and fear, one self-consciously smiling, for she had got the message and had thought perhaps that by offering the use of her body she could escape. Poor thing.

'They were all photographed in a prearranged sequence, Louis. First the clothes and the modelling, the girls modestly getting undressed and dressed behind a screen.' Kohler tapped a photo. 'Then, having got used to the camera, a few shots in evening gowns on the staircase with the chandelier's glimmer in the eyes and diamonds around the neck and wrists—are they really diamonds?'

'Perhaps, but then . . .'

'Paste perhaps. So, okay, it's something to think about, seeing as there's gold or silver jewellery elsewhere—it is gold or silver, isn't it? Hey, it looks like it.'

'Then a few more shots in the bedrooms, Hermann, and on up the stairs to the attic but never were any photos taken in the rooms up there. Never.'

'But into the main bathroom and finally, the insistence that it would really be best if a shoulder was bared or a bit of thigh.'

'Still no gun and no threats,' muttered St-Cyr. 'But to ease the minds of nervous young ladies whose stations in life might not have matched this place, there would have to have been more than just words of reassurance. The presence of another woman perhaps?'

A man and a woman, and a kid from Belleville . . . 'Good. Yes, that's very good, Chief. Having to work with me is toning you up, eh? So, come on, my fine *flic* from the Sûreté, let your big brother from the Gestapo show you a little something else.'

'The balcony off the attic?' mused St-Cyr.

'*Verdammt!*' snorted Kohler. 'And here I thought I was going to be one up on you.'

From the french windows of what might have been a bedroom or the sitting-room of an attic suite, they looked out into the rapidly fading light across a balcony that ran to a stone balustrade and urns and continuously around the three sides of the quadrangle, servicing every one of the houses and offering a ready means of coming and going.

'I'll quietly ask of the neighbours, Hermann. Nothing so alarming here as your presence, I think. Not just yet.'

'Then I'll chase up the robbery details and see if I can find out if the other girls are listed as missing.'

'Of course, but please don't alert the préfet. To invade his territory is to stamp on his balls and disturb the city.'

Paris and its environs were Talbotte's beat. The Sûreté and its Gestapo counterpart in the fight against common crime had the rest of the country to forage, and in any case, their investigation was totally unofficial.

Intuitively Kohler understood that Louis needed to be alone. 'Take care, *mon vieux*,' he said, gripping him by the arm. 'I'll drop back in a couple of hours and we'll go over to Chez Rudi's for a bite to eat.'

The head was shaken, the battered brown felt trilby pushed a little further back off that broad brow. 'There's no time. None, Hermann. Meet me at my place.'

'The club, I think. Won't Gabi be back?'

'Yes, yes, all right, the club. I must pay my respects.'

To a woman who loved him but to a love that had yet to be consummated.

Kohler thought to have the last word but turned away only to call back up the stairwell, 'Hey, I'm going to slap a *verboten* notice on the door and leave you a bit of wire to tie it shut. Okay?'

The hand of acknowledgement would automatically be lifted in salute he knew, the pipe and tobacco pouch taken out with feelings of doubt—short on rations again. Ah *nom de Dieu*, I'd better find him some, swore Kohler inwardly as he got into that big, black, b . . . e . . . a . . . utiful Citroën of Louis's.

It had been repaired at last, and repainted. No more bullet holes, broken glass and shot-out tyres. So, good. Yes, good.

As the tyres screeched on the rue de Valois and then at the corner of the rue de Beaujolais, St-Cyr followed him with his mind's eye and grimaced furiously.

Right to the main branch of Crédit Lyonnais over on the rue Quatre Septembre, he grimly followed the sound of the Citroën— there were so few cars on the streets these days, a hush like no other. Then all the way back again to fix a forgotten notice to the door, leave the wire and gather up the photographs to stuff them safely in the boot!

At last St-Cyr was able to pack his pipe and strike a match. Well, strike three of them in succession because they were so terrible but they'd always been that way, war or no war, Occupation or no Occupation. Like taxes, the government made them.

Letting the silent house come to him, he willed away all thoughts but those of Joanne and the other victims and heard in that terrible loneliness their earnest cries for help.

* * *

French banks were a bugger—Kohler was positive of it! They opened and closed at their convenience, took offence when none was intended, and had three hour lunches when they damned well felt like it, even in wartime.

But this one was different. Below stone carvings, in front of bronze plaques, two *flics* in dark blue kepis and capes stood guard in the snow with iron-cleated boots and black leather truncheons, a bad sign.

Flashing his Gestapo shield and looking grim and determined, he blithely rocketed between them and in through bronze doors too heavy for old ladies to open. Shit! The place was all but empty.

Surrounded by a floor whose sea of mottled grey marble lapped a magnificent staircase of the same and rose in plush red carpeting, he looked up into the frescoed vault above and then slowly brought his gaze down to the mezzanine.

Two superbly sculpted golden Venuses flanked the préfet of Paris, two of his detectives, the suave, bespectacled manager of the main Paris branch of Crédit Lyonnais and an assistant. There was a huge tapestry on the wall behind them, a gift no doubt from the impoverished silk weavers of Lyon in hopes of sales.

For perhaps ten seconds the gathering was overcome by the intruder and speechless, then Talbotte ripped himself away and bellowed, '*What the fuck do you think you are doing here?*'

Ah *merde* . . . 'My chief wants me to look into things,' sang out Kohler so that his voice would echo too. It was a lie of course.

'Your chief . . . ? Piss off. You've no jurisdiction here. Boemelburg . . .'

'Cash is cash, Préfet. The Resistance may have knocked off this little nest egg to buy guns and explosives from naughty boys who shouldn't sell them.'

'The terrorists?' snorted Talbotte, doubling a fist. 'Don't be an imbecile, Haupsturmführer. It was a straight gangland snatch and shooting. The *coup de grâce* at one metre for misbehaviour.'

In other words, pushing the right bell at the wrong time! 'Done with an eleven millimetre service revolver, Préfet?' sang out Kohler like a buzzard trying to pick the bones before the lions closed in.

Talbotte shrugged magnanimously. Yielding a little information could not matter. A gram or two of the flesh so as to discover why Kohler had shown up unannounced. A little of the blood.

'Yes, yes, an eleven millimetre most probably. Ballistics are still working on it.'

'After four days? Hey, that's a typical Resistance gun, my friend. I'd better jot that down and let the chief know of it.'

'*Nom de Jésus-Christ,* now wait a minute! We are not sure of this.' Talbotte turned to the others and raked them with a hiss. 'A moment, you understand? Let me deal with this one personally.'

Clapping his fedora on one of the Venuses and throwing his overcoat over the other, the préfet launched himself down the stairs with both fists at the ready. Blue serge suit and tie and all the rest. Dressed like a banker too.

Of medium height, square and tough . . . ah *Gott im Himmel,* yes . . . the préfet was nearly sixty years of age. There was Basque blood in him somewhere . . .

The swift, hard dark eyes of a gangster savaged the intruder. The bully, the street bastard and top cock of the dung heap, roared up to the mincemeat from Wasserburg and snorted garlic at him.

'Why are you and that fart of yours not in Lyon?'

'Oh that. We wrapped it up in style and slept all the way home on the train. Smooth as silk. We're raring to go.'

'So, where is Louis?'

A smile would be best and the offering of a cigarette. 'Busy.'

'You shit! I don't smoke with traitors, Kohler. *Traitors!*'

The insult echoed. It crashed all around them, shocking Kohler. It referred to a previous case, a lesson he had not quite learned . . .

'What happened in Vouvray was justice, Préfet. *Justice!* If you were anything of a cop and not so fucking corrupt and in bed with the SS and their friends, you'd know all about it.'

This was heresy. The cigarette was still shaking. Clearly Kohler was terrified his confrères might still wish to punish him for far too zealous an attention to 'justice', especially when one of their own had been involved.

And just as clearly the Resistance still thought his partner and friend—a known patriot—was a collaborator, ah yes!

Talbotte wagged a reproving finger. 'You should not have got the Organization Todt to repair Louis's house, *mon fin*. This Resistance you speak of may well have planted the little bomb that accidentally killed Jean-Louis's fornicating wife and child instead of himself but they will come back if I should give the nod, eh? The nod.'

The shit. Louis's wife had been fooling around behind his back but had decided to come home.

'The explosion took out all the windows,' breathed Kohler, 'to say nothing of smashing up the front of the house and getting his neighbours angry at him for costing them their windows too.'

'Which you had the Todt replace as well, and at cost to yourself.'

'So what? It was personal.'

Talbotte lit up and blew smoke through flaring nostrils. Kohler's French was really very good. 'So out of charity to the two of you, let us agree to co-operate a little, eh? Let us show the good will among police forces so that your Führer will be pleased.'

The hypocritical bastard! Kohler chanced an uncertain glance up the stairs to the spellbound audience. The préfet's gaze never left him. Hooded under thick black brows, the eyes waited.

A shrug would have to do. Louis wouldn't like it but . . . ah what the hell. 'So, okay, let's co-operate. How many held the place up?'

Still the eyes didn't shift.

'First you tell me why you are interested in this affair?'

'My chief . . .'

Talbotte flicked ash at him. 'Your *chief*, as you call him, was just here. The Sturmbannführer Boemelburg is convinced the terrorists had nothing to do with the matter because, Inspector, I have said so and what I say goes.'

'*Bon.* So, how many were involved? Three . . . was it three?

One to watch the street, one to hold the gun on the employees and the last to . . .'

'I'm still waiting, Inspector. Why have you such an interest in something that can concern you not in the slightest!'

The sparrows on the mezzanine hadn't moved. The Venuses gazed sublimely down upon the world . . . 'All right. A small affair. A girl is missing. She may have seen something.'

'A girl. So, good. Yes, that is good. Now a little more, I think.'

'Her name, eh? You first. Were there three men or was there a woman with them?'

'This girl, perhaps?' asked the Chief of Police pleasantly enough. 'Please, is this what you wish to know, Inspector?'

Ah *Gott im Himmel*, the bastard . . . 'Just, was there a woman with the men who robbed this bank?'

Talbotte filled his lungs with smoke and held it in only to release it slowly through the nostrils as a dragon would before eating a peasant and his pig.

'Then ask someone else but do so in the street.'

The fingers were snapped, the voice thrown back over a shoulder and up the stairs. 'You and you, accompany the inspector to his car and switch on the ignition for him. If he resists, give the sieve to his brand-new radiator and abort the tyres to remind him that in Paris it's not only the gangsters who do things properly!'

The birds took wing, drawing their guns as they came down the stairs.

The banker blinked and wiped sweat from a worried brow. Now why was that? wondered Kohler. A banker in trouble *after* the fact!

Out on the street, he grinned and said, 'Okay, okay, you win, eh, until we meet again.'

The custodian of the gates to the garden of the Palais Royal couldn't remember seeing anyone remotely resembling Joanne Labelle. 'In here, a girl like that?' he said. 'Ah no, no, Inspector. I would most certainly be aware of such a one.'

You snob! grimaced St-Cyr, disliking the man intensely for

looking down on the citizens of his beloved Belleville but nodding in agreement several times. 'How stupid of me. A girl like that in a place like this . . .' He waved the snapshot Dédé had given him. 'Other girls perhaps but not such a one as her, especially as there were ten degrees of frost and the garden would have been all but deserted.'

Vincent Girandoux drew himself up until his dark blue cap with the gold braid and badge of authority all but touched the roof of his tiny kiosk. 'Inspector, the domestics aren't appreciated in the garden. Nannies are, of course, and the nurses, the companions of the elderly ladies who live here but . . .' He teased a cuff of his dark blue greatcoat with gold braided epaulets and brass buttons down a bit. 'But if the tenants thought for a moment . . .'

'That you were disloyal? Now listen, she was not someone's mistress. She was . . .'

The dark horn-rimmed bifocals leapt. 'I *didn't* say anything about mistresses!'

'Okay, okay, so those are all more classy. Please, I come from Belleville myself, eh? She's just a girl we are looking for.'

'Why?'

'That doesn't concern you but . . . Ah but if she's been murdered, it's entirely possible we'll have to summon you to testify.'

'Murdered . . . Here? Let me see the snapshot again. Why doesn't she wear an overcoat and galoshes?'

The photo had been taken in the fall of 1940. 'Imagine her in a beige double-breasted overcoat with the collar turned up. Give her a golden yellow mohair scarf from Hermès, monsieur, and a cocoa-brown beret. Gloves of brown suede—pre-war of course—and most probably not winter boots but rubbers over shoes with medium heels. Pumps.'

'Silk stockings?'

The quality of the scarf had done its work. 'Perhaps. Yes, it's entirely possible but, like the rest, they would have come from long before this war.'

'Then the clothes would have been handed down.'

Their eyes met. The detective waited, then said guardedly,

'Hand-me-downs and recently made over yet again to suit, yes. They were my first wife's and I gave them to the girl's mother in the spring of 1934 when that first wife left me because she could no longer stand the nights and days of never knowing if I would return from work alive. She just walked out and left, and one day I came home to find her gone.'

Had it been a warning, wondered Girandoux and if so, was it but an affair of foolishness then, this matter of the girl? The affectation of one who had adopted the position of surrogate father or 'uncle'. 'The girl was afraid, Inspector. I noticed the coat, the scarf and gloves, yes. She was quite handsome but . . .'

'When . . . At about what time? Please be as precise as possible.'

'At . . . at about 1.15 or 1.20 perhaps.'

About half an hour after the robbery. 'And she was afraid?'

'Yes. A frown, the constant looking back over her shoulder. Once a pause beneath the trees to watch the gate for a few minutes. Five, I think. Then again under one of the arches, and once more from the arcade in front of the shop of Monsieur Meunier, the engraver.'

'Please, this shop, which is it?'

A Pétainiste through and through, a man who liked order above all else, Girandoux removed a black leather glove to place a forefinger on the plan of the garden that was tacked to the wall precisely in front of the plain wooden table and chair that were the sole furnishings of his office, apart from a calendar whose days had been meticulously X'd.

'It's at number 27, Inspector.'

Directly across the gardens from the house . . .

Perhaps the frost was the cause of the moisture in the detective's eyes, thought Girandoux, perhaps the knowledge that the girl had quite possibly been followed and most certainly must have known of this.

'Was she with the Resistance, Inspector?' he hazarded. One never knew quite what to say in these times.

A copy of the Paris weekly *Je Suis Partout* was sticking out of the worn leather briefcase on the floor. The lunch packet was empty.

Pro-Nazi and violently anti-Third Republic, the weekly reflected the views of such fascists as this one, thought St-Cyr. The lighted candle would give the illusion of warmth. The black-out curtain was drawn.

'Inspector . . .'

'Yes, I understand perfectly, Monsieur Girandoux, custodian of the gates to the garden of the Palais Royal. Is it that you've missed out on the reward of 100,000 francs by not notifying our German friends of such a suspicious character? *If* she had been apprehended, and *if* forced to confess, then of course the money would have been paid and you could rest a good deal easier knowing you had rid the world of such a terrorist. But, ah but, you see, monsieur, she wasn't of the Resistance, was not even suspected of such of thing.'

The man heaved a grateful sigh. St-Cyr thought to ask further questions—they desperately needed to know what had happened—but he couldn't bring himself to do so and was angry his feelings should intrude so harshly.

Without another word, he snuffed out the candle and left the bastard in the dark.

Meunier, the engraver, was more co-operative and with good reason. To the quiet, steady trade of engraving cigarette cases and bits of silver and gold for German officers, had been added the engraving of embossed and gilded notices for official receptions and calling cards. 'Beautiful paper, tireless and exquisite workmanship,' said St-Cyr. 'I commend you, m'sieur, and your son. That is your son in the workshop, is it not?'

It was. 'His chest, Inspector. The lungs are not very good.'

'So, free of the call-ups of '39 and '40, and free of the forced labour in the Reich.' There would be an exemplary doctor's certificate stating absolutely that the boy's health wouldn't for a moment allow such activities.

The speckled, grey-black, neatly trimmed aristocratic beard didn't move. The dark eyes behind the gold-rimmed glasses were limpid.

'I've nothing to hide, Inspector. This,' Meunier indicated the displays, 'is but a living. Were I to have shut up the shop of my great-grandfather and gone south into the Free Zone, I would simply have forfeited everything. Is that not so?'

It was, for the Germans would have taken over and sold what they could or rented the shop to someone else and pocketed the rent, since that had been one of the first ordinances of the Occupier. Get back to work or else.

Meunier had been bent over his desk patiently working on a copper plate, with an array of wooden-handled engraving tools before him and a jeweller's glass to one eye. Now he reached for his jacket and, putting it on, buttoned it up over a grey vest and waited. The shop was warm, a rarity in these days of so little coal. A bad sign, since it implied outright collaboration.

The son tried to continue to operate a small hand-press. A notice in heavy bond for the Kommandantur perhaps, or the SS over on the avenue Foch since it was the holiday season.

'A small matter, monsieur,' said St-Cyr. 'Did either of you see this girl on Thursday last at about 1.20 p.m?'

The engraver didn't even look at the snapshot.

'Is it about the house of Monsieur Vergès, Inspector?'

'Monsieur Vergès?'

'Yes. Directly across from us. The girl studied the house for some time, then entered the shop to ask whose it was. Monsieur Vergès hasn't been back since the exodus of June 1940. I told the girl there couldn't possibly be anyone there and that she must have the wrong address.'

To offer information so readily was just not usual, especially not in these desperate times. 'And how did she react to what you said?' asked St-Cyr cautiously.

'Distressed. Flustered. At first certain that I hadn't told her the truth, then casting anxious looks through the windows towards the house. This . . . this morning when Paul arrived to open the shop, he . . . he noticed the curtains had been removed. Has something . . . ?'

'Ah yes, the curtains. The house is empty.'

'Empty, but . . .'

'But what, m'sieur?'

'But . . . but Monsieur Vergès can't have sold it, Inspector? The house has been in his family for generations. He swore he would never do so even though his only son is one of the droolers and was never allowed to show his face here.'

One of the droolers . . . *les baveux*. A special branch of the *gueules cassées*, the broken mugs of World War I whose faces had been horribly mutilated by shrapnel and the bullets of snipers and machine guns.

Without a lower jaw, or only a part of it and often no lips, one drooled constantly and wore always a towel around the neck to catch the saliva.

'Surely Paris and the garden could have been allowed the son, monsieur?'

The detective had obviously been a soldier himself.

Reading the engraver's mind was easy. 'A sergeant in the Signals Corps,' said St-Cyr guardedly. 'I've seen so many of them, monsieur. *Begging* in the streets. Shut up because . . . ah because one's family and friends soon became so ashamed of the gah-gahing, they turned their backs on those heroes and loved ones in revulsion.'

And you're still bitter about it, thought Meunier, warning himself to go carefully. 'Monsieur Vergès is the kindest of men, Inspector. The boy was to have been married but when his fiancée saw what had happened to his face, she screamed in terror and ran from him, refusing absolutely to have anything more to do with him.'

A quite common response and quite understandable though regrettable. 'So, let us proceed to the matter of the house and the girl in this snapshot. Did she stay with you long?'

Meunier hesitated, but immediately regretted doing so and was flustered. 'Ah, not long, Inspector. She asked again about the owner of the house and left in a hurry.'

'But . . . but she thought she was being followed?'

'Followed? Pardon?'

Was it such a catastrophe?

Swiftly Meunier went to close the door to the workshop and

shut out his son. Then he came back to stand on the other side of
the counter. 'She said nothing of being followed, Inspector.
Nothing!' he hissed.

'And did you not sense this?'

'No, I did not. I saw a girl who didn't belong in a place like this
and had obviously been given an incorrect address, a girl who
couldn't understand that such a mistake had been made. When I
told her the owner wasn't there, she showed me a letter she had
received in answer to an advertisement she had found in *Le
Matin*.'

So, the fish is fresh, thought St-Cyr. Now for the sauce. 'And
what did the letter say? Come, come, monsieur, an answer is
required.'

'That . . . that she was indeed to go to that address. This I
cannot understand, Inspector, but at the time, I said there still
must be some mistake as I hadn't seen Monsieur Vergès in over
two-and-a-half years.'

'And do you think she went to the house?'

As if the confrontation were over, Meunier began to relax. 'Of
that I have no idea. She left without thanking me and I paid not
the slightest attention until . . .'

'Ah yes. Until your son told you the curtains had been taken
down.'

'Yes, not until then,' came the testy reply.

'And were the curtains there yesterday?' asked St-Cyr cautiously.

'It was Sunday, Inspector. Though we're very busy, the Lord's
Day is sacred.'

'Saturday then?'

What has happened in that house? wondered Meunier. 'Yes,
the curtains were there on Saturday. I myself saw them and can
swear to this.'

Then there's no need for me to speak to your son, is that it?
thought St-Cyr. 'Tell me about this Monsieur Vergès, monsieur.
Where does he live?'

'Near Provins. He has a house there which has been in his
family for over two hundred years.'

'A house. A château?'

Meunier thought a pause would be best. He would draw himself up. 'I really wouldn't know, Inspector. One never asks.'

'Come, come, m'sieur. Monsieur Vergès would have used your services on a number of occasions, especially to announce the engagement of a son.'

Ah damn the Sûreté and their meddling! 'Le Château des belles fleurs bleues.' The Château of the Beautiful Blue Flowers.

Lupins probably, or violets along the wooded banks of the Seine. 'And the name of the fiancée who ran away?'

'Angèlique Desthieux, but surely that business happened so long ago, it's of no consequence?'

It would be best to give the engraver a moment and then to quietly tell him, 'In crime everything is of consequence. The announcement, please. You will still have a copy of it.'

Desthieux . . . It rang no bells until Meunier just happened to say, 'She was a mannequin for one of the top fashion houses. Freelance also.'

A mannequin . . . Startled, the detective threw him a look of savage puzzlement. 'She was *what*?' he demanded.

Unsettled, Meunier thought to shrug the matter off. 'Oh, she was from before that other war, Inspector. Very beautiful, very elegant. Tall and slender, with long chestnut hair and large dark brown eyes . . . Monsieur Vergès's son was very much in love with her. I used to see them strolling in the garden from time to time. It was the young Monsieur Gaetan who, at his father's wish, asked us to do the announcement.'

A drooler . . . a girl with long chestnut hair and deep brown eyes . . . 'May I keep this for a little?' asked St-Cyr of the gilded announcement. 'Please, I'll take good care of it.'

'Certainly. I have two others. We always keep three or four and always I seem to be thinking I ought to throw them out but can never bring myself to do so.'

'*Bon.* Now, please, m'sieur, a word with your son for I greatly fear you have tried to mislead me and that he's the one who really let the girl into the shop and spoke with her.'

Crestfallen that the information he had sacrificed had not

accomplished what he had intended, the engraver sadly nodded in defeat. 'He's a good boy. Lonely—aren't all such boys lonely when everyone says he should have done his duty and he can't find the will to forgive a father's love? He's the only son I have, Inspector. No one else can carry on the name.'

'Then let me speak to him. It will do no harm and go no further than the three of us.'

Reluctantly Meunier opened the door to the workshop. The boy had removed his glasses and apron and, though brushing tears from sensitive eyes, stood proudly waiting to be carted off to prison.

Ah *maudit*, what have we now? wondered St-Cyr, not liking it at all.

Dumbfounded, the father stood in silence gazing at his son as if for the first time.

The boy whispered, 'Papa, forgive me.'

'For what? For talking to that girl?'

St-Cyr nudged the father out of the workshop and closed the door. He thought to say to the boy, You fool, he thought to say so many things but a sad weariness had overcome him and all he said was, 'I'm Chief Inspector Jean-Louis St-Cyr of the Sûreté. My partner is from the Gestapo.'

'The Gestapo . . . ?'

The boy blanched. For perhaps ten seconds the pale grey eyes in that thin, angular face met his as the ghastly reality of those two words sank in.

Paul Meunier was delicate, thin and tall. A boy, a young man—one always spoke of both in the same breath—of about twenty-six years of age.

'My family,' he blurted. 'My father, my mother and my sister . . .'

'They will all be shot, as will yourself,' said St-Cyr, not sparing him but hating himself for having to adopt the guise of the Occupier, 'unless, of course, we can come to some agreement.'

'Agreement?' It was a yelp. The boy wet his pale lips and, at a loss as to what to do with his right hand, pushed back the silky light brown hair that had fallen over his brow.

'Look, my interest is in the missing girl, Joanne Labelle.'

'Not in the papers?'

'Don't be an *idiot*! Don't offer information like that!' *Merde alors*, must God do this to him, a simple detective? 'Listen, *mon ami*, one can read your mind so clearly! Forging papers. Making a hero out of yourself so that the girls will think more highly of you. Hey, do you know something, my fine martyr? I *don't* want to know who you forged them for.'

He doesn't want to know . . . ? 'My father, he . . . he forbade me to go into the army.'

An impatient hand was tossed. 'Forgive him. That's the only thing you can do. Now listen, I want you to shut up about these forgeries. Sure I know the Resistance must be using you, but I have to walk the knife edge always, so the less said the better.'

Was the inspector involved in something himself? wondered Meunier. Was it best to let him go on thinking that it was the Resistance he had done the forgeries for and not Mademoiselle Marie-Claire de Brisson, the banker's daughter? The nights and nights of patient practice and experimentation until she was satisfied and it was done. Three sets of documents with *laissez-passers* for Provins and Dijon. The travel papers had been the hardest to forge, the others not so bad, and in time, perhaps, the Resistance would be able to use him once a suitable contact was made.

'Your partner . . .' began the boy.

St-Cyr told himself the Resistance should never have used this one, that the boy would drag them all down, himself as well if mentioned. 'My partner, yes. Hermann Kohler of the Gestapo.'

'Will you . . . will you be telling him that I . . .'

'That you are a forger for the Resistance? Perhaps I will, perhaps I won't. I leave you to worry about it, eh? So watch yourself and don't try to leave the city. Now tell me about Joanne Labelle. Tell me everything. Try to forget about my partner.'

Kohler let a breath escape slowly as he compared the head-and-shoulders photo in one of the card-index drums of missing persons with a photo from the house, then moved on to the dossier Émile Turcotte had pulled for him.

On Thursday, 3 July 1941, a girl named Reneé Marteau had

answered an advertisement in *Paris-Soir*. She had been an out-of-work mannequin with nearly two years' experience and had, apparently, seized on the advertisement as a means of getting herself back onto the circuit.

Long chestnut hair and deep brown eyes all right. A bit small in the bust, but what the hell, that wasn't everything when you had smashing legs, a nice smile and a gorgeous posterior.

He turned a page and found the first of six grainy black-and-white police prints that made him turn away and nearly lose his lunch, though that had been eaten hours ago.

On 15 August 1941 her nude and badly battered body had been found washed up downriver in St-Cloud just past the Citroën works. It had caught against the mooring cable of a refuse barge that had been machine-gunned during the blitzkrieg and had sat on the bottom ever since. Weeds were in her mouth and nostrils. Mud was smeared in streaks over pale white skin that looked cold.

She hadn't been in the water long. Perhaps twenty-four hours at the most. A vagrant had found her. Hair all chopped off so that only tufts remained. Throat cut. 'A slice from the right and savagely,' hissed Turcotte who had never been at the discovery of this corpse or any other, and not even at the morgue. 'The breasts removed for good measure but we feel this was done before the killing.'

Verdammt! swore Kohler. What the hell was he to tell Louis?

Records occupied the whole of the sixth and top floor of what had formerly been the Head Offices of the Sûreté Nationale but was now that of the Gestapo in France. Screams in the cellars, dread on the rue des Saussaies and the rue du Faubourg Saint-Honoré right in the very heart of the city, only whispers and dark looks up here where seventy or so French detective-clerks in grey smocks foraged round the clock in shifts for news or filed away another bit.

The Sûreté had never thrown a thing out. Second only to the records of the Gestapo in Berlin, the whole damned place had been taken over lock, stock and barrel in June 1940. A treasure trove of criminals and their crimes to which, as a measure of

Germanic efficiency and consolidation, had been added the files of the Préfecture of Paris. Talbotte had seen fit to keep copies for himself but had been reluctant to object. He had known his place and still did only too well.

In addition to the ten or fifteen million dossiers and cards dealing with outright crime, there were the millions of other bits and pieces that might eventually prove useful. One never knew. Apply for a passport or a visa in pre-war days, or even now, or a new set of papers, and you got a card here. Apply for a hunting licence in days past when such a thing was possible, and you got a special card, complete with registration number. Nice for the Occupier. No problem in finding stray rifles and shotguns that should have been turned in. Apply for a marriage licence, birth certificate or divorce—yes, here divorce had been legal before the war, though now Pétain and the government in Vichy frowned on it, the hypocrites. Age, date of birth, sex, race, colour of eyes, nose, height, weight, religion, address and those of the closest relatives, place of residence, job, education . . . it was all here, locked up in silence until the wheel was spun, a drawer opened or the pen taken up.

The labyrinth of missing persons was discouraging. To all those who had been listed because of suspected or proven crimes, were added those who had simply walked away without telling anyone. Then there were the thousands who had died or become separated from their loved ones during the blitzkrieg, when the roads had had to be 'cleared' of refugees for the advancing Panzers and the boys in their Messerschmitts and Stukas had had a field day.

Émile Turcotte was lord and master here, a hawk-eyed, miserly little bastard with no sense of humour, the rake of a guardsman's moustache and, too often, the defiant gaze of a wounded librarian. They'd got through all the usual refusals far too quickly. The préfet had tipped him off and had told him to co-operate or else, so as to bleed this Gestapo of information.

Well, that was fair enough, though Turcotte was not a servant of the préfet but one of their own and ought to have known better.

'Shall we spin the wheel again?' quipped the librarian.

Kohler snorted and sadly shook his head. It had taken them nearly an hour to find this one. For now he had enough on what must have happened to the other girls.

And Joanne? he wondered. Would there yet be time to save her and if so, what would they find?

'Look, I need a bit on that robbery. For a start, give me what you have on the manager of the main Paris branch of Crédit Lyonnais.'

This, too, the préfet had warned of. 'That is not possible.'

'It had better be. I'm not used to threatening my fellow workers but if I have to . . .'

The acid seethed. 'The last time you . . . you tried to steal my tobacco tin for Louis!'

That had been about a month ago. 'Then this time I'll simply requisition it.'

The dark olive eyes flicked away in uncertainty. Kohler was trouble. 'A moment,' grumbled Turcotte. The préfet, he . . . he wouldn't like it but . . .

'No moments,' grinned Kohler, clapping a hand firmly on a thin shoulder. 'Hey, *mon fin*, I think I'd better come with you in case you run into an accident.'

Such records were in another section, and even that God of Louis's could never have found them, but Turcotte had a nose for it and the memory.

When he pulled the file, right away the banker's name came up: André-Philippe de Brisson, the address: 35 rue de Montpensier, almost directly across the garden of the Palais Royal from the house.

'Eighteen million, Inspector,' muttered the old woman abstractedly. 'Poor Monsieur de Brisson will be beside himself and will forget absolutely to tell his daughter to let the cat in. It is the toughs these days, the police.'

'Ah no, madame, surely not the police,' urged St-Cyr. One had to speak loudly.

'Yes, yes, the police.' She would purse her lips and glare at

him. She would have to dismiss the girl. One could not have
one's days interrupted by the Sûreté. How shameful.

The maid had let him into the house which was next door to
the house of Monsieur Vergès. The hour of the apéritif had come
and gone with two glasses of well-watered port he had not been
given a chance to share.

Little had been accomplished. The bank manager's house was
across the garden. 'The daughter, Madame Lemaire?' he hazarded. 'Does Mademoiselle de Brisson let the cat in through one
of the attic windows perhaps?'

'The cat . . . ? What cat?'

'The robbery, madame. You were only just saying . . .'

The thin shoulders beneath the mound of sweaters and shawls
quivered with indignation. 'Please do not interrupt me,
Inspector. I know perfectly well what I was saying.'

The woman drifted off into silence and left him waiting, though
not purposely. Fortune had passed by, leaving faded, once plush,
wine-purple armchairs with holes in their arms and loose threads
trailing to the floor to join frayed tassels.

There were two of these armchairs, one on each side of a
smoke-blackened grey marble chimneypiece; no fire, no fuel
tonight. A cross, a small ormolu clock, a photo in its frame, two
plates of dubious value and a vase from someplace occupied the
mantelpiece beneath a gilded Louis-Philippe mirror that had lost
the top left corner of its carving. An accident years ago.

A pair of flanking, gilded sconces, mounted on the cracked,
pale yellow walls, held stubs of candles in each of their three
holders. He felt the stubs had been left for propriety's sake
though the thought of melding all six together would have presented a dilemma whenever it registered.

Impatient at the continued delay but telling himself to go easy,
he cleared his throat and said, 'The robbery, madame?' But now
the grey eyes that had only this past moment been so fiercely
defiant, drifted into memory at the thought of food as she touched
the faded menu at her side.

'The ninety-ninth day of the siege, 25 December 1870,' she
said, wistfully reading it.

The Franco-Prussian War. The winter of 1870-71. How old had she been? he wondered. Fifteen or twenty, no more . . .

' "Hors-d'oeuvre: *Langue de kérabau en gelée écarlate. Cervelle d'éléphant. Animelles de zèbre à la crème sur canapés.*" '

Jellied water buffalo tongue, elephant brains, and zebra testicles sliced, in cream, and on little wedges of toast.

The city had been ringed by the Prussians. Napoleon III had been taken prisoner. No food could enter Paris . . . 'Madame . . .'

'Please do not interrupt me, Inspector. I read this every day to remind myself of the brave and to beg God to let them return since men such as yourself have not stopped the Boches.'

A purée of emu with croutons, a consommé of kangaroo thickened with tapioca, garnished with dried royale and sprinkled with chervil, no doubt. On the ninety-ninth day of the siege, the Paris zoo had been emptied and the contents shared.

The menu was perhaps from the restaurant Le Grand Véfour that was off the north-western corner of the garden with an entrance on the rue de Beaujolais. It had been founded in 1760, was still open and still much the same. A classic. Balzac had eaten there.

Duchess potato croquettes dipped in egg and breadcrumbs and fried in very hot, deep fat . . . Camel stew, braised shank of antelope . . . 'Madame, an important investigation. A girl is missing. To prevent a tragedy it is imperative that we . . .'

A girl . . . 'She is waiting in the doorway. Nanette, please show the inspector out.'

Baked mongoose, stuffed lemur with truffles . . . As a young woman, madame would perhaps have had the second service and have sipped a Romanée Conti 1856 by candle-light while the city, besieged, prayed for the brave to defend its honour.

'She's like that always now, Inspector. My mistress is really a very dear lady who has been extremely kind to me. She doesn't mean to be difficult.'

Marianne, his dead wife had been a Breton, thought St-Cyr. This one, too, had the fair cheeks and china-blue eyes, the blonde hair that was like silk and the warm if hesitant manner.

'What will you do when she passes away?' he asked as they

paused by the door to the outer hall and stairs. 'Please, I know it's a matter you've told yourself many times you must face.'

The girl's eyes were downcast. Moisture gathered rapidly in them.

'I . . . I don't know, Inspector. Madame, she has no one but me. No one any more. They're all dead, don't you see?'

He nodded gravely and said, 'Permit me, then, to give you my card. Please, I'll see what I can do to help.'

'But me? Why me? Why should you do such a thing?'

She had instantly thought the worst. 'Because I know what the alternatives are, mademoiselle, and can perhaps find a suitable situation for you with two dear friends who may just be looking for a little help. It's not impossible. Both are older women of great experience and understanding. They have a shop on the place Vendôme. Look, I must visit them soon and will broach the subject so that when the worst should happen, we will have a little preparation.'

She tried to smile but tears flooded from her. He gave her his handkerchief, she muttered, '*Merci*,' and when her cheeks were dry, her eyes still moist and bringing back such memories to him of Marianne, he said, 'Did you see who came to remove the furniture from the house next door, the house of Monsieur Vergès?'

It would be best to nod quickly. 'Four men in two *gazogène* lorries from the firm of Dallaire and Sons last night.'

Sunday evening . . . Her chest lifted, a breath was held. He would be brief since there was more. 'At about what time?' he asked.

There was a firmness in his voice that made her realize she would have to tell him. 'At 6.07 p.m. I had just taken Madame her first glass of port and had returned to the kitchen to see what I could do best to make her supper a little more attractive.'

After dark, then. 'Some parsley, perhaps?'

The girl brightened. 'Yes. Why yes, that's it exactly!'

'And did you call the matter of the movers to her attention?'

'No. Ah, no. I . . .' She would lower her eyes because he would not think well of her now. 'I knew how upset she would have been, Inspector. Monsieur Vergès has always been so very kind to her. Though he doesn't come to his house any more, his presence is still felt. Flowers . . . flowers are still sent each year on her birthday.'

Then she has someone after all, but you're afraid of him—was that it? he wondered, looking her over. The girl was no more than twenty-two years of age and had been with Madame Lemaire for the past five years. Though probably not entirely innocent, she was still a 'good' girl and had not put herself on the streets as had some. 'The son of Monsieur Vergès, Mademoiselle Nanette? The sender of the flowers perhaps. Did he ever come to the house next door?'

Stricken, she threw him a look of anguish. 'No. Ah no, Inspector. Not that one. Not that I . . . I know of.' Swiftly she crossed herself while dropping her eyes and saying inwardly, The drooler . . . the drooler . . .

He would have to be gentle and must soften his voice. 'Then tell me what you heard from that house, Nanette. You were waiting for sleep perhaps. Madame had already . . .'

Her shoulders straightened. Her chin lifted. Her gaze was steady. 'She goes to sleep very early, Inspector, but like a lot of old people, often awakens in the night and is sometimes up for hours.'

'What did you hear?'

The Inspector would hate her for it. 'A woman crying. My room . . . It's in the attic at the back, you understand.'

Overlooking the balcony and the garden. 'And did you tell Madame of this crying?'

His gaze demanded the truth. 'No, I . . . I was afraid to. Madame has a heart murmur, Inspector. Sometimes things upset her and . . .'

'And you were afraid she would be very upset since neither Monsieur Vergès nor his son apparently ever came to the house.'

'Yes.'

The tears were very real and many. The lovely lips quivered with remorse. He hated to do it to her but had to know. 'How often did you hear this crying?'

She mustn't tell him everything. She mustn't! 'Sometimes

every night for days but . . . but then it would stop and . . . and there would be peace until . . .'

He couldn't keep the sadness from his voice. 'Until a few days or weeks had passed, or a month or two perhaps, when again there would be much weeping but not, am I right, from the same person?'

So much was registered in the girl's eyes. Fear, doubt, anxiety, shame. 'What has happened in that house, Inspector? Please, you must tell me.'

Ah damn, what was she hiding and why was she too afraid to tell him?

'Nanette . . . Girl, has he gone?' came the voice of Madame Lemaire.

'Yes . . . yes, madame! I am just bringing the supper.' Frantically the girl turned to him. 'Please, Inspector, her heart.'

'I'll be back. Say nothing of this to anyone. Your life may well be in danger.'

After he had gone, she pressed her forehead against the door and wept. She hadn't told him of her attempts to find out what had been going on in that house since the Defeat. The Defeat! She hadn't told him what she had seen.

Taking the business card from her apron, she opened her blouse and slid it down under her brassière until it nestled against the plump warmth of her left breast.

'I will sew it into the lining,' she whispered. 'I will keep it with me always. And when I have to wash the brassière?' she asked herself, with all the practicality of her ancestors. 'Then I will put it under my pillow at such times.'

He would hate her for what she had seen and said nothing of.

2 THE BOY WAS WAITING IN THE FREEZING DARK-
ness of the rue Laurence-Savart beside the gate to
number 3. He had been there for hours.

'Dédé, what is this?' asked St-Cyr. 'You'll catch pneumonia.'

'It's nothing, Monsieur the Chief Inspector. Nothing.'

'Of course, but you know I would have come up the street to
visit with your dear mama and papa, and your brothers and sisters. We agreed, isn't that so? A wash, a cup of bouillon and then
the conference. That's why I'm here. How are they bearing up?'

'Terrible, Chief Inspector. *Grand-mére* is saying Joanne has
been violated and murdered, and that her nude body has been
left out in the cold for the crows to peck out her eyes and the rats
to eat their way up her . . .'

'Ah damn that old woman, she ought to know better! Come
inside immediately. Is the gas still on?'

St-Cyr unlatched the gate and pushed it open. The Germans
often turned the gas off for the stupidest of reasons and for others
too: the acts of terrorism that were gradually becoming more frequent and bolder. Each day the gas was on for but a few hours
and he had lost track of those times, for he was seldom home for

long. 'Dédé, please answer me. Men must be brave at such times.'

Men . . . 'It . . . it's off, Chief Inspector, as is the electricity and the water, the full job, but . . . but I've brought you a thermos of soup and some bread.'

'Ah *bon, c'est bon*. You must thank your mother for me. Now let's go inside and I'll fill you in on the latest developments.'

It was freezing in the house but fortunately the Organization Todt had stacked sufficient kindling and bits of board from the repairs for a decent fire. The stove was soon warm. The soup was excellent, a family sacrifice he appreciated.

But what did one say to a ten-year-old boy who adored his oldest sister because she loved him and made him feel special, since he was caught in the middle so to speak, having both older brothers and younger sisters to contend with?

Out of respect, the boy had pulled off his knitted hat and placed it on the table. St-Cyr took in the sallow cheeks and hollow eyes, the high forehead and narrow chin that would, in time, fill out if allowed.

It was the lack of milk, cheese, vitamins and minerals. No milk could get into the city from the farms of plenty, except for that sold on the black market or directly to the Germans. There were no potatoes in a land of them. They had all gone to the Reich.

But of such hardships there must be no mention. He grinned and threw his hands out, shrugging too. 'So, progress, *mon vieux*. Great progress. Joanne was not killed in the house to which she went for the interview.'

Not killed . . . 'But . . . but she has gone to the Théâtre du Palais Royal for the interview?'

Why was it boys of this age always seemed to have such large eyes? Beseechingly they demanded absolute truth.

'A letter was left there for her, Dédé. Joanne then went to a house.'

'Where?'

'That I can't say. For now it must remain confidential so as not to jeopardize the investigation.'

Confidential . . .

St-Cyr leaned over the table, pushing a small tin of age-old mints a little closer. 'Go on. They help.' He nodded towards the mints. 'My partner proves his usefulness at times. Take two. One for each cheek. Don't crush them up. They last longer.'

The mints were taken but one was dropped through nervousness, moving St-Cyr to say earnestly, 'Be brave. There's still hope. After three days, she was taken from the house to another place last night. We're working on it and I expect to have further answers when I meet my partner in an hour or so. We're not sparing the clock on this one. Joanne was special.'

The Chief Inspector had not yet removed his overcoat and scarf or galoshes, hat and gloves. He ate the last of the soup with the thoroughness of the determined, and when it was gone, wiped the bowl and spoon with the last of the bread just as they did at home.

'It saves on the washing-up, eh, Dédé? Now listen.'

He shoved plate and spoon aside and brushed a few crumbs into a hand before eating them. 'She got to the appointment early. She used her head and looked the house over first. Very cleverly she let others know where she was going. This has made our job much, much easier. It tells me Joanne has her wits about her and will, perhaps, leave further clues for us to follow.' *Merde alors*, how could he lie like this to the boy?

Further clues . . .

'We've gathered a great deal of information, Dédé, in a very short time thanks to her quick-wittedness.'

The Chief Inspector used the candle flame to light his pipe, tilting both away from each other so that the wax fell not into the bowl of the pipe but onto the table. For a moment there was silence as he drew in those first few puffs and wished for the luxury of contentment, but his mind was churning.

'She would have got off the Métro at the station Bourse, Dédé. From there, she would have walked west along the rue Quatre Septembre, approaching the scene of the robbery. The time . . .'

'12.15, Monsieur the Chief Inspector. I followed in her steps and . . .'

'Pardon?'

There was such a look of hardness in the Chief Inspector's eyes. 'We . . . that is, myself and the other boys, decided to follow in her steps.'

'To where?'

Had they done the wrong thing? wondered Dédé apprehensively. 'The bank and . . . and then back towards the station Bourse and down past the Bibliothèque Nationale to . . . to the Théâtre du Palais Royal.'

This in itself was trouble, but one must go easy. After all, how else were the boys to stand the awful waiting? 'The bank then. At what time would she come close to it, before retracing her steps to turn down the rue de Richelieu and make her way to the theatre?'

Disappointment registered and then a massive frown. '12.27 perhaps, so she might not have seen anything of the robbery, Monsieur the Chief Inspector.'

'Good.'

'But . . . but Joanne, she has had plenty of time? She might have . . .'

'Window-shopped, is this what you mean? Those shops . . . those places, Dédé, they make us feel uncomfortable. Besides, the prices are far too high for her, myself also.'

Again there was that frown. 'But Joanne was going to have to model such clothes, Monsieur the Chief Inspector? Seeing them is to learn something of them, is it not? We . . . we think she would have taken a little of her time for this.'

Though he would have to check it out, he knew the boys were right. 'So, she might well have been in position at 12.47 when the robbery and shooting took place . . .'

'Did one of them follow her? That is the question,' said the boy with all the gravity of his tender years.

'You should become a detective, Dédé, but I wouldn't wish the life on my worst enemy!'

Someone had followed her, thought Dédé. He was almost certain of this now. Why else the sudden outburst from the detective? Why else the compliment? But had it been one of the robbers?

If not, who could it have been? 'Was she followed, Monsieur the Chief Inspector?'

'Ah, Dédé, you have me. Yes. Yes, she was followed but by whom?'

More he couldn't say. Concluded, the conference ended with his gruffly pressing the tin of mints into the boy's hands and telling him to share them up. 'Don't go around looking for any more answers, eh? Wait for my instructions. I may need you for something special.'

But then at the door, he said, 'Stay out of trouble. It's dangerous. We don't want to ruffle any feathers until we've found Joanne and got her safely away.'

St-Cyr was thinking of Paul Meunier, the son of the engraver, as he closed the door. He was thinking of the world he found himself in. One of watchers upon watchers. Why the hell had someone followed her? Had it been someone from that house making sure she was alone?

In pencil, with a fine and very artistic hand, Paul Meunier had deftly sketched Joanne as he had seen her in the shop, even to etching the worry in those lovely eyes, the strain of her not knowing why she was being followed though certain that she was.

Giving life to her, so much so, he could still hear the sound of the pencil on paper and how the younger Meunier's breath had quickened as the girl had grown before him.

To have such a remarkable recall was not common. Clearly the engraver's son should have been free of the shop and allowed to follow a career as an artist.

Young Meunier had broken all the rules of his class and his father's establishment and had offered Joanne a cup of coffee which the girl had taken standing up with, yes, two heaping tea-spoons of white sugar and milk. Yes, milk.

Some have all the luck, especially engravers of cigarette cases and other knick-knacks for the Germans.

Now where was Hermann? Suddenly the need to see him was all-consuming.

*   *   *

Pigalle was usually fun, but the Bar of the Broken Cat, in a cellar off the rue Fontaine, was most definitely off-limits to the Occupier. Kohler wet his throat as he stood in the entrance. The music had stopped and so had all talk and motion.

From a smoke-filled sea of tables, huddled gangsters stared at him while in the distance, a three-piece orchestra waited. There was only trouble for him here and he had walked right into it. A 'friend' at Gestapo Paris-Central had given him the address. A *friend*, the laughing bastard!

Where the girls clung dolefully to each other circling round and round on glass that scratched and scoured the music, there was now only an electrified stillness. Not even a look from half of them, the breath held.

He wished that Louis was with him. Louis was good in situations like this. But Louis wasn't with him and they needed answers quickly if they were ever to find Joanne alive.

The préfet had his informants, his *mouchards*. The 'word' from Gestapo HQ, such as it had been, was that the one who would have the most to say could be found here. Henri Roland Péguy, one of the *durs*, the hard ones who had spent time in prison and would wear the three dots on the web of skin between the right thumb and index finger. M.A.V.—*Mort Aux Vaches*, Death to the Cows, the cops. Ah yes.

He had last been in the Santé awaiting trial for the murder of two pensioners from whom he had been trying to squeeze their life savings. But that had been in the fall of 1940. The jails had been emptied of their most useful occupants who had then gone to work for the SS and the Gestapo.

Péguy had been passed over in the first rush but then miraculously sprung by the very man who had put him there, the Préfet of Paris, though that little bit of information was supposed to remain a secret for ever.

Now the secret was in jeopardy and Péguy waited.

He was a mean-eyed, hard little bastard of forty-four with one prominent gold tooth, the upper right lateral incisor. Hence the nickname of 'Fortune'.

Kohler found him at last, three tables back of the postage

stamp dance floor, holding court with four others amid a clutter of wine bottles and cigarette butts. 'Now, look, all I want is a little information,' he said quietly.

There were five empty bottles and spills of red wine on the linoleum table-top.

'Eat dung. Kiss your mother's ass.'

'Don't be tiresome.'

A flick-knife came out; the blade leapt! Fifteen centimetres of highly polished, hardened steel straight from the Reich and bearing the much-coveted logo of the SS, the death's-head.

A man of few words, then, but with them, the sickening realization that, though it was forbidden to kill any member of the Occupying Forces, there was one exception. Hermann Andreas Kohler. Fair game and no one's loss.

'Put the knife away. Please. Let's not get heavy, eh? Just a few small questions,' breathed Kohler.

A bottle fell, the table quivered, neckties and faces were blurred. Kohler grabbed another bottle and smashed it. The sound of breaking glass shattered the silence. A girl screamed but was slapped into silence.

Péguy got slowly to his feet to face the spines of glass. '*Give me room,*' he hissed, tossing the words out of the side of his mouth.

The others backed away. Soon there would only be the two of them on the dance floor, ringed by spectators all thirsting for blood. *Mine!* thought Kohler. Ah *merde.*

The table was flipped out of the way, the knife flashed. Kohler lost the broken neck of the bottle. Blood ran from his right forearm, flooding over the back of his hand. 'You cut my overcoat?' he said, feeling no pain. A puzzle.

'*Now the liver!*' spat Péguy. 'You have no friends.'

To one side, revolvers had come out but were not yet pointed at him. Was it but a taste of things to come when this lousy war should end and everyone else had gone home?

'Look, I'll walk out of here. Okay? No problem. No questions. Nothing said.'

The knife didn't move. Balanced lightly, it was held close in, with the elbow braced against the base of the ribcage and the muscles knotted.

Slowly Kohler pulled off his scarf and gathered it as best he could around his bloodied hand. If he drew his pistol, the bastards with the guns would even the score. Ah Christ, there was nothing for it.

'Don't say I didn't warn you,' he said. 'I'm bigger. I don't like to pick on little guys.'

The knife flashed, the wrist was grabbed, Péguy taking to the air to land on his back with a crash that broke the floor and sent the bottles spinning.

Kohler swept up one and smashed it.

The Frenchman began to back away on his ass, to throw his pals looks of desperation. So, a court of last appeal and everything not exactly going one way, snorted Kohler inwardly. The rest of them had figured it out by themselves.

The bastard scrambled up and made a run for it through the parting crowd. Kohler got to him in the toilets. Throttling him from behind—seizing him by the belt and lifting—he crammed the pomaded, black-haired, jerking head into the stained trough of the urinal and shrieked, *'Kiss it, you son of a bitch! Kiss it and puke!'*

Blood ran from battered lips to mingle with the piss and other things. 'Now talk,' he whispered, letting up a little and catching a breath. *'Talk!'* he shrieked in good Gestapo form.

Down on his knees, with his face still squished to one side and his eyes fighting for a way out, Péguy spat blood and his gold nugget and winced. 'Air,' he managed, vowing to rip open Kohler's other cheek and cut off his balls. 'Air.'

'Okay. Don't choke on your puke.'

Straddling him, Kohler eased up a little. 'So, what did you find out for our friend?'

He waited. He shook the bastard. 'The robbery, eh?' he hissed. 'Eighteen million straight in from Lyon that very same day, am I right?'

Vomit joined the blood. There was a ragged gasp up the nose. A breath was caught and swallowed. 'My knees . . .'

'Fuck your knees. You're one of the préfet's *mouchards*, piss-head. Where did the money come from, when did it arrive and who the fuck knew about it?'

That was too much to ask. The préfet would kill him. '*Silence. I keep the silence!*' came the watery hiss.

'Jesus, a hero!' shouted Kohler, slamming him back into the trough. 'I'll piss on your head, you little fart!'

'Lyon that . . . that same morning by banker's dispatch. Eighteen millions, in 1000- and 500-franc notes. New francs.'

'*Ja, ja.* Now who told who about it?'

'We . . . *we do not know that yet!*' shrieked Péguy, struggling to escape.

He was throttled like a dog and forced to kiss the urinal but there was nothing more to come on that aspect. 'So, now tell me about the suitcases. Start with those and see if you can remember everything.'

Kohler let go of him suddenly. He would give him time to think that maybe . . . just maybe it would be possible to get up.

Then he cocked his pistol and pressed its muzzle to the back of the bastard's neck. 'A girl is missing, you greasy son of a bitch. A friend. The robbery may have nothing to do with it. We'll have to see. Just start talking or we'll have an accident.'

Kohler . . . Kohler had a pretty little pigeon named Giselle le Roy . . . 'Two suitcases. Leather. Alligator. Louis Vuitton 1934 to '36. Two men, one woman.' Péguy angrily spat blood and other things. 'The men to take the money, the woman to watch the street. One motorcycle for the getaway.'

'Come on. Two big, heavy suitcases and two guys on one motor cycle? Hey, you can do better than that. Why not throw in a *vélo-taxi* just to speed things up?'

A bicycle-taxi.

A nostril was cleared. 'They . . . they stole a car.'

'Talk louder.'

'*A car!*'

'Good. Let the others in there know you're telling me everything, eh? Then it won't be Talbotte who cuts your throat but your friends.'

'My usefulness. . . . Please, the préfet is counting on me to . . .'

'Aw, stop whining and get on with it. A car in Paris? A German car?'

The bastard nodded but banged his forehead and cursed Kohler's ancestors until the gun was pressed a little closer and he was told that, since Talbotte had not wished to co-operate on such a delicate matter, there had been nothing for it but to ask his sources. 'It's simply your tough luck, *mon fin*, so spit it out.'

'Then yes. *Yes!* The car of one whose mistress was in a shop across the street. They forced her driver to take them to Pigalle and they ditched him here.'

'Now wait a minute. Whose car was it?'

'Ah *nom de Jésus-Christ, foutez-moi la paix!*' Bugger off!

Kohler waited.

'The . . . the Sonderführer Franz Ewald Kempf.'

A special officer, Section II of the Propaganda Staffel, in charge of news releases for the Luftwaffe. An arrogant smart-ass, a real ladies' man. 'Pigalle in broad daylight?' scoffed the Gestapo's strong-arm. '*Maudit salaud*, don't be such an utter idiot!'

'Montmartre, up on the hill . . . a farm lorry, a *gazogène* . . .'

That was better but still not good enough. Kohler leaned down to whisper in his ear. 'Is your ass as tight as your lips, or do I have to bring one of your friends in here to find out for myself?'

Both nostrils were cleared. There was some choking. 'A court-yard off the rue des Amiraux. Number 9. The driver was knocked out and left in the car. They . . . they walked away.'

'With two big suitcases like that? Near the goods yards? Hey, you must think I don't know my way around.'

Péguy swallowed. 'Two rucksacks. They . . . they left the suit-cases but these were then taken by someone else and we have not yet been able to find them.'

'Did they leave a little of the cash as hush-up money? Well . . . ?'

'Yes, yes, most probably. Maybe a bundle of 500s. We do not know as yet!'

'Didn't the chauffeur get a look at them?' ·

'One wrenched the rear-view mirror aside, the other put the

gun to the back of his head. Things moved too fast. He was hit pretty hard and has suffered a concussion.'

'So, tell me about the two men.'

'They . . . they were dressed as mackerels but . . .'

'Dressed like pimps so as to point the finger elsewhere? Good *Gott im Himmel*, how dumb do you think I am?'

'As *maquereaux*!' spat Péguy desperately.

'Hey, *mon fin*, pimps don't have the guts to rob banks, nor would they smash a teller's face with lead. Come to think of it, why that teller?'

'He . . . he reached for the . . .'

'*Ja, ja*, the alarm bell. Hey, look behind the shit to find the ass that left it. Why that teller?'

His nose was broken, raged Péguy silently. His teeth were smashed. 'He . . . he may have recognized one of them.'

'Or?'

There was a sigh, that of a departing soul perhaps.

'Or known of the shipment and . . . and foolishly passed the word so as to obtain the pay-off.' Marseille . . . could he manage to go into hiding there?

Again Kohler leaned down. 'Don't even think of Marseille, *mein Schatz*, my treasure. You'd stand out like rotten fish. Hey, you're really very good. If you had udders, you'd make a farmer happy. But let's hope your milk hasn't turned, eh? Because if it has, I'll be back. Oh by the way, those two guys. How old were they?'

He'd kill Kohler if he could! 'Thirty . . . thirty-two to thirty-six, no more, not much younger.'

Things must have happened pretty fast. 'And they didn't talk or act like pimps, did they? Well, come on. Empty the udders so that I can put you out to pasture.'

The head was shaken. A hair was savagely spat. 'Well-educated, eh?' asked the Gestapo.

The head gave a nod. 'So, good. Yes, that's very good,' said Kohler, straightening to stand over him. There was only one language a bastard like this would understand. 'Don't move. I've got to put the pistol away and take out the other one.'

Giving it a moment in which Péguy cringed and waited himself, he said, 'The woman. The one who watched the street. Let's not forget her.'

'She . . . she lost herself quickly.'

'Just walked away? No bicycle? No motor cycle or *vélo-taxi*?'

'None.'

'How old?'

'Thirty to thirty-five, maybe a little older.'

'Okay. Was it a Resistance job?'

'We . . . we don't know. Perhaps not. It . . . it's too early to say.'

'So you told Talbotte no.'

The head leapt, the bastard tried to face him.

'*Yes, yes*, I told him no! Do you think I want trouble with those people? If they find out I've squealed on them, they will slice me up.'

It had best come softly. 'Maybe that's what you deserve.'

Péguy raked his mind for details. Giselle le Roy liked to dance in the Bal Saint-Séverin and to while away her time watching old movies in any of three most favoured cinemas. Sometimes she would go around the corner to pay Madame Chabot a little visit and to talk over old times. Since she could no longer offer the use of her body to anyone but Kohler, the girl was bored.

In boredom would there be vengeance. The sword with the serpent entwined.

'Thinking about tattoos and vowing you're going to kill someone close to me, eh?' snorted Kohler. 'Hey, I'd watch it if I were you. Ah *merde*, the battery's dry. You're in luck!'

No piss.

For good measure, he leaned on Péguy's head and ground it into the trough a last time. 'Don't even think of touching Giselle or Oona. I'll kill you if you come within a block of either of them. *If* your friends out there allow you to leave. If. *Bonne chance*, you're going to need it!'

The battered lips quivered with rage, the bloodshot eyes were smarting. 'I . . . I will have the protection of the préfet and they will know it.'

'Then I pity you for its worthlessness. *Au revoir, mon fin.* Sleep lightly.'

The Cluny was at 71 boulevard Saint-Germain, not all that easy to find in the darkness. Kohler stood in the middle of the street. Hell, there was so little traffic, a drunk could have slept out here.

From time to time the squeaking wheels of a frost-pinched *vélo-taxi* would struggle by, but for the most part the night left him alone. His right arm was stiff—nothing more than a flesh wound, but close. They had patched him up at the Hôpital Laennec and had asked why he hadn't gone to one of his own clinics.

He had simply said the hospital was nearer and had warned them to say nothing. But the confrontation in the Bar of the Broken Cat was troubling him and not just because one of his confrères had given him a bad tip and some in Gestapo Paris would like to be rid of him, but because this war had to end and when it did, those who were left behind were going to have to pay for it, rightly or wrongly.

Only too well he knew the French passion for 'justice'. 'Giselle,' he said, searching the dark outline of the cinema's billboards where once, in good times, the lights would have been lit up until three or four in the morning. 'I'm going to have to do something. Oona's in it too.'

Sentiment rushed in on him. He liked and admired them both, often for quite different reasons. They made him feel at ease with himself when all around him he could see so clearly what was going on. They never once openly questioned their relationship though deep within themselves they must be asking what was going to happen to them when the Germans went home.

Sure as hell life would be made damned miserable for all who had fraternized with the enemy. And Louis? he asked.

The Resistance would go for Louis, disregarding entirely that he had had to work for the Occupier or else. False papers, new IDs ... travel permits? wondered Kohler. Spain, maybe Portugal? Somewhere warm and near the sea. Then maybe after the rubble and the hatred had cleared, a small bar, a quiet little shop, nothing fancy, only peace.

A farm for Louis, since even a recent case in Provence had failed to make him shut up about going back to work a land he had never farmed like some, his partner namely, except as a boy on holiday.

Flinging his cigarette down in disgust at himself, Kohler said, 'Use your brains, idiot, not your balls! Let them go while they still have a chance. Set it up for them and say goodbye.'

Giselle was sitting in the middle of the cinema, about three-quarters of the way towards the back because her eyes couldn't take anything closer. Shoulders that were so lovely when naked were hunched. No heat in the damned place, of course. Half-hidden by the cheap fur collar of a thin overcoat, she stared raptly at the screen, was completely oblivious to all the others around her who smoked, necked, fucked, slept or did other things. Ah yes.

She was totally lost to a film she must have seen twenty times since its release in 1937. Another ancient rerun the war and the censors had allowed, the latter because, asses that they were, they had thought it reflected unfavourably on the French!

Pépé le Moko. The story of a little thief who was wanted by the *flics* and had taken refuge in an Algerian kasbah. Christ! the wonder of celluloid. A kasbah no less, and no knife in the guts from another thief!

Apart from this, it was a good film, but he hadn't the time for it and when he ousted the man next to her, Giselle didn't even look up or pay attention to the disturbance but only stared at the screen.

A tear trickled down a soft cheek, another followed it. 'Giselle . . .'

'They . . . they have arrested him. He . . . he is now going to kill himself rather than face prison.'

Quickly she crossed herself and kissed her mittened fingertips, was all broken up about the ending just because the fantasy of hope had turned out to be the harsh reality of life.

Handcuffed, the thief cut his own throat with a penknife. End of Pépé. Would that all such thieves and punks would do the same.

'There . . . there will be no escape when this war is over,' she said, a torn whisper as she dried her eyes.

The film was late due to a 'power failure'. It was nearly 11.00 p.m. when the Métro would close. Everyone else didn't bother to stand for the anthem of the Occupier but beat it. They were soon left alone in the dark. 'Look, I'll do what I can, *chérie*. You know I will. Hey, I was only just thinking about it.'

She had short, straight, jet-black hair with a fringe, strong, decisive brows, good hips, lips, legs and all the rest. Magnificent violet eyes, a lovely milk-white throat.

She was only twenty-two years of age, half Greek, half Midi French, could pass for someone else. Was not stupid and would use her brains.

'The *résistants*, the 'patriots,' will kill me,' she said. 'They will strip me naked, Herr Kohler, then they'll beat me as those from the rue Lauriston did not so long ago, isn't that correct? And then they will stone me to death.'

The rue Lauriston . . . She was refering to a previous case. 'Hey, what's with the Herr Kohler bit? It's Hermann you're talking to.'

Entirely not her fault, she had been badly roughed up in that other episode by gangsters of the French Gestapo and still bore the bruises and the memories of it.

'Come on, let's pick up Oona. I have to see Louis. It's urgent.'

She shook her head. 'It's finished, Hermann. Your little ménage is over. Me, I am going back to work so as to be fucked by Frenchmen!'

'Oh no you're not.'

'Am I too good for my fellow countrymen, Herr Haupsturm-führer?'

'Of course not. You're too good to be a whore.'

'And you—you are saving me from that? You with your great big Bavarian cock?'

'Come on. A girl is missing, Giselle. We have to find her before they kill her.'

* * *

The Club Mirage was on the rue Delambre in Montparnasse. Squeezed among the thirsty tunics of Fritz-haired men in grey-green and navy or air-force blue, St-Cyr tossed back the pastis with a gulp and fiercely thrust the glass across the bar. 'Another,' he said. Eight hundred Wehrmacht troops on leave hooted, cheered and ogled the chorus line of naked girls and grandmothers who should have known better, while the band, preferring noise above all else, blew their guts out.

It was pandemonium—*Kultur* with a capital K! Under char-treuse floodlights, emerald ostrich plumes and brilliant red pasties moved in a layered haze of tobacco smoke, farts and sweat that had a life of its own.

Leon Rivard, the one with the face like ground meat, tossed him a quizzical eye but knew enough not to ask what the trouble was. 'This one is on the house,' he shouted. 'The last one also.'

'*Merci.*'

Downed again. A fire in the belly and the brain. A real tough guy who was pissed off at something. Ah yes. 'Hey, Gabrielle isn't mad at you, Inspector. She just cut her holiday short to come back to work. Okay?'

'It's Chief Inspector St-Cyr to you, and she's far too good a singer for a dump like this.'

Rivard grinned. One of two brothers who owned and ran the place, the Corsican fluted, 'Just as you please, monsieur,' before fist-wiping the zinc and refilling the glass a fourth time.

The girls up on stage were thrusting their bottoms at the troops. The roar grew deafening. St-Cyr added a drop of water for propriety's sake and gloomily watched as the pale yellowish-green of the pastis became milky. 'Hermann,' he grunted disconso-lately, as he fingered his glass in thought. Everything with his partner would have to be out in the open this time. There must be no secrets if they were to find Joanne. He would have to tell him the engraver's son had been forging papers for the Resis-tance. He would have to trust Hermann not to turn the boy in. There might be a connection to something the Bavarian had uncovered.

The pastis, pre-war and 90 proof, was kept under the bar not only because of its rarity but because most Germans found its strong taste of liquorice revolting. The girls were gone, the stage empty, the hush expectant. Perhaps a minute passed but not an eye was diverted. Even the thirsty who thronged the bar had put down their glasses or rapidly shaken their heads when more was offered.

In the shimmering, sky-blue, sleeveless sheath that was her trademark, with diamonds at her wrists and neck, Gabrielle Arcuri walked on stage. Thousands of tiny seed pearls, in vertical rows on the fabric, rippled, electrifying the place with her gracefulness and fluidity. Tall and willowy, she had an absolutely gorgeous figure. The hair was not blonde but the soft, soft shade of a very fine brandy, the eyes not just blue but an exquisite shade of violet.

She clasped her long, slender hands before her as a schoolgirl might and shyly smiled, then broadly grinned and shrugged as if, having suddenly made up her mind about them, she could now accept them into her heart. 'Mes cher amis, I have a song for you of love. Of lovers who have been separated by trouble and now do not know if each still has in them the love for the other that was once there. They meet in a cinema under the cone of light from the projector. Cigarette smoke filters up into this light but the film, it means nothing to them. Nothing, you understand. They are sitting side by side, not even daring to hold hands, not knowing what the other is thinking.'

She sang. She gave herself to it totally and the song brought tears to every last man in the place. She held them in the palms of her outstretched hands which implored them to understand the tragedy of life, of war, of hardship and separation.

A breath was caught, a note was kept until her lungs threatened to burst and all at once there was a collective sigh and then a single shout, the voices of men who knew of the battlefields and wept for home. She brought the house down.

'Louis . . . Hey, Louis, sorry I'm late.'

It was Hermann. 'Your arm? What's happened, please?'

'It's nothing. A punk called Péguy.'

'Fortune? Ah *merde*, did you . . . ?'

St-Cyr saw that Oona and Giselle were with him. He touched his lips with the tip of a troubled tongue and plucked nervously at his moustache. 'Fortune isn't to be trusted, Hermann. Exactly how well did you destroy him in the eyes of his friends?'

'Completely.'

St-Cyr turned swiftly to the barman and hissed, 'A table. Quickly!'

There were objections from the troops. Even the chanteuse had to wait while they were seated but laid the soft down of a pacifying voice over the ruckus by asking the displaced to join her on stage.

She put her arms around them. They grinned shyly and stood with her like great dumb drunken blockheads not knowing what to do.

With her fingers trailing in their departing hands, she smiled at each of them, then sang as they left the stage, mollified and coddled in the cocoon of her generous nature.

Giselle le Roy could only remember standing naked before men such as these, hearing their hoots and thrusting catcalls, their hush as her bruised and battered body had been exposed to them by the gangsters of the rue Lauriston.

Hermann had covered her. He and Jean-Louis had come to the rescue, but now it was as if those two didn't even remember what had happened here not long ago and were oblivious to her feelings.

I *am* a whore—*putain, fille de joie,* cunt—she said to herself. It is expected of such women that they should have no feelings. It is part of the profession.

Yet they had just spoken of an engraver's son. Hermann had leaned closely to Jean-Louis and had asked, 'Could the boy do some work for me?' He had given a nod towards herself and Oona, so they were not unaware of her after all.

In return, Jean-Louis had grimly understood and said, 'Let's see about it. A good thought.'

False papers. *Laissez-passers,* the *ausweises* of the Nazis. A little trip somewhere. Escape from Paris and the only place she had ever known.

Two tears fell, blurring her vision so that the lights became as the last of a sunset and she saw herself on a tropical island walking alone along a beach beneath tall palms, waiting for the night to come and trying to believe she was safe from the coming storm.

Unlike Giselle, Oona van der Lynn watched her 'protector'—what else could she, an illegal Dutch immigrant from Rotterdam, call Hermann Kohler? Having lost her two children during the blitzkrieg and had her husband murdered while under interrogation by the French Gestapo, she had had no other choice. But war makes instant friends and lovers just as quickly as it separates them. Hermann was a good man, and perhaps he did love her a little, if one could call it love, for he was home so seldom and Giselle ... why Giselle did require attention.

The girl was amazingly beautiful but sat woodenly staring up at the stage, unconscious of the looks she was getting from the crowd, remembering how it had been and wondering what the future held. Ah yes.

To be blonde, blue-eyed, tall, slender and forty years of age was not to covet Hermann Kohler or get jealous of Giselle le Roy, though sometimes those sorts of feelings intruded. One was only human and yes, of course one worried for that same future. At any moment the rifle butts could come even at Hermann's door. Giselle and herself could well be dragged away and 'deported'.

One must live for the present and accept the situation as it was.

The two detectives had drawn a sketch of the quadrangle of the Palais Royal and its environs and were deep in conversation over it. Hermann was in his element, smoking, tossing glances up at the stage, grinning, drinking beer, thinking that he would like to get a hand between a pair of legs up there, yet all the time his mind was flitting back and forth, recalling little things, projecting on into the future.

Jean-Louis always questioned everything. A thinker, he was not at all interested in the naked girls who kicked their legs above his head. She knew he longed to be alone with his pipe and tobacco, his little furnace, so as to examine the disappearances and murders from as many angles as possible. One so committed, he lived only for each case, especially this one. A cuddly man, Giselle had once said and laughed delightedly at the thought of seducing him, for men over fifty made good lovers sometimes, and the girl had thought it might be 'very interesting' to compare the two detectives in such a way.

St-Cyr traced out Joanne's route from the Bourse station of the Métro westward along the rue Quatre Septembre towards the bank which was on the other side of the street. Then back again and south down the rue de Richelieu past the Bibliothèque Nationale to the Théâtre du Palais Royal in the north-western corner of the quadrangle.

She had picked up the final letter and had, at 1.15 or 1.20 p.m., entered the garden and gone into the shop of Meunier the engraver.

Then finally she had walked out of the garden and around to the rue de Valois to knock at the door of that house.

'For three days she's kept a prisoner, Hermann. Three days of . . . ah, I can't bring myself to think of it. Then suddenly they leave and the house is emptied.'

'The photos are then scattered either by one of the kidnappers or by someone else,' said Kohler grimly.

'But the photos only tell us so much. The rapes aren't shown, but were they photographed?'

'For someone else to view?' breathed Kohler, watching him closely. 'Someone who wasn't present?'

St-Cyr nodded curtly and passed a smoothing hand over the rough sketch map he had drawn. Oona van der Lynn was very still, and when he looked across the table at her, he saw her flinch, saw moisture rush into her lovely eyes.

Giselle le Roy was tense and pensive—ashen, so much so that the paleness of her fresh young cheeks contrasted sharply with her jet-black hair.

'A sadist, Hermann? A psychopath—one with money enough to hire those who would do his every bidding?'

'A man and a woman . . .' said Kohler, lost in thought.

'Madame Lemaire's maid, Nanette, heard the crying not just of Joanne, but of others,' said St-Cyr.

Kohler told him of Renée Marteau's body and that the former mannequin had been kept for at least forty-three days. 'Between 3 July 1941 and 15 August. The throat was slit, Louis, the hair hacked off, the breasts . . .'

'Say it, please.'

Ah *merde* . . .'Removed.'

'Months—*years*, Hermann. How long has it been going on in that house? Fourteen girls all with the same colour of hair and eyes, the same height, weight, size of bust . . .'

'Louis, take it easy. Try not to get so close. A man probably took the photos but a woman may have greeted each girl at the door.'

'One whose purpose was to lead them on,' blurted Giselle le Roy, all broken up about it. 'How could *any* woman do such a thing?'

'She was essential,' said Oona, instinctively reaching out to comfort Giselle. 'If she hadn't been at that door to welcome them in, some of those girls would have turned away and saved themselves.'

'Joanne was very nervous. She knew she was being followed . . .' muttered St-Cyr.

'But did she see the robbery?' asked Oona earnestly. 'Could she have identified one of the men or perhaps the woman who watched the street for them?'

'Ah, I wish I knew,' said Jean-Louis.

'And was *that* not the woman who followed her?' asked Giselle.

The girl shrugged when St-Cyr looked at her—she could appear so innocent at times, so fragile.

'If so, then it couldn't have been the one who answered the door,' she said more decisively.

'Then there were two entirely unconnected women,' concluded Oona positively. 'One who watched the street for the bank robbers, and one who opened the door when Joanne rang the bell or knocked.'

Two women   It was a thought.

'They couldn't have been the same because Joanne would have recognized her, Louis,' said Kohler. 'The one she knew was following her must have been the one who watched the street.'

'Did both women follow her, but only that one was seen by Joanne?' asked St-Cyr grimly.

'*Verdammt*, Louis. The one who opened the door would have made damned certain Joanne had come alone!'

'And to do so, she would have had to follow Joanne right from the Bourse Métro to the Théâtre du Palais Royal,' said St-Cyr, 'then leave her so as to get to the house on time.'

'But wouldn't she have seen the other woman, then,' asked Oona, 'and thought the girl hadn't come alone?'

'Perhaps but . . . ah *mais alors, alors* . . .' muttered St-Cyr. It was all speculation.

'Girls with specifics,' said Giselle, giving Kohler the tremulous look of a young woman who was still not certain her lover really cared enough about her to obtain false travel papers for them.

'Specific physical features,' said Jean-Louis, gravely brushing both hands over the table, 'that match the girl who was once engaged to the son of the house's owner.' He fingered a richly gilded announcement. 'Le Château des belles fleurs bleues near Provins. A Mademoiselle Angèlique Desthieux, a mannequin.'

'Ah no,' gasped Giselle, clutching the base of her throat and feeling quite sick.

'A mannequin . . . ?' managed Oona.

'Engaged to Captain Gaetan Edouard Vergès, 13 April 1916.'

'And then?' asked Kohler, hearing the guns of that other war as if only yesterday, feeling the mud, the shit, the shells . . .

'A drooler, Hermann.'

Giselle quivered and couldn't look up but seemed only to shrink into herself. 'The face . . .' she managed. 'The constant drooling as he paws your naked body and then fucks you. No lips, sometimes half a nose, no jaws . . . Nothing but noises, *mes amis*. *Noises!*'

'*Verdammt!*' Kohler grabbed her hand. 'Did you . . . ? Hey, *petite*, have you ever had to . . . ? Well, you know.'

'Me?' She arched her lovely eyebrows at him, pleased that he should care so much but distressed also, for it was not any business of his! 'No, Herr Haupsturmführer, one such as that has never slobbered over these breasts you hunger so much to suckle, nor has such a one ever fucked me. But . . .' Ah! poor Hermann, he was so mortified and embarrassed . . . He must really love her a little. 'But I have heard others talk of it, not at our house. Ah no, Madame Chabot would not allow it. But at other houses.'

'Les *baveux*,' said Oona, watching the two men closely and asking herself what she really felt about Hermann Kohler. Jealousy after all? Envy that Giselle, who had such a splendid young body and was so very beautiful, gave him such pleasure while she . . .

'Madame Lemaire's maid hasn't told me everything,' grumbled St-Cyr. 'Is it that Nanette saw the drooler on or from the balcony of those houses, or is it that her mistress has so filled the poor girl's head with stories of the war, the very sound of crying next door is enough to give her nightmares?'

'The shrapnel, Louis. Clouds of it. The screams, the sounds of those who could no longer scream because their faces had been torn to shreds.'

St-Cyr turned to Giselle. 'The shells exploded above our positions.'

'And ours!' swore Kohler, grabbing his own chin to show what had happened to his face. 'Brilliant star-bursts and then . . .'

'The dark grey snaking tongues of metal,' sighed Louis.

'Of pieces,' said Oona, sadly fingering her cardigan, 'some no bigger than the buttons of my blouse.'

Hermann had withdrawn his hand from Giselle. He had noticed her reaction and had felt a little something for her.

Again Jean-Louis spoke. 'Angèlique Desthieux refused to marry Gaetan Vergès. She was shown his face by the doctors and couldn't bring herself to carry through, but is it that he harbours such a hatred after all these years, he still seeks out only those with her eyes and hair?'

'*Yes!*' hissed Giselle with a harlot's vindictiveness. 'Those who *wished* to become like her.'

Kohler calmly ignored the outburst. 'Vergès couldn't have taken the photos, Louis. None of those girls would willingly have posed for him.'

It had to be said. 'But did he employ the photographer and the woman? Did he wait upstairs in the attic and come down only at the last? Is *that* not where Madame Lemaire's maid saw him and is this not what she's too afraid to tell me?'

They were each silent at the thought. All around their little group the racket soared with laughter, much applause and foot-stamping both on the stage and beneath the tables.

St-Cyr drew in a breath. Still deep in thought, he said, 'A cat wanders, a banker's bank is robbed and right across the garden from his house, a young girl is brutally assaulted. Then ... then three days after the robbery and the kidnapping, the house is emptied by four men from the firm of the Dallaire and Sons—why that firm, Hermann? And how, please, could that maid of Madame Lemaire's have seen the name on those lorries when, at 6.07 in the evening, the street would already have been pitch dark and it's against the law to show a light?'

'Did she go outside to look?' asked Giselle.

'Perhaps but then ... Ah, I must ask her,' said St-Cyr ruefully. 'I must ask her so many questions.'

Hermann found a few dregs in his stein and drained them before shoving it aside. 'Chloroform, Louis. Why not ether?'

A square pad of cotton wool was dragged out and held with trembling fingers as Jean-Louis delved deeply into memory and more sadness came, thought Oona. The sadness of that other war, of things that could never be forgotten.

'Ether,' he said. 'Is our Gaetan Vergès an ether-drinker?'

'Ether, while used as an anaesthetic, can also be taken internally as a narcotic,' said Hermann, looking steadily at his partner and friend, so much so, one knew absolutely he understood exactly how Jean-Louis felt.

'Ether to kill the pain of disfigurement,' said Giselle earnestly, 'or to kill the loss of his lover. And why, please, the kidnapping now? Is it that only under the Occupation he feels secure enough that such horrible things can be done, or have they been going on before the war as well?'

The two men swiftly exchanged glances. Both knew they had best start for Provins immediately, yet should they not look closer first? wondered Oona. 'That balcony,' she said, and then, 'Both chloroform and ether, they ... they must be very difficult to obtain these days and would require special papers. Even then, I do not think such an addiction possible any more.'

Medicines of all kinds were exceedingly difficult to come by. Even aspirins were virtually impossible to buy and only one or two were doled out at a time, if available. 'Boemelburg first, Hermann. We'll have to have his clearance for this,' said St-Cyr. 'We can then take it from there.'

'Yes, yes,' grunted Kohler, 'but the Chief isn't going to like it, Louis. Ah Christ! why can't things be easy for once?'

Unnoticed, the floor show had changed two or three times. Now the man with the rabbits in his hat was accusing his buxom assistant of hiding them upon her person and demanding that she search her top and briefs to hoots of laughter as they reappeared.

The tiny dressing-room backstage was beyond a crowded gauntlet of all-but-naked chorus girls who, while waiting to go on stage, grinned lewdly at St-Cyr, wet painted lips, gave knowing looks or brushed teasing fingers down his arm or across a cheek, asking, 'Hey, my fine Inspector, what's she got that I haven't?' and pressing firm, plump breasts, with pasty-covered nipples against him. Old, young, not-so-young, all sizes, all shapes . . . 'Ah *merde*,' he sighed. 'Please, it's no ordinary visit. A young girl is missing.'

'*Missing*?' teased one with flashing dark hazel eyes and huge lashes. 'What is missing is that you are the only one with clothes!'

There were pink dots on her throat and breasts . . . Measles? he wondered apprehensively. Sequins! 'Please, another time.'

'All of us?' asked one. They were laughing now and whispering to each other.

'Oh, let him go,' said another.

'She's *waiting*, Inspector!' hissed another lewdly. 'But for what, *mes enfants*? The shag? The release of his little burden?'

'And hers!' laughed another. 'But it will never happen, ah no. Not with them. He's always too busy; she also, and too beautiful, too sophisticated, too . . .'

Self-consciously he hurried past them, brushing talcum powder from his jacket and wiping lipstick, face cream and rouge from his cheeks.

'Gabrielle . . .' He burst into the cubbyhole she called her own. The door closed behind him ánd he drew in the scent of her perfume.

'Jean-Louis . . .'

There were only two chairs and she was sitting in one of them with her feet up on the other. She reached out to him and he took her hand in his and, suddenly at a loss for words, stumbled over an apology for not having spent Christmas with her and her son at her château on the Loire as planned. 'Lyon and a case of arson,' he said. 'A tragedy,' only to leave it off and shrug, 'With you there is no need to apologize. How is René Yvonne-Paul?'

'Fine and still wanting to spend time with you but understanding that, like his mother, he must share you with your work just as he must share me with mine.'

'My work . . . ah yes. May I?' he asked, indicating the other chair.

Must there always be this stiffness between them at first? she wondered, but when he sat opposite her, their knees touched and he took both her hands in his.

She squeezed his hands hard and tossing her head in warning, said urgently, 'Kiss me. I want to be loved, *mon cher. Loved!*'

Merde alors! what was this? Releasing her hands, he cautiously stood and looked slowly around the cramped room, searching always . . .

There were two tiny microphones—one behind the dressing-table mirror, on the left up high, the other hidden above the ceiling light.

'A cigarette,' he said, easing himself into the chair to sit looking at her, worried, ah so very worried.

She moved a piece of paper across her dressing-table and watched as he wrote, *What has caused the Gestapo to be interested in you?*

She shrugged and smiled sadly, then shook her head to indicate she didn't know.

Have your contacts in the Resistance any word on the robbery at the Crédit Lyonnais? he wrote and saw her shake her head, and when they held each other tightly and he drew in the scent of Mirage, of vetiverol and bergamot, angelica and lavender, she whispered, 'So far there's been nothing, but the few I work with don't think it was a Resistance job.'

None of the microphones could be touched. Another was located with difficulty in the wall behind the fire extinguisher in a corner. She was Russian. She used an assumed name, had escaped during the Revolution and had later married a Frenchman who had been killed in this war.

One could not question her activities or tell her the danger was too great and that, if it came to the worst, it would be hard for Hermann to turn a blind eye and for himself to help without perhaps first killing his partner.

She understood the risks, he understood her need to be involved. As they sat facing each other, he quietly told her about Joanne—the Gestapo would know of the girl by now. 'She's like a daughter I've watched over,' he said. 'I *must* find her before it's too late.'

Instinctively a hand touched his cheek and she let her fingers trace down to his moustache to press themselves against his lips. He wasn't like the wealthy businessmen or politicians, the generals and other high-ranking officers who took her to dinner, bought champagne, sent flowers and asked her to parties and endless official receptions. He was shabby, somewhat diffident, rough-and-ready, a cop—they had met on another case ... Ah, how should she say it? He knew himself absolutely and didn't try to be anyone else. Yes, he was *not* like so many other men. She felt good with him, good all over. Secure, at ease, at home, so many things. What more did one need?

Chantal and Muriel, he wrote. *I must take the photographs to them.* What photographs? she wondered and saw him write, *Mannequins . . . clothing . . . the manner in which the photos were taken, the sequence, Gabrielle.*

And then . . . *Leave word for me with them if possible. Always a warning if you're in trouble, eh? Simply a Yes if the Resistance knocked off that bank, or a No. We must find out so as to eliminate the possibility or include it.*

He struck a match and burned the slip of paper. He destroyed the ashes by rubbing them in his palms and then blowing them towards the door. They held each other. They wondered when they would see each other again. His moustache tickled when he kissed her ear—never on the lips, not with him. Her voice, the influenza season . . . he was too conscious of her well-being, a worrier.

Without a word he left her and for a time she was alone. Chantal and Muriel had a shop on place Vendôme. They were old friends and knew the fashion business like few others. He would go to them for information and advice as he always did when necessary. She would leave something there for him if she could.

Poor Jean-Louis, she said silently. He is a cop whose partner, though now a friend of mine too, is of the Gestapo. That alone will tear him apart every time he thinks of me.

Lighting a cigarette, she sought out each of the Gestapo's bugs and counted them again before worrying about their interest in her and if there were any she hadn't found.

3 IN THE MORNING, BOEMELBURG WAS WAITING FOR them. They had only just parked the Citroën in the courtyard off the rue des Saussaies, when an orderly approached and gave them the order.

'He isn't happy.'

'Is he ever?' snorted Kohler, hung over and taking a last drag before carefully stubbing out his cigarette and hiding the damp remains in his little tin. A real *Kippensammler par excellence*. The things one did these days to keep nourishment at hand.

Butt-collecting had become a national pastime, a preoccupation shared by those of their German masters who had fallen from grace and were without a regular supply.

'Pharand is to be bypassed. Go straight to the Chief,' said the orderly.

Pharand was Louis's boss, a file-minded, territorial little French fascist who was insidiously jealous of his turf and believed firmly in the system of wealthy friends who had put him at the top.

'Our luck,' snorted Louis. 'Maybe I'll keep my job, Hermann, and maybe I won't.'

It was always the roll of the dice of whim these days. Pharand had lost his cushy office to Boemelburg who had moved in on the day of the Defeat and had kicked him out and down the hall, so that when the little twerp had found the guts to come back to Paris, he had found there had been a few changes.

Humiliated by the loss of status, Major Osias Pharand had elected to make up for it in other ways.

'Don't worry about it, Louis. I'll protect you.'

'*Grâce à Dieu*, that's exactly what I'm afraid of!'

They went into an office that was spacious and once filled with Chinese porcelains, Japanese prints, ivory fans, chopsticks—little mementoes of colonial days years and years ago. Other things too, of course.

But now all chucked out in favour of the utilitarian. Maps detailed every nook and cranny of France with pins and flags. Telexes hammered. Telephones waited. From the office next door came the machine-gun sounds of four secretaries typing reports already at 0700 hours Berlin time, 0600 hours the old time, 0500 hours in summer, Christ!

As Head of SIPO-SD Section IV, the Gestapo in France, Boemelburg had the power of life and death over every living soul in the country. A giant, like Hermann, but well over sixty years of age and with an all-but-shaven grey bullet of a head, sagging jowls and puffy sad blue eyes, France's top cop had been a detective for much of his life, but had included some years in Paris as a salesman of heating and ventilating systems. He spoke excellent French, even to the slang of the *quartiers* and, what was far more important, could think like the French when needed.

Depending on his mood, however, it could either be French or *deutsch*. This time he chose the former. One never quite knew with him, and of course, to have known and worked with him before the war on the IKPK, the International Organization of Police, had been more of a detriment than an asset. Boemelburg had known only too well the capabilities of God's little detective and had put him to work but had given him Hermann as a watchdog.

The voice was gruff. 'So, Louis, a matter of eighteen million and the disappearance of a neighbour?'

Turcotte in Records must have filled him in.

'Walter . . . ', began St-Cyr.

The lifeless eyes grew cold. The frame, big and big-boned, with flesh hanging under a dishevelled grey suit, straightened ponderously.

'Herr Sturmbannführer,' said the Sûreté's little mouse, 'we're not certain yet if there is a connection between the disappearance and the robbery.'

'Then make certain of it. Otherwise you'll devote yourselves entirely to the robbery.'

'And the préfet?' blurted the mouse.

'You leave Talbotte to me, Louis. Kohler, how was the fucking last night? Did you bang the both of them? How dare you tread on such thin ice? A whore and a Dutch alien?'

'I . . . I fell asleep before . . . Well, you know,' shrugged Kohler, managing to look foolish. 'They were both disappointed.'

'Then perhaps we have your undivided attention after all.'

Ah *nom de Jésus-Christ*, was it a warning of things to come? wondered St-Cyr. An old and much trusted friend of Gestapo Mueller in Berlin, it fell to Walter to send them on their way when need arose which was always these days. Alas, and with no extra pay, not even a mention of it. Just the blitzkrieg because that was the way the Germans wanted things done.

Boemelburg indicated a side table and said, 'Kohler, go out to that car of Louis's and bring us a selection of your fourteen victims. Don't waste time. *Use* it!'

He waited for the Gestapo's Bavarian sore thumb to leave, then said, 'Louis, this business mustn't be taken too close to the heart. There's a war on and I have my priorities. Though Talbotte says he's convinced there isn't a terrorist connection to the robbery, I want the matter fully cleared.'

Is that understood? One could read this in the Sturmbannführer's gaze.

'Certainly, Walter.'

'*Can I count on you?*'

Ah *merde*! 'Yes. If . . .'

'If I let you work on the girl, eh? Is it to be a bargain with the

Devil, Jean-Louis? You, a patriot who must betray his own kind or find himself elsewhere?'

There could be no backing away from it this time. If there was a Resistance connection, he would have to be told. It was either that or forget about Joanne . . .

'There can't be any in-betweens, Louis. Either you're one of us or you'll be kept on elsewhere only until such time as your usefulness ceases.'

The brown ox-eyes lifted to a ceiling sculpted in plaster. Doves and whorls, harps and cupids, a naked Venus with snakes in her hair or was it Medusa?

Moistening, the eyes asked God, why must You do this to me? Then they were lowered to Boemelburg, and he lied. 'Yes. Yes, of course, Walter. Joanne first before France. You have my word on it.'

'Gut! Because if you don't inform on the Banditen in this matter and all others, I will personally make you eat those words, even though that same Resistance for the most part still hates your guts and still has you on their list!'

Ah no, their hit-list . . . There were cells and cells. Each was very small and seldom connected to more than one or two others at the most. Gabrielle would not be able to contact more than a few people to tell them the accusation of collaborator was totally false!

Boemelburg's rapid switch to deutsch hadn't been without its cruel effect. The Sturmbannführer was only too aware of her interest in this Sûreté. He would know only too well that Gestapo Central had bugged her dressing-room and probably her flat. But while they might have their suspicions, they were apparently content simply to watch her for the moment as they did so many others.

'Now take a look at the photographs on that table, Louis. Records have spent the night digging them out for me as a favour to you for old times' sake.'

A favour. How nice . . .

In black and white, and corpse by corpse, were the grisly bodies of nearly forty women. Some were so badly decomposed only teeth and bones and shreds of flesh and clothing remained. Others were quite fresh. Some had been shot, others strangled, still others bound and gagged then knifed or smothered. Not all were naked—indeed, most were clothed or partially clothed and in only six were the dresses rucked up, the underwear and stockings yanked down, the blouses and brassières ripped open or otherwise dishevelled.

Long hair, short hair, curly and straight—all was spilled over muddy ground, wet grass, concrete, carpeting or floated among tendrils of weeds. Arms and legs slackly sprawled, heads that were crooked at odd angles, eyes that were open in some cases and blindfolded in others or simply closed.

No sign of Joanne as yet . . . None. 'Are . . . are they all from after the Defeat?' he managed. Could Talbotte be shirking his duties as préfet so much?

'They bracket the Conquest, Louis. Most are from afterwards but it's for you to decide exactly how long this affair has been going on. Ah, it's about time, *dummkopf*!' he shouted at Hermann.

Beneath each photograph on the table was the respective dossier. Some were barely a page or two, others quite thick. It was Kohler who said, 'Most of these can be discarded, Sturmbann-führer. We're looking for potential mannequins of the ages of eighteen to twenty-two.'

'Then look. Spread out the ones you have from the house of Monsieur Vergès, and the next time you think to slap a *verboten* notice on a door whose lock you have smashed, remember to ask my permission.'

'We were in a hurry.'

'Don't backtalk your superior officer! Good *Gott im Himmel*, have you not had enough lessons for one lifetime?'

It was a sore point and nothing more needed to be said. Grumpily Boemelburg spread single photos of each of the fourteen girls out in a row below the others. Then the three of them began rapidly to search for the corresponding photographs or to dig into the files. From time to time there was a grunt, a, 'Ah, there she is,' or, 'No, it can't be this one.'

Eight of the fourteen girls were accounted for. All were naked.

Though some had been left lying face up, others were face down. All had had their breasts removed but these were absent from the scene and had not, apparently, been recovered.

Four were still bound and gagged and had been butchered on the spot, their clothes scattered about the rain-soaked trampled grass of an abandoned field or vacant lot.

Renée Marteau had not been the first to die. At least three others had come before her— one as early as 7 October 1940 and missing since 15 August—fifty-three days and nights of terror.

A gap had then occurred until 21 December 1940.

'Then 3 March 1941, Louis,' said Hermann, 'and then another gap and Renée on 15 August 1941.'

'The day that one went missing, Hermann, but a year later . . . ?'

'Some kind of anniversary?' asked Kohler.

'Perhaps, but then . . . Ah, Walter, Walter, even if there is no connection to the robbery, is not the case of these girls and that of Joanne sufficient?'

Boemelburg reminded him of the robbery's priority.

'Of course. How stupid of me to have forgotten.'

Kohler felt he had best say something before Louis hanged himself. 'It looks like the kidnappings began after the fall of France.'

Not the conquest? Was Hermann trying to be kind? wondered St-Cyr, alarmed.

'Point is, did their murderer figure he could get away with it now?' asked Hermann with all that such a question implied about the Occupation. Giselle had suggested it.

'Or did he feel such women, and what they stood for, had betrayed France in her hour of greatest need and sought to punish them?' asked Boemelburg. There had been a legacy of bitterness after the Defeat of June 1940, the accusations of cowardice all too common. 'There has to be a rationale, Louis. Violent hatred such as this must have its roots in a deep psychosis.'

Walter couldn't yet know of the son of Monsieur Vergès or of the boy's fiancée. 'Have Ballistics come up with anything?' asked St-Cyr.

There was a nod. 'A typical terrorist gun, just as Hermann said to Talbotte in that bank. An officer's gun that wasn't turned in. A Lebel Model 1873.'

And as common as dust.

'But was it from the First or the Second War, Walter?' asked St-Cyr gravely. 'That is the question, since the gun, as you well know, was used in both.'

'But not with any of these,' grunted Boemelburg, indicating the eight of the fourteen victims.

With each of those whose bodies had been found, the hair had been cut off in fistfuls and disposed of elsewhere, with the breasts perhaps.

Four of the bodies had been moved after death, but only Renée Marteau's corpse been found in water, in the Seine.

Two of the girls had been strangled with silk stockings. An axe had been used with the two whose heads had been removed. A single blow in one case, three blows in the other.

One girl had been smothered by having her face pushed into mud. Another had been forcibly drowned, in a bathtub, perhaps and her body dumped elsewhere.

'And one was so badly burned with acid, Louis, she must have died in agony,' said Hermann, 'though not a drop was spilled on her face.'

Ah *nom de Dieu*, wondered St-Cyr, what was he to tell Joanne's parents? Acid . . . A drooler who hated young women . . .

'Louis, I've had the dossiers and the photos copied for you as a gesture of our willingness to co-operate in this matter,' said Boemelburg.

The sad eyes lifted to him. 'And that of the bank teller, Walter?'

'That also. He had a wife and two children. Perhaps the wife can tell you something.'

A nod of thanks would suffice. 'We'll go first to the warehouse of the mover to see what has happened to the furniture from that house, then we'll split up so as to get the work over as quickly as possible and cover more ground.'

'*Bon*. Keep me informed and remember our little agreement.'
'Our agreement. Of course.'

'What agreement? Louis, you'd better tell me.'
'Then perhaps you'd best not drive so insanely. After all, it is *my* car!'
'Piss off! Don't evade the issue. Boemelburg swore you to allegiance. Otherwise it was fuck Joanne and get on with the robbery.'
'Please don't use such crudities. The girl has a mother and father.'
'*And* a grandmother!' They were shouting.
So Boemelburg had put it to Louis, the poor sap. 'Hey, *mon vieux*, if you want it, I'm going to give you the last word to make you feel better!' Kohler tramped on the brakes, hit the accelerator and they rocketed up the hill of Montmartre. No traffic . . . Well, none of consequence. *Vélos*, *vélo-taxis*, one miserable horse-drawn carriage, a Wehrmacht lorry and . . .
'*Ah no!*'
Screech!
'Ice . . . the roads are icy, Hermann. Please. God has just granted us a small miracle. Let us proceed more cautiously since the boy was not crushed under our wheels and is now weeping in his mother's arms.'
'A ball, Louis. Why the hell was a ball rolling out on to the road like that in winter?'
'The street is narrow. We're in an older part of the *quartier*. The people here have to make do. The boy is too little to play elsewhere. The mother . . .'
Kohler pulled on the handbrake. The car idled beautifully. 'Hang on a minute. It's Christmas,' he said and, getting out, went over to the woman who immediately thought she was going to be arrested.
As St-Cyr watched, the Gestapo's Bavarian protector dragged out, from God knows where, a handful of sweets.
The woman was so rigid with fear, he had to take off the boy's hat and leave them in it.

Backing away with the palms of both hands upraised in caution, and looking ridiculous in greatcoat, scarf and fedora, he got back into the car. Breath steaming. Fog on the windscreen.

'Gimme a fag, Louis.'

'I haven't got any, Father Christmas.'

'A *fag, damn it!* Light one for me.'

Hermann was shaking.

The cigarette, retrieved from one of the Gestapo's inner pockets and lighted, began to do its work. At last the giant confessed. 'I don't ever want to have killed a child, Louis. I could never live with that on my conscience. Two wars and I swear I haven't yet. No women either.'

'Me also. So let us proceed more slowly.'

The office and warehouses of Dallaire and Sons were in the industrial heartland of Saint-Denis just off the rue du Landy and by the railway tracks. Depressingly grimy windows shut out the grey light of day. The stench of soot and sulphur dioxide was in the air, stares from workmen down the way who were loading sacks of coal into railway trucks . . .

Bound for the Reich no doubt, but where the hell had they found them? wondered Kohler.

'Are Dallaire and Sons on holiday, Hermann?'

'Pardon?'

St-Cyr indicated the place. A front office in one of twin warehouses. No sign of the *gazogènes*.

'Maybe they're out on a job?'

'Perhaps, but then . . . Ah *merde*, Hermann, unless I'm mistaken, they're not here.'

The warehouses were empty. There was rubbish—when one had cleared the window glass sufficiently to peer inside, the litter became all too apparent.

'Empty since the Defeat, Louis. They probably left for the south during the exodus and simply didn't bother to come back.'

Must God do this to them? 'Now what?'

'Someone with contacts enough to borrow a couple of lorries, Louis. Someone smart enough to have known or taken the time to find this place was empty and then to have used the name.'

'Which will now have been removed from the lorries.'

'Did that little maid tell you the truth?'

There was that shrug Kohler knew so well but then, 'She had no reason to lie about this.'

'Yet she didn't tell you everything.'

'No, but then did that *mouchard* you beat up tell you everything?'

'Péguy? He can't have known anything about the house. We dealt only with the robbery.'

'Then perhaps this is the link we're looking for? The name of a firm that is no longer here but which would cause no suspicion if its lorries were seen by the neighbours.'

'I was hoping we would find the negatives. More photos— other things than we're permitted to see in the prints they left us. Shadows, an arm, a leg—the woman who helped out.'

'But why empty the house, Hermann? Oh, *bien sûr* there may well have been thoughts of their leaving fingerprints we would find, but all the furniture? And three days later? It doesn't make sense. Even if interrupted, as obviously they were, why clean the place out like that?'

'Maybe the stuff was simply stolen.'

'By someone else? Is this what you're thinking?'

'Or by the kidnappers who'd become used to having such nice things around them, or simply moved by the drooler, the owner's son.'

The drooler . . . ah, *merde* . . . 'We never thought to check the photos, Hermann, but for myself, I don't think we'll find any finger-prints other than our own.'

'Let's see where the bastards from the robbery dumped the get-away car and its chauffeur.'

It was not far. Just back into Montmartre a little way.

The courtyard of 9 rue des Amiraux was so close to the goods yards, they could hear the constant shunting of locomotives. Various small ateliers gave on to it. A carver of tombstones, an ironworker who threaded bolts for the railways . . . All were at it behind closed doors and shutters for it was winter and damned cold.

Only a woman of forty or so, with a thick and tattered black shawl over her shoulders, stared impassively at their entry from a distant doorway.

'No one will have seen a thing, Hermann. It's useless to ask and will take much time.'

'But why this courtyard, Louis? Why not any of the countless others?'

It was a good question for which there were no ready answers, except the nearness of it to the warehouses of Dallaire and Sons, its obscurity and a knowledge of the area. 'Two men, two very fine suitcases crammed with banknotes which were hastily emptied, then left for someone to steal,' said St-Cyr.

'While the chauffeur, bound and gagged, was out cold,' snorted Kohler.

'Why didn't they kill him? A perfect witness?'

'Maybe they were afraid to, seeing as he was a member of the Occupying Forces.'

'Then who freed him?'

'Perhaps the mistress who borrowed the car can tell us, Louis. Perhaps the chauffeur himself. And if not either, then the owner of the car and the guy who's fucking her, the Sonderführer Franz Ewald Kempf of the Propaganda Staffel.'

'Have fun. I'd best return to the house of Monsieur Vergès for another look around and a quiet think.'

'Do you want the photographs with you?'

Good for Hermann. 'Some of them. Please drive by the house you have so kindly had repaired for me. I'll collect my briefcase but make the selection elsewhere, I think. Yes, that would be best.'

'Chez Rudi's then, for breakfast. Hey, I can smell the coffee and the croissants, and to hell with ration tickets and your principles. The soul needs to be fortified before tackling the ass of the mistress!'

Hermann always had to have the last word. One ought to object. Privation was a national pastime and heroic but . . . ah, heroes were not always so and the meal would be good. Perhaps a simple thermos could be provided and a few sandwiches? He would leave the details to them.

'You okay?' asked Kohler.

'Yes, I'm okay.'

'Those photos the Chief laid out for us, they're not bothering you, are they?'

'A little.'

'Hey, we'll find her. She's going to be okay. I've got a feeling about it, Louis. Joanne's alive but only because the house had to be emptied in a rush.'

A feeling . . . How comforting. St-Cyr stared out the side window at the bleakness of what Paris and France had become. A cinematographer at heart and fascinated by the cinema, he could not help but see with the camera's clear eye the last and final moments of those girls.

He heard them begging for their lives, their frantic screams and saw their pathetic struggles as they tried to escape. It was now nearly ten o'clock. He and Hermann hadn't been on the case twenty-four hours, yet could he not do more? Had the lack of vitamins numbed his brain?

The car had stopped outside his house. 'A moment, Hermann. I'll just dash in. Please tell Dédé we're on urgent business and can't delay.'

Kohler dug into a pocket as the boy came down the street towards him but found the sweets all gone.

The boy was ashen.

He rolled the window down and managed a grin. 'Hey, kid, she's alive. We're going to get her soon, eh? Unharmed. Not a hair touched.'

Without a word, the boy stood watching him, unyielding in denial until at last Dédé said, 'You're lying,' and turned away.

Coming quickly from the house with his briefcase, St-Cyr caught him by the shoulder. The boy swung on him in tears, in rage, but stopped himself from cursing the only one who could help them.

'Dédé, listen to me. It's serious. We've had a major setback this

morning but are working on it and hope to have something positive very soon.'

The flat was three storeys above the boulevard de Beauséjour,
not a stone's throw from the Bois de Boulogne and the apartment
of Louis's chanteuse, which was just to the north on the boulevard Emile Auger at number 45. A tidy neck of the woods that
smelled all too evidently of old money and young inheritors with
too much time on their hands.

Gabrielle was an exception.

Kohler finished his cigarette in the car at the side of the road.
Becker of Gestapo Central's internal records hadn't liked fishing
for details on the Sonderführer Kempf. 'Betrayal of a sacred trust'
and all that shit. Money had had to change hands. Lots of it—
5000 francs to put it bluntly.

One could never quite get used to paying for information that
ought rightly to have been given freely by one's own associates
and subordinates, but what the hell? It was the Occupation. All
the rules had had to be rewritten. Paris was expensive.

He thumbed open his wallet and saw that he had exactly 20
francs left for house money and everything else. Pay-day had
been and gone and would not come again until 5 January at the
earliest, unless the Führer decided to make it later.

Mademoiselle Denise Céline St. Onge was twenty-seven years
of age, a graduate of the Sorbonne with a degree in Ancient History and French Literature, absolutely useless to her should she
have to earn a living as a riveter.

There was a villa in the south of France at Le Lavandou where
the parents had retreated for the Duration. A brother resided in
the Reich as a guest at a POW camp. Another fed the daisies in
summer.

The Sonderführer didn't live with her but sometimes stayed
the night. Her place or his, whichever was convenient or gave
that added little thrill.

It was nearly noon and time she was up. A maid noticed the
Gestapo shield in his upraised palm, a finger to his lips as well,
and let him in.

Flustered, she went in search of her mistress and left him to a tapestry-hung salon with sofas, deep armchairs and throw cushions in cream and gold silk on Persian carpets. Bibelots were scattered like pleasureful playthings, bronze-green trinkets from ancient tombs—were they Sumerian? Venetian glass beads—he knew a little about very old glass from a recent case in Provence. Gold signets with hieroglyphics, clay tablets too. Egyptian. Falcons, slaves and snakes among other things.

There were books, of course—mostly on ancient Egypt. Hell, who really wanted to read about the present? A linen-draped table was in a corner by a sofa that still held imprints for two. There were snuffed-out candles on the table, late-night caviar and champagne probably and, with the drapes open as now, a view of the night sky over the Bois. How lovely. Heat on. No shortage of coal. Soft murmurings of passion.

Amid the clutter on the mantelpiece, there was an invitation to an auction of works of art at the Jeu de Paume, 31 December, viewing from 2.00 to 5.00 p.m., sale at 8.00 p.m. and a late supper afterwards at the Ritz.

Hermann Goering had done the inviting. Well, not actually. An assistant of course. But, still, the Reichsführer himself and supreme commander of the Luftwaffe.

Probably flying in for a little bit of fun in spite of the disaster at Stalingrad. A busy man and an avid collector.

The heavy and embossed bond had the deckle edges of quality. The gilding and black lettering were really very nice.

There was a discreet logo on the back. 'Our engraver,' he said, a whisper . . .

Nearby there was a chummy photo of Kempf and his lady friend outside the Alcazar, 8 rue du Faubourg-Montmartre and in daylight of all things. Kempf was a typical blond Aryan in uniform with a nice grin. No battles for this one. He had come in after the blitzkrieg. Thirty-two years of age and married, with the wife and kids back home in Köln and under the ashes, incinerated by the RAF's firestorm of last May 30 and 31.

The grin must have been from before the loss, the photo taken in the early spring. A man from an old and well-established family who had suddenly lost everything in that fire. A man then, wondered Kohler, with a grudge to bear and a need to recoup his family's fortune?

It was a thought, but how long had the romance been going on and how heavily?

The shadow of a woman's wide-brimmed hat was behind and off to the right of the couple. Hats like that had been all the rage this past spring and summer, but not the year before. And hadn't it been a marvel the way the girls had used just any old thing to make hats like new? Amazing really and very chic.

The hat must have belonged to a friend, but not to the photographer, since it would have cast a different shadow.

'Inspector . . . ?'

Black silk crêpe clung to Denise St. Onge like a second skin but below the lower thighs, sheer black see-through lace fell to the ankles exposing lovely legs. Flowered white ceramic clasps held the twin straps of high-heeled, black leather shoes. There were thin straps over bare shoulders—nice shoulders—a nice chest, with a faintly ruffled neckline, long, slender arms, long fingers, thick, dark brown hair brushed and pinned tightly and parted on the left, a high, smooth brow, not a wrinkle, angular face, thinly arched and well-plucked brows and large brown eyes. Deep brown and grave. Could they melt iron or were they always so hard?

'Inspector, what is it you want with me?'

Mein Gott, the accent was lovely. 'A few questions. Nothing difficult.'

'Then please sit down. An apéritif, or is it that you mustn't drink while on duty?'

'A glass of wine would be nice. White, if you have it.'

'Certainly. Excuse me a moment. Jeanne has had to do the shopping, you understand.'

She had deliberately sent the maid away and he was all too aware of this, she felt. He didn't offer to get the wine for her but took the opportunity to study her and was impressed, ah yes. Most men who liked looking at women were. It didn't please her, of course. He was trouble, and trouble wasn't wanted at this moment in her life.

When she came back with a bottle, two glasses and a corkscrew, Kohler watched her hand them to him as her lovely red lips gave a little pout.

There was a diamond-encrusted bracelet on her left wrist, loose and slipping down over a slender hand. Ear-rings to match that dangled, framing arrogance betrayed but only for a moment.

'The Château Grillet, 1939 ... To think they could even bottle anything then,' he said wistfully.

'Wine must never be wasted, Inspector. Not even if it's a bad year.'

Actually it had been a pretty good year for wine, among other things. 'It's all the same to me,' he said and grinned and yanked the cork out. 'I prefer beer. I'm from Bavaria.'

'Yes, I gathered you were, but how is it, please, that you speak our language so well?'

He tossed his head. 'Oh that. I was a guest of your country from 17 July 1916 until the Armistice.'

'Ah, a prisoner of war.' She, too, tossed her head and then, accepting the glass he held out to her, took it without touching his fingers.

Enfolding herself fluidly on to the sofa with knees together and towards him, and one elbow resting on the back so that she sat sideways, she tilted her forehead a little forward in the manner of such women, to study him better.

The hand whose elbow rested on the sofa, plucked at the bracelet of the one that held the glass.

'So, a few questions, Inspector. Nothing difficult.'

'It's about the robbery.' She was making him feel like a dolt with that look of hers!

'Yes, I gathered it would be about the robbery but you see, Inspector ... ' The lovely shoulders were raised. 'I couldn't possibly help you since I saw nothing of it.'

'I thought so. There you are, Mademoiselle St. Onge. That's Gestapo Central for you. Send a poor detective out on a wild-goose chase. *Sacré-bleu*, another waste of time!'

He downed his wine. She wasn't fooled in the least and took but a sip of her own just to wet her throat. Would it hurt to offer him a crumb? she wondered. Would it help or merely cause more suspicion? Ah, what could she say about him but that he was most definitely suspicious.

For this there was no apparent reason, and she put it down merely to his manner. He wished to unsettle her, as he would all others he had to question no matter how innocent.

She took another sip and let him watch her lovely throat. 'Harald wasn't killed, Inspector, and for this I'm truly grateful and much relieved.'

'Harald?' he asked.

'Yes. Franz's driver.'

'Franz?'

'Oh come now, Inspector! How else could you have found my name and address if not from that same Gestapo Central who would, I'm sure, have told you of my lover?'

'The Sonderführer Franz Ewald Kempf.'

Again there was that teasing little pout and then a shrug. 'He lets me have the use of his car from time to time.'

The inspector set his glass aside just as Franz had once done while sitting in that same armchair, watching as she had undressed, she touching herself, he searching her splendid body for its every soft nuance, his eyes rapt, the grin of hunger on his lips until at last . . .

But Franz didn't do that any more, though the detective could not know of this.

'Tell me about the driver,' he asked, having not read her mind at all.

'There's nothing to tell.'

Kohler saw her swallow. Her wineglass was forgotten. 'How often do you have the use of the car, Mademoiselle St. Onge?'

How often were things still going on between her and Franz, was that what he really wanted to find out? 'Once or twice a week, it depends.'

'Usually for the day?'

'Yes.'

He took out his cigarettes and offered her one but she refused. There was a lighter on the side table. SS and of stainless steel. A gift he studied but didn't use. Indeed, he put it down and thought better of having a cigarette himself.

'Do you often go to that shop in the rue Quatre Septembre?' he asked.

At 12.47 p.m. on a Thursday? Was that what he wanted? It was. 'Not often. Only sometimes.'

'Once a week?'

'Perhaps.'

'Here, let me refill your glass. The wine's really okay, isn't it?'

He got up so swiftly, he was all but on top of her. He stood there tall and big and brutal, yes, yes—a scar down his left cheek, a duelling scar?

Inwardly she shook her head and told herself this one doesn't do things like that. He has no use for them and is of far too humble a birth. A peasant.

She covered her glass with a hand and said, 'Ah no, Inspector. I have sufficient.'

'Then maybe you'd better tell me how often you visit that shop and why.'

To blink her eyes up at him, to fill them with tears, would be of no use. 'I'm usually there once or twice a week. Sometimes, as at this time of year, far more. You see, I own the shop. It's called quite simply Chez Denise.'

'That's nice. We're getting on a lot better. What do you sell?'

'Clothes.'

'Only clothes at an address like that?'

'Designer clothes, things of quality.' Again there was that pout and shrug. 'These days there is not so much and it's very hard to find suitable stock, so we remember.'

'*Soie sauvage?*'

Wild or raw silk. 'Yes. Yes, I do like to have it.'

'I'll bet you do,' he snorted but didn't return to his chair. Instead, he remained standing over her with the bottle gripped by its neck. He had big fingers, thick and coarse, fingers that when doubled . . .

Kohler gave her a moment. She wouldn't back down, was too highborn for that. 'So, mademoiselle, you would leave the car of your lover outside your shop and there's a good chance you did so often enough that others would see this and note that the car would be available.'

'I . . . I don't know what you're implying?'

'You don't? *Gott im Himmel*, forgive me. You either told a friend the car would be there at 12.47 p.m. with its engine running, or someone else, another friend or acquaintance, knew you would be there because you always were.'

'The . . . the times varied.'

'Oh no they didn't. Your little life is like a clock. Sleep until noon, get dressed and drop into the shop to see how things are going, then off to lunch at Maxim's with your lover.'

'He . . . he wasn't in the car. Harald . . .'

'You and his driver were to pick him up at the Propaganda Staffel over on the Champs-Élysées at number 52.'

'Is . . . is that so wrong? These . . . these days, Inspector, what is a girl to do? Make friends, yes? Fall in love. Sleep with her lover.'

'And borrow his car from time to time. Hey, I almost forgot.'

She waited. Her heart was racing. The interview wouldn't stop, not now. Questions, questions, always more and more of them from this one who could know nothing of her and Franz, that Franz no longer loved her, that he only wanted to . . .

When he handed her the photograph from the mantelpiece, she took it from him with trembling fingers he didn't notice, or did he? He set her glass aside and she heard him say, 'I like your perfume. What is it?'

Her perfume . . . 'Mirage. A little something special from a shop I know of and would wish to have some day on place Vendôme.'

Ambition then, was that it? wondered Kohler. Louis would be intrigued, for Louis not only knew the shop and its owners well but also that same perfume since it had been made especially for a certain chanteuse who always wore it.

'Who took the photo?'

'A man. He's of no consequence. I don't even know where he

is now.' She could tell that Herr Kohler hadn't cared about the one who had taken the photo, that he wanted something else . . .

'Whose was the hat?' he asked.

She could shrug and say she didn't know. A passing girl perhaps, a casual acquaintance but, ah it would be of no use. He had that look about him, that look of . . . 'A friend. Inspector, is this necessary? She had nothing to do with that robbery. My God, that photo was taken months ago!'

He would wait until she gave the name to him. He had that same look about him. Not brutal as so many of the Gestapo were, but unyielding in resolve. Like concrete.

'Her name is Mademoiselle Marie-Claire de Brisson, Inspector. We . . . we were at the university together. The . . . the Sorbonne, of course.'

The banker's daughter . . . *Jésus, merde alors!* 'Don't leave the city. I may want to talk to you again.'

Without another word he showed himself out and only after he had gone and she was replacing the photograph, did she notice the invitation and realize he would have seen it.

Hurrying over to the windows, she watched the street and saw him think better of getting into his car. He looked both up and down the street, then chose the direction which offered the most potential, and went after her maid. Ah no.

Kohler found the girl shivering in the Jardins du Ranelagh, but over on the avenue Chemin de la Muette. She was looking off down the avenue past an old man and his dog, straight towards the Bois de Boulogne in the near distance.

She didn't turn when he came up behind her. Christ, it was bleak. Normally quite lovely in summer, the gardens reminded him of Siberia, though he had never been there.

'Mademoiselle . . .'

The girl was shattered. She thought it was the end for her. 'I know nothing, monsieur. She tells me *nothing!*'

He turned her towards him. She wasn't any more than eighteen. The face was thin, the eyes afraid. 'Look, Mademoiselle Jeanne, I'm not going to hurt you. I only want the answer to one question. Does your mistress loan things from that shop of hers to a friend?'

'Sometimes.'

Kohler gently lifted her chin so that their eyes met. 'Which friend? Mademoiselle Marie-Claire de Brisson?'

'Yes.'

He nodded curtly. He took her by the arm and walked with her the short distance to the tearoom on the avenue Raphaël but he had no money or time for such things.

She saw that his thoughts were far away but then, having decided, he said, 'Jeanne, go in and have a cup of that stuff they call tea. Take your time, then go back and swear to that mistress of yours that we never met. *Never*, do you understand? It's very important. I'll do my act for her if she's still watching my partner's car. I'll help you out, kid, so don't forget.'

Louis, he said to himself. Louis, I think I know where Joanne is. If I need help, you'd better come running. *Mein Gott, mon vieux,* I only hope I'm not too late because I'm going to have to take the time to walk up to that car of yours as though I couldn't find her maid. I'm going to have to drive slowly away even though I know I haven't a moment to lose. The banker's daughter, Louis. I can't have Mademoiselle St. Onge telephoning the woman to warn her. I can't.

From time to time as he moved about the empty house, St-Cyr looked out on to the rue de Valois to see the austere façade of the Bank of France. It was there as if to remind him of the robbery, yet was that event but a distraction hiding what they needed most to know?

'Two men and a woman,' he said aloud but softly to himself. 'It doesn't fit with what we know must have happened here. Bank robbers don't fool around taking pictures of kidnapped girls. In any case, why the delay of three days? Why *wait* until then to leave? Why clean out everything?'

As always these days, crime had to be viewed through the Occupation's prism, warped though that was most certainly. A crime such as the robbery could have been perpetrated by the

Germans for their own ends but they could have used French gangsters so as to disguise the fact.

It could, of course, have been done by those same gangsters for their own ends but without them letting their German masters in on things.

It could have been a straight crime unconnected to either of these parties, in which case each would want to know who had done it.

Then, too, the Resistance which, a year or even six months ago, need not have been factored in simply because they were such a very, very tiny element, had now to be considered since the war in Russia had driven the Communists in France to actively resist the Germans. Though not all of the Resistance was Communist, a good part of it was to the shame of everyone else.

In any case, the Resistance now could well have learned of that shipment and robbed the bank out of necessity or to teach someone a lesson. Monsieur André-Philippe de Brisson perhaps.

Uncomfortable at the thought of the Resistance teaching people lessons, he took out his pipe but elected to ration himself after all.

'Something's bothering me,' he said. 'Ah *merde*, why can't I put my finger on it?'

He felt the thing was so simple, it was staring him right in the face, yet when he looked at the walls all he saw was the wallpaper and then . . .

Faintly the outlines on the walls revealed where the owner had hung his paintings. In room by room they showed so clearly. Some had been larger than others, some of moderate size and some really quite small—had these last been photographs? he wondered and thought they must have been, but had the paintings been of value? Would Monsieur Vergès have left such things here, knowing the Germans, if they should discover the house without occupants, would requisition the premises and use it for their own?

Somehow Monsieur Vergès must have taken measures to see that the house remained unoccupied even by his German masters.

But had the paintings been of value and was this why the house had been emptied?

Then why scatter the photographs of those poor unfortunate girls? Why not simply take them away with everything else?

Again he was forced to admit that the finger of suspicion pointed at the drooler, at the son.

With a decisive thoroughness that pleased him, St-Cyr measured and recorded the size of each of the outlines, stopping only at the smaller of them.

Then he stood in what had been the grand salon, willing himself into Joanne's shoes.

She had lived in her imagination as a little girl. Oh *bien sûr* she had always been very interested in the goings-on around her, a most curious and analytical nature, but right in the middle of something, she would be a shop-girl taking orders over the counter of the local *pâtisserie*, a dancer suddenly or a sword-fighting pirate, a waiter. This last recollection was vivid.

Joanne had tilted her little head to one side while holding a small pad and pencil and, while she could not then read or write, had asked what they would like to order and had written it all down with quick, deft strokes and had made suggestions as to the more expensive items, particularly the wine. She could only have picked this up by watching some big pavement café from the wings The family had had no money to sit in such places and order such things.

'She ought to have been an actress,' he said. 'I had forgotten how well she could drop into any part she chose to play.'

She would have seen the paintings—indeed everything else in this . . . this lovely house. She would have marvelled at the furniture, have hesitated at first to touch a thing. It was all so far removed from the life she had known.

She would have been submissive, shy, hesitant always—worried, oh my yes. Could she do it? Would they find her unsatisfactory?

He would have to force that little maid next door to tell him what she knew. He must question the neighbours on the other side of the house—no one had been in when he had rung the bells. He would have to question the banker's daughter about the cat, ah yes.

Suddenly furious with himself for not making faster progress, St-Cyr dug out the smattering of photographs he had gleaned from the heap in the car and realized he ought to have had the complete sequence.

The clothes Joanne had modelled had been very good. *Très chic* for these times and quite classy but things . . . ah what could he say about them? The styles . . . ? Skirts, blouses and sweaters, suits that were really very good but did not quite fit perfectly. Trousers, evening gowns, sequined sheaths, peignoirs and lingerie then . . . why then, nothing.

Though he found it uncomfortable, he forced himself to study her naked body knowing that if ever they should meet again, he would have the utmost difficulty facing her.

She had lovely breasts, full and not too big or too small. Had she been proud of them? Of course, but she would seldom have seen them, for good girls, even ones who wanted to become mannequins, didn't spend long before the mirror. Christ and the Blessed Virgin, God and old Father Taverner, the parish priest, saw to that. And if not them, her mother and father, the crowding of an overcrowded house, and if not that, her grandmother.

Joanne had been left-handed so, while in photos of the other girls a single bracelet had been worn naturally on the left wrist, with her, she had instinctively chosen the right wrist.

She was lying on that *chaise-longue* staring up into the camera.

In another photo she lay on it but with her head and shoulders hanging just over the edge and her arms straining to stop herself from sliding on to the floor.

Mon Dieu, she was so beautiful it hurt to look at her knowing what had happened to the others.

The bracelet had been removed. She was totally naked, her legs taut and straining too, her eyes clamped shut in fear, a lower lip bitten, the cheeks tense.

Quickly he found the shot of her backed into that corner, having just been told what was to become of her. Somehow she had snatched up the bracelet and had put it back on the right wrist, yet when he examined similar photos of three of the other girls, they had not worn the bracelet.

Fishing in a pocket, he dragged out a small lens and was grateful that the photos had been enlarged. In raised relief, figures appeared on the bracelet. Though their outlines lacked resolution, he saw a naked young woman kneeling with her head uptilted and a hand grasping something so as to hold it in her mouth.

Was she sucking a cow's teat?

In another, a falcon-headed figure sat in judgment while a jackal-headed figure weighed something on a tall and quite simple beam balance.

The figures had been copied from the tombs of ancient Egypt. There would be hieroglyphics—snakes, scarabs, birds of various kinds and yes, the scales of truth, the weighing of the heart and the suckling so as the soul could enter the otherworld nourished and reborn . . .

He swallowed hard as he looked at that thing.

Joanne had worn the bracelet in hopes someone would see it. Though he couldn't prove this, he felt the photographer and his assistant had, perhaps, been too distracted to notice.

If so, that could only mean they had been afraid of discovery and in a hurry.

Cramming everything into his briefcase, he raced for the door, caught himself only at the last moment to leave a brief note for Hermann.

Then he headed for the rue Quatre Septembre with a vengeance, Dédé's words echoing in his head. '*But . . . but Joanne, she has had plenty of time? She might have . . .*'

Window-shopped so as to see the type of clothes she would have to model. Of course!

Hermann . . . Hermann, have I found the answer?

4 'EXCUSE ME, MONSIEUR, BUT IT WILL HAVE TO BE another time. I'm going out.'

The banker's wife was in her early sixties, still quite handsome, and wearing a dove-grey suit that was perfect for her. Good-naturedly Kohler grinned and tossed the hand that held his fedora. 'Ah, of course, Madame de Brisson, I quite understand but another time is just not possible. It's an emergency.'

The blue eyes behind their gold-rimmed spectacles hesitated. 'Emergency? But . . . but what is this? What emergency?'

'Gestapo, Paris-Central. Kohler, Haupsturmführer and Detective Inspector. Please step aside.'

'Most certainly not!' she quivered.

The rounded shoulders were bunched for battle. So, okay, he would let her have it. 'Your daughter, madame. We have reason to believe she's engaged in a criminal conspiracy.'

'Our daughter . . . ? Marie-Claire . . . ? But . . . but that is impossible, monsieur. What could the girl have done?'

Moisture was rapidly gathering in her eyes. 'Why not tell me, eh? Suddenly you feel sick, madame. What's she been up to?'

'*Nothing!*'

The reddened lips trembled, the rouged and powdered cheeks tightened. 'Then step aside and we'll have a look. Her flat first, then down the stairs to yours. Anyone leaves and my partner out there on the street has orders to shoot on sight. No questions. Just bang, right in the face!' Louis was nowhere near but . . .

The pearls were clutched. 'Marie . . . Marie-Claire couldn't have had anything to do with that robbery, monsieur. It's monstrous of you to even suggest such a thing. *Absurd!* Adopted at birth, a treasure to her dear mother and father . . .'

Adopted . . . 'Go on. Please do, Madame de Brisson, or shall I first go through the house and then that flat up there?'

'You . . . you've no reason to suspect her. She . . . she's innocent.'

'Then you've nothing to fear.'

'Have you a magistrate's order?'

It was a last line of defence and he had to give her credit for trying. 'Don't be silly. Be thankful I haven't brought along the troops to knock hell out of this place.'

The salon de Brisson was rather nice though he saw it only in passing. Fluted columns with scrolled volutes and acanthus leaves held up a ceiling whose ornate mouldings made him think of Rome. A grand piano, Louis XV armchairs in silver with dove-grey fabric were tastefully scattered. The alabaster head of a woman sat on the mantelpiece beside a large bouquet of silk flowers, both reflected in a superb mirror. Then he was in a hallway with doors opening off it, a library, a study, a billiard room, kitchen, pantry, stairs up the back to the attic, to what formerly had been the maid's quarters, the cook's or nanny's.

He skipped the second floor and went on up to the third floor and a change of scenery. Avant-garde, more of the *demi-monde* and the Left Bank.

Instead of oil paintings on the walls, there were mounted black-and-white photographs. Lots of them. Scenes of Paris, of the gardens, the Champs-Élysées, pigeons, old people, flowers, children . . .

He drew in a breath, then went through the attic *pied-à-terre*, swiftly opening doors, checking the two bedrooms, the small sitting-room, kitchen, bathroom, toilet, et cetera, even to opening tall armoires that were crammed with clothes. Good stuff too. Evening dresses, sheaths, blouses, skirts and suits, and then, ah *Gott im Himmel*, a small dark-room. Shit!

The banker's daughter was an amateur photographer who developed and printed her own photographs.

Joanne Labelle was nowhere in the flat. Hesitating, for he had felt so certain he would find the girl here before it was too late, Kohler went down the front stairs to Marie-Claire de Brisson's private entrance on the rue de Montpensier, then back upstairs and down the service stairs into her parents' home.

'Nothing, monsieur. There is nothing, is there?' said Madame de Brisson, still looking ashen and so close to tears he had to ask himself, what was she hiding?

He wanted to shriek at her to spit it out while there was still time. Instead, he sighed and pulled off his overcoat. 'Let's go upstairs to your daughter's flat, madame, and you can tell me all about her work as a photographer. Oh by the way, where is she?'

'At work, of course. Where else would she be?'

'Work?'

Was it so surprising? 'Yes, the shop of a friend, Chez Denise. It's on the rue Quatre Septembre directly across the street from my husband's bank.'

For hours, it seemed, St-Cyr stared at a bracelet in the window of the shop called Chez Denise. Was it the twin of the one Joanne had worn in that photograph or exactly the same one?

As Dédé had suggested, he had followed in Joanne's footsteps and had window-shopped westward from the Bourse Métro station. But he mustn't let the bracelet's presence disturb him so much he gave away what he now knew and jeopardized her life. He must go into this shop and ask a few simple questions about the robbery—the jewellery only in passing if at all. Yet for the moment he could but stand here seeing that thing among a cascade of others, on deep blue satin near white antique lace and a soft woollen evening dress that was such an intense reminder of pre-war days.

The bracelet was of delicately wrought gold and blue enamel

in the style of ancient Egypt, with mummiform coffins, scarabs and winged gods. Tutankhamen's tomb had been discovered in early November 1922, spawning a roaring trade in such things. There had been a good ten years of them but since the mid-thirties such pieces had seldom been seen.

There were necklaces of lapis lazuli, turquoise and gold in which the sun god appeared in the form of a scarab that was worshipped by two naked servant girls holding funerary urns of embalmed organs. The heart, the lungs, the brain. There were rings and brooches, pendants and ear-rings, some of which he was certain had been worn in other photographs. A pharaoh's fortune but why display it like this if it was involved? It made no sense.

The stuff had to be old stock that had been brought to light by the Occupation. Few, if any, today could be making such things. The gold alone precluded this.

The shop, and others nearby, were on the very northeastern fringe of the fashion district that encompassed the rue de la Paix, the place Vendôme and extended southward to the rue du Faubourg Saint-Honoré. Yet could it have occupied a prominent place right in the heart of the trade? Had the owner seized on the Occupation to lift it from the fringe?

The clothes were really quite exceptional, given the extreme shortages. There was, as in most such places, that flagrant acceptance of the black market and the two-tiered economy. Those who could buy and, sadly, those who didn't even have enough for food and ate sparingly since the rationing system was so lousy and niggardly.

A classic Chanel-type bolero was to be worn over an exquisitely uncomplicated little dress of black silk crêpe de Chine. A Schiaparelli-like purple satin dress with plum-green Ottoman friar's cape was complemented by scarves, berets, hats and gloves, all of which were displayed with flare and feminine eloquence by a person who had a real eye for such things and left no detail to chance.

But the styles and the fabrics—indeed the whole of the window—were of the 1930s. It was as if, not only would the shop

work within the system and flaunt this in the faces of all, it would
show people what things had once been like before the war.

Determined to find out what he could without jeopardizing
Joanne, St-Cyr let himself into the place and stood there looking
around. The shop was not overly large but very elegant. There
were several customers—not all were German officers and their
mistresses. There were the wives of bankers and investment bro-
kers, of industrialists and others who profited from the Occupation. Their men, too, some of them and . . . ah yes, a smattering
of lesser types and their girlfriends.

'Monsieur, can I be of service? A little something for your wife
perhaps?'

Must she look at him as if she saw *flic* written all over him?
'The owner, please, mademoiselle, or the manageress.'

'Ah! then you will want Mademoiselle de Brisson.'

'Mademoiselle de . . .'

Was he ill at the thought, or merely alarmed? she wondered
apprehensively. 'De Brisson, monsieur. Excuse me a moment,
please.'

That the banker's daughter should work directly across the
street from her father's bank was troubling enough, but to add the
presence of the jewellery in the window . . . *Nom de Jésus-Christ!*
what was he to think?

With difficulty, much apology to a client in the Kriegsmarine,
and a troubled glance his way past trousers of grey tweed with the
generous legs of the thirties, Mademoiselle de Brisson sought
him out. The knitted, forest-green woollen dress, with its ribbed
collar and long sleeves, accentuated the green eyes and made the
pixie-like cut of dark red hair far more attractive than they might
otherwise have been. She was perhaps twenty-six or twenty-eight
years of age, a little taller than himself, of good figure but not
beautiful. The rather plain and sharply chiselled face was made
bright by the use of cosmetics—indeed, everything about her had
been used to good advantage. But still there was a brow that was
too high, a nose too broad and long for smallish ears. The lips
that forced a smile did so awkwardly under scrutiny and he had

to ask himself, Does she think it cruel of me to look so closely at her? and answered, Yes, it upsets her a great deal.

Her voice was harsh. 'Monsieur, to what do I owe this intrusion? I . . . I'm very busy as you can see. If you would like to wait, I could perhaps . . .'

A backless, white piqué evening dress with green and white taffeta halter attracted him momentarily. The intricate embroidery of a brightly coloured blouse caught his fancy. He told her who he was and said, 'Your shop is impressive, Mademoiselle de Brisson. I had no idea it was still possible to achieve such elegance.'

'Then you should understand that to forget is to survive.'

Not only was there the acid of a swift rejoinder but a nervousness that made him edgy. *To forget is to survive* . . . Survive *what*, exactly, he wondered? 'A few questions, Mademoiselle de Brisson. On Thursday last your father's bank . . .'

Impatient with him, her voice remained harsh. 'Look, I know nothing of that business! I've already told the police all I know. Mademoiselle St. Onge, the owner, and I were in the office at the back discussing things when one of my girls came to tell us what had happened.'

'Yes, of course. Perhaps you would be good enough to conduct me to the office, mademoiselle?'

'So that everyone in the shop will think I've done something wrong? Is this what you wish? Ah *mon Dieu, mon Dieu*, the nerve! I saw *nothing*!' She stamped a foot. '*Nothing*! Denise . . .'

'Mademoiselle St. Onge?'

Ah damn him for picking that up! 'Yes, the owner.'

'Is a friend?'

'Yes. Yes, a friend, but it's strictly business between us when she comes to the shop. There are always things to be discussed.'

A nod would suffice. He would ask how Mademoiselle St. Onge had taken the news of the robbery.

Why must he watch her so closely? she wondered. Why must he be so suspicious of her? 'Mademoiselle St. Onge was extremely distressed, Inspector, both for the sake of the driver and for the car since it was not hers.'

Uncertainty registered in her eyes. She waited for him to ask whose car it had been and when he didn't do so, was troubled and had to ask herself, Why has he come if not for that reason?

St-Cyr set his shabby fedora on the nearest display case and, taking out pipe and tobacco pouch, appeared as though prepared to stay until closing and afterwards if necessary.

'The fabrics, Inspector. The perfumes. It is requested that there be no use of tobacco in the shop.' She gave him a tight little shrug and forced herself to apologetically grin. 'Of course we cannot ask our German friends to comply but with ourselves . . . Ah, I am sorry. Each day I hunger for my cigarettes and tell myself I must wait.'

The urge to ask what she was afraid of was almost overwhelming, but he would have to wait until Hermann was with him. He couldn't jeopardize Joanne's life.

His shrug said, Okay, it's all right about the tobacco. I quite understand. A nearby café will suit just as well. Shall we?

Ah, it said so many things.

'Tell me, Mademoiselle de Brisson, how is your father taking the loss?'

Startled, she blurted, 'My father . . . ? Ah, I . . . I suppose not well. Eighteen million . . .'

'You haven't asked him?'

Was such a lack of familial discourse so questionable? 'My father and I don't discuss things, Inspector. Though I live above the house of my parents, I see little of them. I live my own life.'

He began to move away from her and she didn't like him doing this since it said he was questioning everything she said. *Everything*, ah no. A grey woollen jersey skirt and Hermès block-printed silk scarf attracted him, then the pleated front of a white silk blouse, then the perfumes where he lingered and asked if they manufactured some of their own.

When she said no, he told her he had a friend in the trade who did this. 'She's really very good,' he said, but didn't tell her the name of this friend or that of her shop and its location. Instead, he left her out in the cold so that she would wonder what this friend of his would say about Chez Denise and would be unsettled. Gossip was always trouble, jealousy rampant, and compliments too hard to come by but why had he done it to her? Why?

Several of the customers and salesgirls were now stealing little looks at them. An oberleutnant, a hauptmann, their women ...

Suddenly having made up his mind, the detective turned to confront her. 'Your girls, mademoiselle. Every one of them must be questioned. Look, I'm sorry but it's necessary. A teller was shot and killed. Someone obviously knew that car would be waiting in the street. Let's begin with the one who brought the news of the robbery to you and Mademoiselle St. Onge.'

She must force herself to give him a hard, shrewd look. She must! 'Very well, if that's what you wish. Juliette is the one you will want first.'

'Did none of them see a thing?' he asked, caught off stride.

Her little smile must be cruel so as to put him in his place and stop him in his tracks. 'None, Inspector. One of the girls from the shop next door came to tell Juliette who was, herself, busy with a customer.'

He would have to accept this for the moment. He would have to show the face of defeat, that of the humble detective who would now have to go away and think about it so as to put her at ease. 'What time is it, please?'

Automatically she glanced at her wrist-watch but had to pull the sleeve up.

The watch was worn on the back of the left wrist but had he seen the scars? she wondered. Had he? '3 ... 3.14, Inspector.'

St-Cyr gave her that little nod he reserved for those whose actions revealed rare insights into their characters. He wouldn't ask about the jewellery yet or if she had told her friend and employer or anyone else of the shipment of cash from Lyon. For now he would have to leave it.

'You have an eye for display, Mademoiselle de Brisson. The shop is lovely. Everything is displayed to best advantage so that the whole collection produces at once intense feelings of delight in its elegance and refinement.'

How cold of him. 'We deal in nothing else, Inspector, and nothing less. Chez Denise is that happy marriage of employer who knows what she wants and employee and friend who carries out her every wish.'

Two women . . . 'I'll show myself out. Please return to your customers. I'm sorry for the inconvenience.'

Just to prove to the customers there was nothing wrong, she forced herself to shake hands with him, and only at the last did her slender fingers betray what a herculean task it had been.

Long after he had left the shop she remained staring at the door, knowing he had seen the scars on her wrist and dreading what they would cause him to believe.

Still in the attic *pied-à-terre*, Kohler forced himself to slow down and think as Louis would have done. Marie-Claire de Brisson was a tidy thing. Everything about the flat suggested great attention to detail—too much so, he thought.

The girl had been adopted at birth. While at the Sorbonne she had become close friends with Denise St. Onge.

She had also taken up photography—was very good, he thought but, in so far as he could determine from a search of her dark-room and filing cabinets, had given it all up in the late spring of 1940. There were no more recent photographs on her walls or in her files. The bottles of developing solution looked unused in years though none had any dust on them. Perhaps she had wisely thought the hobby too dangerous, too open to question by the authorities? She would have needed a permit in any case. Perhaps the very cost of film on the black market had deterred her.

There were two Leicas, a Hasselbad and a Graflex press camera but all had been packed away. There were lenses, lens tissues, even spare packs of film still unopened and ready but bearing the dates of 2 April and 13 May 1940.

Stubbing out his cigarette and forgetting to pocket the butt, Kohler got up to move about the bedroom, searching the photographs on the walls both here and then in the rest of the flat.

There was in all of them nothing but beauty. Not a hint of the tragedies of life. Children in plenty, but only those with happy faces. Old people smiling. Flowers. Birds nesting. Leaves in autumn in the Luxembourg Gardens.

It was a puzzle, for if she photographed only beauty, how could she have photographed those girls? And in any case, knowing what he now did, he had to ask himself, Was she even aware of what was going on across the garden?

There were no fashion photographs, not even a hint of them. The clothes in the armoires were very chic and, though they looked like some of the clothes in the photographs of the victims, he couldn't recall sufficient detail to match them.

Opening the french doors, he let himself out onto the balcony. Stone urns, that in summer would hold geraniums, now were cold and bleak but marked the balustrade with regimented regularity round the three occupied sides of the quadrangle. The daughter would have stood out here at night, looking over the garden and beyond the rooftops to that of the Bank of France. She would have had a cigarette. There would have been the sounds of crickets and cicadas in summer, little intrusion of traffic—hell, the city was so damned quiet at night it was like a tomb and dark if for no other reason than that it was illegal to show a light in any window.

When he found a clutch of frozen cigarette butts in the left of the two urns that abutted her turf, he knew she hadn't just stood out here in summer. Most had lipstick on them and most had been stubbed out in anger or fear.

There was no sign of Louis across the way. He, himself, had sent Madame de Brisson downstairs to her own house thinking the woman would be sure to summon her husband from the bank. This she hadn't done even though she'd been afraid.

Returning to the flat, he began to search in earnest for the secret compartment the daughter must use to store her negatives, prints and film. It wasn't in the dark-room, or in any of the other rooms but lying atop the cistern in the water closet.

It was not film or photographs of naked girls whose breasts would be removed but a series of 'Letters to Myself' all neatly bound in leather.

Wednesday 23 December 1942
I hear his footsteps on the stairs and know my father is coming
up to see me again. The sound is like a hammer in my tortured
brain. It makes the chasms open and I see myself as a girl of ten
caught between the pinning walls of his arms. I feel his hands
on my naked body. I smell the sweat of him, the pomade, the
garlic too—whatever we have had for supper that night. Which
night? Ah, Jesus, Dear Sweet Jesus, I cannot remember, for each
time the agony is the same, and each time I weep and pray and
vow I will never tell a soul.

From the rue Quatre Septembre to the rue de la Paix and down
it to the place Vendôme was not far. Never one to miss the
beauty of the city he loved more than any other, St-Cyr tried to
slow his steps but, ah, it was no use. Mademoiselle Marie-Claire
de Brisson filled his cinematographer's mind in living colour.
Against the lovely long view that ended in that tall bronze
column with its statue of Napoleon as Caesar on high, he saw the
girl naked in the bath, slashing her wrists with a razor.

Three times, on the left wrist—so, a very determined attempt
and one she still tried hard to hide. Blood flowing out to stain the
scented bathwater while, with eyes fixed on the wounds, she
watched her life drain away until . . .

She had been found, but by whom? Her mother, her father,
her friend and employer Denise St. Onge or by someone else, a
lover perhaps?

The scars, though not recent, hadn't been that old. Though he
couldn't be sure of this, he thought perhaps no more than six
months or a year at most.

A broken love affair? Girls sometimes killed themselves for the
silliest of reasons. 'But not this one,' he said and paused.

The traffic flowed around him—pedestrians whose shoulders
jostled. Now a well-dressed, middle-aged woman in a hurry, now
an old man with a brown, paper-wrapped parcel under one arm.
Antiquarian books, the sale rejected, the disappointment and
what it meant all too clear. No food.

There were a few *gazogène* lorries, two of which were parked outside very expensive restaurants, lots of the inevitable *vélo-taxis* filled with German soldiers and officers on leave, staff cars, Gestapo cars . . . ah, one had only to look at these last to tell them apart from all others.

Had it been the only time Marie-Claire de Brisson had attempted suicide?

She'd been clever and hadn't run across the street to her father. She'd known the Sûreté would be watching for just such a thing.

But had she tried to kill herself because of what had gone on in the house of Monsieur Vergès? That was the question.

Hermann might have an answer, but Hermann wasn't with him.

The shop Enchantment was on the east side of the octagon, facing across place Vendôme towards the Ritz Hotel where a gigantic swastika hung above two helmeted sentries with bayonets fixed. Requisitioned by the German High Command, the Ritz was a place for generals and other high-ranking officers. Pedestrians were everywhere and, though that *joie de vivre* could not quite be snuffed out, most kept their heads down and hurried about their business, for then there would be far fewer questions. Ah yes. Always one must look as if one knew exactly where one was going and was about that business and no other.

The Germans like order and efficiency. It hadn't taken the Resistance long to learn this simple lesson.

The shop was very classy, very chic and upbeat and very expensive and busy as always. A place of lingerie, perfumes, lace and silk, bath oils, creams and soaps, et cetera, and the most beautiful mannequins in the business, all shop-girls too, for Muriel Barteaux chose them not only for the shapes of their bodies and their posture above all else, most certainly, but also for the quickness of their minds.

'Chantal, it's good to see you looking so lovely.'

That little bird from yesterday gracefully turned from a customer, a lieutenant with whom she had been discussing the weather—she never served the customers herself, one must not do such a thing—to delicately touch in hesitation the silk chiffon scarf she wore then press a hand to the base of a throat that bore few wrinkles—one did not speak of such things. 'Jean-Louis . . . ? Is it really you, *mon cher détective?*'

The eyes were clear and large and of a lovely, warm shade of brown—very sensitive as now.

Gabrielle has informed her of my problem, he said to himself. And taking Chantal's hand, brought it to his lips. 'How marvelous you are,' he said and meant it.

She let him kiss her on both cheeks. Her laughter, though tiny, had a bell-like quality that pleased. Well into her seventies, Chantal Grenier and her lifelong companion had run the shop for over fifty years. As toddlers they had both experienced the Prussians at the gates of Paris in that winter of 1870–71 and, conditioned by such a momentous event, had been wary of Germans and the economy ever since.

He knew they must have a hoard of gold coins stashed away for a rainy day. They had weathered at least three, or was it four, major devaluations of the franc and an equal number of inflations, and all else, very well. They owned the building and had the flat directly above the shop.

The coins would be illegal, of course, but one must not take too seriously the proclamations of the Nazis and those of tax collectors.

Whereas Chantal seldom strayed from the place Vendôme and its little world of refinement, Muriel did the buying, the organizing, the tough jobs, though it was to her that fell the job of manufacturing their own perfumes.

'So,' she said, on drawing away from an embrace that could have been better had he been more presentable, 'the wreckage of Provence and Lyon returns to the bosom of Paris but what is this? What have you done with the new hat, coat, suit, shoes, gloves, shirt and tie we provided?'

The others had been ruined on another case. 'Criminals are no respecters of detective's garments.'

The pencilled eyebrows were sharply raised. 'Apparently not, but you are forgiven. Let us send them to the cleaners at once.'

'Ah, another time, Chantal.'

That little head was perfectly tossed. 'There is no time at present?'

'Ah, no. A matter of great urgency. Is Muriel in?'

'My Muriel? Is it that you wish to see only her and not myself?'

'No, no, of course not. But the matter is for the toughest, Chantal. For myself, you understand, I would not wish to bruise a sensitivity I cherish always.'

Ah, he was such a gentleman. Handsome still, if only he would take better care of himself. Wounded in the heart, divorced from the first wife, a widower from the second—it was such a tragedy that business of the bomb that had been meant for him, but for the best.

'Your lover was in to see us. It was she who told us to expect a little visit from you. How may we be of service? Please, the shop is at your disposal. I have steeled myself to whatever infamy you must reveal to my Muriel.'

The shop went on about its business. Swathed in its cocoon of undergarments and scent, of pastel shades and lace like air, he watched the girls amid the gilded statues of Venus, Diana and Aphrodite deal with plod-minded, shy German officers and their French mistresses. Other women also, as before at Chez Denise, but wealthier and far more sophisticated. Really classy, class-conscious and discriminating. Not the fringe of the fashion trade, but the centre.

'Let us go into the office, Chantal, but please, my dear, dear friend, if at any time you feel the matter too much, leave us to it. This business I have, it is not pleasant.'

Delicately she touched the back of his hand and fixed him with a gaze that in itself implored understanding. 'I am of sterner stuff, my dear detective. I was once eighteen myself, Jean-Louis, and once, yes, abducted by two men. Ah,' she raised both hands to stop him from saying anything, 'the matter is closed. I mention it only so that you will understand my reasons better.'

'You are a friend.' Nothing else needed to be said. Taking her by the arm, he walked that cloud of rose-pink silk and chiffon through the displays past bemedalled, monocled and jackbooted

Prussian giants who fingered lace and satin as if they were explosives about to detonate.

Muriel Barteaux was waiting for him in a cloud of cigarette smoke.

Kohler left Madame de Brisson to her house and her own thoughts. Indeed, he didn't say a thing to her about the daughter's 'Letters to Myself'. Moving purposefully, he entered the garden of the Palais Royal and soon found himself among the lindens.

The daughter had had every reason to take revenge on her father and get out of Paris, but had Louis got it all wrong about the Resistance, had she been the one to ask for the forged papers? Had she played look-out in the rue Quatre Septembre for the two men who had held up her father's bank? Sweet revenge and eighteen millions?

Storming into the engraver's shop and flashing his Gestapo shield, he demanded to see the invitation he had found on Denise St. Onge's mantelpiece, the Reichsmarschall Goering's invitation for 31 December, to the Jeu de Paume and the Ritz. 'There's been a mistake. I've been sent to check it out.'

That ought to put them off. The son stopped what he was doing in the back shop, the elder Meunier scrambled up from behind his desk. 'A mistake . . . ? But that's impossible, monsieur?'

'Orders straight from the top, eh?' Kohler thumped the counter. 'Well let me tell you, my fine goateed little printer, the Reichsmarschall's a very busy man. It's not every day he gets to ferry supplies in to a sinking army the Soviets are about to annihilate. Winter does something unkind to aircraft engines and ground crews in summer fatigues. It's the frostbite, I guess. Now give me the invitation. Make it two of them and shove over. I've got to have a word with your son in private.'

'My son . . . ?'

Was it such a ghastly request? 'The invitations.' He snapped his fingers and lifted the counter flap to let himself through. 'My partner's keen on art auctions and late suppers at the Ritz. I want to surprise him.'

Nervously Meunier found the things and handed them over. 'Your partner . . . ? Was he the one from the Sûreté?'

'*Ja, ja,* that's the schmuck. A real asshole and lazy. Now hurry up.'

The boy had come to stand in the doorway. 'It's all right, father. I will tell him what he wants.'

'*You fool!*' cried Meunier, lunging for the Gestapo. '*Run, Paul! Save yourself!*'

It was all over. Kohler eased the elder Meunier into a chair and patted the collar of the grey business suit. 'Take it easy, eh? You're too out of shape. Hey, I've had lots of practice. Make yourself a cup of that coffee your son gave Joanne Labelle. Try not to think it's the end of the world. Look, I'm sorry if I frightened you.'

The elder Meunier shut his eyes and bowed his head in defeat. Things had been going so well for them, but Paul had had to listen to that woman, to that Mademoiselle Marie-Claire de Brisson . . .

Kohler turned to the son and said, 'I hope you see the shape he's in. Now spit it all out and quickly. I have to find my partner before it's too late.'

'Three sets of documents were forged. Identity cards, work permits, military discharges and *laissez-passers* to Provins, 24 December, for two men. The third set consisted only of a *laissez-passer* for Mademoiselle de Brisson dated 1 January 1943, and a certificate stating that she was allowed to travel to Dijon for reasons of health. A past history of repeated bouts of pneumonia.'

To Dijon, of all places? Dijon was synonymous with rain, but the son had had it all rehearsed just in case the Gestapo should come for him . .

'My father knew nothing of it, monsieur. Nor my mother and sister. Only myself.'

How helpless. How utterly naive and stupid to think that by saying this he could save them.

Sadly Kohler gave him a nod. 'Tell me about the two men. Their assumed names, ages, height, weight, all other such details.'

The boy didn't back away from it. Still thinking that the only hope for his family lay in the truth, he said, 'Both were engineers, one electrical, the other mechanical. I'll write it all down for you and sign it.'

'Their ages? They'll be false but approximate.'

'Thirty-two and thirty-six. Both wounded during the invasion of 1940 and subsequently released with medical discharges. Raoul Chouard and Claude Deschamps, both lieutenants in the infantry. Both were assigned to the Provins municipal works department. Chouard has blue eyes, blond, curly hair. Deschamps has straight black hair and dark brown eyes. There were scars, the wounds of course. These could not be faked, could they?'

'Yes, yes, write it all down. Don't bother to sign it.'

Kohler took out a cigarette and, lighting it, went out to the father. 'Here, you need this more than I do. Look, Monsieur Meunier, let me give you a piece of advice. Get out of Paris while you can. Claim health, sickness in the family—hey, use your German friends and if not them, then get your son to do a job for you. Lyon, Marseille, Toulon—choose a city in the south. Things are still better there, but go.'

'Leave?'

Was it such an unthinkable thing? 'Yes.'

Since the travel permits for the two men had been dated 24 December, they must have ditched the car and headed straight for the appropriate railway station, the Gare de Lyon.

Marie-Claire de Brisson had specifically asked that her *laissez-passer* be for 1 January 1943, the day after the auction. Dijon, *verdammt*! What did it mean?

The boy was thin, tall and not a runner. Too sickly an occupation, thought Kohler ruefully but his judgement had to be harsh if their lives were to be saved. 'Listen to me carefully. You can't possibly tell when someone will blow the whistle. Eighteen million are involved and maybe the murders of fourteen girls.'

'Murders . . . ? That house . . . ?' faltered the boy.

'Look, if you know something, tell me.'

'Mademoiselle de Brisson, she . . . she came here often at night to see how the papers were progressing and to offer me advice,

Inspector. I . . . I sometimes wondered if she had just come from seeing someone or something she . . . she did not like. She was often most distracted and . . . and sometimes very upset.'

'Who let her in through the gates?'

'I did. The shopkeepers have spare keys so that we may come and go if necessary but it's not something that is commonly known.'

It still wasn't much. 'At any time did she say where she'd been?'

'A party, a dinner, the flat of her friend or simply her own place and a small gathering. Once she was most distressed at not being able to find her mother's cat. She said that Madame Lemaire's maid must have taken it in again and that she would have to speak to the girl, but I do not know if she ever did.'

'The men you forged papers for, did she know them well?'

The boy shrugged. 'They were friends, that's all I knew. Friends who needed help. Nothing dishonest—they hadn't done a thing, she said.'

'Spit it out.'

'They . . . they had to leave Paris so as to avoid the . . . the forced labour in the Reich.'

'And she paid you the going rate?' he asked harshly. '1000 francs for each identity card and 3000 for each set of the other documents?'

'5000 for each job. She was very kind to me, Inspector. Very pretty, very well dressed. Once she came in a black evening dress, more often a simpler sweater, skirt and blouse, but always the perfume.'

You sap, thought Kohler but only nodded and said, 'She sweet-talked you, so what else is new? Women have been doing it for thousands of years. But you're certain it was Mademoiselle de Brisson?'

'Yes. Yes, of course.'

'Paul . . .'

Stricken, the elder Meunier stood in the doorway.

'Father, what is it?'

'There are others.'

'Others?'

'The screech of brakes, the sounds of . . .'

'Ah *Gott im Himmel*, run!' swore Kohler, cursing their luck. 'Go! *Vite! Vite! Merde*, idiot! Don't just stand there blocking the way!'

They ran. He watched through the windows. Father and son entered the stark rows of lindens but didn't know which way to turn. There was the shrill blast of a whistle, then hard steps on icy gravel, the hammering of many boots and steel-cleated shoes on the paving stones of the arcades.

Paul Meunier dragged his father after him as they ran towards the fountain that was out of sight near the far end of the garden. Kohler thought to shout to the *flics* in dark blue and the boys in field-grey that they should slow down and take things easy. Then he realized the latter would toss a few bursts from their Schmeissers his way, shattering the shop windows and himself, ah Christ!

There was a burst of firing—oh how he knew that sound. The father would see his son suddenly throw up his arms in shock and watch as the boy collapsed. He would try to pull the son to his feet. He would plead with the boy as the dark shapes swarmed after them among the trees.

In his mind's eye Kohler saw that the boy didn't move. In panic, the father tried to make up his mind. They were almost upon him now. He would turn. He would start to run again. The light wasn't good. He would hit a tree and stumble backwards fighting for balance . . .

Another burst and another ripped through the commotion.

Kohler swept up two blank cigarette cases that had been waiting to be engraved. He gave the troops a few seconds to gather about the bodies, was ready when an SS-Hauptsturmführer entered the shop with some others, pistols in hand.

'*Idiots!*' he shrieked at them. 'I had those two right where I wanted them and you had to come along and spoil it!'

There was surprise at his presence in the shop, there was suspicion. Tossing the cigarette cases on to the desk, he said gruffly, 'Kohler, Gestapo Central, you *dummköpfe*. Pick up the pieces and while you're at it, tell me who gave you the buzz-word and when?'

The SS-Hauptsturmführer didn't like him being here at all. For several seconds Kohler saw reassessment being put to the test, then at last the pistol was slid away.

'It was an anonymous call, Herr Kohler, at 1507 hours.'

Not that long ago. Had it been Madame de Brisson? 'Was it a woman or a man, Haupsturmführer? Well, come on?'

'A man.'

Had she telephoned the banker who had then called in the alarm? he wondered, or had she called the daughter who had got someone to do it for her? Kempf, perhaps, or someone else?

Marie-Claire de Brisson wouldn't have asked anyone to do it for fear of bringing the Gestapo down on her head should the Meuniers have talked . . .

'Herr Kohler, how is it, please, that you knew those two were hiding Jews?'

Jews, not forgers? Ah *verdammt*, then it could have been the daughter after all, or her father, or Kempf or someone else! 'Let's just say I had my suspicions. Don't wreck the place. They aren't here.'

Picking up the two cigarette cases, lovely pieces really, he gave the bastards an abbreviated version of a Heil Hitler and left the shop.

Darkness had fallen. Suddenly exhausted and badly in need of a drink, he made his way to the street.

The boy's mother and sister would be deported. There wasn't a thing he could do for them and he knew it, was thankful Louis hadn't been with him because Louis would have insisted they try to help them.

When he found the note Louis had left for him in that empty house, he knew where his partner was but wouldn't intrude. 'Kempf,' he said to himself. 'I'll go and find that bastard and ask him about his girlfriend.'

Muriel Barteaux grimly passed her stern grey eyes yet one more time over the photographs that covered her ample and very cluttered desk.

'First, there are the clothes and the way they were asked to model them, Jean-Louis,' she said, her voice one of gravel. 'And then there is the matter of the photographs and the manner in which they were taken.'

He waited. More than a hundred years of accumulated experience was before him in these two so vastly different women. The office held remnants of fabric from ages ago, sample books, pattern books, patterns and perfumes—he loved to explore this world of theirs, renewing old memories and finding new things always. But for today they had the business at hand.

'The clothes are good copies, not originals,' said Muriel. 'The delicate ecru silk of this dress is very feminine. I like the cut of it, the tiny pleats, full sleeves . . . even the allure of this *décolletage* of crocheted lace.'

The pudgy, beknuckled and beringed fingers automatically reached for her smouldering cigarette without even a glance at the ashtray. The grey pinstripe suit, with its broad lapels, had ample pockets that were always useful for keys, scissors, measuring tapes, cigarettes, order books and other things.

'This crêpe georgette is really quite elegant, don't you think, dearest?'

Still stricken by the horror of row on row of murdered—yes, murdered—girls, Chantal Grenier could only try to answer but without success. 'Be brave, little one,' said Muriel. 'Why not attend to the tea? You know we always take it together in here at the close of each day. There's a good girl, there's my love.'

They waited while that little bird in pale rose chiffon hurried from the office. They heard her give a ragged sob and retch, and knew she would go straight upstairs to the flat and stay there until composed.

'Louis, if this has anything to do with that shop of Denise St. Onge, then we should begin with it,' said Muriel firmly. 'Mademoiselle St. Onge fancies herself at the very pinnacle of the fashion trade yet still refuses to stock originals—they're *too* expensive. That one uses copiers, not originators and sticks to the styles of the thirties. That, in itself, is fair enough if one doesn't wish to rise to the top. But she shouldn't run her business on the knife edge of bankruptcy and should pay off her creditors and suppliers, not threaten them with the Gestapo if they don't cough up or give her more time.'

He was grateful for the information and sighed deeply to show his appreciation. The pipe and pouch were taken out. They could now get down to work.

'Does Mademoiselle St. Onge have a line of credit at that bank of Mademoiselle de Brisson's father?'

Muriel nodded. 'The word is that Denise will only be allowed to stretch that little friendship so far.'

'The father has been after his daughter to speak to her boss?'

Again there was that nod. 'Denise St. Onge will never rise to the top, not if those among us who care are around to stop her.'

'The shop is good.'

'And why not when you've friends who can ask others to make certain you get the best materials available?'

'But . . . but you all do this? You couldn't survive otherwise.'

'But not in the way she does, Louis. We don't threaten and we do try to pay up on time and sometimes even in advance.'

'Tell me about the modelling.'

'A woman, not a designer, told them how to model these. Her judgement wasn't always right—that is to say, she didn't accurately match each of these girls to the clothes they were asked to wear. There are subtle differences. Some girls just can't wear certain things. Also, this girl is a little too tall for that skirt. They should have lowered the hem but didn't bother to.'

Muriel picked up another of the photos. 'Well off the shoulder is lovely if you have good shoulders. If not, then less of the shoulder is exposed. It's only natural. To each figure, the patient adjustment so that the dress, the suit, slip or whatever looks its very best. Spaghetti straps and mid-thigh slits take talent. These girls were instructed by someone who was very positive about what she wanted but blind to the subtleties of variation or in far too much of a hurry.'

Slivers of emerald satin, midnight lace and blue silk undergarments showed between the photographs as if to emphasize the horror of what had happened and to call all such frivolities into question.

'It was definitely a woman in your opinion?' he asked.

'A woman,' she said, not backing away from it. 'Look at each of these girls as they came to bare themselves. Go on, don't be ashamed. I know you enjoy the naked female body as much as I do. It's a work of art, a gift from God, not a curse.'

'They . . . they are hesitant but . . .'

'But she has reassured them, and they have done as she asked. The woman was a partner in this business, Jean-Louis. I could be wrong, but you have asked my opinion. Shall I give you another?'

'The photographer?'

'Was an amateur.'

'Ah *nom de Dieu*, how can you be so sure?'

Immediately she gestured with a hand, letting the stub of her cigarette cling to her lower lip. 'Photography, like good painting, good modelling, good anything, isn't just experience but art which is that joyous combination of the soul, the subject, the camera or whatever, the light and the lighting, the *mood*, Jean-Louis. The willingness to give everything even if it takes for ever. Intuitively there is an understanding of this. One either knows how to do it or doesn't. For me, it can't be taught. I think one has to be born to it. Picasso and Braque would probably agree most heartily.'

Muriel had paintings by both artists in her collection. Like all good collectors, she had bought early so as to encourage the artists and had held on to their works even in hard times or when profit tempted.

'An amateur photographer,' he said.

'A good one—oh he's had some experience. I won't deny that, but he shows his lack of judgement by trying for special effects that only distract. The reflections of this girl in this vitrine, the shadows that are cast on the breasts of this other one—did he think to show that fate was closing over her life like the Nazi shadow over Europe?'

'A man?'

'*Mais certainement.* A woman would have concentrated on the tragedy of those lives even though she took part in the killing.

There is . . . there is also the suggestion of an eagerness I do not like.'

'Pardon?'

The rheumy eyes were sad. 'The photographer and his assistant, Jean-Louis. Were they both about to humiliate and destroy these girls right after their final entrapment had been recorded?'

'Have sex with them?'

'*Yes!*'

Their tea came. Composed at last, Chantal followed one of the shop's mannequins in. The girl said a quiet, shy hello to St-Cyr. She was an absolutely gorgeous creature—exquisitely formed, with superb hazel eyes and wavy, curly hair.

Wearing only briefs and a flimsy brassière, she asked how he took his tea and said, 'It's Darjeeling. May I suggest it clear?'

'You are absolutely beautiful, mademoiselle, and very, very charming.'

'She's very special,' said Chantal. 'Spoken for, of course, and exceptional in her work. Dominique, darling, I bring you in only to refresh my Muriel's eyes and to illustrate to Monsieur the Chief Inspector that, in my humble opinion, only two of the girls in those photographs had any hope of ever being mannequins.'

'Two?' he asked.

'Your little Joanne, Jean-Louis. If you find her alive, you may send her to us so that she does not have to search the newspapers *ever* again for such . . . such advertisements!'

'And the other?' he asked. Anger was helping Chantal to overcome the tragedy.

'Renée Marteau, of course. Had we known Renée was desperate for work, we would have taken her in. She was good—very dependable, very keen to please and very professional. Indeed,' said Chantal fiercely, 'I have to ask, Why should she have answered such an advertisement? Why would she not have come to us or to others?'

Something had to be said however feeble. 'Perhaps she did? Perhaps you were not in the market at the time?'

That wasn't good enough. With her teacup in hand, Muriel

went over the photographs again. 'Chantal, please come and help me. Your eye is often better.'

'This one, I think, dearest. The lips, that smile—it's so like Renée's. The forehead, the eyes . . . ah, the hands, Muriel, and the way she holds them. Exactly. *Exactly!*'

They both looked up at him. 'Did Renée have a sister? A younger sister perhaps? *This* girl,' asked Chantal.

He felt so helpless. 'I . . . I don't know.'

'Then you must find out. It may well be that Renée followed in her sister's footsteps to find out what became of her,' said Muriel firmly, holding up the photo.

Two girls, taken from one family . . . Was it possible? A terrible tragedy in itself . . .

'This the police may not have realized,' said Chantal quietly, 'and thought, instead, that poor Renée was simply out of work and looking for a job.'

'The jewellery?' he asked with a catch in his throat.

'It's not new but stock, perhaps, that has been rescued from another time,' said Chantal.

'The twenties and the early thirties,' said her companion. 'Eighteen carat gold and superbly crafted. Far, far better than most of such pieces we have seen, but perhaps first brought on to the market after the demand for such things had fallen off. Timing is everything, luck but a figment of the imagination.'

Their shop had never carried jewellery so whoever had first offered it for sale, would not have come to them. 'Mademoiselle de Brisson . . . ? Have you anything to say about her?' he asked.

'She's good at her job,' confessed Chantal, 'and we would wish she were employed elsewhere but that one . . . ah, what can be said? She refuses all offers and stays with her friend. Perhaps it is that such loyalty stems from an attraction to Mademoiselle St. Onge, perhaps from something else, a debt still unpaid. Together their little shop must float or sink.'

'Could it have been two women?' he asked, 'The one to instruct the girls and the other to photograph them?'

'Mademoiselle de Brisson and Mademoiselle St. Onge?' asked Chantal.

It was a thought repugnant to them. Vehemently they shook their heads, but he could tell they would have to think about it.

And he would have to be satisfied with that for now. As he gathered the photos, he said, 'There is one further matter.'

They waited and when he handed them the announcement of the engagement between Angèlique Desthieux and Gaetan Vergès, Muriel gripped Chantal's wrist and said, 'Steady now. Be brave. Don't embarrass yourself again with tears.'

It was Chantal who sadly said, 'They made such a beautiful couple, Jean-Louis.'

Muriel lit another cigarette and fiercely blew smoke through her flattish nostrils. 'Angèlique would have put even our Dominique to shame.'

'She had such gorgeous hair and eyes. That deep chestnut shade of hair, long and thick and lustrous, the eyes . . .'

'Dearest, please,' said Muriel.

'She was lovely,' whispered Chantal. 'Is it that you can still remember her nakedness, my Muriel? The sweet and delicate breath, the loveliness of her composure—grace in every movement, even the simplest turning of the little finger? Her laughter, her smile, her warm and outgoing nature? The exceptional quality of her skin—isn't that what you once said, Muriel? The texture of *boiled* almonds that have lost their overcoats!'

Even after all these years Chantal was still fiercely jealous. Muriel chose the mannequins. Muriel . . .

'She came to us, Jean-Louis, and we used her but only for special occasions,' said Muriel tartly. 'Angèlique Desthieux was very good *and* very expensive.'

'She had an agent who guarded her talents as the Shah of Persia his harem!'

'*Chantal*, stop it! This attitude of yours will get us nowhere.'

'An agent, Jean-Louis. A business manager.'

'Albert Tonnerre,' snorted Muriel with obvious dislike.

'Luc,' whispered Chantal. 'Albert Luc Tonnerre. Though a ladies' man and a seducer, a deflowerer of silly young teenaged girls, he . . . he has fallen in love with her several times, Monsieur Louis. Love, he has called it. *Love!* The fornication! And if you ask me, she believed him. Oh yes she did! It was most unprofessional of him, especially since she was pledged to another.'

Muriel tapped the announcement and said, 'To the son, the drooler.'

'What happened?' he said, suddenly at a loss to fathom the depths of their memories.

'Did she take up again with Monsieur Tonnerre after she had rejected the horror of her fiancé's face?' asked Muriel, harshly giving him his very thoughts. 'No, she did not.'

'Someone ... someone threw sulphuric acid into her face, Jean-Louis. Where once there had been beauty and such inner calmness, there was now destruction, the end of a promising career, and ... and the banishment of her young life to the house of her parents in Dijon.'

5 ALL ALONG THE CHAMPS-ÉLYSÉES, THE RUSH-HOUR traffic struggled valiantly against the darkness and the ice, while up from the Seine came a freezing ground fog that gave the ether of surrealism to the fatalistic winkings of so many pinpricks of light. Still deeply troubled by the shootings of the two engravers, Kohler watched the traffic for a chance to cross. Swarms of bicycles and *vélo-taxis* were forced to part for occasional cars and *gazogène* buses or lorries. White studs on the paving stones formed a *passage clouté*, a miniature runway beckoning pedestrians to take their chances.

Occasionally there was the sound of a bell or a shout. For the most part, though, progress was mute and determined. Several thousand people were on the avenue. All over Paris, along every major artery, it would be the same, but now even the passengers in the *vélo-taxis* had ceased to laugh and think it all a great joke.

Had the Sixth Army fallen? he wondered apprehensively. Had his two sons been killed or taken prisoner?

Suddenly the need to know was too great. Recklessly pushing through the crowd, he started to cross the avenue. The Propaganda Staffel could never keep a lid on news like that. The BBC

London would trumpet it loud and clear. '*Ici Londres,*' Here is London calling . . .

Though it was illegal to tune into that waveband, lots did. There would be whispers—open hostility among the French and smug looks of triumph that would say, Now it is our turn, monsieur. Our turn . . .

He was nearly hit by a bicycle. The man skidded onto his side, the crate clattering beneath the wheels of a honking bus.

'*Monsieur*, attention!' shrieked the traffic cop, the shrill blast of his whistle and frantic flagging of the arms somehow bringing traffic to a standstill.

'My sons,' blurted Kohler. 'Jurgen and Hans, they're . . . they're only boys.'

He hadn't realized he'd spoken *deutsch*. For a moment he stood in the centre of the avenue, collared by a French *flic* nearly half his size. Ah *nom de Jésus-Christ*, the lights, the pinpricks—everyone was watching. Breath billowing. Waiting. Poised. Angry . . .

The man whose bicycle had been ruined, dragged it up and began to scream invective. A woman went to calm him. '*Gestapo!*' she shrieked and the street went to silence.

Nearly 150,000 Wehrmacht troops had been killed at Stalingrad in what must surely be the fiercest campaign of the war. House-to-house fighting, unbelievable hatred on both sides, and still there were nearly 100,000 men trapped in a pocket no more than 50 kilometres in diameter with all their equipment and virtually no supplies.

'Look, I'm sorry,' he said to the *flic*. 'If he'll give me his name and address and not think he's about to be arrested, I'll see that he gets another bike.'

The *flic* raked him savagely with a glance. 'Beat it, idiot! Can't you see you're but one against many?'

The Feldwebel on the desk at number 52 gave him the latest news. 'No change, Haupsturmführer. We're still waiting for a miracle.'

They were still holding out. Ah damn Goering and his fucking Luftwaffe, ah damn the Führer for biting off too much and not realizing gains should always be consolidated.

The Propaganda Abteilung was spread over several floors. Newspapers, films, books, radio broadcasting, the theatre and the arts—even the allocation of paper—had offices here. News bulletins streamed in from the Reich. The Staffel selected these for distribution, censored the French reporters' columns and told them what and what not to print or say, then rewarded those who obeyed and punished those who didn't. Anyone who was anyone in the media and the arts had to come here for permission. But at 1800 hours, though there were staff about, and the censors worked in shifts until midnight, the place had emptied like a sieve.

Sonderführer Kempf was in charge of Luftwaffe news releases from an office on the fourth floor at the back. Never one to trust the elevators—the French ones particularly—Kohler climbed the stairs and fought to overcome the sudden weariness of it all.

The boys would die at Stalingrad—he had that feeling. Christ! why did it have to be that way?

Gerda . . . his Gerda . . . would leave him for a conscripted French farm labourer.

There would be nothing for him back home when this lousy war was over, just as there would be nothing for the Sonderführer Kempf, ah yes.

One of the grey mice, the *Blitzmädchen* from home, held the fort in an outer office. She had started in on the hors-d'oeuvres—a custard tart with blackberry jam and white icing sugar—while having a coffee and typing up yet another heavily censored news release.

Wiping jam from her hairy upper lip with the back of a hand, she threw him a watery look of surprise and said, 'He isn't here. What . . . what has he done now?'

Kohler gave her a wolfish grin of thanks for such a choice little insight. 'Relax and finish your supper. It must be a bitch having to work late every night.'

She thought this over while tidying her hands. He asked her name.

'Fräulein Schlaak, Herr . . .'

'Kohler, Kripo. Gestapo Central.'

Common Crime . . . A giant with a savage scar—had he been
a soldier? Had it been shrapnel? There were the scars about the
face and hands but shrapnel had not caused the one from the left
eye to chin. A duelling scar . . . ?

'Barbed wire,' he lied, throwing himself into a chair. 'Ah *Gott
im Himmel*, Fräulein Schlaak, I've just seen some poor bastard
crushed to a pulp under the wheels of one of their lousy buses.
You wouldn't have a drink handy? I'm about done in.'

He did look badly shaken. Sonderführer Kempf would not
even notice a drink was missing. 'Schnapps?' she asked. 'There is
a bottle in . . .'

'Hey, that would suit me fine. Stay right where you are and I'll
get it. The bottom right drawer?'

'The . . . the cabinet.'

As she watched from the doorway, the giant downed three
straight glasses and then took another before offering her some,
to which she vehemently shook her head and gushed, 'The
reports. I . . . I must finish them.'

'A cigarette?' he asked.

She indicated the desk and watched helplessly as he took a
fistful, then lit up. 'So, take your mind back to last Thursday the
24th, fräulein, and tell me where he was.'

Wariness showed in her dark blue eyes. 'The truth, eh?' he
asked. 'Hey, it's not too hard, seeing as he isn't around and will
never know I've been here if I put these back.'

One by one he replaced the cigarettes and tidied the desk.

'The . . . the press briefings are always on Tuesdays and Thurs-
days, Herr Kohler. Sonderführer Kempf, he . . . he must always
be on hand for those.'

Kohler blew smoke towards the ceiling. He'd try a long
shot and see what happened. 'But he wasn't here last Thursday,
was he?'

Her throat rippled. The tightly corseted bosom swelled then
deflated with a sigh. 'No . . . no, he . . . he was called away but
Harald, his driver, had the car and that one, he . . . he was
kidnapped.'

'The robbery. *Ja, ja*, we know all about it. So, where was the Sonderführer when the bank was being robbed?'

'I . . . I don't know, Herr Kohler. The . . .' She thought madly. 'The dentist, I think.'

'Did he come into the office at all on that Thursday?'

'No . . . no, he didn't. I . . . I gave the releases to one of the others.'

'Then let's have a look at his appointment book. Maybe that'll refresh your memory.'

She winced. 'He . . . he complained of pulled muscles—the racket ball, the "squash", he said. He . . . he went for heat treatments and a massage; afterwards a swim at the health club and then . . . then to lunch at Maxim's.'

A nice life. '*Gut*. Now tell me where I can find his driver.'

'Harald has gone home on a five-day pass to see his wife who is pregnant.'

'How convenient.'

There was a photograph of Kempf's wife and two children in better times, another of the Sonderführer astride a handsome gelding, yet another of him in a racing car. A regular playboy. 'When you asked, What has he done now, fräulein, to what exactly were you referring?'

He waited. Trapped in the doorway, she sweltered under the scrutiny of faded, lifeless blue eyes.

One by one the cigarettes were again removed from the box.

'Gambling, the . . . the expenses—the borrowings against his pay cheque for dinners and holidays everyone knows he . . . he cannot possibly afford, not now that he . . . he has lost everything. The wife, the children, the house of his father and mother, the family business, everything.'

Kohler indicated he understood and was sympathetic. 'Did Mademoiselle St. Onge ever come here?'

'Sometimes, when . . . when she needed help.'

The woman looked as if she was digging her own grave. 'Relax. What sort of help?'

'Help with her creditors and . . . and suppliers. The Sonderführer has many contacts.'

'Did they ever talk about having a little fun?'

'Fun?' she bleated.

'A threesome,' he said. 'Two women and your boss. The one perhaps much younger than Mademoiselle St. Onge. A teenager perhaps.'

Fortunately the telephone rang and when she had grabbed it and understood who was calling, she blurted, 'Gestapo!' and thrust the receiver at him.

It was the Sonderführer just checking in. 'The Press Club,' said Kohler, hanging up. 'A *rätskeller?*'

'In one of the cellars of the Lido. He . . . he usually goes there for a drink after work.'

'So let's have an answer to the fun, eh? Two women and one man. Your boss.'

'I . . . I wouldn't know about such things. I'm only his secretary.'

'How long have you been with him?'

She could feel the Gestapo's breath on her forehead, Herr Kohler was now that close to her. 'Since . . . since the beginning. Since the summer of 1940.'

Kohler nodded. 'Once again I'm going to ask you, Fräulein Schlaak. A young girl with chestnut hair and deep brown eyes, Mademoiselle St. Onge and your boss for a little fun. French girls who didn't matter.'

The puffy eyelids blinked. Fragments of conversation came to her from over the past two years. Had it begun right after his arrival? First that cousin of his, this Mademoiselle St. Onge— beautiful, leggy, smartly dressed and knowing her way around— and then . . . then other girls. *Ja, ja.* Lots of them. Mademoiselle St. Onge had seen it, too, in his eyes, in the way he had looked at her and had . . .

'I cannot say, Herr Kohler. I do not know of such things.'

'He would have left the office early, would have stayed out late and not used his driver.'

She shook her head but when Herr Kohler had left the office, she felt as if gutted and wept openly until another tart was found but the coffee was cold.

The Sonderführer was so handsome and well educated. Very

sure of himself, very well placed and with lots of important friends. The Reichsmarschall and Reichsführer Goering himself had personally seen that an invitation to yet another art auction had been sent over from Luftwaffe HQ Paris but this time there was a late supper at the Ritz. Mademoiselle St. Onge and the Sonderführer were to attend both the auction and the dinner together. They were still friends. The woman still clung to him. Women like that always did even though often ignored.

'You should get yourself a man,' he had said to her several times, to his *secretary* who was such a credit to him. But he had never *once* asked her to the Press Club for a drink.

St-Cyr didn't like it one bit. The emergency call from Hermann to the shop of Muriel and Chantal had said only that he was to come at once.

The Lido had an entrance in the middle of the Arcade des Champs-Élysées. As a warren with escape routes it was ideal. In addition to the dancing-saloon, floor show and rotating stage, there was a swimming pool where the girls and customers could take the plunge. Lots of distractions, then, and cellars off the main area. Sewers below. Back stairs as well. *Pour l'amour du ciel*, what the hell was up?

Hermann was standing next to the brass railing that sealed off the most expensive tables nearest the stage. Girls—women— naked from well below the bellybutton and up, except for ostrich plume head-dresses and sequins, went round and round in a tableau reminiscent of a circus, while others, on swings high above the decorated pool, cavorted to music as the chorus line kicked their gams and jostled their boobs and the crowd, mostly officers, collaborators, SS or Gestapo and their girlfriends ogled them and grinned while still others bathed to hoots and shouts.

'If you can tear your eyes away from that Alsatian wet nurse, *mon ami*, please tell me why the urgency?'

'Louis, *verdammt*, idiot! What took you so long? The bastards may have buggered off. I can't watch everything myself.'

The gaze hadn't altered. Hermann was clearly agitated and in need of calming. 'What took me so long? Discussions, of course,' said St-Cyr drolly. 'Besides, you have the use of my car; myself, that of my feet! The place Vendôme is . . .'

'Don't get bitchy! Look, I'm sorry I had to tear you away from those two old girls in the underwear trade but *nom de Jésus-Christ, idiot*, we have trouble.'

A cigarette girl in meshed stockings rubbed shoulders, spreading her wretched scent of cheap perfume, garlic and toilet water. Fake flowers were being sold in lieu of cigarettes. 'Trouble?' bleated St-Cyr.

At last the Frog was listening. 'This one is an excellent shot with the pistol. Three times champion of the Reich. *Two* Olympic gold medals. Rides in the steeplechase, plays polo when there isn't snow and ice, drives a racing car, swims the marathon, fucks like a tiger and was absent from his job the day of the robbery. *Absent*, idiot! Absent!'

A German . . . Must God do this to them? 'Kempf?' asked St-Cyr. Hermann was keeping his eyes on the entrance to a distant cellar beyond the stage and to the left.

'Have you got your shooter?' he snapped. Being Gestapo, it was Hermann's responsibility to take charge of their guns and only release them when needed.

'My shooter,' mused St-Cyr, wishing his partner would slow down long enough for a little conference. 'Ah yes, Inspector, my revolver. The Saône, remember? The ice and that little swim we had to take? I lost it in Lyon on that last case.'

So he had. 'Wouldn't Stores issue you another without my okay? Hey, you're making me feel sick—you know that, don't you? The son of a bitch is over there in the Press Club's *rätskeller*. He's with a Frenchman, one Michel le Blanc of *Paris-Soir*, a reporter. Their . . . their descriptions, Louis . . . They exactly fit those the engraver's son gave me.'

The dancers smiled and kicked their stockinged legs. The girls above the pool peeled off everything so as not to spoil their costumes . . .

'Forged papers?' asked St-Cyr. Had things come to a head so soon?

'Ah yes,' snorted Kohler. 'Kempf is the blond, blue-eyed, curly-haired playboy in Luftwaffe blue whose new name is Raoul Chouard. Le Blanc wears a grey business suit, white shirt and dark blue tie, all pre-war. Straight black hair, dark brown eyes and maybe three or four years senior to our boy, so about thirty-six years of age and bang on for the robbery. New name, Claude Deschamps. I couldn't get a line on him. Becker at Gestapo Central knew nothing of him when I called in but promises to do a little digging if I pay him 10,000.'

'*Hermann, we need to talk!*'

'Later. Somebody gave the SS and the French *flics* the anonymous nod, Louis, and they put paid to your engravers. Bang, bang.'

'Dead?'

'Yes, dead, damn it! Accused of hiding Jews. Now do you understand?'

The Press Club's *rätskeller* had once been a wine cellar. Broad archways of red brick rose to a dirty white ceiling from which single light bulbs hung on long black cords above crowded tables and chairs. A roaring trade was in progress. There was much tobacco smoke, loud talk, argument, little liaisons—a hand up a skirt—and both French and German men and women. One happy family.

A French girl was kneeling on the Sonderführer's table with arms stretched out to the sides, balancing a stein of beer on her pretty head. Nice legs, no stockings—hell, they were as scarce as diamonds these days—beige skirt hitched above the knees, a tight little behind and rosy cheeks.

It was le Blanc who gave the warning, Kempf who said, 'Ah, Herr Kohler, it's good of you to find us.'

The stein teetered. The girl started to reach for it. Kohler swept the thing off her head and said, 'Beat it! I have to talk to them, eh? Go piss in a barrel or something. You're drunk. It's too early for that.'

His French was very good and at first she didn't understand if this was what was really wanted of her and threw the Sonderführer an uncertain look.

St-Cyr took her by the arm. 'Pay no attention, mademoiselle.

See that you get a couple of beers for my partner and a pastis for me, eh? Now cheer up. It's really nothing. Put the drinks on the Sonderführer's tab and have another for yourself. We've business. A few questions. Nothing complicated.'

Unsteadily she fled. Kempf laughed. Le Blanc was uneasy.

'So, *mes fins*,' said Kohler, turning the back of her chair towards them and sitting down, 'a few small words into the shells of your tender ears. Let's begin with last Wednesday midnight and take it straight from there through Thursday. Who you slept with, where you slept. Give names, addresses and times. Be specific. You're both under arrest.'

Doucement, Hermann, go easy. It's too early for such things, is it not? muttered St-Cyr to himself. Sometimes Hermann could be so impulsive.

Kempf moved to find an inside pocket of his open jacket. '*Don't!*' breathed Kohler. 'I want answers. Dead men can't talk.'

'But of course. I was only getting my cigarettes. Perhaps that one could assist.' He gave a nod.

'Louis, see what he's got inside the jacket.'

There was no gun, only a silver cigarette case that was beautifully engraved and signed *With much love, Denise*.

Meunier had engraved the thing. Meunier.

It was Kempf who grinned and asked, 'If it's not too much trouble, Herr Kohler, of what are we accused?'

Hermann took out his bracelets and laid the handcuffs on the table. 'Armed robbery and murder.'

'*He means it, Franz!*' hissed le Blanc warily.

'Shut up, *dummkopf*! Robbery, Herr Kohler? Come, come, where's the proof? Surely it's within my rights to loan a certain lady the use of my car?'

'Not in wartime. Look, I'll be blunt. Your description and that of your little squeeze-box exactly fit those of the robbers. We've eyewitnesses who will swear to it. Photos as well.' This last was not true, but what the hell? How were they to know?

'Photos?' blurted le Blanc—they were still speaking French. 'That's not possible.'

Hermann grinned. 'Then you tell me why it isn't.'

Kempf finally took a cigarette from his case and lit up. The Bavarian was making a nuisance of himself, the French *flic* with the moustache was simply studying the proceedings intensely. 'There are no photos of us, Herr Kohler. I was not even near the Crédit Lyonnais at the time of the robbery and neither was my "concertina", as you put it. We were on our way back into the city from le Bourget. Fräulein Schlaak had to be told something, since the reason for my absence was top secret and those were my orders.'

'Yet you didn't use your car for such a purpose?' asked St-Cyr quitely.

The Sonderführer's look was cold. 'We had a briefing to attend. The Graf von Stenglin had come straight from Berlin to inform us of the latest situation in Russia and to discuss policy. Monsieur le Blanc was joining Denise and myself for lunch at Maxim's so I asked him to come along, but he waited in another room.'

Was it all so clear and tidy? 'What time was the briefing?' asked Hermann, failing to hide the note of disappointment and not following up on how they had got to the aerodrome.

Kempf drew on his cigarette and studied these two *Schweine Bullen* who had thought they had the world by the balls. 'From 0800 hours until noon. We were,' he said tiredly, 'a little late for lunch.'

The son of a bitch! 'If you're lying,' said Kohler, 'I won't just have your balls.'

Their drinks finally came. Le Blanc watched as the one called Louis tossed his off neat without even looking at it. Had the Sûreté noticed something, some small inflection or nervous habit? What really was going through that head of his? That the Occupation afforded opportunity and licence to pursue the dark side of human existence? That robbery and murder could have official sanction? Yes, yes, that was what he was thinking. Then he'll find the girl Franz got to kneel on the table. He'll ask of the waiters and discover that one of them was paid to act as a look-out to warn them of Herr Kohler's arrival.

It wouldn't take them long to discover that the briefing had lasted but an hour and that the Junkers Ju 52 had been late due to bad weather but that even so, they had been free by 10.15 a.m.

Then they'd find that the car to le Bourget had belonged to the Kriegsmarine's press officer and that they had simply hitched a ride because Franz had wanted Denise to have his car for the day. Ah yes, but they still wouldn't be able to discover the truth.

'So, are we still under arrest, Herr Kohler?' asked Franz. *Merde alors*, thought le Blanc, why couldn't he take the arrogance from his manner?

'Do you both play squash?' asked Kohler. As sure as that God of Louis's frowned on detectives, these bastards had been up to something and still were. Had they been fucking Joanne? Was that why the smart-assed smugness, or had they merely stolen the money?

'Squash,' said Kempf with a grin. 'Michel lets me beat him but gives me a good run for his money.'

Self-consciously le Blanc tossed his head a little to one side and shrugged.

'Oh come now, Michel,' snorted Kempf, looking at him. 'I always knew you were better at it than I, but you know your place. You're a realist and that is good. Does that one?' he asked, turning to Kohler and pointing at Louis. 'Or is he one of the stubborn?'

'*Hermann*, leave it!' hissed St-Cyr.

'Of course, but if he asks around about you, Louis, I'm going to haunt him, and in any case, we're not finished. Don't either of you leave town. Clock in at 0700 hours on the dot to Sturmbann-führer Boemelburg personally and provide him with a typed and signed itinerary for each day. We'll want to contact you, so make it easy for us.'

'Boemelburg . . . ?' began le Blanc, definitely not happy about it.

Kohler stood up. 'The Big Chief himself, schmuck. He's a personal friend and old acquaintance of my partner.'

Swiftly he retrieved the bracelets but left the beers untouched. 'Louis, let's take in a bit of the show. I need to forget what I've just had to deal with. My boys are dying because of crap like this.'

Later they sat in the car discussing things in the freezing cold and darkness at the side of the Champs-Élysées, knowing Kempf and his friend had realized they would be followed and had slipped away.

'Provins is only about 80 kilometres from Paris, Hermann. Kempf and le Blanc could have gone there under the assumed identities, hidden the cash, and come back easily under Kempf's auspices using their own identities and no one really the wiser. They could be using the Château des belles fleurs bleues. Vergès and his son might no longer be alive.'

Uncomfortable at the thought, Kohler fiddled with a cigarette. 'It doesn't make a bit of sense having a man-shy thing like Marie-Claire de Brisson working with those two humpers. By rights that third set of papers ought to have been for Denise St. Onge, not her.'

'Then is it that she asked Mademoiselle de Brisson to have those papers forged for her friends, Hermann, or is it that Mademoiselle St. Onge doesn't even know of them?'

A man had turned in the alarm on the engravers. No doubt he had spoken fluent French. But had Denise St. Onge been the one to warn her lover there might be trouble?

Kohler recalled the photograph on her mantelpiece of her and Kempf and how the hat of the banker's daughter had cast its shadow behind the couple to spoil the snapshot. In just such little things were there sometimes answers.

'Did Mademoiselle de Brisson lie to me about being in the back of the shop with Mademoiselle St. Onge?' asked St-Cyr. 'Was her employer and friend watching the street for the robbers or following Joanne, or both?'

'Then why scatter the photographs if you're a part of it?'

Why indeed. It was a problem.

Kohler lit the cigarette and took two deep drags before sharing it. 'Was that teller silenced, Louis? Did he recognize the Sonderführer from an earlier visit with Mademoiselle St. Onge, a visit perhaps to put pressure on the banker to extend her shop more credit?'

It was a possibility, but an idiot could have hit the teller at that range.

Again they came back to the woman in the street. Had she felt Joanne a threat and followed her simply for this reason? If so, then there might be no connection to what had been going on in that house, only its final interruption.

'An amateur photographer,' said Kohler. 'A good one but one who, on the surface at least, hasn't used her cameras since before the Defeat and in any case takes only sweetheart photos because . . .'

A cloud of cigarette smoke filled the air. 'Because "To forget is to survive." Our Mademoiselle de Brisson said this to me at the shop and now you have supplied the answer as to why she said it.'

'But if sexually abused, why the desire to abuse and kill girls who want to become mannequins and then, only those with chestnut hair and deep brown eyes?'

'To do to others what she herself has had to endure, Hermann. To get back at what has happened—it's common enough, but is Mademoiselle St. Onge aware of her friend's abuse and using it in some way? The girls, that house . . . ?'

'Or to extend her credit at the father's bank?'

'Yes, the bank, or is it that the daughter herself has warned the father that if he shuts down the shop of her friend, he ends her own silence?'

There were other problems. The presence of the jewellery in the shop window; similar things among the bric-à-brac of Mademoiselle St. Onge's flat—hieroglyphics, tablets, seals . . . Egyptian things—she had often loaned clothing from the shop to the banker's daughter.

'So, what about the drooler?' asked Kohler, clearing a patch of frost to stare out at the street. 'Do we write him off as being completely innocent?'

St-Cyr heaved a troubled sigh. 'The drooler, ah yes, Gaetan Vergès and his fiancée, Angèlique Desthieux. It's still possible the drooler could have waited upstairs until the initial photographs had been taken and Joanne was then completely naked.'

'The poor kid.'

'A mannequin with chestnut hair and deep brown eyes,' said St-Cyr of Angèlique Desthieux, 'whose career ended abruptly when someone threw acid into her face. She had a business agent, one Albert Luc Tonnerre who fell in love with her in spite of her betrothal to Gaetan Vergès.'

'Did the drooler know him?'

'Most probably.'

'Then that's one more reason for us to visit the château,' breathed Kohler, lost to old memories of that other war, to unparalleled suffering and what it had done to decent men. Changed their whole personalities, made some men hate so much they would . . .

'There is another reason,' said St-Cyr. 'Monsieur Vergès senior had a number of paintings in that house. Were they stolen and is this not why the house was emptied so quickly?'

'The auction . . . the invitation to the Jeu de Paume and the Ritz.'

'And afterwards, on the morning of the 1st, the banker's daughter quietly leaves Paris for Dijon and the home of the drooler's ex-fiancée.'

They had both avoided one thing, and Kohler knew he would have to mention it. He started the car—he'd give it a moment to warm up. Christ! It was nearly eight o'clock. 'One of the victims died of acid burns, Louis.'

'Ah yes, but the acid was deliberately not thrown in her face. It was poured on the rest of her. That's what puzzles me.'

Silenced by the thought, they drove slowly to the Palais Royal and round past the Bank of France to leave the car in the rue de Valois which was even darker than the Champs-Élysées.

Louis would talk to Madame Lemaire and her maid, leaving the Gestapo half of their partnership to speak to the neighbours on the other side of that empty house, then they would both have a few quiet words with the banker and his daughter.

'Inspector—Madame, she is still at her supper. Could you . . . ?'

'Come back a little later?' asked St-Cyr. 'Ah, no, Mademoiselle Nanette. Murder seldom allows the luxury of such lapses and it is, I fear, your murder I'm worried about.'

'Mine? Ah no. No!'

He slid into the vestibule, into that tired remnant of a once proud house and touched a finger to his lips as she sat on the little bench Madame Lemaire used when putting on her over-boots or simply resting after coming in from the street. 'Please, it's best we talk and that you give me straight answers.'

Moisture made her large blue eyes all the clearer, reminding him again and poignantly of Marianne, his dead wife. 'Nanette, why didn't you tell me that on the night the furniture was taken from next door, you went outside to see whose firm it was? You couldn't have seen this from the windows above the street.'

The darkness . . . the black-out. He would pry the answers from her now and she would have to tell him. Then he would despise her and not ask his friends if they could find a position for her in their shop when Madame passed away. 'The noises, Inspector, I . . . I was worried so I . . .'

'When you heard those lorries, you took your life into your hands. Did you not realize how dangerous it was to go out there?'

Her eyes were wiped with her fingers. 'No one saw me. I . . . I was careful.'

'Were there really four men and were they all French?'

'Yes.'

'No women?'

'No. Ah . . . Perhaps. I . . . I can't really say. Forgive me, but I can't.'

'Did they say anything to each other? Come, come, there is very little time.'

'Only that they must be careful not to make much noise, that they must look as if they were simply doing a job. They . . . they had papers to . . . to prove who they were and why they were there. One of them said this to the others and warned them to let him do the talking if the police or the Germans came by.'

More forgeries . . . the papers would have been taken from the firm's warehouse in Saint-Denis. St-Cyr drew in an impatient breath. The girl must be made to realize he wasn't happy with her answers. 'Did that one have a name?'

She shook her head. 'They said so little and I . . . I was afraid to stay too close to them.'

He would have to let it be but had to ask, 'Has Madame ever mentioned the name of that firm?'

There was a startled look he would not forget. 'They . . . they . . .'

'Well, what is it?'

'Dallaire and Sons used to do all the moving business for the houses of the Palais Royal. Madame, she has told me that when Monsieur de Brisson and his wife and daughter moved in ten years ago, it . . . it was they who did the moving.'

And now you've trapped yourself, thought St-Cyr, because, *ma chère* Nanette, you didn't ask this of your employer until *after* that house had been emptied. 'What made you ask her? Come, come, you saw something else. I know you did. Was it then or earlier? Much earlier? People coming and going, a girl . . .'

She gave a nod and took a deep breath. 'The cat. I . . . The cat came to the window-doors of my room. I . . . I let it in.'

'When?'

'Late last spring.'

'The cat of Madame de Brisson?'

'*Oui.* It wanders. I . . .'

How pale she was and so preoccupied she didn't even hear Madame Lemaire asking for her. 'You were lonely and frightened,' he said. Her eyes were downcast, the lashes long and damp. 'You took the cat in for a little company, Nanette, and Mademoiselle de Brisson came for it.'

'She had seen me looking out my windows while holding it. She demanded that I return it. I did so.'

'*And?*'

'And she told me never again to step out on to the balcony to retrieve it or anything else. She . . . she has said she would report me to the authorities if I ever went out there again, and . . . and that she would tell them I was illegally in the city. *Illegally* when I have worked for Madame these past five years and am a *good* girl!'

There was a sudden rush of tears that made him want to comfort her but he must not do so.

'Could Mademoiselle de Brisson have felt you had seen something you shouldn't have in the house next door?'

The apron was used to blow her nose and wipe her eyes, making him ask himself, Why must God remind him of how unhappy Marianne had been? The long absences, the loneliness of the house at 3 Laurence-Savart. The feeling of still being a foreigner trapped in the big city never knowing if he would return alive from yet another murder case or robbery.

'Well?' he asked harshly. 'Nanette, tell me what she thought you must have seen.'

'There . . . there was a gap in the curtains—just a little one. A girl with . . . with her hair in tufts. *Naked* and . . . and chained by the wrists and ankles so that she . . .' The girl broke down. 'She was stretched out, Inspector. *Stretched!* Reaching for the ceiling and . . . and leaning well forward over the lamp with . . . with her legs spread widely and her ankles tied to . . . to the floor.'

'The lamp?'

The girl dragged in a breath. 'Painted blue and without its shade. Its *shade!*'

'*When?*'

Would he arrest her? 'Late last spring. She . . . she had fainted. She . . . she looked as though she had fallen asleep but was still chained up like that with . . . with a rag stuffed into her mouth and . . . and her eyes blindfolded.'

'Yet you said nothing to anyone? *Nothing?*'

The girl was frantic. 'I *couldn't!* I would have been arrested and sent home!'

Was there more? he wondered. The sound of crying, this one awake at night listening to it and *knowing* what was going on!

He must be firm. 'Did you see anyone else in that room?'

She shook her head as if her life depended on it, was so ashamed.

'Who did you see on the balcony, Nanette? Was it only Mademoiselle de Brisson or was there someone else?'

The girl bolted and ran from him. He heard her on the stairs, heard her fling herself on to her bed, heard weeping as if she herself was one of the victims.

She lay with her face buried in the pillows. Madame Lemaire

was now shouting at the top of her ancient lungs and banging her cane. A decanter fell . . .

'M . . . Monsieur de Brisson,' blurted the girl. '*De Brisson!* He watched at my windows for the longest time and . . . and finally he went away.'

'You didn't draw the curtains?'

'I was waiting to see if anyone would come to the house next door. I was sitting in a far corner of my room, in darkness. It was not so very late. Perhaps only eleven o'clock.'

You fool! he said but to himself. Again he asked when this had happened and again she said. 'In the late spring. Just a few days after Mademoiselle de Brisson found me with their cat.'

'Did Monsieur de Brisson go into the house next door? Come, come, Nanette, now is not the time to hesitate or hide the truth.'

'He *must* have! He went that way, Inspector, and not back towards his house. For the longest time I waited, but then the telephone rang and Madame . . . I was so afraid it would awaken her but . . . but when I answered it, they hung up.'

There were the usual things in the bedroom of a girl such as this. A heavy white flannel nightgown was folded over the back of a chair. There were no slippers. Like so many these days, she would wear two or even three pairs of woollen socks to bed.

Letting himself out on to the balcony, St-Cyr made his way next door to peer into that empty house and test its lock and door handle.

How was access gained? Had Monsieur Vergès left a key with someone? The banker? A notary—this would be the most logical—but how had he kept the Germans from requisitioning the house?

Kempf? he asked. Had Kempf seized on the use of the house and made certain no one in authority would interfere?

If so, then the Sonderführer and Denise St. Onge most probably had visited Mademoiselle de Brisson in her attic *pied-à-terre* as early as September of 1940, and it was then that the possibility of using the house had been conceived.

'Access could simply have been a matter of breaking in and replacing the glass, he muttered to himself.' Once a spare key was found in the house, they could come and go at will, or perhaps they changed the locks.'

Through the darkness all he could discern was the line of the rooftops across the garden and more dimly beyond them, those of the houses on the rue de Montpensier. Leaving the girl with a warning to say nothing to anyone, he went downstairs and outside, to enter the house from the street.

Empty, it had its own feeling as if the walls, the voices of those girls, cried out to him.

Shining his pocket torch briefly on the ceiling, he found where the ringbolts had been—the holes had been plastered over and painted but this had been done in haste and the plaster not allowed to dry.

The holes in the floor had simply been filled with sawdust and wax.

If only Madame Lemaire's maid had spoken up. How many would have been saved? Two—would it have been two or three?

But he couldn't find it within himself to blame the girl. He understood only too well how fragile her position was even after five years of service.

As far as he could determine, the attic window-doors hadn't been forced nor had a pane of glass been broken and replaced. They had had a key, then, right from the start. A key . . .

Hermann was waiting for him beside the Citroën. 'Nothing, Louis. A bookseller and his assistant in the attic flat who claims he is nearly deaf and that the assistant doesn't stay the night. Homosexuals who won't say a thing for fear of drawing attention to themselves and getting a one-way ticket to nowhere. A medical doctor, his wife and son in the flat below who must be out having supper, then the owner of a department store who says he saw and heard nothing. Absolutely nothing!'

'Good. That makes life easier for us. I've just cracked a bank and must transfer my accounts to another.'

'Monsieur de Brisson?'

'The same.'

✳   ✳   ✳

The descendants of the Kings of Prussia ate in uniform—blue, grey and black or the business suits of the mighty—amid the sumptuously warm glitter of the restaurant. Gilded, trifold, mirrored screens reflected the gaiety of bejewelled mistresses and wealthy friends. A banker, the owner of a racing stable, a judge—all sat before framed tapestries of barefooted, docile girls, a lamplighter, a gatherer of grapes.

'Sliced testicles of water buffalo in sauce lyonnaise,' seethed the Sûreté as they followed the maître d' among the tables. 'Braised anaconda steaks in cream with poached cobra eyes! Hermann, *mon vieux*, you must leave this one to me, eh? Let me have the son of a bitch on little wedges of toast!'

'Be my guest!' grinned the Bavarian. 'Remember I've got the only shooter.'

'His is between his legs!'

Oh-oh, the Frog was really hopping.

Louis pushed the maître d' aside so as to make the introductions himself. 'Monsieur de Brisson? Madame, mademoiselle, please forgive this slight intrusion into what I know must be a private family supper.'

'Georges, what is the meaning of this?' demanded de Brisson of the head waiter.

'Don't fuss,' hissed St-Cyr. 'It's not his fault. Tip him generously and see that he finds us two chairs before the embarrassment of our visit causes you grief.'

The chairs were brought. The *truite aux amandes pochée au vin blanc*—the poached trout with almonds—looked superb. Cooked in white wine first, then dipped in egg yolk, rolled in thinly sliced almonds and lightly browned in butter and olive oil, the meal made a poor detective sweat with desire. Where had they managed to get all the ingredients?

Kohler lifted a bottle to examine the label. 'The dregs of a Romanée-Conti 1915, Louis. *Jésus, merde alors*, where were we then, eh? Cleaning the dust and shit from the shelling out of our eyes and ears, or was it the remains of some poor bastard's guts?'

'Hermann, *please*! A few simple questions.'

André-Philippe de Brisson was in his early sixties. The immaculately tailored grey suit with dark blue tie and handkerchief went with the image. The dark blue eyes which, from behind gold-rimmed spectacles, returned his gaze were those of a banker about to dismiss a dishonest employee.

'Monsieur,' began St-Cyr.

The knife and fork were at last carefully set down on his plate. 'Inspector, what is the meaning of this? You have no right.'

A tough one. 'Monsieur, eighteen millions have been stolen from your bank and a teller killed. Surely it is in your interest to co-operate a little?'

'Here?'

Still handsome, suave—eminently successful and master of all that was around him—de Brisson appeared to be a man of little patience and much arrogance. 'Here, there, what does it matter,' said St-Cyr, 'so long as the money is recovered and the criminals apprehended?'

'Then contact me at my office. I will have them roll out the carpet of welcome.'

Was he a friend of the préfet and of Pharand, the boss of this humble servant of justice? Probably. Ah yes. A self-conscious grin and a little shrug of apology would therefore suit. 'Unfortunately time does not allow us the luxury of polite custom. The Sturmbannführer Boemelburg wishes my partner and me to settle the matter as expeditiously as possible.'

'Boemelburg. Ah very well, you may proceed.'

The closely shaven, rounded cheeks would smell but faintly of an aftershave. The puffiness beneath the eyes suggested late nights and too much work, the receding hairline a vanity that regretted such a loss. 'The shipment from your head office, monsieur. Is it customary for such large sums to be transferred to Paris?'

Though the one from the Sûreté concentrated almost totally on him, the one from the Gestapo kept looking from Marie-Claire to Bérénice. *Maudit salauds*, what were the two of them really after? 'The German authorities, Inspector. They wish us to put the notes back into circulation as soon as possible so as to save on the printing costs and paper. Once every two months Lyon ship to us. Oh *bien sûr*, it was nothing new. Merely routine.'

'Eighteen million?'

'In October seven million. In August only four.'

'But always on the 24th of the month?' asked Louis still meeting the steely gaze of the banker.

'Unless it's a Sunday or a Wednesday, the half-holiday. In which case, the next working day. Inspector, what is it you wish me to say? That someone outside of my immediate staff had learned of the shipment and been so indiscreet as to let someone else know of the matter?'

'Could that have been possible?'

'Never!'

'Then could your teller have recognized one of the two men from a previous visit?'

The cheeks were blown out in exasperation. Immediately the face came alive with the preposterousness of such a thing. 'Ah no, no, of course not! Monsieur Ouellet, he had merely reached for the alarm button which was just beneath the counter and to the right of his cash drawer. A brave man—he'll get a citation for sure—very conscientious and due for a promotion to head teller as soon as the post came free. Isn't that correct, my dear?' he asked the wife, disturbing at once her stony gaze and silence, and awakening the downcast eyes of the daughter, their little mouse.

'Yes, of course, my dear. You are correct,' said the woman.

As always? wondered St-Cyr. How could such a positive-looking woman have stood for the continued sexual abuse of her daughter? A fine-looking woman but one who, in the company of her husband, was so used to taking a back seat, she couldn't force herself to rise above it.

'It's sad,' went on the banker. '*Ma chère*, you must come with me when I visit with his wife and children. Perhaps a hamper? A few little things . . . ? Inspector, you see how it is. At the Crédit, the employees really count. My wife and I were very fond of Monsieur Ouellet.'

'Certainly.' But why lie about it, wondered St-Cyr, if not to hide something else?' 'The suitcases, monsieur. Why suitcases? Why not banker's dispatch cases?'

'Why, indeed, Inspector? Ask Lyon, don't ask me. Maybe all the cases were in use.'

'Had they ever used those suitcases before?'

'No. No, of course not but there is always a first time, is that not correct?'

'Louis Vuitton and alligator leather, monsieur? Their choice was admirable to say the least and very handy for the thieves, but what I can't understand is why those two men discarded them?'

'Then why not ask *them*, Inspector? Maybe they can tell you.'

Patiently Kohler watched the proceedings, still wondering if Louis would confront the banker with the statements of Madame Lemaire's little maid and the daughter's 'Letters to Myself'. Mademoiselle de Brisson obviously feared the worst, though she could only know of his own visit to her flat, not what they had discovered.

The golden mohair dress fitted Marie-Claire like a glove, even to hiding the razor marks on her wrists. The green eyes that still looked down at her plate held nothing but despair. Was she knitting her fingers in her lap? he wondered. Was she swearing to kill herself and not botch the job this time?

'Those two men were nothing but gangsters,' said the father. 'Nothing but rubbish, Inspectors! The *dregs* of a society that, if given half a chance under our German friends, will shape up, eh? They had no reason to kill Adrian. He was such a kind man and so good with his children. There are six, or is it seven? Ah, I can never remember. It was always a little joke between us.'

'Of course,' said the Sûreté who had taken to studying Madame de Brisson. 'There was a woman in the street, monsieur?'

Madame de Brisson! sighed Kohler inwardly, and the banker setting up the robbery of his own fucking bank and having the wife play look-out even though she was a bit too old for the part, or was she?

'Talk. Nothing but talk.' The banker shrugged and tossed his hands and head. 'You know how it is, Inspector. One witness says this, another says something else—ah! it was all over in a few seconds. The gun, the demand, the cash, the shot, the car and zoom, those bastards were gone!'

It would be tiresome to again say Of course, thought St-Cyr. The urge to do so was almost overpowering, but one must go carefully. The age of the woman in the street had been put at between thirty and thirty-six years. Then why, please, he asked himself, was Madame de Brisson sweltering? Was she about to choke on a fishbone even though her trout had not been touched since their arrival?

De Brisson didn't like the silence. 'There was a young girl who window-shopped, Inspector. Eighteen perhaps. Yes, that was the age. Another supposedly stood watching this girl and the street. The woman who reported this to the police could give few details except to say that the girl at the window was aware of the one who watched.'

Gravely Louis tidied the table-cloth in front of himself though it needed none. He looked away across the restaurant, seemed bent on deciding the best course of action. All around them the diners went about their business. The place had now settled down and would take little notice of them until they left.

'Mademoiselle de Brisson, is there anything you can add that might be of help? I know you were not a witness, but ... ah, some little thing perhaps? One of your girls taking too close an interest in the car your employer borrows from time to time? Perhaps someone saw something out front? A window-shopper like this ... this ... How old did you say she was, monsieur?'

'Eighteen.'

It was such a fiercely perturbed answer. 'Eighteen,' acknowledged the Sûreté gruffly. 'Repeated visits, mademoiselle, so as to case the bank of your father?'

'Inspector, it was a simple hold-up,' breathed de Brisson impatiently.

'Not with eighteen million, monsieur. No, it was an operation that involved meticulous planning. Of this my partner and I are certain. So, mademoiselle, have you anything to say? Did anyone notice this girl looking in the window of your shop?'

What did he really know? she wondered harshly. The Meuniers

were dead—*dead!* The Gestapo had shot them before ... before
Paul could ... could say a thing. A thing! These two could know
nothing of the papers. Nothing! 'We get thousands looking in our
window each day, Inspector. Sometimes it is only a glance in
passing, sometimes a searching for hours on end as the mind, it
fantasizes.'

'The girl, mademoiselle, had long brown hair—was it brown,
Hermann? Is that what the préfet said?'

'Dark brown, Louis, and brown eyes, I think.'

'One of so many, Inspector,' said Madame de Brisson tightly.
'It can mean nothing. Absolutely nothing.'

'Or everything, madame,' said the Sûreté with that little shrug
Kohler knew so well. 'You have a cat, madame?'

'A cat? Why ... why, yes.'

And now you look as if you had just swallowed your canary.
Again he would gravely tidy the table-cloth and pass smoothing
fingers across it waiting always for the silence to do its work.

'My cat, Inspector? What ... what has Samson to do with the
robbery?'

Moisture had collected around the stern blue eyes behind
their glasses. Guilt, fear—the horror of what she had done—was
it this that made her tremble? 'Your trout, madame. I greatly fear
my partner and I have spoiled your supper but, as you have a cat,
well ...'

He left it unsaid. 'Hermann, *mon vieux*, we have work to do.
Monsieur, madame, mademoiselle, please forgive the intrusion.
Merci.'

Outside on the rue de Beaujolais Kohler exploded. 'You had
me believing you were going to slam that bastard against a wall
and cut off his balls before confronting the daughter with the
forged papers!'

'Ah, no, Hermann. It's best, is it not, to add the spices only at
the moment of tenderness so that the bouillon becomes the
sauce when quickly thickened and allowed to simmer but for a
little while?'

'Hey, for a moment there you had me worried.'

* * *

'Dédé, ah *mon Dieu*, what are you doing on my doorstep at such an hour?'

Wrapped in a blanket, the boy stood up and shook the snow from himself. '*Grand-mère*, she is saying she has had a vision in the night of Joanne, Inspector. Naked, ravaged and with . . . with her . . . her breasts cut off.'

'Ah damn that old woman! Come in. Quickly. Light the stove. Here . . . here take this thermos. My partner knows another Bavarian who has a restaurant. It's a little soup, Dédé. Ham and lentils with red kidney beans. There's a handful of croutons in my overcoat pocket. See that you restore the body's temperature, eh? while I find a little something from my days as a soldier. Be sure to use the bread. Mop up the dregs. Keep nothing. I'm not hungry.'

The boy would do as he was told but was there no way to shut that old woman up? The breasts . . . How *could* she have said a thing like that to the family?

Down in a cellar too dark and dank for comfort even though it was his own, he moved a wine barrel, one of several from the days when he had once tried to make his own wine, and found beneath it yet another barrel.

Moving it, he got down on his hands and knees with his pocket-knife and prised out a stone in the floor. The revolver in the tin box, a Lebel Model 1873, was just as he had left it on the day of the Defeat. Well-greased, in its holster and with two boxes of cartridges.

The gun was heavy—indeed, it was almost as effective as a club. Though some had been modified to eight millimetre, this one still used the eleven millimetre, black-powder, low-pressure cartridges that were slightly less in calibre than the .455-inch cartridges of the British Mark IV Webley.

Hermann wouldn't expect him to be armed and would probably find something, yet this could not be guaranteed in time and the sacrifice would have to be made.

Returning the army holster and one box of cartridges to their hiding place, he went back upstairs. The boy must have been ravenous. The bowl was clean, the thermos dry. Not a crumb of bread remained. Dédé saw the gun in his hand and couldn't take his eyes from it. What could he let him tell the other boys? 'It looks like the police revolver I lost in Lyon, Dédé, the same as the gun that was used in the robbery. But this one ... It's not quite thirty years since I had to use it in that other war. Please, it's a private matter between us, eh? Just you and me. No others.'

'Is it that you know where Joanne is?'

'Ah, I wish that were so. We've made great progress, but must now visit a place of flowers.'

'A cemetery?'

'Ah, no. No. Beautiful blue flowers. Lupins perhaps or violets, but in spring.'

'And the robbery?' asked the boy. 'Is it that Joanne has perhaps seen something and this is why she was kidnapped?'

Would it hurt to lie a little so as to give hope? Though he wanted to, he told himself he would have to be honest. 'We simply don't know yet. But the robbery and the kidnapping are connected. I'm almost certain of it.'

'Then you have a suspect?'

'More than one.'

'Male or female?'

'Both.'

The gun, the man, the detective stood before him across the table. How many times had he and the other boys seen the Chief Inspector trudging home to an empty house and a wife who slept elsewhere with another, a German officer? How many times had they kicked the soccer ball to him only to find he had stumbled and fallen asleep from exhaustion to look like a drunkard lying on the pavement?

He had lost his car, his great big beautiful black Citroën to a Boche, a Bavarian. His bicycle—his precious Sûreté *vélo* with the five kilos of brass for a lock—had been smashed on a case and then stolen. Yes, *stolen*. A smashed bicycle!

A collabo, they had called him behind his back, the people of this street he loved so much, but only because he had had to work for the Boches, the Krauts—*les Allemands,* the pork-eaters and sneezers, the pickled cabbages, the Schlocks.

Yet only he and his partner could save Joanne.

'Dédé, what is it?'

A hand was extended formally. 'Nothing, Monsieur the Chief Inspector. Only that I am with you.'

'Good! Now go home and tell that grandmother of yours that if she opens her mouth again, I'm going to have her arrested for selling thread on the black market—ah, don't deny it. We're friends and these days one does what one has to. Just tell her I want no more of her visions in the night. They make me uneasy and that's not good when I might be up against a man who can shoot a pea off a post at thirty paces!'

6 ALL OVER PARIS, THE SNOW WAS SOFTLY FALLING TO deepen the hush of darkness but lift the city from its misery.

At 2.00 a.m., Gabrielle Arcuri pushed open the iron gate at 3 Laurence-Savart and made her way up to the front door but turned to look back. The houses were cheek to jowl beyond the low wrought-iron fence with its cement posts and fake Louis XIV urns. The staff car of a German general waited and would do so patiently. A little bite to eat, a glass of champagne with that one, nothing else because ... ah because there never could be anything else with them or anyone but ...

Belleville, she said to herself. Jean-Louis will never leave it and only a fool would ask him to.

Inserting the key Hermann had given her as a Christmas present, she unlocked the door and pushed it open. Jean-Louis wasn't asleep. From the tiny vestibule, she could see that he was in the kitchen at the back, the only light. There were shadows on the walls ... a roaring fire in the stove behind him ... a scandalously wasteful fire.

In his suspenders, trousers and brogues, and wearing a faded blue plaid work-shirt, brown tie and revolver in its leather holster, he remained unaware of her, so deeply was he lost in thought.

Row after row of photographs were spread across a table whose rustic look and size suggested a farm somewhere. There was so much she didn't yet know about him.

He was searching the faces of the victims, was 'talking' to each of them. A cup of acorn-and-barley 'coffee' had long been forgotten.

'Jean-Louis . . . ?'

'Ah! Gabrielle, it's you. How did you get in? The club, has it closed early? What time is it? Hermann, he . . . he's picking me up at 3 a.m.'

She told him of the key and that she had developed a small catch in her throat. 'It's nothing serious. The voice simply needs a little rest.'

Maybe it dawned on him that, had he been asleep, she might have come up to him. Maybe he regretted this was not so, but all he said was, 'Joanne tried to tell us of the shop. A bracelet, Gabrielle. This one.'

He waited for her to join him but they didn't hold each other or even touch in greeting. Instead, still lost in thought he continued, 'She was followed by a woman whose reported age was between thirty and thirty-six but . . .'

'But bundled against the cold and wearing a hat, lipstick and rouge,' she said decisively, 'that woman could have been much older.'

'Madame Bérénice de Brisson, but does it fit?'

'She would have caused little notice if she had entered the bank of her husband, Jean-Louis.'

'Yes, the perfect look-out if . . . if the husband is the one who set the robbery up.'

'Was he broke?'

'Or being blackmailed?'

Quickly he told her what Madame Lemaire's maid had seen late last spring. 'Did he know of what was going on in that house? Were the kidnappers aware of this, so much so they would tempt him with a little gap in the black-out curtains?'

'A blue lamp . . . the shadows of that poor girl on the ceiling above her . . . how could he not have said something?'

'Perhaps it is that he participated?'

Startled, she asked uncomfortably, 'And Madame de Brisson learned of it?'

'Perhaps, but then . . . ah, it's all speculation, the racing of a mind tormented by doubt.'

He flung photograph after photograph before her. 'Joanne is still missing,' he said. 'We've been on this case constantly since Monday afternoon. It's now just the start of Wednesday. If I fail, I fail not only her but Dédé, Gabrielle. Dédé. At my worst moments, the boys seemed always to be there up the street, watching me trudge home. They would call out, "Hey, oo-oo Monsieur the Chief Inspector," and kick the soccer ball to me and I would work it up the road and try to get through them. Those boys . . . they respect the law because of me. *Me!* I simply can't fail them. I mustn't!'

She touched his hand. 'You will find her. I know you will,' she said, but one couldn't comfort him. What he needed was answers. 'The Resistance say they have no news of the robbery and think it wasn't the work of known criminals or the Gestapo and the SS.'

'Amateurs?'

'Perhaps, but good ones except for the killing of the teller which they feel may have been a mistake.'

She would know only so very few of the Resistance and couldn't possibly have questioned many. 'Be careful,' he said. 'Don't take chances. I may not be able to help you and neither might Hermann.'

He told her of Marie-Claire de Brisson's 'Letters to Myself' and said he hoped the girl wouldn't destroy her diary, that they might soon need it.

Saddened, she said, 'The father takes what he wants and has total disregard for her as a person.'

'She was adopted at birth and is the loyal servant of her employer and friend, so much so, Gabrielle, she asked Paul

Meunier to forge travel papers and documents for two of Mademoiselle St. Onge's friends.'

Gabrielle drew in a breath, her lovely eyes alive with interest.

Jean-Louis told her of Kempf and le Blanc. She said, 'Let me see what I can dig up on the one from *Paris-Soir*. Maybe he's the one who fielded the placing of the advertisements and thought of using the Théâtre du Palais Royal as a letter drop and blind.'

St-Cyr ducked his head in appreciation but also to indicate the photos. 'Are all of the clothes and accessories from that shop?'

Sadly she had to tell him, 'I never go there but can begin to check.'

'Mademoiselle de Brisson also had a set of papers made for herself,' he said, 'but for Dijon on the 1st of the New Year.'

'Dijon?'

'The home of Angèlique Desthieux, and a permanent residence under her own name, not a *nom de guerre* as with the other two.'

Gabrielle gave a little toss of her head. 'Muriel and Chantal spoke of her. Was it her fiancé who threw the acid into her face?'

'And poured it over this one?' he asked, finding the photograph for her. 'Or was it someone who wishes us to blame the drooler?'

Sickened by the sight of the corpse, Gabrielle turned away and felt him reach out to her in comfort. 'Forgive me,' he said. 'I'm used to such things.'

He waited and at last she said, 'Apparently Angèlique never named the person who ruined her career. She refused absolutely to blame anyone but herself for having rejected her fiancé so shamefully.'

They were both silent. She touched a suspender strap and, leaning down, for she was a good head taller than him, lightly kissed his cheek. 'You really will find Joanne and bring her safely home. Like Dédé and his friends, I have confidence.'

There were tears in his eyes as there were in her own. 'Five-and-a-half days, Gabrielle. For five-and-a-half days now she has had to live in hell, never knowing if she will be killed.'

'Is she with the things from that house?'

'I'm certain of it! But not with the paintings, if they were taken and placed at auction.'

'The paintings . . . ?'

He told her of the outlines on the walls of that house. She reached out to him again. 'Then we'll visit the Jeu de Paume together and by then, perhaps Monsieur Vergès or his son will have described them to you.'

'If they're alive.'

She kissed him again and held him tightly. She knew he couldn't telephone Vergès or attempt in any way to find out if indeed the father and son were still alive for fear of jeopardizing Joanne's life. 'Take care, *mon cher détective*.'

'And you. Until the 31st, then,' he said. 'Here, let me help you with your coat.'

Was he burning the last of the scrap boards so as to enjoy a final fire in case he didn't return?

'It could be perfect for us, Jean-Louis.'

'Yes, perfect. We'll have to take a little holiday in the spring. Always my mind, it goes back to late last spring.'

'Last spring?'

'And a suicide that didn't succeed.'

'Ah! I almost forgot. Muriel said to tell you Mademoiselle de Brisson was found in her bathtub by Denise St. Onge.'

'Not by the father?'

'No, not by the father or the mother. Denise stayed with her at the hospital until the crisis had passed.'

'And then paid frequent visits?' he demanded.

He was so intense. 'Of course. It's what friends do, isn't it?'

'Friends or those who wish to make sure she keeps her silence.' His mind ran away from her lost among dates, and only as he muttered them to himself, did she understand they were the dates eight of the victims' bodies had been found.

'7 October 1940—missing since 15 August, Gabrielle. 21 December '40; 3 March '41; and Renée Marteau on 15 August '41 . . .'

'And then?' she asked and saw him look up as if startled by the intrusion.

'26 October '41; 18 December '41; 14 February '42 and 6 May '42.'

The late spring . . .

They looked at each other. He didn't ask. She answered softly, 'Jean-Louise, Marie-Claire de Brisson was taken to the hospital on the night of the 5th. It was all hushed up but there was talk. Muriel said everyone in the fashion business eventually heard of it.'

He reached for a photo but kept it from her. 'And this one died of acid burns. Acid all over her body but not on her face.'

Just before dawn it was very cold. Darkness hugged the wooded escarpment which formed the north-western fringe of the Côte d'Or but snow among the vineyards on the slopes below gave some light and to this were added the tiny, isolated winkings of fires in sheet-iron barrows between the rows.

Louis was beside himself with worry about what they would find at the château near Provins, but first there was a visit with the former mannequin in Dijon.

Kohler let the perfume of the fires come to him. They had been on the road for hours. Fontainebleau Woods and memories of a murder case there and trouble, much trouble, then Sens, Joigny and Chablis and yet more shared memories but just before Montbard overconfidence, sleepiness or the distraction of not knowing what they would find had caused him to take a wrong turn. Louis had been adamant they should take the left fork. The Bavarian half of the partnership had won out, and they had come down off that escarpment to meet the fabled *route du vin* well to the south of Dijon. There they had pulled over, to walk off the stiffness and fatigue.

A former convent stood stark and bleak among the vineyards, having probably been there since at least the seventeenth century. More modern presses would have been installed and expanded cellars in the caves below, but still there would be the prayers for the *vendange*, the harvest of each year, still that supreme sense of continuity. Wars might come and go but always there would be the vines and always the wine.

Breaking out the coffee and biscuits, Kohler filled two tin mugs from the hamper Rudi Sturmbacher of Chez Rudi's had provided, and added a generous dollop of cognac.

'Quit fussing,' he called out.

'I'm not,' came the shout from down the road. 'I'm restoring the soul. That escarpment you ignore so patently provides the microclimate which is so necessary to the vines, Hermann. Moisture from its run-off carries lime to enrich the soils. The southwesterly face prolongs the day, further lessening the effects of frost *and* extending the time of harvest so that more sugar can be gained in each grape.'

Ah *Gott im Himmel*, another tiresome lecture and travelogue but a good sign his spirits were up.

St-Cyr approached. 'When I was a boy, Hermann, I dreamed of living here. My aunt had a farm near Beaune.'

Kohler ignored the passionate outburst and got down to business. 'So, tell me all about that shooter you're wearing. If Gestapo Central wouldn't issue you one, where's the store?'

One had known it was coming. One had just not known when it would be asked. 'My service revolver. A slight oversight, Inspector. It's nothing. In the haste of the Dèbâcle I merely forgot.'

An offence punishable by lengthy imprisonment, deportation or death, to say nothing of having kept it since the Armistice of 1919 and discharge from the army! 'Then see that you use it when needed and shut up about it.'

'Of course, but please don't be so pious. You've a spare pistol taped to the inside calf of your left leg. The tape is itchy. Don't scratch so much if you want to keep the weapon secret.'

'*Verdammt!* Did Giselle tell you about it?'

'Or Oona? Plain detective work. Use a tensor bandage, not tape, and tell me where you got the pistol.'

'Fair's fair, eh? Provence, *mein Kamerad der Kriminalpolizei.* Up in those hills to the north-east of Cannes and from a certain Italian. It's a Beretta nine millimetre Parabellum, the 1934 model and b . . . e . . . a . . . utiful. I'm really quite proud of it.'

'And stolen! Ah *nom de Jésus-Christ*, you can't be trusted!'

'Hey, I brought it along for you. You should have kept that revolver quiet and trusted your big Bavarian brother to take care of things!'

'I did, but couldn't guarantee it would be possible for you to find me something.' Had Hermann really made such a sacrifice?

'So, what else is new?'

'The changing pace of the war, Hermann, and the need for extra weapons others don't know about.'

To this there was no response. The coffee, though welcome, was drunk as if tasteless when really it was excellent and very real.

The biscuits were dry.

'Franz Ewald Kempf, Louis.'

St-Cyr accepted the proffered cigarette and found his matches.

'The fags are his,' said Kohler—they had been through everything countless times on the road south. 'Kempf accepts a position with *Berliner Tageblatt*, summer of 1937, as a reporter covering the Luftwaffe, but doesn't take the wife and children along to Berlin. Likes beautiful young women. Plays around and never mind the tears. Spends like a mogul, drives his racing car, plays polo. Becomes assistant editor in the fall of 1938. Joins *Auslands-presse-Abteilung der Reichsregierung* in the spring of '39, the foreign press relations office.'

'Just in time for the invasion of Poland,' muttered St-Cyr, still hoping to catch the first light on the escarpment.

'On June 1940 arrives in Paris as a special officer.'

'Is one of Goering's boys but obviously a little more than that.'

'Wants to curry favour with the big cheese so gets himself and his girlfriend invited to an art auction and supper,' snorted Kohler.

'Have they paintings to sell that are not theirs?' mused St-Cyr, still looking off towards the escarpment. 'He has been with the girlfriend since arrival. That's a long time for him to be with one woman, is it not?'

It was! 'She's a distant cousin and a girl who likes her fun. Did they meet in Berlin before the war?'

There was as yet no light among the distant trees. Again Hermann asked about Berlin—impatient, must he always be so

impatient? wondered St-Cyr. A shrug would be best and then . . .
'Perhaps, but if so, is the love affair as strong as it once was, and
how is it, please, that Denise, who has lost a brother to your soldiers and has another in a POW camp, can take up with such a
one as Kempf?'

Ignoring the need to save it, and wishing Louis would quit
watching the fucking escarpment, Kohler tossed his cigarette butt
away. 'That affair's as strong as ever. Success demands it, and success is sweet. She's a realist, *dummkopf.* A realist!'

Mornings were never Hermann's best of times. If only he
would open his eyes to the beauties around him. If only . . .

'Louis, for Christ's sake . . .'

'Ah yes, then, Hermann, a realist but would that woman do
the unmentionable to keep her lover?—that is the question. Has
she taken steps to protect herself and the Sonderführer?'

The first light was now at last among the most distant trees and
for a moment the Sûreté's little Frog insisted on remaining silent.

Then the hand that had gripped his partner's arm fell. 'Did the
banker become aware of his daughter's plans to leave, Hermann,
and is this not why the engravers had to die?'

'Or be arrested.'

'Or did Kempf call the anti-Jewish squads but do so in
French?'

'Okay, so let's not avoid it any longer. What about Marie-
Claire de Brisson and Dijon?'

'That is what concerns me most, Hermann. Is it that she plans
to kill herself so that no one, not even Mademoiselle St. Onge,
can stop her?'

'Maybe Angèlique Desthieux can tell us.'

'That is my earnest hope but we will, of course, not ask her
directly but feel our way so as to decide later.'

And Joanne? wondered Kohler. What of Joanne?

The street was narrow and crooked and right in the heart of old
Dijon. Uniformly shuttered town houses presented nothing but
massive, arched wooden doors that led to each courtyard, while
smaller doors in these saved the muscles and the back when no

carriages needed to enter. Number 22 was no different from all the others.

'Though a city of nearly 90,000, Hermann, Dijon is strictly provincial. Dank, cold, grey and eminently respectable. If you thought Lyon was close, my friend, here you have things to learn.'

It was all so typically Burgundian, thought St-Cyr. Rich in its own right—the food and the wealth of humour had been superb—but confined and scornful of others. 'To return here from a life in Paris, would be as it was for Napoleon at Elba. Stables downstairs all along one side of the courtyard, with an enclosed staircase zigzagging upwards to connect each part of the house. Living quarters at the front and back. Two storeys here, three at the back with garrets there as bad as any in Paris. No flowers, for it's not a city of them. Shards of bottle glass sticking out of the top of every free-standing wall as if, down through the centuries there has been a legacy of acute distrust of one's neighbours.'

Footprints in the snow revealed the single crosses that had been cut into the soles of the clergy. Wherever a foot was placed, a cross. It said something about the Dijonnais, thought Kohler uncomfortably.

'This house is next to the Bishop's, Hermann, but still the two courtyards abut along a wall whose crest of broken glass defies all but the foolish and is far too high for most to climb in any case. Our Mademoiselle Desthieux came back from the joys of Paris to gaze out on what could just as easily have been the prison yard of the Santé!'

End of lecture. 'The street's perfect for a *rafle*.'

A round-up and house-to-house search. Trust Hermann to think of it when they had so much else to concern them! But Hermann was really just mocking the Gestapo.

'Bung the barrel at both ends, Louis, then stave it in with an axe and let the pickles pour out on to the paving stones.'

The stones, ah yes. They were treacherous beneath three centimetres of newly fallen snow.

There were sparrows in the courtyard, feeding in a circle that had been swept clear and sprinkled with millet. Far down the courtyard, the house rose to tall french windows whose shutters were open.

A well, a pump, was here even in the centre of the city, the house perhaps 300 years old . . .

'She's seen us, Louis. She was watching the sparrows. Our mannequin.'

A housekeeper soon appeared, a no-nonsense type, short, rotund, all red bluster, blue darting eyes and a tangled mop of grey and unruly hair. 'Messieurs, out. Out! Hurry! Hurry! You cannot come in here.'

The richness of the accent was sauce to the air. Her breath billowed. An iron soup ladle was fiercely gripped in the left hand. Three leeks had been thrust into the generous waistband of her apron.

Kohler grinned—the French never ceased to delight and take his mind off other things. 'Let me, Louis.'

'Don't be an idiot! When presented with such a firm resolve, go easy, eh? Madame, I am Jean-Louis St-Cyr of the Sûreté Nationale and this,' he indicated Hermann, 'is my partner from the Gestapo.'

She drew in her shrouded bosom. 'I don't care if you are two of the Bishop's disciples from Galilee, monsieur. No visitors are allowed. All appointments are by letter and all are refused.'

Stubborn to the very bone. 'Oh *bien sûr*, we are aware of this, madame, but the Préfet of Dijon, he has . . .'

'That one should know better.'

Better of too many things was implied. Ah *merde*, must she be difficult? 'It's a matter of great urgency, madame. A young girl has been kidnapped. Your mistress may be able to help once she learns that the girl resembles herself at the same age and that she is the latest of fourteen such girls, all others of whom have been savagely violated and murdered.'

Her bosom was swiftly crossed. Dark droplets of soup or sauce stained the snow beneath the ladle. The sparrows had fled.

'Murdered . . . ?'

'Yes,' grunted Kohler. 'Inform Mademoiselle Desthieux that it's an order from Sturmbannführer Boemelburg, Head of the Gestapo in France.'

The blue eyes beneath their shaggy mop gave Hermann a look of utter coldness, then turned to St-Cyr. 'If it is as this one says, monsieur, I will advise Mademoiselle Desthieux. The father has been dead for some years. The mother wanders in the mind so much, Mademoiselle Desthieux must be careful she is not disturbed.'

'And herself?' asked the Sûreté.

The look was one of scorn but with interest in visitors from afar, especially detectives. 'She alone will decide. Excuse me a moment. Please stay exactly where you are. The front half of the house is occupied by *les Allemands*, a captain and his orderly. Two corporals are in the rooms between. Had the snow not fallen last night, you would, I am sure, have seen the tyre marks of their motor cycles or those of the captain's car.'

Meaning, if Hermann and he had been observant, as detectives should have been, they would have noticed them anyway.

A nod would suffice and was given. After the woman had left them, Kohler hissed, 'Why didn't the resident Préfet warn us, Louis?'

St-Cyr surveyed the occupied parts of the house and shrugged. 'To understand is to comprehend the Burgundian, *mon vieux*. Their character is not defined simply by their food or even by the manner of its eating. The préfet was certain the captain would stop us. Mademoiselle Desthieux is special and her privacy to be guarded not just by her housekeeper. No doubt the father was once mayor or one of Dijon's other leading figures. That is why the daughter is sheltered, not only for her past and fame or infamy, but out of deference to the memory of her father.'

'And that of her "guests", her lodgers, eh?' snorted Kohler. 'Don't try to fool yourself too much.'

The woman received them in the attic at the back of the house. The narrow staircase seemed never to end. A candle warmed the glazes she used to decorate the porcelain plates before her with a design of fillet lace. 'It's a living, Inspectors. A local works keeps me busy.'

The left eye was without lashes or eyebrow and permanently closed over its empty socket. From there down across the lips and chin, the scars were deep, red and glazed. There were others on her neck and no doubt her chest.

But the other eye and the hair . . . ah *mon Dieu*, thought St-Cyr, it was as if all those missing girls pleaded with him to confide their stories to her.

'How can I help?' she asked. There were so many things crowding them. The scars, the ruin of her face, the stacks of unpainted plates, the simple work table with its candle and tiny pots of colour, her chair, the windows and the confines of an empty courtyard below.

'Why is it you choose to work up here, mademoiselle?' asked the Sûreté when, of course, he already knew the answer.

'So as to watch the comings and goings of my father's house. One has to these days, is that not so?'

She looked with apology at Hermann and saw him nod. Nervousness made her hesitate, but then she leaned down to blow out the candle and took up a rag to wipe her hands.

A new design, or one remembered, covered the back of her left hand with a delicate tracery of dark green and gold, but all too soon this vanished.

'Well?' she asked, removing her apron. They were making her nervous and she didn't like this because . . . ah, how could she put it? They were themselves nervous and trying to feel their way. Then she had been correct to meet them here and not in the salon.

Kohler noted that from the right, apart from a few scars, she was still a very handsome woman. Tall for a Burgundian. Even in a heavy beige sweater, white blouse and dark brown skirt, she had that certain quality, that tremendous sense of presence only a top mannequin possessed.

'Can we begin at the beginning?' asked Louis with apology in his voice, so much so she couldn't help but note its sincerity.

Fingers touched her lips to feel their scars. 'The beginning . . . ?' she blurted. 'Which beginning?'

St-Cyr handed her the engagement announcement. It took but a moment for it to register. Angèlique Desthieux turned suddenly away to face the stacks of plates in their straw-filled racks. 'What has Gaetan to do with this?' she gasped.

'We don't know, mademoiselle,' confessed Louis.

'I was only twenty and did not understand what the war could do to a man.'

'Of course. We were both caught up in it, mademoiselle. We both know how you must have felt.'

'*Do you?* I *screamed* when I saw what the Boches had done to him! I *shrieked* my silly head off and had to be taken from the ward. I cried out, Inspectors, and yelled at God, *I hate You for what You've done to me. To me!* Not to them.'

It was all coming back, Ward 5 at the Val de Grâce in Paris, and *les baveux*. 'They . . . they had no lips, no jaws, no noses or even eyes, some of them. There were towels around their throats to keep their constant droolings from soiling their pyjamas. Vacant, horribly twisted faces—faces that stared hatefully at me from among the bandages. The . . . the doctors showed me Gaetan's face and . . . and I shamed myself and my father and mother in front of all of them, messieurs. Me, who was so beautiful. Even in my nightmare, I could feel the hunger in them for a woman and felt violated as I screamed.'

After the Great War, veterans' groups had proliferated out of a desperate need. The droolers had taken the motto, Keep smiling. Don't become a victim. The *aveugles de la guerre* were those who had been blinded; the *ailes brisées* were the broken wings, the disabled aviators with their terrible burns.

The *gueules cassées*, the broken mugs.

'Did Gaetan Vergès hate you for refusing to marry him?' asked Louis.

'*Is that why the acid in the face?* No! No, a thousand times, Inspector! Gaetan understood.'

Her back was to them. The eye was hurriedly wiped, the nose touched with a handkerchief. Her shoulders quivered.

'Then who threw the acid?' asked Hermann.

'*Why must you ask?* I have said all there is to say, messieurs! That business, it is closed!'

'But must be reopened,' said Louis. Clearing a space on the table, he laid out single photos of each of the missing girls then quietly told her why they had come.

'So many?' she asked, trembling at the sight of them and what their hair, their eyes and ages must imply.

'If Gaetan Vergés didn't throw acid into your face, Mademoiselle Desthieux, who could it have been?'

'Luc.'

Ah *merde*. 'Albert Luc Tonnerre?' he asked, tossing Hermann a look of alarm.

They must know something of her past, but who had told them? she wondered. 'My former business agent was among *les baveux*, Inspector. It's God's irony that the two men in my life should have been disfigured by the same cloud of shrapnel. I didn't know this at the time of my visit to the ward of that hospital. I discovered it only later when the letters began to come.'

'The letters . . . ?' asked Kohler uneasily.

'Letters of such hatred, I destroyed them and told no one.'

'Not even when the acid . . .' began Kohler.

'It was thrown a year later. By then the letters had stopped. I had my life in Paris. I didn't even *think* I was in danger.'

'The Gare de Lyon?' prompted St-Cyr.

'How is it that you knew?'

'I didn't. I merely guessed. The platform would have been very crowded. Hundreds of soldiers heading for the Gare de l'Est and the war, or returning homeward on crutches and stretchers, the ambulances and nurses, a few civilians . . .

'Believe me, I saw nothing. I was *blinded. Burned!* I screamed in agony just as they had done. I panicked and tore at my face, my beautiful face. My lips were on fire, my skin, my cheeks, my eyes . . . I rolled and thrashed about and finally someone pinned me down and I fainted. When I awoke, I was just like them.'

'How close in friendship were Tonnerre and young Vergès?' asked Louis.

'Very. They were comrades in arms, Inspector, two of the droolers.'

'Could your fiancé have . . .'

'My ex-fiancé.'

'Could they have decided it together?' he asked.

She had to sit down before them. She must try to compose herself and tell them how it really was. 'It's a question I've had the years to answer, Inspectors, and yet my answer has always been the same. Gaetan would never have harmed me. He was far too gentle and kind—not bitter, I think, as so many would have been, but philosophical. If he had even in the slightest suspected Luc of such a thing, he would have gone to the authorities.'

Yet she had so readily given them Tonnerre's name. 'Then could it have been another of the patients on that ward?'

This was a question that deeply troubled them for they had the life of this one girl to consider and the deaths and mutilations of the others. 'Luc must have had an alibi Gaetan was positive he could accept,' she said blankly.

Ah *nom de Dieu*, it was evident she had counted on Vergès coming forward to accuse his friend! 'Was it Tonnerre who threw the acid, mademoiselle?' asked St-Cyr, determined to settle the matter.

Her gaze was unrelenting. 'That I will never say, Inspector. You see, I'm now one of them.'

'Not quite.'

How cruel of him! 'No, not quite, but in spirit.'

They prepared to leave. The Frenchman gathered the photos, the other one held the briefcase open. Both were disappointed in her responses. Both had a young girl to find before it was too late.

'Inspectors, I . . . I've not seen or written to Gaetan since the summer of 1917 when I saw his face so clearly I can still recall it.'

'The letters, then, had begun to arrive in the fall?' asked Louis and saw her nod.

He wouldn't leave it alone. She had best tell him. 'But then they stopped on the day of their anniversary, the day the shrapnel hit them.'

'Pardon?' he asked.

'Both were wounded on 2 October 1916, Inspector. I saw the damage the following summer, and in the fall of that year, the letters stopped on that very day, 2 October 1917.'

'Then the acid the following summer, Louis. 1918 . . .'

'Yes, yes, Hermann.' Would it help to show her the photo of that one girl? wondered St-Cyr and took it out.

'Oh!' she gasped and turned away.

Kohler took hold of her by the shoulders and said they were sorry. 'Could Tonnerre have done it?' he asked. 'We need to know.'

'Poured acid on her like that?' she asked, distraught. 'Luc . . . Luc liked the young ones, the younger the better. I once caught him in bed with . . . with two fifteen-year-olds. He had tied up one of them and had gagged her. He was going to . . .' She swallowed hard and shook her head. 'Paris — he will have found himself a place there and will be living on his pension, even though the memories of the good times will constantly remind him of what he once had and was . . . was able to do.'

Two fifteen-year-old girls . . .

St-Cyr put the photo away and closed the briefcase. For a moment he seemed undecided. Again he threw Kohler a troubled glance. 'A daughter, Mademoiselle Desthieux,' he said, and she dreaded what must come next. 'Whose child was it that you gave to the Sisters?'

The child . . . 'Gaetan's. She . . . she was such a tiny thing but I couldn't bring myself to tell him what I had done. You see, by then I knew what I faced and that I couldn't marry him and keep her.'

'Did Tonnerre know of it?'

'*How could he have?* No one knew except . . . except Aurora, whom you have met, and my parents.'

'And the doctor or the midwife and the Sisters.'

'Yes, but Luc could not have known!'

'But could he have found out?'

She shrugged. She said bitterly, 'I suppose he could have. I've never seen her since. I don't even know where she is. I *don't*! I wish I did but,' again she shrugged, 'wishes are for fools.'

'Mademoiselle, the Paris house of Monsieur Vergès . . . could Luc Tonnerre have known it well?' asked Louis, keeping up the pressure.

'The girls . . . ? Is that where they were taken?' she asked. It was. She could see this in the look he gave. 'We all knew it well, Inspector. Gaetan, Luc, myself and others. Those were very happy times. Well, mostly they were.'

'The paintings . . . Can you tell us anything about them?'

What did the question stem from? she wondered. 'Dutch and Flemish Old Masters, a Dürer, a Cranach—Vermeer. I remember there were two small sketches. Heads. Lovely things. They were in the study.'

'Impressionists, too?'

'Yes. Monsieur Vergès loved to collect beautiful things, Inspector, as did his father and grandfather before him. I . . . I was one of them—everyone used to say this, but for his son. I . . . I accepted it as his way of saying he was happy for Gaetan and myself and very pleased.'

'Anything else?' asked Louis.

Was it safer ground for her? she wondered. 'Some lovely marble sculptures and bronzes. A fifteenth-century Eve that was absolutely adorable and had longer hair than mine. Two Gobelin tapestries that were exquisite, Savonnerie carpets . . . Inspector, why are you asking? Has something happened to Monsieur Vergès? If so, Gaetan . . . what's to become of him?'

'This we don't know yet, mademoiselle. The Impressionist paintings . . . ? Manet perhaps?'

'A lovely study of a young mother and daughter. The mother is waiting for the train to bring the father home and sits with her back to the iron rails of the fence, while the daughter in a white halter dress with a soft blue bow clings to it and looks towards the locomotive where only a cloud of steam can be seen.'

'Any others? Choose any one.'

He was so intent. 'A woman, a girl with . . . with her breasts and shoulders bared but wearing a hat in which are tucked some red flowers. There was also a study of Renoir's, a young woman reading a book.'

It was enough and when she heard him say, 'Bon,' she could not help but sigh with relief. The whole interview could not have taken any more than fifteen or twenty minutes. They had come all the way from Paris and must be very anxious.

'I feel quite empty,' she said and tried to shyly smile.

It was Louis who said, 'Not quite, mademoiselle. Are you absolutely certain the child was Gaetan Vergès's?'

Ah no . . . 'Inspector, if you are implying that I slept with both of them, then you are very wrong.'

He would take a breath and hold it. He would simply say quite firmly, 'I wasn't.'

Could it really be important? Was he so insensitive? 'Then I must admit she wasn't Gaetan's and I must ask that you keep this to yourselves. Now you know everything, Inspector St-Cyr, and you leave me nothing for myself.'

'Nothing but the blessings of relief at having told another, mademoiselle, and perhaps helped to save this one.'

From his jacket pocket he took a simple pencil sketch, very finely but quickly executed. 'That is Joanne Labelle,' he said, 'and the boy who drew it is now dead because he did something for the daughter you gave to the Sisters in the early summer of 1917.'

Must he take from her everything? 'In June, Inspector. The . . . the 12th, not three days after she was born and I had begun to love her. Luc Tonnerre had a way with him. He . . . he was very handsome and debonair. He and I . . . Well, what can I say? But he was no match for Gaetan whom I came, in my months of trial and secrecy, to love with all my heart and soul. Of course I cheated Gaetan and must live with myself always for such foolishness and cruelty, and perhaps he would have discovered the child some day, but had things been different for us, Gaetan would have forgiven me and taken her to his heart. That is the kind of man he was, the man I knew.'

'Whereas Tonnerre would only . . .' said Louis.

Why must he force her to say it? 'Would only hate me.'

* * *

'Louis, how the hell did you know she was lying about the child?'

'She answered too readily, Hermann. She didn't deny its existence which she could so easily have done. Remember, she had promised herself to Vergès. If the child had been his, it should have bound her to him no matter what, and it hadn't done so.'

'She would have been too ashamed of herself to tell us.'

'Precisely! But Tonnerre must have known of the child. When our mannequin rejected Gaetan Vergès, she rejected him even more so. Hence the letters of hatred and then the acid.'

Louis gestured with a hand. 'You have no doubts?' asked Kohler.

'None. A crime of passion from a man who, though he didn't truly love her, had been rejected for another, only to have her reject the two of them.'

'Then that's a good enough reason for Gaetan Vergès to hate the very sight and thought of girls who look like her and want to become mannequins.'

'Ah, yes, I'm afraid it is, Hermann, and we shall have to ask him.'

Kohler thought to let it be—Louis was apprehensive enough about what they might find at the château, but . . . 'She said Tonnerre liked the young ones, Louis. She said it as if a woman betrayed.'

St-Cyr fought down his doubts about what must have become of Joanne. 'She was once probably very much in love with Tonnerre—did the two of them play around in that house when the son's back was turned?'

The happy times . . . 'Played loose and easy and took a few photographs, eh?'

'Perhaps. It's just a thought. Somehow there must be a reason for those sequences, Hermann. A start at least.'

'That war was hell, Louis. It did things to normally decent men.'

'Yes, hell.'

'Are you still certain someone could have waited upstairs in the attic rooms until the last of the photos had been taken?'

Must Hermann ask it? 'Not certain, ah, no. It's only a possibility. But if a drooler, then ... why then, was each girl forced into having ...'

Poor Louis couldn't bring himself to say it. All choked up, thought Kohler, cursing the case and the stresses it caused.

Both were exhausted and for a long time they didn't speak. The Citroën held the road beautifully. The countryside to the north of Dijon passed rapidly behind them. Town after town, village after village all seen in winter from an empty road upon which there was not even a Wehrmacht convoy.

Joanne ... thought St-Cyr with a sinking feeling in the pit of his stomach. The Château des belles fleurs bleues was well to the south of Provins. For too long they had been feeling their way closer to the Seine. There had been ploughed fields, then scrub pasture that had been let go. Then woods and finally a broken signboard, a mere grey-weathered arrow and this road, this lost track of icy solitude among tall and crowding hornbeams whose smooth, blue-grey bark was forbidding in the late afternoon light ... 'Ah *merde alors*, Hermann. There are the gates at last.'

Shit!

Two giant beeches stood on either side of a high iron gate that had defied all entry for years. Nothing special. No coat of arms. Just matching curls of ironwork above.

'Have we been led up a blind alley?' breathed Kohler, cursing their luck. The snow was perhaps eight to ten centimetres thick and undisturbed. The road beneath it had been full of pot-holes and large boulders. Not an easy drive, though he knew the aching in him stemmed, not from the hours behind the wheel, but from thoughts of Joanne and what they might well find.

At last the Citroën stopped and, to the cooling of its engine, came the quiet of the forest and then the musical tinkling of tiny birds and still-falling sheaths of ice from branches stirred by the softness of a wind. A thaw. One of those freaks of nature that, in the dead of winter, turned the land briefly to spring and misery.

Paris would soon be awash and shrouded in fog. Then it would freeze.

Kohler got out and eased his cramped muscles and back. The newish padlock and chain were heavy, the *propriéte privée défense d'entrer* notice all too clear.

Louis couldn't keep the uneasiness from his voice. 'Is the son really an ether-drinker? Is it that his affliction is so bad, Hermann, even here he has had to be hidden?'

Uncomfortable at the thought, they approached the gate and looked through its bars to yet a further extension of the lane and, as yet, no sight of the château.

'We may have to spend the night,' cursed Kohler exasperatedly. 'This fucking lock hasn't been opened in years, Louis. What the hell's been going on?'

'Is there a road around the gate? I seem to remember we passed one.'

'We'd have to back out. We're going to have to anyway.'

'Let's leave the car and climb over. The foot-gate will also be locked.'

It was, though here the original lock was still in use and the key, no doubt, hanging in the kitchen perhaps or in the caretaker's cottage.

About a kilometre of lane led between giant sycamores whose spatulated bark formed a stark camouflage against the snow-covered lawns and formal gardens that had been let go. Branches that had fallen had simply not been cleared.

The 'château' was a large manor house of buff-grey sandstone with a blue slate roof and turret, high-peaked dormer windows in its attic, and shuttered french windows below at the front, no shutters at the sides.

'The drapes are all drawn, Louis. The house has been simply closed and left. Our Monsieur Vergès must have gone south.'

'Or into the grave. Ah *nom de Dieu*, what are we to make of it, eh? It has an uncomfortable feeling, *mon vieux*. I've seen too many places like this and found too many old people in them, with all the jewellery and silver missing.'

'You're full of surprises. Why not retire and write a book about it, eh? *My Life as a Detective!*'

'Please don't joke. It isn't helping.'

'Then quit talking about bludgeoned old people!'

They tried the front door, the side door—found all were locked and no answer came to persistent ringing of the bell-pull.

The house was of a ground floor, one storey and then the attic but above this last, the single turret rose another storey so as to provide a good view of the grounds. Had it ever been a happy house? wondered St-Cyr. Built perhaps as early as 1725 and well before the Revolution, it had been occupied, no doubt, by the same family ever since. 'It's a typical *maison de maître*, Hermann. The family mansion or master's house of what was once a working farm.'

From a walled *potager* of perhaps a hectare, they stood looking at the place wondering what to do. The house appeared to be empty and unfeeling. No smoke issued from its chimneys. The silence was uncomfortable. There were no footprints but their own.

'Well, do we break in or not, Louis? I vote we do.'

The walls of the kitchen garden were tall and had been built to withstand the centuries. Mottled by slabs of pale brown sandstone, they rose to steeply pitched roofs that were flagged with coarse slate. Trellises clung to the walls—beans, roses, hops . . . 'Everything needed to sustain life would have been grown here, Hermann.'

'Look, you're no goddamned farmer, so stop kidding yourself and gassing on about cabbages. Hey, my fine-tuned ear, I hear no chickens or pigs. Where the hell are the old man and his son?'

'And Joanne, if indeed she is here?'

Louis was staring emptily at the house that rose to its tower just beyond the wall of the kitchen garden. The stables were behind the house and an attached wing of it. To the left, and beyond, there were more tall trees—a long line of lindens, so a drainage ditch over there, thought Kohler. A woods to the very left, extending to the bank of the Seine and the carpet of violets in spring.

'I'm going in, Louis, are you?'

'Yes. Before it gets too dark for us to find what we must find.'

'There's no sign of the lorries from Dallaire and Sons.'

Was it the offer of hope? 'Not yet, but there may be.'

Merde, he was taking it hard! 'Mademoiselle de Brisson didn't ask Paul Meunier to forge transit papers for two loads of furniture, Louis. The boy would have told me if she had.'

'Certainly. But our droolers, Hermann? What of them?'

Dear God, if You're really up there, hide the truth from him, begged Kohler.

When they found the lorries in an open-ended, timbered barn the size of a medieval market hall, they knew the worst.

'Dédé,' blurted Louis. 'What am I to say to him, Hermann?'

'Just let me have a look, eh? Stand back. That's an order.'

'From my big Bavarian brother who hasn't the stomach for it? Don't be an imbecile, Hermann. This is my case, my task. *Me*, I brought you into it on your holiday!'

Verdammt, he'd be crying in a minute! 'Joanne may not be in either lorry. Maybe she got away?'

Were all Bavarians so sentimental?

The roof-timbers towered above them. The vacant nests of summer's swallows were grey below with splattered droppings. Light filtered in through the gaping doorways.

So, we have trouble to face, said St-Cyr grimly to himself. Let me find Joanne and then her killers.

They opened the rear doors of both lorries and stood before the tangled contents of Louis XVI armchairs—superb pieces in giltwood and dark green velvet upholstery—a *Régence* sofa that was covered with exquisite needlepoint, lamps, tables . . . a Louis XV *bergère* in antique brocatelle silk, twin *tabourets* . . .

Everything had been hastily crammed into the lorries. Just to climb over the obstacle course would take hours. Arms, legs, shelves, mirrors, crates of crystal and porcelain wrapped in towels, sheets and drapes that had been ripped apart in haste. Clothing too.

Only by standing well back was it possible to see if anything had been disturbed on arrival.

'There,' said St-Cyr. 'That dining-room table. Some of the things on top of it have been pushed aside.'

Squeezing himself into the lorry, Louis somehow managed to work his way towards the front until he reached the other end of the table. 'A chest, Hermann,' he called out, looking down over the edge. 'It's open.'

'Is she . . . ?'

There was a grunt, grim with determination. 'No. No, she isn't here. There's vomit, there's hair—lots of hair.'

'*Christ!*'

'There are some short lengths of cord.They've been cut with a very sharp knife.'

Deftly Kohler hoisted himself up into the lorry. Shoving things aside, he clambered awkwardly forward until he reached Louis.

The chest was just big enough for the girl to have been folded into it with her chin on her knees and her arms wrapped around the lower part of her legs, wrists tied to the ankles. 'Ether?' he asked sharply.

The outline of her nestled body still lay deeply in the hair of not only herself but the other victims. No clump was more than three or four centimetres long. 'Each girl was forced to kneel beside this chest, Hermann, and while they cut off her hair, she had that of the others to look at.'

'The *bastards*, Louis! Ether?' he asked.

'Most probably. Even so, she would have lost consciousness for only from two to ten minutes.'

'Unless they forced her to drink it. Then she would have been out for an hour or two, maybe more.'

Much safer as an anaesthetic than chloroform when inhaled, ether did have its unpleasant side. Instant vomiting on regaining consciousness. When drunk, its burning taste tightened the tongue and throat, giving a tingling sensation while suffusing the body with warmth and producing feelings of extreme excitement, joyfulness and elation, then deep intoxication.

'Does it heighten sexual arousal and make one uninhibited?' hazarded Kohler uncomfortably.

'Were they in the habit of feeding it to their victims so as to gain their co-operation?' demanded St-Cyr, the catch all too evident in his throat. 'Ah, I do not know, *mon vieux*. It's fortunate they didn't gag her. She'd have choked and drowned.'

There was so much hair in the bottom of the chest . . .

'Is it that they wanted to keep her alive for more of their fun?' asked Louis.

'The house,' said Kohler.

'The torches . . . We left them in the car. Ah, damn!'

'There'll be candles—a lantern. Me first, you second and that really is an order.'

'Ah, no, Hermann. For Dédé and for Joanne, it must be me who finds her. *Me!*'

Kohler knew he was going to have to watch over him. 'Then we go together, eh? Side by side.'

'Until the doorway or the staircase becomes too small for both, Hermann. Then I go on alone because this is a matter between my friends, my God, the killers and myself.'

THE SIDE DOOR FINALLY GAVE A LITTLE. AS-
saulted by a stench of rotting food, St-Cyr threw
back his head and gagged. 'The kitchen, Hermann! Ah *nom de Jésus-Christ*, give me room!'

The stench was fruity, pungent, deep and stinging. Of green
beef, high fish, eggs, chicken guts and a black sop of once-wet
mushrooms that had oozed from their canvas collecting bag to
web the tiled floor around it.

'Louis, what the hell has happened?'

'A moment.' The Sûreté's hard-soled brown brogue hit the
plain plank door. Crashing against something, the door wedged
itself on a faience shard the shape of a half-moon. A *soupière*—
Nevers, thought St-Cyr, giving the tureen's provenance and
seeing it once lovingly placed in the centre of a table ringed by
straight-backed open chairs, all in that plain but beautiful style of
the provinces.

The kitchen was a shambles. No shelf or cupboard was full or
even half-empty. Everything lay about or on the floor. The old,
black-iron stove and row of brick ovens held copper pots and

pans once used, then bashed in or turned upside down in rage, their contents burnt to tar and dusty cinders grey with age.

There was garbage everywhere. Bags and pails overflowed. Filthy tea towels and washcloths lay crumpled on the floor, on the stone drainboard beside the sink, or clung tenaciously to the pump handle, a wallpeg, or the edge of a side table and chair.

'The son has had to live alone, Hermann, and has tried to care for himself. Soup, soup and nothing more solid than more puréed soup. The father must have died some years ago.'

Kohler had never seen anything like it. Gingerly they began to pick their way into the house. The ceilings were low and of whitewashed beams and plaster. The walls might once have been decorated in the subdued colours of the country, with flowers everywhere and paintings. Portraits of long-deceased relatives in gilded oval frames were now smashed—smashed to smithereens! The chairs, the sofas, the desk with its once beautiful marquetry, all were broken and ripped. 'A rampage, Louis?' he asked, his voice empty.

'Living, I think, from day to day—two years, three perhaps. Ah, it's so hard to tell, Hermann. Night by night and week by week Gaetan Vergès must have destroyed every last link with his ancestors. This . . .' he indicated the once-proud salon, 'was not the refinement of Paris, but was once lovely all the same. It was here, from the family farm, that the money must have come to maintain the house in Paris. Vegetables and poultry, roses for the perfume trade and as cut flowers in the markets and shops. Is the son now dead?'

A *fauteuil*, upholstered with tapestry, had been thrown in a demented rage at the mantelpiece mirror. Other pieces had been broken up and fed into the fire which had then been left to go out.

'He is or was a man in great and constant pain, Hermann.'

'An ether-drinker.'

There were books on horticulture and beekeeping whose pages held badly stained and futilely thumbed lithographs. Apples, pears . . . Many of the books were open and had been thrown as if in disgust that the recommended treatment, a spraying of copper sulphate perhaps, had not controlled whatever pest had infested the orchards. A fungus perhaps, or aphids. No bit of floor space was uncovered. Pages and pages of manuscript in pen and ink held the love letters, the poems, the diaries even of his ancestors and, *yes*, those letters from him to Angèlique Desthieux . . .

My dearest Angèlique . . . At dawn the assault will come again. We are waiting.

It was dated 29 September 1916.

'Louis, let's check the rest of the place and get out of here.'

A rudimentary barometer with calibrated gaugeboard had been spared and still hung on the wall beside the doorway to the main hall, forgotten in his passage from room to room. The main staircase curved continuously upwards through the filth. Its iron rails had been painted a dark green, as had all the stairwell trim and footboards, but the much-scuffed steps themselves and the curved balustrade were of unpainted oak.

A single, gilded and superbly carved pine cone, a symbol of fecundity, stood upright on top of the Napoleonic newel post. No paintings hung on the walls of the stairwell. All had been pulled down and either smashed underfoot or simply flung aside.

Step by step they picked their way through the half-light. Vergès was not in any of the rooms whose beds, room by room, had been slept in until too filthy when, at last, he had found it necessary to move on to another room.

Clothing lay scattered everywhere—suits, coats, shirts and neckties, the uniform he had worn on parade, the medals with their ribbons . . .

At one end of the corridor there was a bathroom with a copper-plated Napoleonic tub, brass taps and water heater; at the other end was the tower with its spiral staircase in dark green again and unpainted oak.

The room at the top of the tower was large, with windows facing the four corners of the compass. A small desk, a chair, an armoire and commode, a simple cot in whose lumpy mattress of striped grey and white fabric the mice had made their nests and left their urine.

The floor was littered with more pages of manuscript—a diary of the war perhaps. Smashed and scattered. Ink nearly everywhere. Pens and countless nibs, more letters . . . *Angèlique, I can never forget you* . . .

There was a porcelain wash-basin and jug on a night stand. The jug had been split by the frost.

'Louis . . .' Kohler grabbed him. *'Don't!'* he hissed.

The girl was lying on her side, folded up on a heap of soiled blankets beneath a far window, one of whose shutters had somehow come open. Her back was to them, the wrists were tied to the ankles so that her chin rested on her knees.

She looked so cold. She did not move. Her skin had the pallor of bluish grey wax. Her hair had all been hacked off, and the double twist of stout white cord had bitten so deeply and savagely into her neck, the skin was pinched, the windpipe crushed.

At the moment of death, she had evacuated herself but these discharges were now frozen.

Her tongue was caught between clenched teeth. The lips were lead-blue, the deep brown eyes wide open, the pupils dilated.

A bloody froth of mucus and other fluids had erupted from her nose and mouth.

The smell was sickening.

'Joanne . . .'

'Louis, go easy. It had to happen. That's all there is to it.'

'Why?'

'Ah *Gott im Himmel*! We both knew she had very little chance. Sure, we kidded ourselves by hoping but . . .'

The Sûreté's look was desperate. 'Dédé, Hermann. How am I to tell him?'

'I'll do it.'

Louis blinked. He fought to think, then said, 'No, no, I will. Go and look for the drooler. See if there's a cottage. Cross the kitchen garden and take the path towards the river. Leave me alone with her. *Please!'*

'*Jésus merde alors*, Are you sure?'

'Yes!'

A last doubtful glance revealed Louis among the rubbish,

standing over her, hat in hand, eyes clamped shut. Beaten, defeated, all alone and begging himself to find the strength to be calm and detached.

It's impossible, said Kohler sadly to himself. Without another word, he went downstairs to stand in the snow-covered drive among the overgrown stubble, wishing things hadn't turned out as they had.

From the kitchen garden, he looked back up at the tower. The open shutter moved, recording but the faintest of breezes. Though he couldn't be certain, he wondered if her killer had not called down from that window to someone in the garden, It's done. She's gone.

It wasn't pleasant to look at Joanne. More than once St-Cyr had to back away. He had found a kerosene lantern in one of the lower bedrooms and had carried it up into the tower to hold it over her.

Light flickered on the walls. The time of death would have to be established by the coroner. Was Armand Tremblay still in charge of this district? Tremblay was a good man and would not attempt to hide things no matter how uncomfortable to the Occupier or damaging to the Vergès's family honour.

Rigor had set in. Everything seemed to suggest death very early Monday morning, 28 December—either on arrival at perhaps 3.00 a.m., or somewhat later that day.

There were bruises on her buttocks, thighs and knees, those of fingermarks also. The bruises on the knees were from having fallen or banged into a chair.

Others on her breasts and upper arms and shoulders suggested she had been grabbed and mauled in those parts and perhaps thrown from assailant to assailant. A small cut above the left eye confirmed the thought. She had been struck across the face several times. There was a scratch behind the right ear and this extended down the back of the neck for about seven centimetres. Other scratches were on her seat and inner thighs, her stomach and groin. More than once her legs had been forced apart, a child, a curly-haired little girl on a street in Belleville who had looked quizzically up at him and said, 'But, monsieur, you cannot possibly like what you do?'

'I must not close your eyes, Joanne. Dr. Tremblay must see you exactly as you are. It's best that way.'

The froth from her lips was of blood, spittle and fluid from the lungs, not semen though they would have done that to her as well. Gingerly he leaned down to smell the froth. Had she been drugged with ether—forced to swallow it? Had they shoved one of Vergès's rubber feeding-tubes down her throat and made her drink the damned stuff to get her to co-operate?

Was it merely the workings of his imagination that brought the smell of ether to him?

Again, only the coroner could pin this down. The ether could also have been administered through the rectum. She was their property. They had had total control over her. She would have tried to scream, to . . .

'Stop! Please, stop,' he said, admonishing himself. 'Try to think. Try to remain calm.'

He moved the lantern back a little but had difficulty nestling it among the soiled blankets where other girls had lain and died perhaps. The dark hairs of her nostrils hadn't been clipped—she had still been such an innocent when she had gone to that house on the rue de Valois.

The flickering of the light was reflected in her eyes, it . . . 'What's this?' he asked, a whisper. 'You can't possibly have a gold tooth. Your family's far too poor.'

Searching—dragging out the pair of reading glasses for which he had unfortunately found an increasing need of late, St-Cyr examined her lips.

There was a small gold wire caught in the froth. He thought of Tremblay, thought he must not disturb a thing but said, 'I can't leave this, can I, Joanne?'

With a pair of tweezers, he teased the thing and gradually it came free. As he held it up to the light, he sighed and said, 'Good. Good for you, *ma brave*. You were defiant right up to your last moment and this is something I must tell Dédé, for it will help him and he'll take pride in what you did, as will I.'

The ear-ring must have fallen to the floor or been set on a table or chair perhaps. Unnoticed, Joanne had taken it into her mouth, the only way she could have hidden it.

A tiny turquoise scarab dangled from the end to match those on the bracelet and the other things she had seen in that shop window.

'Denise St. Onge?' he asked. 'Was Mademoiselle St. Onge witness to your killing, Joanne, or did she leave this room, this tower and this house before you died?'

Or was she even a part of it?

Though webbed with blood, the thing caused the cinematographer in him to see her secretly taking the ear-ring into her mouth—the girl was naked, bound hand and foot, held perhaps. He saw Denise St. Onge in a sleeveless black silk dress wearing such a pair of ear-rings, saw her slowly taking them off as a woman would who was about to have sex. *Sex!*

He saw her putting the ear-rings aside and shook his head. 'I mustn't conjure tricks of the imagination. I must stick to the facts. The droolers?' he asked. 'Did they make Joanne wear the ear-rings and other pieces, only then to remove them from her and set them aside?'

Old stock, Muriel Barteaux had said of the jewellery, things brought to light to service the Occupier who would pay handsomely for such trinkets to send home to their wives or give to their new mistresses.

Muriel and Chantal were looking into the matter and might possibly have something for them.

Carefully wrapping the ear-ring in the handkerchief he kept for such things, St-Cyr pocketed it.

On examining the fingernails of Joanne's right hand, he found a black hair caught in a small tear in the middle fingernail. This hair was further caught between that finger and the index, and between the ankle and that hand.

Had Gaetan Vergès jet-black hair? he wondered. Had she been high on ether? Had she run her hands through the drooler's hair as they had had sex, not love? Never love.

'Michel le Blanc,' he said. 'Le Blanc has jet-black hair.'

The knots suggested a man of some strength, or two persons. 'A man and a woman?' he asked, settling back on his haunches to see Joanne lying there so still and cold, a child.

'You're not alone,' he said. 'Believe me, we *will* find out who did this and then we'll bring them to justice even if one is not a drooler but a member of the Luftwaffe's Press Service, another not a drooler either but a reporter on *Paris-Soir*, and the third a woman and owner of a certain shop or even the daughter of a well-known banker or that one's wife!'

Right in the small of her back, shading gave the pressure point of her assailant's knee as the cord had been savagely twisted.

Needing the lantern now, he had to take it with him. As he stood over her with it, he saw her chained to the attic ceiling of that room overlooking the balcony round the garden of the Palais Royal, asked, 'Did they put a blue light on the floor, Joanne, and let it shine up over your blindfolded eyes?'

Did André-Philippe de Brisson see you like that? Did he put his hands on you and is this not the final link to the robbery?

Kohler hesitated. At dusk, the three-room cottage of stone and timber looked quaint and peaceful amid the snow and open woodland at a bend in the Seine. No smoke issued from its chimney and this worried him but what else was there about the place?

A rowboat had been drawn up and overturned on the simple dock of weathered poles and planks. Reeds, now brown and old, rose thickly through the shore ice. There was no loosestrife to bugger everything up and choke off the food supply the water-fowl needed. 'Cleaned out,' he breathed. 'A hunter?' he asked of the son, of Gaetan Vergès. There was something about the place that gave him the shivers.

Tepees of dead branches had been gathered by wagon and left to await use years ago — how many years? he asked, recalling the lane between the sycamores and the final approach to the main house.

There was a good stack of cut firewood—oak and beech—under a shed with a plank roof, but the wood looked untouched for at least a couple of years. A man's bicycle, gently rusting, was leaning against the wall nearest the front door. Heavy timbers framed the doorway and extended out so as to form a covered entrance. Two wrought-iron squirrels shared an iron walnut above a mud-caked bootscraper next to a sisal mat. The mud was not quite dry—hell, nothing really dried out in this climate so close to the river, unless indoors by the fire.

Easing the door latch down and finding it unlocked, he let the door swing slowly open. The place was all but dark, the smell . . . ah *Gott im Himmel!*

Again there were beamed, low ceilings. A massive stone hearth, directly opposite the door, held charred logs and a good bed of ashes. There was an iron pot on an arm that could be swung in over the fire, a spit that, when its rope was unwound by the counterweight, rotated.

There were chairs, tables, a roll-top Napoleonic desk, brass candlesticks, fishing rods, an old shotgun that should have been turned in to the authorities. Smooth bore, both barrels, and unloaded.

Carefully he put it back. In contrast to the main house, the cottage was immaculate but whereas the former had been lived in continuously, this had been left until . . .

A shoe, a sock—the turn-up of a trouser leg—caught the last of the light. Nervously Kohler drew the Walther P38, then realized how stupid the gesture was and slid it back into its shoulder holster.

The man was lying face down on the carpet behind the table that separated the fireside from the rest of the room. A service revolver, one of the old Lebel Model 1873s, was clutched in the right hand.

Grey and splattered across the carpet, greasy and frozen—streaked with congealed blood—his brains had been blown out, the bullet having not only entered the right temple but having been cut before firing with the Cross of Hope for divine forgiveness.

A pocket-knife, lying on the carpet nearby, showed shavings of lead and it was as he looked at these, that the light finally slipped away without his realizing it.

'*Verdammt!*' Fumbling with his pocket matches, Kohler lit first one and then another and another of the candles.

Still shaking, he lit a cigarette and for a time stood there trying to get a grip on himself. 'It's finally got to me,' he breathed and was glad Louis wasn't with him. 'I've had it. Death, death, *death*! That's all I ever seem to get!'

A fleeting memory of his sons came to him. A wagon, a trip into Wasserburg to market, one of those rare times when papa, who made the money that had kept the farm alive, had come home from Munich. Papa on a visit. The big detective. 'Shit!'

There was a photograph among several others on the desk. Kohler picked it up and turned it over to read the inscription. *Luc and I at the École Militaire, 10 March 1914.* The saps. They should have gone AWOL and beat it to Algeria and the desert or headed south to the Congo.

Another photo showed Angèlique Desthieux and Gaetan Vergès, the happy couple. It was signed *From Luc who relinquishes all claim with regrets and kind regards, Paris 3 July 1916, Jardin du Palais Royal.*

There was little left to resemble the once handsome young man in that photograph. The face which remained was without the lower jaw, most of the upper jaw was horribly twisted to the left and up, the skin flayed by a mass of deep scars among which grew small forests of bristles. One eye was completely gone and most of the nose.

The plastic surgeons had done their best—a new science then and finding its way with lots of fodder for experiment. Plates of silver and those of nickel had been fixed under the skin to give some semblance of form to shattered cheekbones and a forehead that still didn't look right even with a toupee above.

There were no muscles in what must pass for lips—nothing but a slack hole for the spoon or rubber tube that would feed him and slake his thirst for the rest of his life. Constant drooling and no voice. A slate board and chalk or bit of paper and pencil for 'talking'.

'The poor bastard,' breathed Kohler. 'By rights he should have died on the battlefield.'

But had he messed with that girl, with Joanne Labelle? Had he put his hands on her and tried to kiss her? Had he . . .

Trembling at the thought, he lit another cigarette and then a lantern, which he placed near an unshuttered window should Louis come looking for him. He knew they had the night and morning to spend in this godforsaken place—that's all there was to it. Too many things to look for and carefully—yes, God damn it, yes, most carefully.

The coroner would have to be called in, the local *flics* and a photographer. It was all a routine he had come to detest, only now he really knew it and felt it. 'It's finished for me,' he said. 'I don't think I can take any more.'

Boemelburg would simply stare at him and snort or say, Welcome to the Russian Front, Kohler. What was your former rank?

There were dozens of glass containers in a small storeroom that must once have served as a wine cellar and root-store. But all the bottles were empty and covered with a film of dust, though all bore the label of ether.

Clearly Gaetan Vergès had been an ether-drinker but his supply had been carefully budgeted by the father in the main house and doled out only a little at a time. The son had lived here, had fished, shot ducks, gathered firewood, read, written his journals, worked in the family *potager* probably, and each evening had had his cubic centimetres of ether. Maybe twenty or thirty, maybe forty or fifty—just enough to make him feel good for a little while and then to get him to sleep. One hundred, two hundred . . . would it have taken half a bottle or the whole damned thing?

But all that had ceased with the death of the father and the Defeat of France. The source must have dried up, though when the father had passed away, they still didn't know.

Up in the loft, there was a small bedroom—it was all so tidy. There was a portrait photograph of Angèlique Desthieux—she had been a real beauty, a fine-looking young woman. Decent, calm, gentle, not arrogant ... Eminently lovable and adored. Worshipped.

The photos had not all been taken by Luc Tonnerre—some had been done by professional photographers and presented to Vergès as gifts from the mannequin and future bride with love and tenderness.

Kohler eased the bedside table drawer open ... a Bible, a rosary, a simple cross on a neckchain ... a packet of photographs tied with pink ribbon ...

Angèlique Desthieux had had a splendid body. She lay naked on a magnificent Louis-Philippe *chaise-longue* he recognized from the photographs they had found in the Paris house. She was looking up into the camera lens not with fear but lust in eyes that, though lovely, were hard and demanding.

Naked, she stood on tiptoes and leaned against a Louis XVI commode, facing a superbly carved and gilded wall mirror in which were reflected her breasts squeezed between stiffened arms, lips that were parted as if in orgasm, dusky eyelids that were closed, the thick triangle of her pubes ...

In another of the photos, her seat was pinned to the edge of that same commode. She was facing the camera and her gorgeous backside was reflected in the glass, but she was not biting back the tears, ah, no. She wanted to be fucked and everything about her said this. Same, too, with her lying on the carpet both facing up into the camera and with her face down.

Kohler retied the ribbon and slid the packet into his overcoat pocket. All the photographs had been signed *Luc* and had carried the message *Gaetan, mon cher compagnon d'armes, this is how she was and what she was really like.*

Ah *merde* ...

Beside the cross on its chain there was a packet of eleven-millimetre cartridges for the revolver. Several were missing.

Beside the cartridges, there was a small bell jar—the memento the doctors had presented to him on release from the operating table. *Verdammt,* the French! Had they no more sense than to do a thing like this? Perhaps as many as sixty pieces, many of them the round lead pellets so common in the shrapnel of that other war, had been picked from Vergès's body. Varying in size from coarse to fine, from perhaps a half-centimetre to two centimetres, some had little burrs or ragged edges, others nicks—mere imperfections of the casting or deliberate, they had become their own special brand of razor.

When he went downstairs, Louis was crouched over the body oblivious to everything else and intent on memorizing, as only the cinematographer in him could, every last detail.

'I'll go out to the car, and fetch the local boys in blue and the coroner.'

The Sûreté's gumshoe didn't even look up or turn away. 'Insist on Tremblay. Be positive, Hermann. Use your Gestapo cudgel if necessary. I want Tremblay to have a look at this and the other one. Bring the torches when you return. Say nothing of the house in Paris—make up some story. Hey, it doesn't matter, eh? The less they know the better. Total secrecy. A blanket order from Boemelburg. We need to buy us some time, *mon vieux. Time!'*

When the coroner found them, St-Cyr and Kohler were standing in the barn near the lorries with the préfet of Paris.

'The girl has been dead for at least two days, Jean-Louis, the man also,' said the coroner, 'but I do not think he was the one who killed her. There are no rope marks on his hands and there should be since both died at about the same time.'

'*Idiot*, of course he killed her!' roared Talbotte, the préfet of Paris, furiously. 'He was fucking her eyes out, *imbécile*! Banging her ass, her mouth, her cunt until she was blue in the face and . . .'

'Préfet, *please*. I knew the girl,' said St-Cyr, tapping him on the chest. 'I know her mother and father.'

'Louis, go easy, eh?' cautioned Kohler. 'It's Talbotte's beat. We're within his jurisdiction and we need him.'

The Bavarian as pacifier? 'Then tell him to go easy with his own mouth!' snapped the Sûreté.

Ah *nom de Dieu*! tired and still wound up. 'Look, he's taking it hard, Préfet. Back off,' urged Kohler.

'Piss off and suck lemons!' hissed Talbotte. 'The one in the cottage discovered he could no longer live with himself and ended it. That's fair enough. He has saved the taxpayer a considerable expense.'

Louis drew the préfet aside. Alarmed, Kohler hesitated, wanting to go after them but Tremblay, the coroner, judiciously pulled him back and quietly said, 'I know Jean-Louis, and I know Talbotte. Let them work it out between themselves. They hate each other and it's obvious.'

Wise words or those of disaster? wondered Kohler apprehensively. Ah *merde*, the French! they were so territorial. The fingerprint boys from Paris were busy dusting down the cabs of the two lorries. Up in the tower room, a police photographer was doing close-ups of Joanne Labelle, while in the cottage, another caught Gaetan Vergès from every possible angle.

Paris and its environs were Talbotte's beat. No sooner had the Préfet of Provins been alerted, than his phone line to Paris had started buzzing the big cheese himself.

No fool when it came to money, the Occupier, or a chance to keep a finger in his own pie, Talbotte had driven out himself.

Kohler offered the coroner a cigarette which was gratefully accepted as was the light. At fifty-six years of age, Armand Tremblay had seen enough murder-suicides to form his own conclusions no matter how inconvenient. Robust and ruddy-cheeked, with lively dark brown eyes behind wire-rimmed spectacles that had been mended with surgical tape, he looked a man who loved his comforts.

'That revolver, Inspector,' he said, giving his head a little toss and shrugging magnanimously as if to forgive whatever oversights he might make, 'it's just not right. Ah no, no, most certainly not.' He took a drag on his cigarette and blew the smoke aside. 'You see, Inspector, on firing a revolver or pistol, the hand is automatically jerked upwards and only settles back a little unless deliberately pulled down. Then, too, with such a violent cessation of the nervous system there is very often cadaveric spasm, a tightening of the muscles which would grip the revolver as if in life. Unfortunately this one's fingers are slack, whereas all his other limbs, they are rigid from the spasm which has the same effect as normal rigor but comes on instantly at the moment of death.'

'*Merde alors*,' breathed Kohler, knowing he would have seen it himself had he not been so preoccupied with death itself. 'The barrel wouldn't have remained pointing directly at the entry wound. The fingers show the pressure marks of having had their rigidity broken so as to force the hand to hold the revolver.'

'Precisely!' enthused Tremblay, pleased at having got the better, not of a detective, let alone one of the Occupiers, but of the killer. 'These are simple things and they should not have been overlooked, especially if the killer knows anything of guns.'

'Was Vergès forced to lie on the carpet first?'

'*Mais certainement.* One has only to look at him.'

'Then the muzzle was pressed against his forehead?'

'Ah no, not quite. Your Monsieur Vergès has co-operated, Inspector, by first cutting a cross in the bullet that killed him.'

'Pardon?'

'Don't forget your cigarette. Don't waste it. Not these days, eh? It's simple. The cartridges are nearly thirty years old and there's a thin film of grease on them. Monsieur Vergès has this grease on the fingertips of his left hand. He has held the cartridge as he cut the bullet. There are also a few flakes of lead in the grease and a little of the lead has rubbed off on the skin itself. We will, I am sure, find his fingerprints on the pocket-knife and the spent cartridge case but not those of the killer.'

'A friend?' bleated Kohler, thinking of Luc Tonnerre.

The rounded shoulders automatically lifted. 'Perhaps. Let us say a friend for now. An assisted death. A death by agreement but under the laws of even your own country, one of murder all the same.'

'Then why didn't he simply kill himself?'

'Perhaps it is that he couldn't bring himself to do it and needed help.'

'Was he high on ether?'

'It's too early to say. After the tests ... A little patience, Inspector. Then we'll be positive.'

'But you think that might have been the case?'

Detectives were always wanting answers before they could be given. 'There is the possibility but no evidence of the bottle nearby or of the means of drinking it. Oh *bien sûr* there are those other bottles but they've been there for ages, and certainly one could pour it into a glass and down it quickly perhaps, even though it is highly volatile, but with lips like that ... ah, one cannot drink from a glass so easily, can one? And that, Inspector, is all I can say for now.'

'Then which of them died first?'

The Bavarian was so intent. 'This, too, I cannot say since the times of death are very close.'

'But ... ?'

Tremblay sighed impatiently. 'But if pressed, I would say the girl first and then the man, both most probably on Monday morning at perhaps 9.00 or 10.00. I am only guessing.'

'Just after dawn.'

'Yes.'

Louis and himself had been on the train coming back from Lyon with no thought at all of what was to come. 'Louis said you were good.'

'He's too kind.' Jean-Louis had seen what they had just discussed, of course, but had not let this one know, out of deference to his German masters perhaps.

'What about the girl? Was she also drugged?' asked Kohler, throwing a worried glance towards the end of the barn through which Talbotte and Louis had disappeared too long ago for comfort.

'The girl ... ah yes,' said Tremblay, looking at the lorries, then very seriously up at him. 'Inspector, I think what you really wish to ask is was she co-operative in any way, and this I cannot tell you until I have analysed her blood and organs for the presence of ether, or any other deleterious substance.'

'But is it possible?'

'Anything is possible. God made the world that way so that we might find within us the urge to do right, not wrong.'

Tremblay gave a mildly self-conscious smile at his little sermon. 'Personally I do not think such a thing ever entered that girl's mind, Inspector. She may well have been coerced into doing as they demanded of her and that is why she ran her hands through the hair of at least one of her assailants who was not Monsieur Vergès, by the way. No, not at all. The assailant's hair was natural and growing in place.'

'There was an ear-ring . . .'

'Jean-Louis wishes me not to mention it in my report for now but has shown it to me and told me exactly how and where it was discovered.'

'Any thoughts?'

'Besides his own? No, not at the moment. A brave child. Another Jeanne d'Arc.'

'Didn't the Burgundians capture and sell Joan to the English?' asked Kohler, frowning over his knowledge of French history since it was still fuzzy even after a good two years of putting up with Louis.

'Ah yes, the Burgundians to their eternal shame, Inspector, but it was most definitely others who burned her at the stake in 1431 and then forgave her after a new trial in 1456, and in 1920 made her a saint!'

More than 500 years later! It said something about the French. They carried their guilt through the centuries, periodically mulling it over and trying to exorcise the misfortunes of a hot-headed moment. Idly Kohler wondered what they would say about the Occupation fifty or a hundred years hence?

Guilt again? he asked himself, snorting inwardly. Further trials and more of the periodic soul-searching! 'I guess I had better find Louis.'

'I wouldn't. I would leave them. They have things to discuss in private, old cases, new cases, this one, that one, who knows?'

'Blackmail?' asked Kohler darkly.

There was another shrug. 'Perhaps. Who cares so long as it

accomplishes the desired purpose of gaining you both the necessary time to pursue the investigation without undue interference?'

With perfect timing, God used the coarse sieve and turned on the tap. Raindrops drove themselves into the snow and pretty soon they were seeping into a poor detective's shoes whose soles, with all the exercise, had opened, lacking as they were for glue and stitching thread due to the extreme shortages of labour and materials. It was the last straw. *'Préfet, don't give me shit and muscle! I want full details of the robbery! Everything you have!'*

Talbotte's fist was raised. His voice erupted. *'You idiots smashed up my best* mouchard! *I would sooner co-operate with the Devil! The Devil!'*

'Ah, merde, *I have thought that is who you were!'*

A fist lashed out through the darkness. The rain came down. St-Cyr ducked, feinted left, right . . . tried to shout at himself *No, idiot! He's the Préfet of Paris. Don't try to defend yourself! Don't let Joanne's death get in the way of common sense!* 'Look, why can't we co-operate for once, eh? A few small questions. They're really nothing. Boemelburg has assigned Hermann and myself to the case.'

'To the robbery!' roared the préfet. *'There can be no connection with the murder of that little cunt!'*

'Ah yes, the girl in the tower, Préfet. A connection.'

'There is *none* and therefore you and that . . . that turd of a Bavarian have no authority here. *None*, Jean-Louis! Absolutely none!'

'Oh but there is a connection, Préfet, and because of this, we need your help.'

'I'll kill you!'

'Some other time.'

'I'll tip the Resistance off and they will complete the job!'

'And Boemelburg will learn a few things, eh, about a préfet who co-operates but hides the truth.'

'Such as?'

'Ah, don't be so impossible! Gold bars, louis d'or, diamonds and fur coats—two mistresses, one in Clichy on the rue de Neuilly, the other in Les Lillas on the rue de Paris, an Italian, a sweet little thing not twenty, eh, Préfet? Eighteen and the same age as the one in the tower! Hey, those girls of yours are expensive even for a well-paid civil servant such as yourself who has not been doing his job.'

A hand was tossed. 'You have no right to make insinuations! No right! Everything was turned over to the authorities, the SS of the avenue Foch!'

Valuables from Jews who were then deported! Twelve thousand of them had been rounded up by Talbotte and his men and their safe deposit boxes opened. 'Almost sufficient for your retirement and expenses, Préfet. I have a list. After the round-up of last July, I made it my business to find out exactly what you had personally misappropriated.'

'*Bâtard!*' came the shriek. Talbotte lunged at him. St-Cyr crashed into the side of a police van. Fists pummelled him, a head bucked and slammed him in the face. His chin went back . . . The eyes . . . Talbotte's fingers were ripping at his eyes . . .

The fist . . . 'Ah Jesus, Préfet, *give it a rest!* We're *not* trying to take your job away or show you up!'

Blood poured from the préfet's nose. One eye was closed and rapidly swelling. The lower lip was bleeding profusely. A tooth had come loose.

Kohler held the lantern a little higher so as to get a better view of the damage. Grinning hugely, he asked how St-Cyr's hand was and said, 'Hey, I think you've done a job on him. Why not let me do the talking?'

'*No!* He will answer only to me since I have not yet applied the shoes, Hermann. A few simple answers to show that our two police organizations really do work in harmony.'

A real tiger. Ah *Gott im Himmel* . . . Kohler set the lantern on top of the van. Clearly Talbotte felt very threatened about the future, the war in Russia perhaps. 'Start talking then. I'll stand between the two of you and listen.'

Cigarettes were called for and these made it imperative to sit in the préfet's Citroën even though the leather would get wet.

A bottle of brandy was found under the front seat, nestled

between two machine-pistols with spare clips. 'Well, what do you know?' enthused Kohler. 'Nervous, eh, Préfet? Louis, the fucking car's an arsenal! He must be expecting a little surprise from the Resistance. A road-block!'

He took out two stick grenades and, setting one on the floor at his feet, fiddled with the wrong end of the other. 'A simple twist, a yank, drop and run. No car, no préfet. An accident,' he said. 'Now talk. My partner in the back seat is about done in.'

St-Cyr stared at the back of the préfet's head. 'Full details of the robbery,' he said breathlessly. 'Everything you have, you lousy son of a bitch. My hand, Hermann. My left hand! Always it is the left side that gets injured!'

Kohler ... thought Talbotte. Kohler wasn't liked by several in Gestapo circles. The Resistance could finish him off easily if word was passed that an exchange could be made and one or two of their people allowed to 'escape'. No one would care too much.

'Préfet, you of all people shouldn't even think of it,' breathed the Gestapo. 'You'd only get caught in the middle. Why not co-operate? Hey, we'll even agree to give you all the credit and half the cash.'

'The money ... the eighteen million? Is it hidden here? It can't be. Those girls ... Ah, you can't possibly link their disappearances to that robbery.'

Nursing his hand, St-Cyr took it away from his lips long enough to hiss, '*I think I can!*'

'Then the money's here?' demanded Talbotte, wiping blood and rainwater from his lips.

'No. No, it never left Paris.'

'Louis, how can you be so ... ?'

'So sure, Hermann? Ah, nothing is certain until all the information is in.'

Talbotte told himself he had had enough of this shit! 'Those two men abandoned the car and made a run for it, idiot! The Gare de l'Est, the Gare de Lyon ... who's to say once they're gone?'

Louis sat up and leaned forward quickly. '*Yes, yes,* Préfet, but has there been any word of their having been seen taking the train? *Any* train?'

'Louis, what about the . . .'

'The lorries full of furniture? They're certainly a possibility.'

'Yet the money isn't here?' said Talbotte, wondering what Kohler had been about to ask Louis.

'No. No, I do not think the money is here,' said St-Cyr, grateful at having stopped Hermann.

Kohler told himself to let Louis handle things now that the two of them had calmed down. Quite obviously the préfet knew nothing of the forged papers Marie-Claire de Brisson had had made.

'The girl in that tower?' demanded Talbotte darkly. 'What has she to do with the robbery?'

'Nothing,' said Louis.

'Then there is no connection!' snorted Talbotte, only to regret having used his nose so thoughtlessly.

'A connection . . . ah yes, Préfet, that is a quite different matter and for this we need to know more about the woman in the street.'

'The one who stood look-out for the robbers?'

'Yes, that one.'

Talbotte saw Kohler fiddling with the stick grenade. The Bavarian was only bluffing but . . . ah *merde*, he had a reputation for doing just such things! 'She was not so young as thought at first. She was well dressed—that is to say, the overcoat, scarf and hat were of good quality. Not overly expensive, but good. Pre-war. Leather gloves also. Dark blue.'

'Eyeglasses?' asked St-Cyr.

'Yes.'

'Age?'

'Perhaps fifty, perhaps a little more.'

'Try sixty?'

'If you wish.'

'Now tell us about the hat?'

'Felt, grey-blue with a feather. The brim not so wide as the hat you have left out in the rain.'

'My hat? Ah *maudit!*'

St-Cyr looked out at the rain, then ignored the loss. He'd find the hat later. 'Before the robbery she was seen watching the one who is now in the tower, Préfet. Was she seen following her after the getaway?'

'Yes, but before this she approached the girl two or three times, always from behind. The woman was very nervous and seemed to have recognized the girl but they didn't speak. It's felt she was about to warn the girl of something but . . . but then couldn't bring herself to do so.'

'Good!' breathed St-Cyr. 'Then what?'

'The girl hurried east along the rue Quatre Septembre. The woman hesitated and then followed. They turned south on the rue de Richelieu and went into the Bibliothèque Nationale. Only the woman came out and was seen trying to find where the other one had gone. The woman then went south and entered the garden of the Palais Royal and walked along the west arcade.'

Past the shop of the engravers . . .'And her name, Préfet? Come, come, let us in on it.'

The moment must be savoured. 'That we do not know. My informants . . .'

'Are excellent, Préfet. Péguy was most certainly not the only one, nor the best of them.'

'Péguy . . . Ah yes, Jean-Louis, that is a little matter you and I will have to settle another time.'

'Of course.'

'Louis, I'm going to arm this toy for him. Why not get out and ask him again. Hey, I'll meet you after the bang.'

St-Cyr got stiffly out of the car to stand in the rain and wait for the préfet to roll down his side window. 'The name?' he asked. He would not beg, though everything in him said to.

Talbotte shrugged. 'Find out and then we will deal with it, eh? *Us*, Jean-Louis, not you.'

'Don't be so miserable. It's just possible the credit will come to you, so why worry?'

'Why? Because, *mon fin* from the Sûreté, that particular *mouchard* was not nearly as good as Péguy.'

*   *   *

Daylight had come, and with it, solid curtains of rain which screened the open ends of the barn, filling the place with their unnerving sound. Louis was grim. Hands jammed into the pockets of an overcoat that was drenched and cold, he watched impatiently as the *flics* from Provins emptied the contents of the lorries and stacked the furniture. A harpsichord, a gorgeous but fragile piece, had inadvertently lost a leg and every time the instrument was banged against something, the poor Frog would leap.

One by one the paintings and bits of sculpture were carried out and held before him but he would only nod gruffly, after which they were taken away and stacked.

Kohler went through every drawer and chest but couldn't find the negatives and prints of the photos that had been taken in the Paris house. Worried that they had been destroyed, he searched all the harder but to no avail, then stood beside Louis sharing a last cigarette.

'All of the paintings and sculptures Mademoiselle Desthieux told us of are missing, Hermann, the tapestries and carpets also. Either Monsieur Vergès senior sold them some time ago to pay for the care of his son, or they were stolen and we will now find them offered for sale at the Jeu de Paume.'

'Why would he have kept the house in Paris during the twenties and thirties?'

'To escape the farm and the responsibility. To conduct business, to remember, perhaps, the good times they had once had there. Ah, who knows the reasons behind such things? That house, Hermann, has been in the family for generations.'

'Angèlique Desthieux and Luc Tonnerre must have had the use of it prior to 3 July 1916.'

'Those photos of her in the buff . . . yes. Tonnerre must have had a key of his own, and our mannequin was not so saintly as either she or some of her other photographs would suggest.'

'That key was then used after the Defeat of 1940.'

'Unoccupied, the house was perfect,' said St-Cyr sadly.

'We'll have to find Tonnerre and quickly.'

'Those two droolers couldn't have come and gone between here and Paris without *laissez-passers*, Hermann.'

'They couldn't have robbed that bank.'

'No, of course not, since their faces would have been seen, but is it possible, perhaps, that Madame Lemaire's maid saw Luc Tonnerre in the attic of that house?'

'Waiting for the photos to be taken downstairs,' said Kohler. 'Did Tonnerre and Vergès hire the photographer and that woman to help them?'

'Perhaps, but . . .'

At a shout, they were forced to run through the rain to the kitchen of the main house where the former help had been brought from their homes and assembled. A cook, a house-keeper, a gardener and caretaker, all were greatly distressed and very afraid.

St-Cyr took off his soaking hat and let it drain over the clut-tered sink. Kohler emptied his shoes and squeezed the turn-ups of his trousers, then dragged off his overcoat and draped it over the back of a chair. He, too, drained his hat.

The préfet of Provins had been instructed to report to Talbotte on the interviews, but was now told to leave. 'We will call you when we need you,' said Louis. 'Let these good people speak freely, Préfet. None of them were responsible.'

It was only in bits and pieces that the truth came out. Mon-sieur Vergès senior had died in the fall of 1939 and from then on things had deteriorated rapidly. 'Occasionally, at first, Monsieur Gaetan's friend would come by car from Paris,' said the care-taker, ducking his ancient head and clutching his black beret in deference. 'They would "talk", Inspector, in the only way such as they can talk. Very serious, always close. The walks, the fishing, the ether at night—yes, both took it, and the friend brought it in two-litre bottles—three or four of them, sometimes more. The cognac *aussi*, of course. Five or six bottles at a time.'

'Then the withdrawal,' hissed the cook, a wasp of a woman, thin and tall and nearly seventy. 'That one,' she spat. 'He would drive away and leave Monsieur Gaetan without another drop to tide him over. We could not buy ether—how could such as we have done such a thing? The brandy of course. Oh *bien sûr* a little cognac, no matter how rough. But the ether, ah no. Doctor Audet was against it. The liver, the kidneys . . .' Her hard, little eyes said, You can see how it was. Do you need us to say it?

'Without it, Monsieur Gaetan, he . . . he would slip into despair,' said the housekeeper, who had obviously known the son since his birth. Her tears were constant and silent, and she had remained a little detached from the others as had been her station in life.

'But he didn't go on periodic rampages through the house until when?' asked St-Cyr gently.

'Until just after the Defeat, monsieur,' grumbled the gardener. 'Until after he had *dismissed* us in July of 1940. We who have always been so kind to him and have never avoided his gaze or turned away from that face of his!'

Florid, pug-nosed and pockmarked, the man was quivering with indignation.

'Was the dismissal after a visit from his friend?' asked Louis.

They glanced at each other. The cook said, 'Yes!'

'*Bon*, that, fits,' said St-Cyr, wishing he had tobacco with which to stoke the empty furnace he had taken from a pocket. 'But there is a small problem. Since the Defeat, cars are no longer common. Did Luc Tonnerre still drive his?'

Again they glanced at each other as only country people can, swift with alarm and hidden meaning. Each shrugged in his or her own way.

'Come, come,' urged St-Cyr. 'We haven't all day and must return to Paris.'

'Always since the Defeat, he . . . he has walked in from the main road, Inspector,' confessed the gardener. 'He has come alone but without the ether or cognac.'

The detectives waited for more. At last the cook could stand their silence no longer and said, 'But I have heard a car passing my house, Inspectors.'

They were both startled, and that was good, she said to herself.

'When exactly did you hear this car?' asked St-Cyr cautiously.

Was it too much to hope for a little break, a smile from God perhaps?

Shrewdly the woman tasted the triumph of her little success. 'Late at night— 1.30 or 2.00 the old time. In the beginning, early in October 1940, within the first week.'

'It has come and gone every once in a while for these past two years, Inspector,' acknowledged the caretaker. 'Always late at night, always leaving well before dawn. A big car with a powerful engine and the lights blinkered for the black-out.'

Had the caretaker been out illegally trapping rabbits? wondered Kohler, and thought he had. 'How many in the car?' he asked. 'Come on, don't clam up now. I'll only have to run you in . . .'

'Hermann, *please*! A simple walk in the night doesn't mean hunting with a ferret and the pâté or stew at morning! How many in the car, monsieur?'

Both detectives were looking intently at him. Would they understand how difficult it had been to even see the car? 'I . . . I can't say for certain, Inspectors, but think there must have been more than one person.'

It was the gardener who said there had been smoke coming from the house at dawn. 'At first I thought Monsieur Gaetan was burning old tyres but as this is now forbidden because of the shortages, I . . . I found the smoke did not smell of burning rubber.'

'Thick and black and full of soot?' bleated the Sûreté. 'When . . . ? What day, what month?'

Again they looked at each other swiftly. There was hesitation, a curt nod from the cook to the gardener, a 'Tell them, Monsieur Romand. You must.'

'Always at dawn the last of a fire that must have begun some time before. First seen in the fall of 1940, in late November, Inspectors, then . . . then in mid-March of this year and . . . and again in September, on . . . on the morning of the 12th.'

'Three times, Hermann.'

Boemelburg had given them photos of eight of the victims' bodies. Joanne made nine and now . . . another three?

Next to the stove there were brick ovens with sheet-iron tops that, in the earliest years, had been used to do the cooking. Louis opened the nearest firebox door to a spill of wood ashes and fragments of bone.

'Part of a femur, Hermann. Part of a tibia ...' He crouched and peered into the firebox and lifted the lantern close. 'Also a piece of a pelvis ... some ribs—these have been sawn. A jaw, fragments of a skull, some teeth.'

They were enough. 'We only need two more, Louis, and we'll have accounted for all fourteen of them.'

8 PARIS IN THE RAIN AND SLUSH WAS MISERABLE, thought St-Cyr, the rue des Saussaies silent and unfriendly. Boemelburg was not pleased to see them. Rain poured down the windows that overlooked the court-yard where their car was parked. The Chief studied the gobs of slush that accompanied the rush of water while Hermann and he, like two errant schoolboys in steaming overcoats and shoes, sat uncomfortably in front of the antique limewood desk to which the bare planks of expediency and enlargement had been thoroughly nailed the day Boemelburg had taken over the office.

'Kempf, Louis,' breathed the Chief as he studied yet another gob of slush. 'The Sonderführer comes from a very old and wealthy family—Prussian to the core, you idiots. He's a cousin of the Reichsführer Goering or were you unaware of this?'

Ah *nom de Jésus-Christ*, a cousin! 'Walter, over the past two years . . .'

Boemelburg didn't turn from studying the weather. He would be very formal with these two. 'Don't interrupt me, Chief Inspector St-Cyr, and please don't assume a familiarity you shouldn't just because we once worked together in the old days.'

'Sturmbannführer, there were . . .'

'Louis, we were speaking French. Please let us continue. Your German may be excellent and admirable but my secretaries have ears, or hadn't you noticed?'

Irritably a hand was passed over the all-but-shaven grey and bristly dome. 'Kohler, use your brains and close the door. This is serious.

'Kempf . . .' he went on without turning from the rain. 'How could you have asked the Sonderführer and his friend, this . . . this French newspaperman, to file daily itineraries with my office each morning at 0700 hours?'

Hermann made the mistake of grinning and said, 'I thought it a good idea at the time, Sturmbann . . .'

'You *thought* it a *good* idea but you didn't consult me? Me who has the power to send you to join your sons? Ah *Gott im Himmel, dummkopf*, Kempf's wife . . .'

'She's dead, Sturmbann . . .'

A fist was clenched, the weather outside forgotten, the voice like steel. 'Dead or alive it makes no difference. Kempf's wife was once a favourite of the Reichsführer.'

Shit! 'When the Sonderführer showed up at 0700 hours with his little bit of paper and his grin, Hermann, I called Gestapo Leader Mueller for some background. Since we're old friends, Mueller very kindly filled me in and asked me to consider the Russian Front for you and Louis.'

In these overcoats and shoes? wondered St-Cyr ruefully. Must God always frown on a poor but honest and hard-working detective?

Kohler saw Louis idly fiddle with a button that had come loose. He heard Boemelburg quietly saying, 'This had better be good. A bank was robbed. The Resistance may be involved. The murders of those girls, no matter how close any of them were to you, Louis, cannot intrude.'

It was now or never thought St-Cyr, and always such things were a gamble. 'The two are connected, Sturmbannführer, if only through the woman who watched the street for the robbers.'

'*Droolers!*' stormed the Chief. 'Did you not think Talbotte would come running to me? Did you have to assault—yes, assault—the préfet of Paris? *Don't* hide your hand like that!'

'Walter, may I remind you that over the past two years fourteen girls have been taken from their simple lives, brutally assaulted, mutilated and ruthlessly murdered!'

Boemelburg placed both hands on his desk among the mounds of papers. 'And what do you want me to do about it? Let the two of you make a fool out of me?'

He sat down heavily. Everyone knew the word was out that he was to be retired soon, that he was becoming *forgetful*, and that in a policeman, a former detective and Head of the Gestapo in France, such a thing could not be tolerated.

But Walter was far from forgetful. 'Kempf and le Blanc exactly fit the descriptions of the robbers, Sturmbannführer,' said St-Cyr. 'Forged papers were made out using assumed names but bearing their photographs.'

'Have you seen them?'

'No, not yet but . . .'

'But, *what*, Louis?'

'But the boy who made the papers gave Hermann their descriptions and we have no reason to doubt his word.'

'Then bring the boy to this office and let me hear what he has to say before we put him up against a wall and shoot him.'

'He's already dead, Sturmbannführer,' interjected Kohler. 'Someone called the anti-Jewish squad and they nailed the son of a bitch and his lousy father.'

'*Good!* No forged papers, no proof. Only the word of one who could well have been lying to put you off.'

'And if we can produce the papers, Sturmbannführer?' asked St-Cyr quietly.

'Then I'll agree to study them but will reserve my decision on the matter until I've consulted Berlin.'

Dédé was standing in the rain getting drenched. The peaked hat, with its big earlugs, let the water pour off into the upturned collar of the heavy, grey, herringbone overcoat that didn't fit too well and had been handed down several times.

He wore no gloves or overboots, just watched as the Citroën came slowly to a stop on the rue Laurence-Savart. A side window was rolled down. 'Dédé . . .'

The boy's expression was grave. 'Monsieur the Chief Inspector, I have a message for you. A *vélo-taxi* came to deliver it from a shop on the place Vendôme. Two ladies, I believe.'

'Old friends, yes.' He took the hurriedly passed envelope. 'Dédé, the news isn't good.'

'Not good?'

Ah damn it! The hollow eyes, that gaunt look of despair . . . 'No, not good. Joanne is dead. I'm sorry. My partner and I, we . . . we were too late.'

'Too late.'

It's . . . It's one of those things, Dédé. We hoped, we prayed, we tried hard to find her but . . .' St-Cyr held him by the lapel lest he run away. 'But we were still on the train from Lyon when it was done.'

'How?'

Why must God do this to him? Why? 'By the rope. By strangulation. Joanne, she has . . .'

'Died quickly, Monsieur the Chief Inspector? Is that how it was?'

'Don't hate me for failing you. Joanne, she has left us two very important clues and with these we will soon find her killers and bring them to justice.'

'Clues . . . ?' asked the boy desperately.

'An ear-ring and a hair. We have also established that an older woman watched her in the rue Quatre Septembre and then followed her but lost her in the Bibliothèque Nationale because Joanne was far too clever for her.'

'A spy?'

'Ah, no. A woman who wanted to warn your sister of the danger but couldn't find the courage to do so.'

'Then she's as guilty as are the killers!'

'Yes, every bit as guilty.'

The boy didn't run home with the news. Shoving his hands deeply into the pockets of his overcoat, he trudged up the street, pausing often to look back at that great big beautiful black car. 'Ah *merde*, Hermann, could I not have told him more gently?'

'Go and get changed. I'll see what I can do.'

'No. He needs to be left alone.' St-Cyr tore open the scented envelope and quickly read the note from Muriel. 'Luc Tonnerre, Hermann. In the early thirties he handled the jewellery some of his confrères in *les baveux* made for a living. Among the pieces were those whose motif was that of ancient Egypt. These pieces were exceptional and of eighteen carat gold and very expensive, but they came on the market too late and found few buyers.'

Luc Tonnerre had not made things easy for them. Ruefully St-Cyr sat in the car and stared at the entrance to number 48. Like so many others in the maze of narrow, Louis-Philippe *passages* just to the north of the boulevard Bonne-Nouvelle, this one had an iron-and-dimpled-glass fanlight above a heavy stone lintel, and an open slot of a doorway no wider than two wheelbarrows.

Rain screened the far end of the cluttered *passage*, a trap if ever there was one. Plugged drains created innumerable lakes. A broken downpipe gushed a torrent half-way across the lane. 'Ah *nom de Jésus-Christ*, Hermann, number 48 F(e) will be at the very back. Will he be watching for us?'

Ateliers faced on to the *passage*. A bookbinder's, a bootmaker's— these could barely be discerned from their ancient signboards. A plumber who would be hard pressed to find lead pipe and solder these days and would just have to make do. 'There are lots of doorways, Hermann. Perhaps if God is willing we can pick our way along unnoticed.'

Louis didn't sound convinced. They started out, the rain came down. Dinner-jackets that should remain dry beneath trench coats began to feel umbrella douches. Polished black shoes were quickly filling. 'Son of a bitch!' grumbled Kohler, fingering the Walther P38 in his pocket. 'We're dead men if he sees us!'

Dodging puddles and leap-frogging from doorway to doorway, they advanced quickly up the *passage*. The lace curtains were tattered, the flat on the second floor. Geranium pots relieved themselves through the holes in their bottoms. A dilapidated lean-to covered the entrance. Three steps led up to a cramped landing, then there were more of them off to the right.

Umbrellas clutched and pouring their streams onto the worn linoleum, they rushed the stairs, barged through the main door, passed a ragged hole in the plaster—just a hole in the wall, a window . . . The concierge's *loge*! 'Messieurs . . .'

'*Christ!*' leapt Kohler. 'Don't do that!'

'Tonnerre, monsieur, and quickly!' hissed St-Cyr. 'The key, idiot. Is he in?'

'In?' bleated the man, quivering. 'Yes. Yes, that one is in and has been for the past few days.'

Reluctantly he gave them the key, refusing to meet their eyes. 'Drunk,' he said. 'Noisy as usual and then the silence. Let him sleep it off.'

'Drunk since when, exactly?' asked the Sûreté cautiously.

'Since Monday late.'

'It's now Thursday afternoon.'

'I haven't disturbed him.'

'*Verdammt*, Louis!' Kohler snatched the key and took the stairs two at a time. The flat was nothing much. Two dingy rooms, one of which was used both as kitchen and bedroom . . .

Fully clothed and still in his overcoat and scarf as if he had just come back from the Château des belles fleurs bleues, Tonnerre lay on his back on the soiled bedspread with his head propped by pillows that long ago had lost their slips.

Above him, strapped to the peeling iron headboard by a dirty band of heavy elastic, was an empty two-litre bottle of ether.

A worn, red rubber tube led from this as a siphon to dangle its end just above his left shoulder. There was a stopcock, a thing of metal that had pinched off the flow. An empty bottle and a closed stopcock . . . Closed?

'*Maudit*, let's open the windows!'

'Ah *nom de Dieu*, Hermann, are we to think he killed Joanne, then his friend and then himself?'

'It's too easy. It isn't right. Why fake the suicide of another if you intend to kill yourself?'

'Why close the stopcock when the bottle is empty?'

Caught by the rapidly expanding cloud of shrapnel, Tonnerre had not been blinded in one eye like his friend but had, through some whim of Chance, lost both ears, part of his cheeks and nose, the lips and lower jaw and, probably, most of his tongue.

'Two litres, Hermann. It's a lot if one is not accustomed to it and has found it hard to come by of late.'

'So why is the stopcock closed, *mien lieber* Sûreté? If he passed out with that much in him, how the hell could he have closed it and why?'

'Precisely,' breathed St-Cyr. Both hands would have been needed. Ether, like alcohol, could be consumed in quantity by the confirmed addict. Highly inflammable and volatile, it evaporated rapidly. Like alcohol, it, too, left little or no stain but would dissolve grease and was, indeed, used as an industrial solvent. 'The pillows, Hermann. To the left of the head. A faint line of grease from the hair. The pomade of too little washing, dissolved quite recently and then redeposited on evaporation.'

St-Cyr traced the line out but Hermann was looking decidedly green. 'Ah *merde*, go into the other room, idiot! Leave me with him.'

Kohler fled saying, 'I'm going to talk to that concierge, Louis. I've got to get a breath of air!'

The door slammed. St-Cyr heard him hesitate in the corridor and knew he was leaning against a wall trying to still the panic. 'It's been happening too much of late,' he said gravely to himself. 'He desperately needs to get away from this business for a while.'

But could they ever do so? They were practically the only flying squad left in the Kripo and the Paris Sûreté, the only ones to handle things such as this. Common crime.

Tonnerre's hands were badly scarred but showed no signs of rope marks, of having strangled Joanne. None at all.

Both the index and the middle finger of the right hand were missing—lost to the shrapnel. In that instant of destruction, he had tried to shield his face. Had he groped for the friend he had deceived, the friend to whom he had given nude photos of his lover and written: *This is how she was and what she was really like*—Angèlique Desthieux, the mannequin they had each wanted in their own way, so much so, that this one had thrown acid into her face.

She had had a child by him. Marie-Claire de Brisson.

Wine, cognac and ether . . . Soup — endless soup and humiliation. The scorn and laughter of ordinary people who ought to have known better. Their turning away in horror. Had the daughter known of him? Had she ever seen and spoken to him?

They would have to find out.

St-Cyr let his eyes search for details and asked softly with a sigh, 'But if the right hand is disabled, monsieur, why should the tubing not hang to the right of you so that your left hand might better operate the stopcock? Is this why some of the ether has spilled on the pillows? The remaining fingers of your right hand, were they not too clumsy, the mind deadened and long past any feeling of well-being?'

And in any case, why close the stopcock on an empty bottle? No, it was not right.

Caught in the black bristles of poorly clipped whiskers that could never be properly shaven, were tiny, short white cotton fibres. 'A pad . . . Ah *grâce à Dieu*, that is why the spill of ether. That is why the stopcock is tightly closed.'

When he heard the door open, he called out, 'It's murder, Hermann, but like everything else about this case, things are not quite as perfect as they should have been.'

From four to five per cent of ether in air was required for anaesthesia, about 100 to 140 milligrams per 100 cubic centimetres of blood—far more of it than of chloroform. Perhaps four times as much. 160 to 170 milligrams of ether per 100 cubic centimetres of blood would cause respiration to cease. The victim would never know.

'He hasn't struggled, Hermann. He came in, lay down here and got dead drunk, but if allowed to, would have slept it off.'

'Whoever held that pad over his face knew exactly how much to use. Lots!'

'Did the concierge say this one had had a visitor?'

'No. He said there's a back door to the house and another *passage* leading to it!'

'The visitor had come and gone. If they themselves could obtain the address from the association of *les baveux*, so could someone else. There'd been several changes of address over the years, nothing out of the ordinary for a badly disabled veteran, to the shame of the nation. Furniture and things that had been acquired before the Great War had had to be sold off bit by bit.

There were only a few changes of clothing, a few framed photographs—none of Angèlique Desthieux. A camera that had been smashed long ago lay in pieces in a cardboard box as if kept in hopes of repairs and to remind him of the past.

'Torn-up prints, Louis, of her in the buff,' breathed Kohler crouching over the box. 'Negatives of her playing around in that house. Every piece of furniture that was used in the later photos, a few of the same poses but none of the clothes or the jewellery since those came later.'

'And none of the more recent photos?'

'None. If he was in on it, Louis, why hasn't he got them? Why hasn't he been leering over them in his quiet moments between girls?'

Why indeed.

A well-thumbed passbook was fixed with a drawing-pin to the back of a bureau drawer. 'Crédit Lyonnais, Hermann. Within easy walking distance, as is the Palais Royal. Pension cheques, the disabled veteran's allowance.'

'Then why hide it?'

There was a grim nod of agreement. 'Payments of from 3000 to 5000 francs from time to time.'

Kohler took the proffered passbook and, quickly glancing through it, frowned. 'Tonnerre drove a car to the farm before the Defeat but he couldn't have had the money even then and must have had to borrow one.'

'But from whom?'

Kohler indicated the passbook. 'This thing only goes back to January 1939. We'll have to ask the bank to give us the records. We'll put it to Monsieur André-Philippe de Brisson that we absolutely have to know.'

'Try last May,' hazarded St-Cyr. 'It's just a hunch.'

'The 6th, Louis. The day the body of that girl who had the acid dumped on her was found. The day after . . .'

'After Marie-Claire de Brison last tried to kill herself, Hermann, and Denise St. Onge rescued her.'

'A deposit of 5000 francs. Wednesday 6 May 1942.'

'Now let's see if we can connect the deposits with any of the other girls.'

Try as they did, there was no apparent connection. Sometimes only a month would pass between deposits, sometimes two or even three months and once, only a matter of a week. '3000 francs both times,' breathed Kohler.

Tonnerre had obviously been getting money from someone but it had all started well before the kidnappings and the killings, before the Defeat.

'Gaetan Vergès?' asked Hermann.

'Or Madame de Brisson, our woman in the street?'

There was no sign of the jewellery Tonnerre had once tried to sell for his friends and fellow droolers. No list of clients, no bills of sale. Nothing, not even a photograph. 'Denise St. Onge could just as easily have gone straight to the source,' offered Kohler, 'but if so, then did this one tell her of it?'

'Things of elegance and refinement for the shop, Hermann, because to forget is to survive.'

'And the boss knows exactly what she wants.'

At 3.37 p.m. it was early yet for a woman of substance to view paintings at the Jeu de Paume. Denise St. Onge was not puzzled or particularly alarmed by the visit of two detectives to her flat on the boulevard de Beauséjour. She was simply bemused. The thick, dark brown hair that had been cut and waved was worn without pins or parting and a trifle impudently. The angular face that was quite beautiful was cocked to one side as she looked quizzically at them.

She was sitting in one of the deep, soft cream armchairs of her salon that overlooked the Bois de Boulogne, had drawn up her long, black-stockinged legs, her gorgeous legs, and had wrapped her arms about them. The black silk gloves extended well above her elbows, the dress, of black silk, was bare at the shoulders and neck and held by two thin and fragile-looking spaghetti straps.

There was a lace-fringed slip around splendid thighs. There were black briefs and garters—she wanted to be disconcerting. Again St-Cyr swept his eyes over those long legs, again the black, high-heeled shoes and the lower part of the dress, a very fine crêpe de Chine that, in this light, had a silvery look to it.

A gold necklace of thin, triangular plaques held turquoise scarabs. There were small gold ear-rings to match. A bracelet too.

A very beautiful and self-possessed woman of twenty-seven years of age, now pouting with indecision.

At last she said, 'Inspectors, what you ask is confidential. Marie-Claire is both valued friend and employee. She couldn't possibly have known who her natural father was. Those things are kept secret, aren't they, with the nuns, the Mother Superior . . . ?'

'Yes, quite secret,' said St-Cyr. 'It was just a thought, mademoiselle. In cases such as this, all avenues must be explored.'

'But this . . this Monsieur Tonnerre couldn't possibly have had anything to do with the robbery of her father's bank?'

'That's a question we have to settle,' went on Louis gravely. 'You see, mademoiselle, a young girl was kidnapped at the same time. My partner and I are, unfortunately, faced with the two problems.'

'Eighteen million and the disappearance of a girl . . . ? How old, please?'

'Eighteen. One million, mademoiselle, for every year of her life.'

'But . . . but you haven't found her? She . . . she's not dead, is she?'

The knees were hugged. Louis tossed his head back and shrugged. 'The matter is still in God's hands but we're working on it.'

They fell to silence, the two of them. The Bavarian, who had come to see her previously, had the better view of her legs and could see more deeply up them when he wanted, which was constantly. A bold man, one bent on unsettling her. The one from the Sûreté had hit his hand rather badly—in a fight? she wondered. The skin over the knuckles was tight and swollen, the hue decidedly yellow but red also and throbbing still. He really did look tough, and wasn't that a gun bulging beneath his dinner-jacket?

'Mademoiselle de Brisson . . .' began the Sûreté as if still in doubt as to how best to proceed, 'could your friend have told anyone about the shipment of such a large sum to the bank of her father?'

She would swing her legs out and, putting her elbows on her knees, rest her chin in her hands and look at them both but only for a moment. 'Marie-Claire . . . ? Ah! you can't know her. She hardly speaks to her father, Inspectors. They're estranged. Oh *bien sûr*, she lives above their house. It's because of the rent. The bank pays for the house so the rent, it is modest.'

'Someone learned of that shipment, mademoiselle,' said Louis.

'Someone who knew that car you borrow would be ready and waiting,' said the one called Kohler, reminding her of his previous visit when he had most emphatically said the same thing.

'Marie-Claire wouldn't have told anyone of that shipment, Inspectors. She would simply not have known of it. Her father isn't one to reveal such confidential information.'

'Ah, the father,' said St-Cyr. 'Is it that you know him well, mademoiselle?'

Was this how it was to be between them? she wondered. The one asking and then the other, both keeping up the pressure? 'Not well,' she said of de Brisson. Had the one called St-Cyr the eyes of a priest?

'Where were you when the robbery took place?' asked Kohler. The Bavarian had started to look around the salon, letting his eyes drift from her body. 'Me? I was in the back of the shop with . . . with Marie-Claire, of course. A conference. She wanted to discuss several things.'

'Such as?' asked St-Cyr quietly.

'The lingerie, the lipstick, the perfumes—we don't make our own, Inspector, but a shop I know of on place Vendôme, it . . . it has such a marvellous scent. *Très dangereux*, isn't that correct?'

'Mirage,' he acknowledged, curtly nodding at her. 'What else did you discuss?'

Would he ask Marie-Claire ·the same question? *Had* he already done so? she wondered. If so, then perhaps he had already discovered that she hadn't been in the shop at all.

'Why, what else but little things?', she said, giving him a delicate and very shy shrug. 'The girls and their problems—they do get jealous of one another from time to time, Inspector. The need for us to use better mannequins, the . . .'

'The jewellery in the window, mademoiselle?'

'Ah yes, the jewellery. Tonnerre . . . is this what you think? That he has supplied the shop? If so, you are mistaken. Marie-Claire is always searching for things that please me, Inspector. The jewellery suits—you can see I have an interest in such things.'

A slender arm indicated the scattered bibelots, gold signets with hieroglyphs, clay tablets, bits of pottery, bits of gold, silver and bronze.

'They're lovely,' he said, 'as is the necklace you're wearing. Mannequins?' he asked suddenly.

The girl . . . how much did they know? she worried and found the will to say, 'Yes, but we don't use them so much, Inspector. For the time being, we've decided to set the question aside.'

The Bavarian got up suddenly and she saw him pass before her without a downward glance. He went over to the small round table, the one with the scattering of things picked up in the bazaars of Cairo and Alexandria in the summer of 1936. He searched, he paused, he picked up and put down, and at last he asked, 'Could I use the toilet? I need to drain the battery. All this rain . . .' He grinned as a schoolboy would but it was not a nice grin.

'Yes, of course. Jeanne is in the kitchen and will show you where it is.' Were the maid and he old friends? she wondered apprehensively. Had he spoken to Jeanne in the street that time before . . . ?

'Mademoiselle St. Onge,' began Louis, 'your relationship to the Sonderführer Kempf, please?'

'Is he suspected of anything, of this . . . this robbery, this girl . . . ?'

'The girl. Yes, yes,' said St-Cyr as if reminded of it and dis-missing totally any question of Kempf. 'The poor thing suspected nothing, mademoiselle. An advertisement in *Le Matin*. A call for mannequins. No experience necessary. Here . . . here, I have it on me somewhere. May I?' he asked indicating the coffee table between them.

'*Mais certainement,*' she said and saw him quickly begin to empty his pockets. An invitation to the Jeu de Paume just like the one on her mantelpiece . . . a small pencil sketch of the . . . the girl. Was it really her—where had he got it? *Where?* A square pad of cotton—*cotton!* A card announcing the engagement of . . .

'Angèlique Desthieux and Captain Gaetan Vergès, mademoi-selle,' he said, looking at her with those priest's eyes of his! Ah *Jésus, cher Jésus,* how much did they know of this affair and why was he trying to single her out and hold her here while the other one, he . . . he went through the things in her bedroom? *Is this what he was doing,* the one from the Gestapo?

A cancelled ticket for the Métro, a . . .

'Ah, at last,' he said. 'You must pardon me, mademoiselle. I'm not used to a dinner-jacket and find, alas, that its pockets are not as accommodating as those of my suit.'

St-Cyr unfolded the torn little square of newspaper and, glancing over it to give her time to worry, finally handed it to her. 'This is the advertisement, mademoiselle. We've obtained photo-graphs of the girl. Apparently she was asked to pose and to wear certain things.'

'Photographs . . . ?'

Was it such a devastating revelation, so utterly unexpected? 'Yes. Scattered all over the floors of an empty house.'

Sickened, she tried to tell herself he was only bluffing but she couldn't stop herself from trembling and this, why it shook the scrap of newspaper, telegraphing its little message to him. '*Photographs . . . ?*' She blanched. 'Of what, exactly?'

It would only unsettle her more if he were to raise his eye-brows and shrug, so he would do so and claim the matter of little consequence. 'Of this one and other girls modelling clothes as

I've only just said, mademoiselle—jewellery like you have in the window of your shop.'

'Girls . . . ? Jewellery . . . ? My shop . . . ?'

The deep brown eyes had rapidly moistened, the lovely red lips that had pouted only a few moments ago, now quivered.

'Fourteen young girls, Mademoiselle St. Onge, all of whom were photographed in exactly the same poses and wearing the same things—things we believe came from your shop. The jewellery . . .'

'Marie-Claire . . . *She* has purchased it for the shop! *She* was the one to find it. *She* has borrowed things from time to time. Dresses, skirts, blouses . . . I . . .'

'*What*, mademoiselle?'

She shook her pretty head and touched the base of her throat. 'I . . . I don't know how she could possibly be involved in such a thing. Fourteen girls . . . ? So many? What . . . what has become of them, Inspector? Lured by this . . . this advertisement to some house. *What* house, please?'

Anger reddened her cheeks, sharpening the features.

'For now the location of the house can't be divulged, mademoiselle, but you can be certain someone scattered photographs of all of those girls.'

All of them . . . 'I don't know anything of this! How *could* I?'

'That's exactly what my partner and I would like to know.'

She dropped her eyes to the scrap of newspaper in her lap and read it silently.

Wanted by a noted fashion house, girls of suitable ability . . . Hair of chestnut brown, eyes of the same . . .

'My hair, my eyes,' she said, desperate now.

'And your ear-ring, I believe,' breathed Kohler, dangling the thing in front of her face.

'You . . . you had no right to . . .'

'We have every right. Where's the other one?' he demanded.

Furious with them, she raised a dismissive hand, tossed her head and all but shouted, 'How could I know? One loses things like that all the time!'

'Louis, do we take her in and lock her up?'

'The other ear-ring, Mademoiselle St. Onge, where might you have lost it, please?'

'*I don't know!*'

'Hermann, could I see this one, please?' St-Cyr took the trinket and held it to the light, then found his reading glasses and put them on. 'The same,' he sighed, the sadness all too clear. 'Joanne,' he said. 'The last one was very brave, mademoiselle.'

As he unfolded a clean white handkerchief, stains of blood appeared against the cloth and dried little crumbs of it fell to the table to lie on the notice of engagement and others on the invitation to the Jeu de Paume and afterwards the supper at the Ritz.

There was blood on the tiny scarab of turquoise that dangled by its thread of gold to match those that were around her neck and wrist. 'Inspectors, I . . . I know that is mine—*yes!*' she cried and hugged her knees to bury her face in them. 'But . . . but I *don't* know where I lost it.'

They stood over her, these two detectives. She could feel their eyes on the back of her neck and shoulders . . . Ah *merde . . . merde*, what was happening to her?

'Hermann, see that she accompanies us to the Jeu de Paume.'

'*Like this?*' she cried out, looking up at them in tears. '*How* could I?'

'Because you must,' said St-Cyr. 'Because perhaps to save yourself, we may have need of you.'

'I *didn't* do it!'

'But you knew of it, mademoiselle, and for us, that is enough.'

'He . . . he made me.'

'Who?'

'No one. *No one!* I . . . I shouldn't have said that!'

'Hermann, take her. I can't stand to look at her any more. I'm sorry.'

They both heard Louis throwing up into the kitchen sink but when he came back, he was all right. 'The paintings, Hermann, and then the supper, I think, if necessary.'

'Shall I put the bracelets on her?' The handcuffs . . .

'No. She's to appear as though free but must accompany us. We're going as her guests. Please inform her of this.'

'What about Gabrielle?'

'She'll realize that I've been detained, Hermann—police work, always the work—and will meet us there.'

The Jeu de Paume had once been a place for court tennis. Occupying the north-western corner of the Tuileries Gardens, it had, before the Defeat of 1940, housed contemporary works by foreign artists. Now it had become a legend that even the long arch of its glassed-in iron roof, blued with black-out paint, could not hide.

In gallery after gallery there were oil paintings, charcoal sketches and watercolours in gilded, richly carved frames, superb pieces of sculpture, altar cloths, Gobelin tapestries, Savonnerie carpets, displays of estate jewellery and silver, diamonds, topazes, emeralds and rubies, porcelain and crystal.

Everywhere there was the glitter, the animated gestures and loud talk of well-dressed men with fashionable women, old, young, the not-so-young, everywhere the smart uniforms and medals of the Occupier.

It was as if all the boredom of winter, the Occupation and the war had been set aside and everyone who was anyone in Paris was desperate for a good time. Old friends met, new ones were made. Lovers kissed and held hands or sipped the free champagne and smoked cigarettes in ivory or ebony-and-silver holders or chose from trays of *canapés* to loud exclamations, lots of laughter, the delighted oohs and ahs of dumbfounded browsers who had come for the gossip, the excitement, the fun, the titilation and the food, of course. *Canapés au caviar*—little rounds of unsweetened brioche toasted a golden brown, spread with caviar butter and heaped in the centre with black caviar sprinkled with chives. *Paupiettes d'anchois Monselet*—scrolled anchovies stuffed with the yolks of hard-boiled eggs on small rounds of toast, covered with anchovy butter. Shrimp, herring and smoked eel with mustard butter . . . pâtés, fresh oysters in the half-shell, *bouchées* . . . puff pastry stuffed with a paste of smoked, Norwegian salmon. Ah *nom de Dieu*! the flavour . . . To refuse such temptations, the price of honour, but one must. The city was starving!

Everywhere there were the dealers, dour and serious, smug and secure in their assessment and mentally tallying their profits. Belgians, Dutch, French—yes, of course! thought St-Cyr angrily—Swiss and Norwegians—Italians. From all over Axis Europe they had flocked to haggle, to buy and cart home the plundered treasures of France, or to sell.

Dismayed—taken aback by the wealth of art that had been assembled—he clutched Denise St. Onge all the harder by the left arm and felt an utter fool, utterly helpless.

Never in his wildest imagination had he believed the theft so great, the rape so deep. 'It's the sale of the century, Hermann,' he said, his voice but a desperate whisper.

'The Einsatzstab-Reichleiter Rosenberg, Louis, with offices at 54 avenue d'Iéna and warehouses wherever they need them. The whole of the Leviton department store in the Faubourg Saint-Martin is being used as a storehouse!'

There were stacks of paintings in addition to those that hung on the walls, stacks of everything. Set up by Hitler primarily to acquire works of art for the Linz Project, his pet dream of creating the world's leading art museum on the banks of the Danube, the ERR handled mostly confiscated works of art. Jews, Freemasons, Communists and other political undesirables, all had to forfeit everything. So, too, uncooperative businessmen, industrialists, private collectors and dealers who refused to sell when they should or who had not listed all their valuables as required by law.

Goering bought in bulk by the railway truckload, traded avidly, selling what he didn't want for Karinhall, his huge country estate just to the north of Berlin. Others bought for the institutes of higher learning in the Reich and for its museums and galleries. Still others bought for themselves or sold, and always the dealers, anxious to burn up the grossly inflated new francs of the Occupation, bought so as to send the money home in the form of something tangible they could then flog to one of the Nazi bigwigs at a hundred per cent profit or more.

'Rembrandt, Goya, Frans Hals and Rubens, Hermann. Not one canvas but ten or more of each.'

'Degas, Manet, Sisley, and Cézanne,' spat Denise St. Onge, desperately searching the crowd for help. 'You can't stop it! You can only join in.'

'Ah yes,' said St-Cyr. 'And isn't that what you did, mademoiselle?'

'I . . . I don't know what you mean?'

Frantically she tried to find a way out for herself. A Luftwaffe waiter, one of many, passed with a tray of champagne in tall glasses. 'The Dom Pérignon, mademoiselle, the Piper-Heidsieck or the Krug?'

She could throw it into St-Cyr's face and run. 'The Dom Pérignon, please,' she said.

'Messieurs?' asked the waiter.

Louis shook his head, Kohler said, 'It's too acid for the stomach. Beer is my drink, his is pastis and the lady isn't drinking because she would only have to visit the toilets and I would have to sit with her.'

'*Bâtard!*' she hissed. 'Franz will be here and so will the Reichs-marschall Goering who is his cousin and *mine*! Yes, mine! you fools. Franz and I are cousins.'

There were Luftwaffe guards at the entrance and at all other doors. There were Luftwaffe security officers everywhere. Hell, the Reichsmarschall's air force handled all transport for the ERR to and from the Reich, thereby ensuring total control of all sales and a first look at all items.

'A moment, *mon vieux*. *Don't* let her out of your sight. I must find the one who purchased the forged papers,' said St-Cyr.

'The forged papers . . . ?' began Mademoiselle St. Onge. 'For whom? *What* forged papers? *Who* has done such a thing?'

Kohler dragged out his bracelets and put one around her right wrist since she was right-handed and would hit first and hardest with that fist. 'Now my own,' he said. 'Hey, they look good with your gloves. Maybe the two of us will start a new fad and the next owner of your shop can put some in the window.'

'Who did he mean?' she asked, pleading with her eyes. 'Was it Marie-Claire . . . ?' She gasped and held her stomach. 'Marie for Franz and Michel . . . ah no. *No!*'

She swung hard. Kohler grabbed her by the wrist. She spat in his face and tried to knee him in the groin. He forced her left arm back and down until, in shock, disconcerted and wanting to keep their distance, the crowd around them cleared and a small space was left.

She knelt on the floor at his feet, head bowed in despair. 'Franz . . .' she blurted. *'Franz, please help me!'*

Kohler wanted to let her stay there so that everyone could see her but knew the scene would only bring trouble. 'Get up. We'll find a place for you to tidy your face, eh? and you can tell me all about it.' Louis . . . where was Louis?

Several people passed in front of St-Cyr and for a moment his view of Marie-Clarie de Brisson was obstructed, then there she was again. Nervously she jotted down a last note, only to hesitate as if not certain she had written enough. The bared breasts of the painting . . . the hat with its red flowers . . . the shoulders . . . the expression of the woman . . . was it not one of, 'He does not like what he sees of me?'

The breasts were full and round but as to why the woman in the painting was partially disrobed, ah, who was to say? 'It's lovely, isn't it?' said St-Cyr pleasantly, the man on holiday.

'You? Ah! Why . . . why are you here, Inspector?'

Was it so terrible? 'Why, to view the paintings like everyone else.'

Her green eyes darted away to the floor, to the pad and pencil in her hands, to the painting on the wall . . . the painting. 'It's what men look at,' she said sharply. 'Please excuse me!'

'A moment, mademoiselle.' Their eyes met. She trembled. 'Are you planning to bid on this one,' he asked, 'or on the other pieces for which you have made notes?'

'I . . . I was just curious. It's . . . it's a thing I often do.'

'Then you won't mind my glancing over your notes.'

She felt him tug the little notepad from her. She tried not to cry and wished he wouldn't spoil everything for her. *Everything!*

The golden yellow mohair dress was perfect for her, sharpening as it did the rapidly misting eyes, the dark red hair with its pixie cut, the tenseness of cheek, chin and brow. 'A Dürer,' he said of the list, 'a Cranach . . . the two Vermeers, a fifteenth-century, all but life-sized sculpture of Eve, the two Gobelin tapestries that are now hanging in the third gallery or was it the fourth? The painting by Manet of a girl and her mother at a railway station, this study of a woman done perhaps in . . .' He examined the little card on the wall and said, 'Yes, of course, in 1878.'

'Inspector, what is it you want of me?'

Her expression was one of devastation and he knew she didn't wish him to spoil things for her. 'Want? Why nothing for the moment. Will you be attending the sale?'

'Yes, to . . .'

'To record the prices or to bid?'

'To record. It . . . it's all I can do.'

Excusing himself, he drifted amiably off through the crowd and she was left to stare at his broad back and shoulders until, at last, he was gone but then a woman stood close by and she heard her saying, 'Ah, *Sainte-Mère*, it's magnificent, isn't it? The tone, the way the flowers are clustered in the hatband to one side, their colour offsetting everything. What will it fetch, do you think?'

'I . . . I've no idea. Too much, probably.'

'1,250,000, I think. Of the *new* francs, of course.'

The woman was tall and in her late thirties perhaps, though it was hard to tell. Not blonde but hair of an exquisite amber. A gorgeous figure, a sheath of dark Prussian blue silk that shimmered. Diamonds at her throat and wrist, and violet eyes that were absolutely stunning and brought instant envy.

'Gabrielle Arcuri,' said the woman of herself, 'and you?'

The hand was cool and slender, the fingers long. 'Marie-Claire de Brisson. Your perfume, it's Mirage.'

'I love it. But . . . but you must have some! I insist. Please, a moment. Here . . . hold my programme. *Merci*. This bag, it's not my usual one. Tissues, keys . . . Ah, here I have it. Allow me to present you with a little sample. A very dear friend makes it for me and in return I advertise it a little. But . . . but your eyes, Mademoiselle de Brisson? Something has upset you.'

'Nothing. It was nothing.'

'That man who was speaking to you was from the police.'

'Yes. A detective.'

'Ah *merde*, those *salauds* are everywhere these days, aren't they?'

A waiter came and they each took a glass of champagne. The woman who called herself Gabrielle Arcuri offered to dry the corners of her eyes without smudging the mascara and she let her do this for her. They spoke of the sale, of the crowd.

The woman said, 'I hear the Reichsmarschall and Reichsführer Goering will attend. It's bound to be a huge success, isn't it? He always gets what he wants. Though the dealers bid against him and run the prices up, in the end the Reichsführer always wins.'

'Yes, I believe he does.'

'Manet is a favourite of mine. Will he buy this one, I wonder?'

The woman touched her lovely lips in thought as she examined the painting by standing back a little and then by walking right up to it to study the brush strokes. She shook her head but indecision crept in and at last she said with a shrug of her exquisite shoulders that perhaps after all Goering would purchase it. 'Manet was severely criticized for painting nudes with the faces of playing cards, yet this one is a study of introspection. A woman thinking she isn't desirable when, in fact, she's very much herself and perfect.'

They discussed the sale a little more. Marie-Claire saw that Gabrielle Arcuri sipped her champagne with great delicacy. So little was taken, only the lips were wet. A German general with a monocle stopped by to formally bow and kiss the woman's hand. Her smile was at once gracious and warm yet still she managed to hold herself back, remaining aloof and proud but not letting him see this. 'A chanteuse . . . ?'

'It's nothing. It gets me into parties like this. Now I must find my lover before he takes offence and finds another. That one . . . Ah, he's always such a wanderer!'

She was tall and willowy, graceful, regal, stunning . . .

They met at the head of the main staircase, this woman and her 'lover,' *Jean-Louis St-Cyr of the Sûreté Nationale!* They kissed on the cheek and delicately held each other, she admiring his dinner-jacket, he raising his deep brown ox-eyes so that he looked up into that radiant, beautiful face! Had they discovered everything?

Arm in arm, they went down the stairs. She tried to follow them, tried not to let them see her. She *mustn't*! She must find out what they knew . . .

Others got in the way. Others. 'Please, I must get past. You don't understand . . .'

A champagne glass was knocked aside. A shriek rent the air as a dress was drenched. Another glass hit the floor . . .

They were at the foot of the stairs now and though she couldn't hear what they said, she knew he was telling the chanteuse how it must be, that Denise had offered the paintings and sculptures of Monsieur Vergès for sale but that there could be only one buyer. *One.*

'Goering,' whispered Marie-Claire in despair as she was jostled from behind on the staircase and forced to squeeze out of the way and hug the railing. 'Goering.'

Always there was a crowd of hangers-on around the Reichsführer, always the onlookers, but when confronted with a beautiful young woman handcuffed to a man twice her size, Goering lost his grin. The lighted cigar was clutched between his teeth. For perhaps five seconds the leaden blue eyes fought to comprehend exactly what was before them, then cruelty entered.

Desperately Kohler glanced from side to side. Kempf stood to the right of the Reichsführer. Michel le Blanc was just behind the Sonderführer, dark, darting eyes, doubt, fear . . . so many things were registering in the anxious looks he gave.

'The handcuffs,' blurted Goering, taking the cigar from his lips. 'Please remove them at once. That lady is under my protection.'

Baron Kurt von Behr, head of the Paris ERR, was on the other side of the Reichsführer, Andreas Hofer, Goering's chief art adviser and dealer, just behind the Baron.

Kohler heard himself saying, 'I can't, Reichsführer. It's a matter for the courts.'

Denise St. Onge tried to step forward but was yanked back and nearly off her feet. The long beige camel-hair overcoat that had been draped over Goering's shoulders slipped. The dark brown velour trilby that had been pulled well down over the broad brow was pushed up out of the way. *'What? You would dare to challenge my authority?'*

Silence fell. Laughter and excited talk trickled off to nothing. Again Kohler heard his own voice. 'I can't remove them, Reichsführer. Not without the authority of my immediate superior officer and that of Gestapo Mueller.' Louis . . . where the hell was Louis?

Enraged, now florid and quivering with indignation, Goering shrieked, *'Do it!* you *Schweine Bulle. Don't be a dummkopf!'*

Ah *Gott im Himmel!* A bully, a natural-born killer . . . As a boy, Goering had been expelled from school repeatedly because of his excessive temper and wilful behaviour. As a young man in the Great War, he had earned the coveted Blue Max and had commanded von Richtofen's famed *Jageschwader I* after the Baron's death, the legendary Flying Circus. A hero . . .

Kempf tried to intercede. Denise St. Onge took another step towards them and was savagely yanked back again. 'Reichsführer,' said Kohler, 'she's one of the principal suspects in the murders of fourteen girls, in the robbery of the Crédit Lyonnais, in the theft of valuable works of art from a house overlooking the garden of the Palais Royal, and in the deaths of their owner and his friend.'

The cigar was flung at him. Frantically Kohler ducked and tried to brace himself. Enraged, Goering unleashed a torrent of verbal abuse, then screamed, *'Do you expect me to believe such shit? Free her at once or suffer the consequences!'*

Had he taken drugs? wondered Kohler apprehensively. Here was the vain bastard who had promised the Führer faithfully to supply von Paulus's Sixth Army at Stalingrad with daily air drops and had failed miserably. Here was the man who, with others like him, had deserted Jurgen and Hans Kohler, two farmboys who should have gone to Argentina like their papa said.

Kempf leaned closely to whisper something. Startled, Goering turned to him. *'What?'* he asked. 'What is this, Franz?'

'She's a cousin, Reichsführer. You will remember that you met Mademoiselle St. Onge at Horcher's before the Polish Campaign. Denise was paying us a little visit and I was showing her the town.'

Berlin and its most famous restaurant. Ah damn, thought Kohler . . .

'Horcher's,' muttered Goering, blinking to clear his mind and wishing suddenly that the whole affair would disappear and he could get on with the party. 'Of course I remember, Kohler . . . Kohler, if you don't remove the handcuffs, I'll have my men cut off your arm.'

Luftwaffe security types were all around them. Heaving a troubled sigh, Kohler braced himself. 'Reichsführer, I'll do as you request, but must ask that you give me a paper stating I've released the woman into your custody and that I believe her to be guilty of the crimes of murder, robbery, kidnapping and extortion.'

'*I have done no such things, Reichsführer!* I am totally innocent! *Wounded* to the quick by such false accusations!'

'Extortion?' muttered Goering. 'Kidnapping? Franz, what is this? The paintings you promised me . . . ? Andreas, what is this one saying?' He indicated Kohler.

'That he will agree, Reichsführer, to release her into your custody,' said Hofer gently.

'*Gut.* That's all I want.' Goering hunched his shoulders to better lift the overcoat back up on to them. Someone helped. Someone else found him another cigar and offered a light. He inhaled deeply and blew a cloud of smoke towards the ceiling. 'A Dürer, Franz. A Cranach . . . Please, you must show them to me.'

'We're not finished,' breathed Kohler to the woman. 'You didn't just help that cousin of yours lure those girls to that house. You took part in everything.'

The handcuff around his wrist came loose and fell away to dangle from her own wrist. Sucking in a deep breath, she caught it up and swung hard, smashing him across the face. '*Maudit salaud!*' she shrieked. '*Liar!* I did no such thing!'

Kempf and le Blanc gathered her in and took her away with Goering to view the works of art she had put up for sale.

'All of those taken from that house, Hermann,' said St-Cyr exasperatedly. 'The Reichsführer apparently provides forty-eight hours' notice of when and if he will arrive.'

'Then that's our delay, Louis.'

'And that is why the house had to be emptied in such a hurry. Until the notice came, they didn't know if he would show up, even though the invitations had been sent out. Denise St. Onge is haunted by guilt and fear, Hermann, and knows only too well we mean to walk her to the guillotine.'

'Where's Gabi?'

'Gone to the club for safety's sake. Apparently Michel le Blanc was once a freelance photographer but gave it up to become a reporter after the Defeat when there was a temporary shortage of suitable applicants.'

'He has jet-black hair.'

The Sûreté's nod was grim. 'Mademoiselle de Brisson made a list of all the works her boss put up for sale.'

'It didn't take Denise a moment to figure out who the forged papers were for and to put that together with the scattered photographs. She knows Marie-Claire intends to pin it all on them.'

'On her body, Hermann. Unless I am very mistaken, Mademoiselle de Brisson plans to leave the evidence on her when she kills herself in Dijon.'

'Or here, Louis. *Here*. They'll try to stop her. They'll have to. She'll be aware of this.'

'Kempf will leave Denise with Goering.'

'Marie-Claire will head for her flat and then . . .'

'Either try to hide until the train tomorrow or try to kill herself.'

Unfortunately, the place de la Concorde was jammed with parked cars, *vélo-taxis*, horse-drawn carriages and *gazogènes*, and so was the rue de Rivoli. Unfortunately, the Citroën was lost among them and Hermann, still badly shaken, couldn't quite remember where he had left it. Unfortunately, the rain had changed its mind and now fell as half-frozen pellets of ice to make the pavements worse than sheets of glass.

When they reached the house of the banker on the rue de Montpensier, the front door was ajar, the lights off, the only sound that of the pellets as they hit the street behind them. Thousands of them. Some fully frozen, others not. Some bouncing to roll about beneath a distant blue lamp, the only one in the street, others simply breaking.

'You first or me?' whispered Hermann breathlessly.

From somewhere came the sound of an accelerating car and then that of the skid and crash. 'Me, *mon vieux*. It was always my affair.'

'Piss off. I'm better at this than you. Count to thirty and then follow. Work to the right.'

St-Cyr held his breath. The pellets hit the barrel of the gun he clutched. They hit his head and shoulders, the back of his hands, filling the air with their sound and the chill they brought.

At last he could stand the waiting no longer and stepped into the house. It would all be for Joanne and Dédé. Yes, Dédé would have to be told of it. Every last little thing. The smell of the freezing rain, its sound, the depth of darkness, the faint odour of cognac and whisky, was it whisky?

The smell of blood, of death, of powder, black powder—yes, certainly, an old Lebel 1873 just like the one in his hand and the one that had killed Gaetan Vergès and the bank teller.

The sharpness of sulphur, saltpetre and burnt charcoal but faint, so faint . . . a window open or a door . . . a door upstairs.

**9** Try as he did, Kohler could recall little of the salon de Brisson. He took a step and then another—would go right around the room if necessary. Lamps, tables, chairs, vases of silk flowers, paintings on the walls ... Where were the bastards? Chasing Mademoiselle de Brisson out on the balcony, driving her to that empty house whose doors would be locked unless ... A key, of course. She must have had one of her own. How else could she have scattered the photographs without the others knowing?

Crouching, he waited. Feeling the carpet wet but only in little places, he followed these places out across the floor until his fingers touched hair.

Louis ... ? he began. Louis, ah *Gott im Himmel*.

Holding back the urge to throw up, Kohler felt the face, the open eyes and broken glasses. Blood trickled from parted lips. The bullet had smashed the nose.

He found the cushion that had been used. He found Madame de Brisson's purse, its contents so scattered a careless step would have broken a pencil or compact mirror. This made him realize her body had been moved. It made him cringe and hesitate as he wiped his fingers on her sweater and tried to clean them as best he could.

Louis would have gone on ahead of him. Louis . . . Where was Kempf sitting—waiting . . . waiting for them to turn on a light! Yes, yes!

Ah *merde*, thought St-Cyr. Hermann must have gone upstairs.

The surface beneath his fingers was lacquered, and when he explored a little further, he found it must be a grand piano—pianos always had a smell to them. Dusty, of felt pads and wire, of ivory and ebony keys . . . Was someone sitting on the bench?

His heart racing, St-Cyr held his breath. Seldom was darkness so absolute one could not distinguish degrees of change and pick out shapes . . .

The piano was near a corner of the room, next to the windows. It was near the fireplace, too. He could smell damp coal ashes. The fire hadn't been lighted in days, the furnace was on, the radiators were warm . . .

Yes, there was someone sitting on the bench, waiting. Having sent le Blanc after Marie-Claire, had the Sonderführer returned to the salon to trap them?

Edging closer, he tried to better define the shape before him. Was it de Brisson hunched over the keys? The top of the piano was up and braced, the music stand would have to be down so as to allow the freedom to fire across the room.

For perhaps ten seconds, St-Cyr waited. Raising the revolver, he began to ease the hammer back completely, having already had it on the half-cock. The figure moved. The figure vanished. One moment it was there, the next . . .

He stepped back, felt himself come up against the wall. Hermann . . . where was Hermann?

The sound of the freezing rain came to him, the feel of a draught from an open window or door, the stirring of ashes in the grate . . .

Kohler fired twice. Someone fired back. Glass shattered. Marble shattered. That someone ran, hit something, stumbled and fell, got up, fired again and again, then ran out of the room and up the stairs.

'Louis . . . Louis, are you okay?' whispered Kohler urgently.

'Perhaps!' came the hiss.

'Those stairs he took only go up to the second floor.'

'Was it de Brisson?'

'The banker . . . ? I . . . I don't know. Is he in so deep there's no other way out for him?'

'Perhaps he'll tell us, perhaps he won't.'

'It was Kempf,' breathed Kohler. 'I'm certain of it.'

'Then where is de Brisson?'

'Take the back stairs up to the attic, Louis. Leave this one to me. Check it out and wait for me. The stairs are off the kitchen.'

'And what if he gets past you and comes back down again?'

'He won't.'

'Then what if he fires down the stairwell as you are on your way up?'

'He won't because he'll hear you go up the other stairs.'

Kohler waited, and when he heard Louis start up the other stairs, swore and called himself an idiot. Le Blanc could just as easily have come back from that balcony and be waiting at the top of them and if not him, then de Brisson.

St-Cyr was grim. The back stairs were steep and narrow. Up the right side, there was a railing and it was along this that he slid his gun. Nothing could be seen. It was far too dark. No shape, no degree of change. Each step was first felt and then . . . then the weight gradually increased until . . . yes, it could be done and another taken.

When he reached a point perhaps one-third of the way up, he wondered if he should not retreat. The draught, always cold, seemed to have increased. Had the door at the head of the stairs not opened a little? Could he not hear the freezing rain more clearly?

He took another step only to feel the boards sag. Crouching, he waited. The door at the top moved. The draught increased. There was a rush, a . . .

Aiming up the staircase, he waited.

The rush came down the stairs and when it reached him, it

meowed and rubbed itself against his leg. 'Ah *nom de Jésus-Christ!*' he whispered.

Reaching down, he felt the thing and ran his swollen hand over its back, then rubbed it behind the ears and let it rub its face in his hand.

Its whiskers were wet. The fur under its chin was wet and sticky. It was not water, not milk—even with the almost total absence of milk from a city of 2,500,000, in houses such as this, it would have been common enough for the cat.

'It's blood,' he breathed. Marie-Claire de Brisson's? he asked and started up the stairs once more, leaving the cat to seek its mistress.

Once in the attic *pied-à-terre*, the darkness was less. A set of french windows to the balcony was wide open and the night sky, with the falling sleet, was of a still lighter darkness.

The sound of the ice pellets filled the flat as they hit the floor nearest the window. Quickly he crossed the small sitting-room and sought the deeper darkness of the opposite wall. He waited, listened—tried to shut out the sound of the ice.

A corridor led to the bedrooms. There were framed pictures on the walls—photographs, Hermann had said. Sweet things, pretty things, not of death and gunshots and bastards like Kempf and le Blanc or of girls like Joanne whose bodies had been left for others to find and deal with.

There was nobody in the smaller of the bedrooms, not that he could be certain without a light, but in the larger of them, the carpet was wet.

De Brisson must have come upstairs to find his daughter throwing things into a small suitcase—it was still open on the bed. Some underwear ... a toothbrush ... a bottle of pills, a straight razor, a diary ...

The banker lay face down on the carpet and it was clear that the muzzle of the gun had been jammed against the back of his head. One shot.

Mademoiselle de Brisson must have somehow used that second to escape onto the balcony.

The hammering of the ice pellets swept back in on him and he heard them pinging off each other, the windows and the floor. Now a blast, now a lessening.

Le Blanc, he said. Le Blanc has gone after her. Should I follow? Isn't this what they want? Le Blanc will have heard the shots.

St-Cyr went back to the head of the stairs to look down them and raise his gun. Kempf, he said to himself. Kempf will have to come up them.

Or will he? And if not Kempf, then Hermann who would do it so silently no one, not even his partner, would know he was there until he had reached the top and said so.

Withdrawing, he waited as Kempf had waited for them, never taking his eyes from the top of the stairs but thinking of Mademoiselle de Brisson who knew everything and could tell others what had happened.

The scattering of the photographs in an empty, empty house, the purchasing of forged papers for men who had known absolutely nothing of them.

The room was empty, the house was empty and they were going to kill her . . . *kill her!*

Clasping a hand tightly over her mouth to stop herself from crying out, Marie-Claire de Brisson huddled on the floor against the wall. They would grab her by the hair, they would throw her down and jam a gun against her head. She would try to get away, would plead with them. Michel would pin her legs. Franz would kneel on her back . . . her back . . . Bang!

She wept. She couldn't stop herself from shaking. Her father—that bastard who had come up the stairs for her so many times—was now dead. *Dead!*

No more would he come for her.

A shape, a silhouette, appeared on the other side of the tall french doors that opened onto the balcony. Suddenly this shape threw out its hands to stop itself from slipping. Michel . . . was it Michel? He banged against the glass and fought to right himself.

She huddled. She got ready to run. He shook the door handle

and tried to force it. She waited. She dropped the hand that had covered her mouth. 'Michel . . . It *is* Michel,' she said.

He broke the glass, showering it into the room. She screamed and ran, banged into a door frame, went down a corridor in darkness, darkness . . . tried to catch a breath, dragged it in . . . in. The stairs . . . she must find the stairs.

Le Blanc threw himself into the corridor. She grabbed the railing and raced down the stairs with him after her . . . after her . . . Fell . . . fell . . . shrieked, 'No! No!' dragged in a breath and hit the stairs, tumbling down them.

He fired once. Plaster dust flew into her face. 'No! No!' she shrieked again and rolled away until she hit another wall and could go no farther.

'Michel . . .' she managed, dragging herself up. 'Michel . . . don't do it, please.'

There was no answer. In all that house there were only the silent cries of girls who once had been so full of hope, her own ragged breathing, the ache in her chest and outside on the balcony, why, only the sound of the sleet as it hit the windows.

'Michel . . .' She swallowed hard. 'Let me go. I won't tell them anything. I promise.'

How contemptible of her to beg.

Still he didn't answer and when, having hesitantly pulled herself up on to her feet, she stood with her back to the wall, the touch of the plaster was dry and rough beneath her hand, and the waiting was cruel.

Somehow she had reached one of the bedrooms on the second floor. There must be a short bit of corridor and then the staircase. She had pulled herself into a ball as she had rolled away but had no memory of having done so.

Windows overlooked the rue de Valois but these were not nearly so tall as those either upstairs or downstairs.

'Michel . . . I . . . I haven't told them anything. I . . . I have the travel papers and other documents I had made for you and Franz. They're . . . they're sewn into the lining of my coat. I couldn't carry them in my purse, could I? The controls, the checkpoints, the Gestapo searches . . . Here . . . here, I can rip them free for you.'

Her fingers shook so much she couldn't do it. A button flew off, another fell . . . Both hit the floor and rolled away, and she heard the sound of them against that of the sleet striking the windows.

Trembling, she tried to find the exact place where the papers were. The left side of the hem . . . Here . . . here, she said to herself and, pulling it up to grasp it in her teeth, yanked hard and . . .

He was standing in the doorway. She could barely make him out through the darkness. Had he raised the gun, was he about to kill her?

'Mi . . . ch . . . el, *please!*'

He took a step, lurched into the room, ran at her.

Shrieking, she darted aside and felt him grab her by the coat. They fell, they both went down hard to roll madly about, she trying to get free of him, he trying to pin her down . . . down. Gun . . . gun . . . what has happened to his gun? she yelled at herself and sank her teeth into his ear.

He screamed and swung hard. Her head banged against the floor and she lay there panting with her eyes clamped tightly shut as the pain rushed through her.

'*Putain!* Interfering slut!' He caught breath. 'Ah *nom de Jésus-Christ!* I've cracked my forehead.'

Through the webs of pain, she could hear his ragged breathing. He would kill her now, there was nothing she could do to stop it.

Bucking her middle fiercely up, she swung her fists hard, hitting him repeatedly in the face, then scratching at his eyes . . . his eyes and tearing at him as he hit her again and again and tried to grab her arms.

They fell back. She butted the top of her head against his chin and scrambled off him. Raced for the door . . . only to be caught, pulled back, dragged down . . .

Shrieking, she kicked hard and caught him in the face then scrambled away . . . away. The stairs . . . she had to reach the stairs.

When her hand came up against his gun on the floor, she dragged it up and threw herself over on to her back.

Against the sound of the ice pellets on the windows, le Blanc heard her breathing through her teeth. He would pull off his overcoat and throw it over her. He would kick her hard until the gun was empty or had fallen from her hands.

Kohler silently swore at himself. Kempf was good. Since leaving the bedrooms upstairs, the bastard had gone to ground so well there hadn't been a hint of where he was. Only the feeling that he had not yet left the house by going up the back stairs or out the front door and onto the rue de Montpensier.

Off the downstairs corridor there were rooms—a library, a study, a billiard room, kitchen, pantry and those same back stairs . . .

When he stepped into what he felt must be the billiard room, Kohler knew instinctively he had made a mistake. There was nothing firmer to back this feeling up, now only the pitch darkness, the coolness of the draught from upstairs, the warmth of a radiator under his hand, the faint smell of chalk dust and green baize all billiard rooms had, that much stronger, far harsher smell of stale tobacco smoke, of cigars, cognac, pipes and cigarettes . . .

He waited for the bullets to come. Uncertain, his fingers trailed across the table. Finding a ball, he cautiously took it up. Where . . . where was Kempf? Standing over by the cue-rack? Behind a chair, beside a lamp, near the tallyboard . . . ?

Cautiously he sent the ball rolling down the table. If one could play this game, so could two.

The ball didn't go far. When it struck another faintly, that sound was all Kohler heard until a breath was released in a sigh and he realized it was his own. Gone . . . the son of a bitch was gone! Ah *merde*, Louis, watch out!

St-Cyr was torn by the waiting. Time collapsed, constricted— played tricks on the mind, expanding suddenly so as to make minutes seem hours not seconds. He knew he should have gone after Marie-Claire de Brisson, knew he must stay where he was, that Hermann would eventually flush Kempf up the stairs to the attic flat. Or would he?

It had been too long a wait. Something must have happened. Perhaps Kempf had left by the front door and would now be entering the house of Monsieur Vergès from the rue de Valois to find Mademoiselle de Brisson and his friend—Was that how it was? She couldn't hide for ever in that empty house, would be terrified.

Straightening, he eased his aching knees and back and lessened his grip on the revolver.

Again he waited, tormented by the need to follow the girl before it was too late, tormented by not knowing where the Sonderführer was. If he moved back to the head of the stairs and, at some noise, chanced a shot or two down them, he might kill Hermann. Only by staying here could he use the degrees of darkness to satisfy himself that it was the Sonderführer who came up the stairs or Hermann who was much taller, much bigger.

A board gave a little. He held himself ready, said silently, Come up the stairs.

There were no further sounds save those of the incessant sleet, and when, at last, a darker silhouette appeared against the lesser darkness but briefly, he was forced again to wait. 'Louis . . . Louis, it's me. He's buggered off.'

'The girl, Hermann.'

'That house, Louis.'

Her breathing came easier now. As she lay on her back with le Blanc's gun clutched in both hands, waiting for him to rush her, Marie-Claire de Brisson gingerly raised her knees a little more.

The last folds of her dress slid to gather about her middle, freeing her legs completely. Bracing the gun against her inner thighs, the backs of her hands were pressed into her garters and silk stockings and the cold skin above them, the smoothness of her naked flesh.

She heard someone on the staircase and, ripped right out of things, thought it was her father, said desperately, Never again will I let him touch me, and realized it couldn't possibly be him.

Ah no. Franz . . was it Franz?

Craning her neck as far back as possible, she chanced a look directly behind her but the steps had stopped and there was nothing but darkness everywhere.

'*Michel, if you kill me, you will never find the money. I hid it elsewhere. I found it in the storeroom at the shop—I did. I moved it!*'

There was no answer, there were no more steps behind her that she could discern. '*Michel, I'm warning you!*'

The gun leapt in her hands. There was a brilliant flash of fire, the instant image of her legs with knees up, then the acrid stench of smoke and a rush of sound, a loud bang, the sound of plaster falling and, finally, through the darkness and the smoke, the muffled shrieking of Madame Lemaire's maid and the sound of the girl banging on her mistress's wall.

Le Blanc waited. Holding his overcoat by the shoulders, he tried to bring himself to rush forward and throw it over Marie-Claire, to kick her hard and let her empty the revolver before it was too late.

She'll hit me, he kept on telling himself and asked, Where the hell is Franz? What has happened to him?

'*I'll go to the police!*' came the muffled words from next door. '*I'll tell them everything, messieurs!*'

He chanced a step and heard Marie-Claire suck in a breath, heard the hammer click as it descended on the cartridge, saw the flash of fire, the upraised knees, the stockings, the underwear, then heard the bang and felt the darkness closing in on him.

For perhaps ten seconds there was no further sound, then she gave a stifled cry, a sudden furious lurching up of her legs, a kicking, a thrashing. As the gun was grabbed from behind, it went off. Kempf forced her hands down between her legs. She had no strength, could not raise her arms, could not move her head for he was kneeling on her chest and tearing the gun from her. '*Michel!*' he hissed. 'Are you all right?'

'Yes. The bitch nearly got me. What happened?'

'They're on the balcony. Hurry! We haven't much time.'

They dragged her up and took her with them, plummeting

down the stairs at breakneck speed. 'No . . . No! I won't tell you!' she gasped frantically and, racing still, was pulled along and out on to the rue de Valois. 'The shop,' she heard Kempf breathlessly say. 'She must have hidden the money there. She couldn't have moved it.'

'I did!'

They stopped. The freezing rain came down through the blue-washed light of the only street lamp, and the sound of the ice pellets was all around them, striking the frozen ground and each other, bouncing from the lamp above them.

'I'll never tell you. Never!' she swore.

Grimly St-Cyr nudged the door to the shop open a little more. Gone were the slipping and sliding, the tumbles that had barked the shins, torn muscles, bruised a shoulder and hurt an already injured hand. Gone were streets impassable to all but ice-skaters!

Hermann was no better off and was decidedly favouring the arm Péguy had put the knife into long ago, it seemed, and forgotten until now.

The smells of the place came to him as the Bavarian softly closed the door behind them and eased the lock on with a finality that troubled, since there could now be no easy escape for anyone, themselves included. There were the smells of perfume and bath salts, of oils and soaps that only the privileged could buy and the black market provide. Smells of new silk, old silk, warm wool, cold linen, glass display cases, scarves and leather gloves, shop-girls who had gone home hours ago, pencils, cash drawers and bills of sale.

At a nudge from Hermann, he moved to the left, his partner working to the right. Now the front of the shop was behind them and he wondered if he shouldn't check the floor for Marie-Claire de Brisson. Had they killed her, had they left her here? Blood . . . there was the faint smell of blood, but from where was it coming?

Silently St-Cyr moved among the displays—dresses, suits, skirts and overcoats . . . the feel of each telegraphing its identity to him, no sign yet of Mademoiselle de Brisson. She'd been wearing a mohair dress . . .

He touched a plaster bust and felt the lace of a brassière. Delicate . . . so delicate. A spill of silk briefs suggested someone must have thrown out a hand.

Crouching, he searched the floor, gathering undergarments, finding nothing else and wondering if Kempf and le Blanc were in the office at the back? Had they killed Mademoiselle de Brisson, had they silenced her for ever, or would they try to use her as a hostage?

When he found her overcoat on the floor, St-Cyr felt its lining and knew it had been ripped apart.

Kohler ran his left hand over the surface of one of the glass display cases, touching lipstick cartridges, compacts and boxes of face powder, rouge and other things The stillness told him Kempf and le Blanc were waiting, but where? Ah *Gott im Himmel*, was it blood he had just smelled?

It was.

The smell of women and girls came to him as, silently, he moved aside the curtain of one of the changing cubicles and felt inside it.

Nothing. *Verdammt!* Where were they? Behind the shop there'd be the office and a storeroom, a lavatory and powder room—a place for the shop-girls to hang their coats and hats. Kempf . . . what the hell would Kempf do?

Louis . . . where was Louis?

St-Cyr reached the far corner of the shop. Racks of evening dresses were to his left—he felt them, felt silk and satin, lace and chiffon—sequins hard and cold, rhinestone beads and tiny seed pearls in seductive patterns. *Merde,* what had Kempf and le Blanc done with the banker's daughter?

Behind the shop there was a corridor, a dark alleyway to what? he wondered and told himself, The office . . .

But other things too. More changing cubicles. He moved a curtain aside and hesitated. He let it fall back into place.

There were three cubicles and he checked each of them thoroughly. The office door was directly across the corridor.

Gingerly he felt around it but, yes, it was tightly closed.

Kohler came to join him and, crouching at his feet, the

Bavarian ran fingers delicately along the bottom of the door. *A rug*, he tapped out the letters, letting them fall uneasily on Louis's ankle.

Gently tugging at the rug, he moved it just a little and a faint sliver of pale blue light intruded into the corridor at their feet. Louis, he said to himself as he tucked the carpet back in place. Louis, they've . . .

Urgently he tapped out another message in Morse that had been learned by all above the rank of sergeant or Unterfeldwebel in that other war. *Me . . . corridor . . . storeroom . . . time. Kick door open, stand back.*

There must be another door to the office, connecting it to the storeroom behind. As St-Cyr waited, the cinematographer within him could not help but see Marie-Claire de Brisson hanging above that lamp in there, stretched out, spread-eagled over it as all those other girls must have been in that house, naked, their hair chopped off, their breasts . . .

He hit the door. It flew open—crashed against a chair, the wall . . . The desk lamp was on the floor below her . . . below her . . . shrouded with a dark blue silk scarf . . . Ah no . . .

He shuddered at what they had done to her and tried to think—*Think!* he cried to himself. Hermann . . . Hermann, they have . . .

Now the blue lamplight flooded out into the corridor to touch the curtains of the changing cubicles, and the girl's shadow was cast upon the ceiling.

Deep in the storeroom, Kohler took a step and then another. Racks of clothing stood on either side of him. All down the narrow space between them, there was only darkness and then . . . then a faint blue wash of light from beneath the back door of the office, the door through which Louis and he were to have come . . .

He chanced a look towards the corridor where a deeper blue light now shone. He wished he had Louis's sense of smell. Louis could sort things out and tell not only when stale tobacco smoke was coming from a man's jacket but how close it was.

Silently parting the clothes on the rack to the right of him,

Kohler eased his gun-hand through ... Gently ... gently, he warned himself. You'll never get him with these between you. He'll only bolt and run and fire.

His little finger briefly touched a coarser fabric than that of the dresses. Immediately it backed away and the dresses on the rack closed silently as he withdrew his hand.

That's one of them, he said to himself, but didn't know if it was Kempf or le Blanc who had watched the corridor. Louis would have found Marie-Claire de Brisson by now. Had they slit her throat, had they strung her up and cut off her breasts?

There wasn't a sound, only the heavy, close smell of wool and silk, linen, satin and cotton, of things from the thirties, things of quality.

Louis, he wondered. Louis ... but stayed where he was.

Still in the office, St-Cyr could see that all around the shrouded lamp on the floor beneath Mademoiselle de Brisson were the scattered clumps of her dark red hair that had been hacked off. Hairs clung to her pale shoulders, they were webbed in the blood that drained steadily from wrists that were tied together so that she hung suspended from the ceiling lamp by a length, not of rope, but of silk, while her ankles were tied to the front legs of the desk by equal lengths of lingerie. Hairs were caught in the small of her back and over the mounds of her buttocks. They clung to her breasts that, like lumps of butchered meat, lay on the desk behind her.

They had cut her throat and had slashed her wrists.

He crossed himself and silently begged her forgiveness for not having arrived sooner. He knew that, though she might well have told Kempf and le Blanc where the money was, they wouldn't leave until they had killed Hermann and him.

He knew that, though his eyes would have adjusted to the lamplight from the floor, still he would have to open the door to face the darkness of the storeroom and the bullets. Joanne demanded that he put an end to the Sonderführer and his friend. The other victims demanded it too, and so did this one.

Searching the door, he realized that as soon as he approached it, he would break the constancy of the faint light escaping from beneath and that this would signal them to fire.

There were samples of clothing, a small stack of scarves. Marie-Claire de Brisson's dress and underthings lay on the floor.

He picked them up and tossed them so that they fell through the light, breaking it . . .

Kempf fired. Le Blanc fired. The door splintered. Bullets hit Maire-Claire de Brisson's back and seat, bullets tore into her.

Crouched, he waited. He asked, Where's Hermann? Hermann . . .

Kohler let the two of them cautiously approach the door and when, at last, they stood hesitantly near it, fired twice and only twice.

Kempf fell. Le Blanc swung round to fire and he shot him in the face at point-blank range.

Then he just stood there clinging to a clothes rack trying to find his voice and saying at last, 'Louis . . . Louis, it's over.'

But, of course, it wasn't over. Ah, no, not quite.

In the crowded salesroom on the ground floor of the Jeu de Paume, Denise St. Onge found it difficult to watch for Franz and Michel's return. She thought perhaps they would be at the very back but when she turned to look, as she often had, two generals and their lady friends smiled and blocked her view and this made her furious though she always managed a brief smile in return.

The Cranach was being offered. Goering much favoured works by this early sixteenth-century German painter; so, too, did Hitler. The bidding had reached 175,000 of the new francs but neither Andreas Hofer, Goering's buyer, nor Haberstock, the Berlin art dealer who bought for the Führer's private collection, had bid against each other. Interest seemed to be waning. The gavel was being raised . . .

She panicked at the thought of such a low price and tried to find Franz and Michel by looking both ways along the rows of chairs, all of which were occupied by very special people, by dealers and their clients and friends. Others too.

The crowd was equally thick and close and standing twenty or so deep in a semicircle around the sixty or so chairs. Goering was three rows in front of her and a little to her left—at the very front—and she wished she could have sat closer to him, wished that he didn't seem to have forgotten all about her.

There was no sign of Franz and Michel. No sign at all. She couldn't stand up to look for them, couldn't raise a hand or try otherwise to signal to one of the security people for help. What was she to do if . . . if Franz and Michel didn't succeed in taking care of Marie-Claire? Just suppose both had been arrested or . . . or had been killed?

She shuddered at the thought, clutched and unclutched the gloves in the lap of her black silk dress until, on hearing the auctioneer say, 'I have 175,000, mesdames et messieurs. Have I one eighty?' she finally forced her hands to stop.

Goering's slab-hard cheeks were flushed, the blue eyes fiercely intent—*Bâtard*, she shrieked inwardly. You *promised* Franz to bid it up so that we could get a good price and you . . . you would take the pieces back home with you.

Suddenly it was cold and lonely for her. The Reichsmarschall puffed benignly on his cigar and stared up at the painting of three naked girls standing before a knight in armour—armour for God's sake! Wasn't it too heavy for a knight to sit like that on the ground? Didn't knights have to be hoisted on and off their horses?

There was a high cliff in the near background with a turreted castle on its summit, a lake or river far below, with bits of fir forest along the shores and mountains with other castles in the far distance. The whole thing was very brooding, very Germanic.

No art critic, Kohler snorted inwardly at the skinny, tight-assed virgins in the painting and thought the walrus with the cigar an idiot for looking so greedily up at them. 'He's got the hots for that bit of canvas, Louis.'

The hots . . .

'175,000, mesdames et messieurs. Do I hear one eighty?'

Her heart sank and Denise St. Onge knew Franz and she had

been betrayed, that Goering, distant relative or no relative, agreement or no agreement, intended to do just as he pleased.

Hanging tapestries, behind and to the sides of the auctioneer, screened a passageway for the assistants as they brought the pieces up for display or took away those that had been sold. This cover extended right to the sides of the hall and she knew that there were doorways there and that Franz and Michel could well have spotted her from behind the tapestries, yet she hadn't caught a glimpse of either.

St-Cyr saw her nervously wipe beneath each eye with a knuckle. Pale ... she was so pale. He heard the auctioneer saying, 'I have 175,000, mesdames et messieurs. Do I hear one eighty?'

The gavel would come down. Denise St. Onge couldn't lift her eyes from her lap, only shuddered as it came down, down and then ...

One eighty, signalled Andreas Hofer who was sitting to the left of the Reichsmarschall and could just be seen by nudging the edge of the tapestry aside.

'I have one eighty. Do I hear one eighty-five?'

She no longer seemed to care, was desperately afraid and shrinking into herself—so much so, St-Cyr wondered if she had seen them.

'Goering buys, Hermann, and Denise sells,' he said sadly, as one of the assistants brushed past them with another painting.

'It's perfect,' breathed Kohler. 'The eighteen million is handed over to the Reichsmarschall and with it he buys what she has to sell and the loot is shipped to the Reich.'

St-Cyr heaved a patriot's sigh, a detective's condemnation of the perfidies of humankind. 'Worthless francs that can't be sent out of France because they're of no value anywhere else; paintings, sculptures and tapestries or carpets that can.'

'Goering then compensates the Sonderführer back home in the Reich, either by repaying him in Reichsmarks that are sound, or he sells what he doesn't want and gives his cousin the proceeds in Reichsmarks less a little commission.'

It was all so tidy.

'And Mademoiselle St. Onge gets to keep the francs less sales commissions here so as to improve her credit balance,' said St-Cyr, watching the woman so intently he hardly heard the auctioneer saying:

'180,000 francs, going once, mesdames et messieurs, twice, three times and sold to the Reichsmarschall and Reichsführer Goering.'

There was cheering, there was applause—the bargain was terrific! 9000 Reichskassenscheine, the Occupation marks. Only 9000!

Denise St. Onge felt everyone was staring at her. Ashamed—mortified—she thought of getting up and leaving, of rushing from the room but Goering ... Goering was leaning back over the rows of seats, squeezing people out of the way, extending his massive hand to ... to shake her own ... her own.

'She *cries!*' he boomed in German and laughed hugely. 'Oh *Mein Gott*, Andreas, I wish others were so easy!'

To show there were no hard feelings, the Dürer went for 2,500,000 francs, an unbelievable price. The fifteenth-century statue of Eve for 2,200,000, the two Vermeers for but a little less.

Goering threw her a look and saw her smile faintly through her tears. He hadn't forgotten her after all, he had simply wanted the Cranach for himself and would instruct Hofer to sell the rest in the Reich for far more than he had paid. There would be no shortage of buyers at home. The mere fact that he had owned the pieces, if but briefly, made them exceedingly saleable at very high prices.

Manet's study of a woman and her daughter brought 1,350,000, the torso of the nude with the hat, 1,400,000, and so it went until the 18,000,000 had been spent.

At a pause for refreshment, she nervously drank champagne but spilled some down her front and tried to wipe it away with her fingertips. At intermission, she searched desperately for Franz and Michel, asking several friends and associates if anyone had seen them, but they hadn't come back from taking care of Marie-Claire, they hadn't.

* * *

The kitchens, deep in the staggered, dingy cellars of the Ritz Hotel on the place Vendôme, were bedlam. Fires belched beneath copper pots, smoke rose from skillets and skewers, while the under-cooks, the *sous-chefs*, ran this way and that to the shrieks of the head cook who threw things when not satisfied. A ladle, an artichoke, a cleaver . . . once a whole bowl of white sauce, the *sauce velouté* most probably . . . Tears in its maker's eyes. Tears!

But the coffee was excellent, the croissants stuffed with Black Forest ham and Edam cheese, with a side dish of radishes, that little touch of home to which only a stein of Münchener Löwen or Würzburger Hofbrau was needed. The milk of Munich.

Kohler wept with nostalgia and pent-up despair, wolfing his supper as if a last meal before the rigours of the Russian Front and the emptiness of Siberia as a prisoner of war in winter or at any other time, ah yes.

'Louis, we can't go up against Goering. What's a few paintings, a few bits of sculpture? Hell, nearly all that stuff at the auction was stolen.'

'Don't be stubborn . . . Is that it, *mon vieux*?' asked St-Cyr, reaching for another croissant as the head cook shattered a soup tureen, maintaining that the gold-and-blue-rimmed Sèvres was required—required!—for the supper. Ah *merde*, a true *artiste*!

Ducking, Kohler tried to ignore the racket though there were at least forty cooks and a dozen or so *plongeurs*—dishwashers, damn it! 'Look, you know what I mean, Louis. Let him *have* the money, let him *have* the paintings. All we want is Mademoiselle St. Onge.'

'And the law, Hermann? What of the law?'

Must they always have this argument? 'You're *not* a priest! You're *not* my conscience! Hey, my fine Frog friend, I'm talking about your ass. *Yours!*'

'Ass . . . Yes. Isn't *that* what this whole affair is really about? Sex, Hermann? Rape, forced masturbation while under the lens, humiliation and hatred in the guise of "fun"?'

'Louis, I'm begging you not only for my sake and your own, but for Giselle's and Oona's and Gabrielle's. Goering's on the downslide. He *failed* to deliver at Stalingrad. He failed in the Battle for Britain. He has a vicious temper but also . . .' Kohler hunched over the table with croissant in hand, 'but also, *mein lieber Franzose*, he's a cold-hearted, cool-headed son of a bitch when he has to be. How the hell else do you suppose he could have won the Blue Max?'

St-Cyr had never seen Hermann like this—oh *mais certainement* they had run afoul of the SS, the Gestapo, the Wehrmacht authorities many times before and there was the slash of a rawhide whip down his face as a reminder of a case not too distant from this one.

But . . . but Hermann was right. If challenged, Goering would react as though stung.

As yet the Reichsmarschall was unaware that the Sonderführer and le Blanc were no more, as yet he still believed the money would be handed over to Andreas Hofer tomorrow morning. 1 January 1943.

Marie-Claire de Brisson had planned it all so carefully. Not revenge for having been betrayed by her closest friend and employer, but justice for herself and all those other victims. The truth. The forged papers that were now covered with blood, the money that had been hidden by Kempf and le Blanc in the storeroom behind the shop but had been found by her and rehidden in a disused part of the cellar only to have it recovered by those two after having obtained the new location from her.

The letters to herself detailing in the neatest handwriting everything that had happened. The items Denise had put up for sale, the photographic enlargements Marie-Claire had managed to make from the negatives and had kept hidden until that house had been emptied and abandoned.

'Louis . . '

St-Cyr grimly nodded. 'We want only the woman, Hermann. The money's to go to Boemelburg who will, no doubt, turn it over to the Reichsmarschall with our compliments.'

'Goodwill and all that horseshit,' mumbled Kohler, reaching across the table to grip him by the hands. '*Merci, mon vieux. Merci.*'

They finished their supper amid the bedlam but in silence and when the last of the coffee was gone and Hermann had wiped the sugar from the bottom of his cup with a finger—real sugar—they dodged and weaved among the racing *sous-chefs* and took themselves upstairs to another kind of bedlam.

'Oysters au gratin, salmon steaks in cream. *Tripe à la mode de Caen*, pigs' feet Sainte-Menehould,' said St-Cyr, aghast at the contents of the menu in his hand. 'Quail under embers, Hermann. Breast of chicken with *foie gras*, goose with sauerkraut, *coeur de Charollais à la façon des Ducs de Bourbon* . . .'

Fillet of beef Dukes of Bourbon, grumbled Kohler inwardly, thinking of Stalingrad and his two sons, and of Giselle and Oona making do with so little. Potato cream pancakes, cauliflower mousse, leeks of Savoy and . . . '*Salmis de Palombe*, Louis?'

'Wild dove in a sauce of red wine. It's a dish from the Pyrenees. Goering is eating his way through the country like a savage eats the heart and kidneys and unmentionables of a vanquished enemy!'

Grimly Kohler reminded him that it had been Goering who had issued the decree of 26 April 1933 bringing into being the Gestapo and letting them have a branch in every part of the Reich. Goering . . .

St-Cyr's nod was curt. 'Please cover the dining-room exits. Let me find myself a vantage point. Let me see her before she sees us so that I can tell Dédé exactly how her downfall was.'

Once the playground of the rich and famous, the Ritz was now used exclusively by the Wehrmacht. Visiting generals and other high-ranking officers came and went as if stiff, fleet harbingers of an uncertain future. Gravely subdued, they were overly polite to one another. Ignoring as best they could the racket from the main dining-room and the Luftwaffe security types who seemed to be everywhere, these 'guests' ducked discreetly into the lounge bar for a quiet drink and to listen to its chanteuse struggle valiantly against the din, or slipped outside to dissociate themselves completely from the Reichsmarschall.

Kohler knew they were embarrassed by the great one's presence and sensed in them his same fears that it was now only a matter of time until the Third Reich collapsed in disarray.

Louis went up the main staircase, that grand, sweeping curve of crimson and black Savonnerie carpet, the black wrought iron of its remarkable balustrade but bars to the Sûreté who, when he stood in front of a hanging tapestry like no other, looked tough and determined, yet sad.

Committed, he didn't turn to look back. He paused to let three U-boat captains descend and then he went on up to the first floor to disappear beyond the brass railing of the balustrade. No king, no general, just a cop on business.

Kohler moved away. Two of Goering's boys followed him and he had to wonder why they hadn't interfered and thrown Louis and him out of the hotel.

But they hadn't done so, and that, too, was a worry.

St-Cyr was troubled. The Luftwaffe security men were leaving them alone. As he walked along a corridor King Edward VII of England must have used, he understood he was being watched but allowed to come and go as he pleased.

Had Goering put in a call to Boemelburg? Had the Sturmbannführer filled the Reichsmarschall in on things?

It was a problem he and Hermann didn't need, for one couldn't soak up the essence of these last few moments and ferret out the truth when one had to always worry about one's back.

Twice he thought of turning and telling them to bugger off. Twice he told himself, They'll only say I have no jurisdiction here.

Yet they were allowing him to proceed.

Built in 1698, and once the Duc de Lauzun's town house, the Ritz had only forty-five guest rooms including its famous Imperial Suite. Not large, quite modest, its success had lain completely in catering exclusively to wealth and fame.

The dining-room was sumptuous, the cuisine always legendary. Beneath glittering chandeliers, amid the din of laughter, loud shouts and much talk, an army of waiters in dinner-jackets moved with precision while a chamber orchestra competed ineffectually against the racket with a sonata from . . . Beethoven? Was it Beethoven?

Two hundred were seated at one long table, others at island tables. Crowded . . . the place was packed!

And in the centre of it all sat the Reichsmarschall, gargantuan, florid, resplendent in his white uniform with all his medals. The Iron Cross First Class, the Lion of Zähringen with swords, the Karl Friedrich Order, the Hohenzollern Order Third Class with swords, the Orden Pour le Mérite—the Blue Max—and with the Grosskreux, the Large Iron Cross Hitler had revived especially for him, at the neck. Folds of flesh, short, curly, wavy hair and hands that pawed as he fed himself.

Flushed with success, Goering ate, drank, drew on his cigar and let his eyes dance over the crowd. Beautiful young women and girls in beautiful dresses and jewels, handsome young men in uniform—Luftwaffe blue, Kriegsmarine blue, Wehrmacht and SS grey and SS black, ah yes. Suits too: art dealers, buyers and sellers. Men on the make, girls on the make. Food in a powder-blue silk lap, wine down a generous bosom as a joke to exclamations of despair that fought to rise above the din but failed.

A broken glass, a shattered plate—the wealthy, the *nouveaux riches*, the *demi-mondes* of Paris toasted the Reichsmarschall's phenomenal luck and drank deeply.

Isolated, cut off, alone and subdued, Denise St. Onge sat six places from the Reichsmarschall across the table, and every time his gaze fell on her and he drank her health, she shuddered.

She looked so tiny in her black silk dress with its spaghetti straps. She hardly touched the breast of chicken that was in front of her and when the fillet of beef Dukes of Bourbon came, she shook her head.

St-Cyr watched her closely from one of the private balcony dining-rooms, letting the cameras of his mind record her every anxiety, for she must by now have realized that the Sonderführer and Michel le Blanc wouldn't return.

And Goering knew it too, which could only mean Boemelburg

really had been contacted and had sent someone to the shop to uncover the truth.

Ah *merde*, what were Hermann and he to do?

When the wild dove in red-wine sauce arrived, she picked at it and tried to eat, for Goering, dribbling dark sauce down the front of his nice white uniform, was devouring her.

At last she couldn't stand him looking at her any more and, colouring rapidly, leapt to her feet, knocking two of her wine glasses over.

Chablis stained the white table-cloth to mingle with a red flood of burgundy. The laughter and talk fled down the table to silence even the island tables around them.

'Eat,' said Goering. 'No one is to leave.'

'I . . . I can't.'

'*Eat!*' he shrieked.

She put both her hands down hard on the table to brace herself. As everyone watched, she picked up a dove, letting the sauce splatter where it would, never once taking her eyes from the Reichsführer.

Sauce clung to her lips and cheeks, a tiny bone caught in her throat. Choking, she clutched her throat, winced, coughed, reached for bread . . . for anything and finally took a proffered glass of the red.

Then she stood there in defeat staring down at her greasy hands, wondering what was happening to her.

St-Cyr drew in a breath. His eyes glazing over as he fought the effects of alcohol and drugs, Goering roughly shoved plates and cutlery aside, wine glasses, too, and those of his neighbours which smashed on the floor until . . .

In bundle after bundle, the 18,000,000 francs were brought in and placed before him and she knew exactly what he was going to do to her.

The robbery passed before her eyes, the good times and the fun, the orgies with naked girls who couldn't count for anything and kept Franz amused while she . . . she knelt beneath them or . . .

'Eat,' said Goering. 'Let everyone see you eat.'

* * *

What had made her do it? wondered St-Cyr. Spoiled as a child, greedy, ambitious, arrogant—ah so many things came to mind but still, could there ever be an adequate answer?

Handcuffed to the arms of a chair and still in her party dress, Denise St. Onge sat with head bowed before Walter Boemelburg. Dragged out of bed at 3:00 a.m., the Sturmbannführer scowled. Her voice was too faint. He had to ask her to speak up but still it remained faint. 'At . . . at first I . . . I didn't stay in the house after the girls had . . . had removed their clothes. Franz would tell me to leave; Michel would . . . would give him the revolver and then . . . then come downstairs with me to make certain the door was locked. They . . . then they . . .'

'A moment,' interjected St-Cyr with a lift of his pipe. 'Where was the Sonderführer while the photographs were being taken by le Blanc?'

'Franz . . ?' she asked, remembering so clearly the look in his eyes as they had searched each girl's nakedness.

Kohler gently reminded her that she had best answer. 'The corporal, here, has to take it all down so that you can sign it. Make things easy for him, eh? We're all tired.'

'Franz . . . Franz usually waited upstairs in the attic rooms. He would hear us as I told each girl what to do. Which dress to wear, which blouse or slip. The make-up . . . It . . . it excited him to listen to us. I would then leave and . . .'

'Go on,' said St-Cyr quietly.

Still she couldn't bring herself to face them. 'Then he and Michel would . . . would play with the girl.'

'They raped them,' said Louis levelly.

'Yes, several times. This and . . . and other things. I . . . I don't know how many times that first day. Maybe twice, maybe three times—enough to teach submissiveness. When . . .'

"When *what*?' demanded Boemelburg furiously.

Startled, she leapt and for a second, looked up but away and then down . . .

Again Kohler reminded her to answer and she did so. 'When they tired of them, after a month, two months—what did it matter?—they killed them. I didn't ask if they'd done so. I . . . I assumed the girls would be let go. Honestly I did. You must believe me. You *must*!'

'We don't,' breathed Kohler.

'You knew they'd be killed,' said the one called St-Cyr.

'All right, I *knew*!' she said bitterly. '*Does that make you feel better?*'

The bitch! fumed Boemelburg. He'd had enough of her! 'They couldn't have been allowed to live, not after what the three of you had done to them!'

Through her tears she looked at him and then at each of the detectives. They would never understand how it had all started or why she had become involved in such a thing. *Never!*

When she was asked how it had begun, anger came to her and she shouted at them, 'How does *anything* like that start? The war was *lost*. My brother Julien was dead. *Dead*, do you understand? My brother Martin was in a prisoner-of-war camp and I wanted him freed—yes, *freed*! Franz could do that for me. Franz . . .'

'How patriotic of you,' snorted Boemelburg. 'Louis, haven't we heard enough?'

'Walter, please. She has to tell us everything.'

'Franz . . . Franz came to see me when he arrived in Paris in the summer of 1940 and I . . .' She shrugged. 'I saw my chance. We began to go out again. It was exciting. He was always lots of fun. He had a job, he had influence. I had none, but I knew him from before, from Berlin. He was a cousin. He was very hand-some. We had . . .'

'Slept together,' said Louis, 'and did so again.'

'But it wasn't enough,' breathed Kohler.

Ashen and trembling, she again lowered her eyes. She knew that no matter how long it took, they wouldn't stop until she had told them everything. 'No. No, it wasn't enough. Not for him. He wanted to do something "different", something "really exciting". One night soon after the Defeat we were in Marie-Claire's flat when Marie asked him about houses whose owners hadn't come back. I think maybe she wanted a place for herself. I really don't know what made her ask such a question. Franz went to have a look. I stayed with her. It . . . it was then that she told me of the jewellery she had found for the shop and of the man who was her real father.'

Kohler filled the Chief in, offering a cigarette. 'Tonnerre had been taking money from Madame de Brisson for years, threatening to tell her daughter he was the girl's father. Tonnerre had a key to the house. They . . .'

'He never missed it,' she said bleakly, not looking up. 'It was nothing to him. Not any more. Only memories of a mannequin he hated, the mother of the daughter he had never spoken to until the day Marie went to ask him about the jewellery. Even then they didn't speak of who her real parents were. Later, Franz and I gave him ether. We got him very drunk on it, very quickly—like lightning, isn't that so? We went through his place, finding first the key and then the negatives of his mannequin naked on a *chaise-longue*, naked and bent over a chair, a table . . . everything . . . everything done in that very house!'

'Those negatives then gave you the idea for the advertisements and you worked out the schedule of photographs and put together the clothes each girl would be asked to wear,' said Louis, lost to the thing. 'Always the same clothes, always the same poses because Tonnerre and Gaetan Vergès were the ones who were to be blamed for the crimes if discovered.' He drew on his pipe, had a sudden thought, asked, 'When did Mademoiselle de Brisson tell you about her own abuse, mademoiselle? Monsieur de Brisson was . . .'

'Fucking her? Is this what you think?' It was. 'Oh *mon Dieu*, you are so wrong! Marie-Claire hadn't been touched by him since the age of fifteen!'

'Yet she wrote of it every day,' sighed Louis, his pipe forgotten. 'And you, mademoiselle? You let her feed on this fear. She was afraid you would tell others, so much so that she would never leave your employ no matter how good the offer.'

Her smile was twisted. 'Monsieur de Brisson came to secretly watch us. He was so hungry, that one. He had such lust in his eyes. Franz caught him on the balcony looking through the gap we had deliberately left in the curtains for him. It was perfect. *Perfect!* Monsieur de Brisson the banker joined the party!'

'Louis, I've heard enough,' grunted Boemelburg.

'Walter, a moment, please.' St-Cyr turned to the prisoner who looked up beseechingly at him through her tears. 'Were photographs taken of the banker with any of those girls?'

Again there was that smile. 'What do *you* think, Inspector? How else could we have found out about the money from Lyon? How else could we have got him to convince Madame de Brisson to help us so that we had them both? He *enjoyed* it! What man would not enjoy a naked girl who has a bag over her head and cannot identify her assailant?'

Merde alors! what had happened to give her such ideas? wondered St-Cyr, greatly troubled by her. Had she been so possessive of Kempf, she had willingly gone along with things?

Sadly he knew this was how it must have been, otherwise Kempf would soon have gotten rid of her and found another.

Again Kohler filled the Chief in. 'Eventually Marie-Claire de Brisson discovered what they were up to. She warned the neighbour's maid to stay away from the balcony for fear the girl would be killed. She made copies of some of the photographs without their knowledge and, after the house was emptied, scattered them for us to find.'

'She had forged papers made for Kempf and le Blanc,' said Louis, picking up the thread of it. 'She hid the money where they wouldn't find it, then wrote everything down so that when she killed herself in Dijon, we would find it on her body. She took a terrible chance they would discover what she was up to, Sturmbannführer, but they failed to do so until the end.'

'Why wouldn't they have scattered the photos themselves, since their wish was to pin it all on the two droolers?' asked Boemelburg.

St-Cyr shook his head. 'Everything was to point to the Château des belles fleurs bleues so as to gain distance from themselves. No doubt the photos were to have been left with Gaetan Vergès's body but . . .' he paused to look steadily at the prisoner, 'but were destroyed at the country house, were they not, mademoiselle?'

Must he act like God? 'Yes, I burned them in the kitchen. Franz was very angry when he found out but . . .' She shrugged. 'Those photographs, they were always such a worry to me. Something . . . ah, I don't know what, told me they would cause us trouble in the end and . . .' Her smile was again twisted. 'I was correct.'

Boemelburg still couldn't leave things. 'Why did Marie-Claire de Brisson wait so long, Louis? Why didn't she speak up?'

There was a sad shrug. The hand, with its forgotten pipe, lifted. 'She didn't know of it until early last May, Walter, when she heard or saw her father returning from that house and then discovered the horror of what they'd been up to.'

'The acid,' breathed Kohler. They had gagged that one and . . .'

She would force herself to face them through her tears. 'We . . . we had spread the girl out in the cellars and . . . and had tied her down. De Brisson . . . de Brisson left us in a hurry and . . . and then Franz said that it had to be done so as to make the motive clear. He . . . he took the acid bottles and . . . and he made Michel and me watch.'

'The daughter then tried to kill herself, Walter,' said the one from the Sûreté gruffly.

She would try to smile at him again so as to tell him he had been right about her in this too. 'But I saved her, Inspector, and I told her she could say nothing because if she did, I would swear that she, too, had been involved.'

'You must have been very careful when going to and from that house,' he said, never leaving her eyes for a moment.

'Careful? We had to be, but these days, Inspector, isn't it always best for others to simply turn away and say nothing?'

She had tried her best to condemn him as being a party to the Occupation but he would ignore it. 'And Joanne?' he asked, lifting his eyebrows in question.

'Joanne Labelle . . . Oh for sure, Inspector, that last one, she told us many times that you were a neighbour and that you and your partner would find and bring us to justice.'

'Kempf or le Blanc took her upstairs to the tower room,' said St-Cyr. 'Which of them killed her?'

'Franz . . . after we . . . we had had one last quick session with her. She . . . she kept on telling us you would . . . Franz hit her several times. He . . . he hated her for saying this. When . . . when it was done, he signalled to me from the window. I was in the kitchen garden waiting for him to do so.'

'You then went to find Gaetan Vergès whom le Blanc was holding in the cottage.'

'Yes. Yes, Inspector. You see Vergès knew all about what we had been doing to those girls. We took him ether, we got him so very drunk—and them too, us also. Why else would he have turned away the very people who had helped him through the years? We made him watch us. We often left him alone with one of the girls and he would, in his drunken state, try to release them, but of course they didn't understand what he was doing and thought the worst. Later, he would realize what had happened and would rampage through the house, destroying everything in his desire for ether and his hatred of himself until, at last, he would fall into a stupor and live in filth.'

'He cut the bullet that killed him, mademoiselle,' said Louis. 'Why didn't he shoot himself?'

'Because he refused to let us get away with things that easily, and because Franz said we would have to make it look like a suicide anyway.'

'And Tonnerre?' asked Louis sharply, his patience all but gone.

'We gave him ether and when he was out, Franz made me soak a pad and . . . and hold it over that horrible face. I wanted to, do you understand? I *wanted* it aɨ to end!'

They were silent for several moments and she didn't know if they were done with her. Then the Sûreté asked, 'The bodies of the other two girls, Mademoiselle St. Onge? Please, we've been able to account for only twelve of them.'

'Buried at the farm in . . . in the kitchen garden.'

Now it only remained for them to ask why the teller had had to be killed and this information she would give quite readily. 'Franz said the teller had to be killed. We didn't argue. I . . . I knew the teller would recognize Franz, since he had seen us on more than one occasion going upstairs to Monsieur de Brisson's office.' She shrugged. 'It had to be done, that's all there was to it. Now I would like a cigarette. May I have one, please?'

Ignoring her, the Sturmbannführer, signalled to the one called Kohler to read through her statement, while the one called St-Cyr fiddled uncomfortably with his pipe and finally put it away.

Troubled, he still had matters to settle.

'On the day of the robbery, Mademoiselle St. Onge, what exactly did you do?'

'I . . . I followed the girl as I usually did with the others until I was satisfied they were alone. I . . . I saw Madame de Brisson about to warn her. I panicked. I hurried to the house and . . . and waited but then . . . why, then the girl came. I couldn't believe it, but there she was at the door.'

'And then?' he asked so quietly she knew he was following every step.

'I . . . I calmed her fears. I gave her a little wine—she said she had only just had a cup of coffee, that a boy across the way had . . . Ah no, the forged papers . . .'

'Paul Meunier,' acknowledged St-Cyr curtly. Marie-Claire de Brisson couldn't have caused the deaths of the engravers. The banker must have called in the alarm. Madame de Brisson must have become aware of her daughter's visits to Paul Meunier and finally told her husband of them . . . 'And then?' he asked.

'Michel came but he was very late and the girl wanted to leave. I . . .'

'Please, the truth, Mademoiselle St. Onge. Joanne was uneasy. She knew she had been followed—isn't that correct?'

'Yes, but I . . . I was able to convince her that . . . that pretty girls often thought such things and that if she stayed, why she'd be sure to get the job.'

'Had you not been there to answer the door and welcome her in—had it been le Blanc or Kempf, mademoiselle—what would she have done?'

Again there was that twisted smile. 'They all needed the presence of a woman to reassure them—isn't this what you wish me to say, Inspector? Yes, yes, a thousand times yes! *Me*, I welcomed them in.'

'Le Blanc finally arrived and . . . ?' he asked, unruffled.

'We began the session.'

'The session . . . Is that what you called it?'

She didn't answer. He asked her again.

'Yes.'

Louis thought for a moment, then sadly asked, 'And how did you feel as you greeted each of those girls?'

Was it so important to him? 'Very excited but . . . but terrified also—afraid that it would all go wrong and the police would come. Fear and sex, Inspector? Is it not fear that sometimes heightens sexual arousal? The fear of discovery, the fear that others are watching as you gratify yourself with another, with a girl who can't escape and must submit, sometimes with a man also and that girl, the three of us—oh I knew Franz and Michel and then de Brisson, too, watched me as I had sex with those girls and with one of them but this . . . this only seemed to make it all the more exquisite and it pleased Franz to watch me. Don't you see, I couldn't have kept him otherwise?'

'Two days, Louis, and then she walks,' breathed Boemelburg. 'No trial, no judge, no priest. The less said the better. Kempf came of a good family.'

There could be no argument. Absolutely none. Gestapo Mueller would demand it.

Two days . . . Shattered by the news, she couldn't stand when released and had to be helped from the office. Heavily sedated, she lay on an iron cot in one of the cells in the cellars of the rue des Saussaies but even then her wrists and ankles were securely shackled so that she couldn't try to kill herself.

As they closed the cell door, it was nearly 5.00 a.m. Berlin time 4.00 a.m. the old time. 'Come on, Louis. Let me buy you a drink,' said Kohler.

'With what?' asked the Sûreté, startled.

Kohler showed him two fat wads of 1000-franc notes. 'Goering will never miss it. Hey, he gets to keep the art work and the money. Fair's fair. These are for expenses. Take one and shut up about it!

'One ... ah yes,' said St-Cyr, and splitting the wad into four parts, tucked it away to be returned in total to the bank in Lyon. 'Dédé,' he said. 'The money can never bring Joanne back but the boy will get the new bicycle she promised him if she got the job.' It would have to come out of his wages but the prices, the black market ...

'Don't be a sap. We'll borrow a bike. I know just where to find one.'

As they crossed the place Vendôme, the ice was treacherous. 'No one in their right mind should attempt to ride a bike in this weather, Louis. Think of it as saving a life, eh? Or avoiding an unfortunate accident!'

Luftwaffe Security Paris had the best bikes in town. Stolen of course. Requisitioned. They borrowed two just in case Louis might need one to replace the one he had lost on another case. They wheeled them through the empty streets which glistened at every rare blue-shaded lamp as if in a place of magic.

Gabrielle Arcuri had just finished her last set when, with the bicycles safely tucked away in the courtyard behind the Club Mirage, they stood at the bar. Without a word she joined them. She didn't ask how it had gone. She simply touched Louis's hand and let her warmth extend to both of them.

They drank in silence, glasses raised to the New Year and an uncertain future.

Two days later the guillotine fell. There were only the Sturmbannführer and St-Cyr as witnesses. Each signed the papers releasing the body to the parents.

Outside the Santé's walls, Boemelburg paused as he was getting into the back seat of his car. 'I almost forgot, Louis. See that Kohler gets this, will you? Read the other one, enjoy yourselves on the coast and keep out of trouble.'

Alone, St-Cyr watched as the car, probably the only one in Montparnasse at that moment, drove slowly down the boulevard Arago. It reached the rue de Faubourg Saint-Jacques and turned northward towards the Val de Grâce, the military hospital where, perhaps, it had all started, this affair of the mannequin.

He glanced down at the pale yellow telex and saw immediately that it was from Army Headquarters Eastern Front. Hermann's two sons were missing in action and presumed dead.

The other slip of paper contained something about 'dolls' in Brittany but he found his eyes were giving him trouble.

Stuffing the thing away, he started out on foot but soon stopped and found a match. As long as there was hope, Hermann would be okay. He couldn't bring himself to tell him the news. He knew that eventually he would have to, but who was to say? Maybe the boys were still alive? Maybe another telex would arrive, cancelling the original.

'For now let him sleep with his little Giselle and his Oona,' he said aloud and to no one but himself. They would catch the evening train to Brest, then they would make their way south along the Breton coast to Lorient. They would certainly not take the car. 'The submarine pens, the air-raids every night, the coast in winter!'

As he looked up with moistened eyes to that God of his in question at this new trick of fate, a pigeon huddled on a window sill. 'We are but soul mates in this world of Yours,' he said, identifying closely with the pigeon. 'Fellow passengers in this lousy Occupation.' Suddenly its wings flapped madly and it fell a metre or so, caught by a foot, a snare . . .

Flapping, the thing was dragged up and into the flat without the shutters opening more than a few centimeters. In his mind's eye the cinematographer saw the neck being wrung, the thin little body twitching even as the feathers were being ripped from it.

Lorient, he read. *Dollmaker arrested in murder of shopkeeper. Most urgent you send experienced detective immediately. Fragments of bisque doll not—repeat not—his.*

Dollmaker . . . a member of a U-boat's crew? An important member—yes, of course. Otherwise Admiral Doenitz would not have intervened. The engine room perhaps? The cook, the armourer, the sonar operator or navigator? Someone who made dolls to while away the hours and was vital to the sinking of Allied shipping.

It would keep Hermann busy, though he badly needed a rest. It would help to take his mind off his sons as the ring of steel closed around the Sixth Army at Stalingrad.